Readers lo

MW01485249

Chasing the Swallows

"It's so well written, its descriptions so starkly believable and filled with hurt feelings that I never once doubted the raw, immediate lives John Inman was laying out before us."

—Scattered Thoughts and Rogue Words

"This was a gritty, realistic story that spoke of great highs and equally deep lows in the life of two men who were determined to remain in each other's lives and love each other fiercely."

—The Novel Approach

Payback

"You'll cry a lot. You'll smile a few times. You might even chuckle a bit. In the end, you'll be glad you read it."

—On Top Down Under Reviews

"I do love my humorous, quirky John Inman books but this serious side of him grips me just as much. In fact this one has just shot way high into my favourite John reads."

—Sinfully... Addicted to All Male Romance

Work in Progress

"I recommend this to anyone who loves to get a good laugh because this book is guaranteed to tickle your funny bone from the beginning to the end."

—MM Good Book Reviews

"*Work in Progress* was just as engaging and romantic as *Serenading Stanley*... this one is going into my re-read pile for when I need a pick me up!"

—Prism Book Alliance

By JOHN INMAN

Chasing the Swallows
A Hard Winter Rain
Head-on
Hobbled
Jasper's Mountain
Loving Hector
Paulie
Payback
The Poodle Apocalypse
Shy
Snow on the Roof (Dreamspinner Anthology)
Spirit
Sunset Lake

THE BELLADONNA ARMS
Serenading Stanley
Work in Progress

Published by DREAMSPINNER PRESS
http://www.dreamspinnerpress.com

For my beta boy. He knows who he is.

Chapter One

HERE IN Nine Mile, kinship still shapes daily life. Familial bonds are strong, and the ties of friendship are lifelong and rarely broken. We seem to possess the tattered remnants of a pioneer culture, with all the spirit and cohesiveness that entails, and at the same time, we find ourselves coexisting with satellite dishes and microwave ovens and shiny computer-driven automobiles that beep and boop and flash annoying little lights at us every time we do something stupid.

The people here are good, most of them. Kind, simple country folks. Many are farmers, and like good farmers everywhere, they have an undying, tongue-in-cheek faith in the ability of God or government, or both, to somehow mangle the next harvest and render it worthless.

In reality, these people haven't changed as much as they might think they have. Their accessories have, certainly, but not the people themselves. Like the pioneers before them, their hearts are strong with reverence for country, family, friends, and church. And the land, of course. With citizens such as these, it is always the land that comes first. Always.

Put simply, they are nice, decent people. On the whole.

Exceptions, of course, can always be found.

And on this, the last day of her life, Grace Nuggett would meet one of those exceptions face-to-face.

It wasn't the sort of day one would choose for the last day of life if one's options were open. The rain had not yet come pelting down, but by the look of that dismal gunmetal sky above our heads, I figured it was only a matter of time before it did. From the occasional grumble of distant thunder, it seemed a safe bet Someone up there agreed with me.

Being the only Methodist minister in Nine Mile, and knowing full well the farmers were scanning the sky for the least little promise of rain to ease the long drought they had been enduring (God did it to them this time, since they couldn't very well blame the government for the weather), I should have sent up a grateful prayer of thanks that the withered crops in the fields would finally get some much-needed moisture. But in reality, all I did was lean against the outside wall of my church, cross my arms, stare balefully at the sky, and sigh. If I were a farmer in need of sunshine, I would have had the pleasure of blaming God for this outrage, but being a preacher in need of sunshine in the middle of a drought, I didn't quite dare. Not that I wasn't tempted.

After two long months with nary a hint of moisture in the air, today, of all days, the sky had finally decided to open up. Sam had warned me, of course. He always does. About everything.

Sam is my go-to guy for all things mechanical, since I'm about as useful as a box of sick hamsters. Sam is also my best friend. We have known each other since we were kids growing up in this one-horse town. Looking at us, one would think we were polar opposites. Sam stands about five foot six, and I'm six four. Sam is well built, and I'm a beanpole. His hair is reddish blond while mine is black. The only thing we *truly* have in common, other than friendship, is the fact that we are both single. Which, of course, opens up a whole new can of worms since every woman at the church is constantly trying to set us up with a female relative or two. Or three. But so far Sam and I have held on to our bachelorhood with tooth and claw.

But that's another story altogether.

"Give the farmers a break, Brian," Sam told me. His voice was a booming, sonorous echo because he had his head buried in the church's old upright piano. He had his head stuck in the piano because he was trying to tune the thing himself since the church couldn't afford to pay an actual piano tuner to do the job.

I didn't say anything, but it sounded to me like he was getting questionable results as far as the tuning went. His words, however, would later prove to be right on key.

"Set the date for the annual basket dinner," he said. "That's the only way the poor farmers'll get any rain, and you know it."

He must have heard my derisive snort, for he poked his head out of the piano and gave me a glare. A dust ball the size of a mouse was stuck in his hair. "Just wait. You'll see. And while you're waiting, hand me that velvet hammer. The one in the toolbox."

I handed him the hammer, and here I was, two weeks later, propped against the side of the church like a tired wooden Indian, the back of my neck heating up, remembering how I had scoffed at Sam's prediction.

Well, to make a long story short, I did see. All too well. As I watched, the good ladies of my congregation, with their starched Sunday dresses flapping like flags about their legs, tried rather unsuccessfully to place tablecloths and napkins atop the plank-covered trestles arranged in rows beneath the elm trees at the edge of the churchyard. Unsuccessfully because as soon as someone neatly spread a tablecloth, the wind would come along and flip it into the grass. Or happily toss the napkins into the air. Or simply poof the poor lady's skirt up around her ears until she was forced to drop everything in an attempt to maintain her dignity, and the moment she did, the wind would take everything—tablecloth, napkins, paper plates and cups—and gleefully scatter them to hell and back.

At my back, through the walls of the old church, I heard the sweet voices of the Methodist choir practicing, yet again, one of the hymns they had chosen for this occasion. Behind the emphatic lead of the ancient upright piano—which still wasn't tuned right, dammit—I heard the choir sing the old familiar lyrics I grew up with.

Shall we gather at the ri-i-iver,
The beautiful, the beautiful r-i-i-*iver.*

Before the verse was finished, a particularly energetic gust of wind rattled the elm branches, and rain began to splatter the sidewalk at my feet and plunk against the tall windows of the church. Then something a bit more insistent began plunking at the window beside me, and I turned to see Sam tapping at the glass from inside the chapel and pointing to the ladies out there beneath the trees as they frantically gathered up the tumbling paraphernalia of our ill-timed basket dinner. With squeals of laughter, they began scurrying, light-footed, through the wet grass toward the church to seek shelter from the quickening rain.

As luck would have it, the food was already in the basement.

"Just in case," Sam had said earlier, with a wary eye on that ugly sky overhead as the ladies began arriving with dishes upon pots upon containers of every sort, filled with heaven knows what but all smelling so wonderful it sent saliva dribbling off the end of my chin as if the gaskets in my mouth had dissolved from the sheer splendor of it all.

As my nephew Jesse, fifteen years old and looking uncomfortably spit shined on this summer afternoon, and his friend Kyle, looking equally clean and miserable, ran past me to help the ladies do what they had to do, I realized it might not be a bad idea if I helped them a bit myself. They weren't paying me to prop up the church. I was supposed to be the man in charge.

Before I could set off to assist the ladies of Nine Mile, a loud crack of thunder made me jump straight up into the air and bang my head on the underside of the electric meter nailed to the side of the church.

One of the ladies squealed in mock terror as she ran for the door, trailing a tablecloth over her head to protect her hair from the rain. Manly enough not to squeal, or so I hoped, I caught one last glimpse of Sam's laughing face in the window as I sprinted for the door myself. Rather than mowing the good woman down in my haste to escape the now cascading sheets of rain, it seemed a bit more gallant to grab her arm and lead her safely, but hurriedly, up the church steps and into the vestibule. There we shook ourselves off like a couple of wet dogs and laughed at the silliness of the situation.

Never one to miss an opportunity to embarrass me, as old friends always seem to do, Sam gave me a good-natured ribbing as I stood in the vestibule, dripping. "Good Lord, Brian! It's raining cats and dogs out there. Let's have a picnic, shall we?"

Sam's aunt Mrs. Shanahan, a rotund lady of eighty-some years with blue finger-waved hair that rolled across the top of her head like a corrugated tin roof, and possessing a voice that could crack obsidian, came to my rescue. Not. Mrs. Shanahan and I were adversaries from way back. She used to chase me out of her scuppernong arbor back in my youthful, barefoot days, and she had been chasing me one way or another ever since.

"Now, Sam. Mustn't pick at the poor man just because he chose the worst day we've had in six months to hold our annual basket dinner. We'll get by. We always do. Old Reverend Morton, now. He knew how to pick 'em. Always chose the prettiest day of the year. I asked him once how he managed to do that year after year, and he said he asked God to set the date *for* him. Now, there was a man of faith!"

He was also a pompous old windbag who inevitably smelled of garlic and cheap aftershave, I thought, rather uncharitably, I suppose, for a Methodist minister. Especially when referring to the man of God who had preceded me at my post for nigh on fifteen years. But it was true nevertheless. Reverend Morton was the dullest man to set foot on this planet since the conception of time, and if he ever spoke directly to God, and God actually deigned to answer, then I was a Kurdish camel driver on the road to popedom.

"But never mind," Mrs. Shanahan yammered on, giving Sam a wink and me a snarl. "We'll eat inside. Lord knows we haven't had to do that for ages. Kind of defeats the purpose of an outdoor basket dinner, don't you know. But what the hey? The food's good. That's what counts. Right, Jesse?"

A hand the size of a thirty-dollar pot roast came out of nowhere and slapped Jesse on the back. I could hear the boy's teeth rattle from the impact. The poor kid looked vaguely appalled at being thusly singled out for an opinion, but he carried it off well enough. "Suppose so," he mumbled to no one in particular. At the same time, he rolled his shoulder around to get some circulation back into it. "I like the rain."

Mrs. Shanahan enthusiastically pounded his back again, this time nearly driving the boy to his knees, which elicited a snicker from his friend Kyle. She appeared oblivious to her own strength. "Of course you do, Jesse!" her voice boomed out. "You and everybody else within shouting distance come from good American farm stock. Ain't a farmer been hatched yet that don't like the rain. In decent doses, that is."

The woman stuck her great arm through mine and dragged me toward the basement steps. "Come on, Reverend. Let's get the tables set up downstairs. Gotta work before we eat, you know."

Sam stood on the sidelines, watching this exchange with laughing eyes and a heart, I'm sure, that soared with happiness. Nothing amused him more than my own embarrassment. If you get to really know Sam, sooner or later he'll tell you about the time I peed my pants in first grade. But let's not get into that.

I was still being dragged along in Mrs. Shanahan's wake when a sudden burst of lightning made her tighten her grip on my arm and hasten her step. She came to life like Frankenstein's monster, I pleasantly conjectured, rather happy with my choice of metaphor, and at the same time, I wondered how the woman could so unfailingly steer my mind into such unchristian corridors. It was a talent at which she positively excelled.

Sam made a face as if he knew what I was thinking, which he probably did. He grabbed Jesse and Kyle around their necks and dragged them down the basement steps behind me. As we headed underground, the sound of thunder receded, to be replaced by the confused babble of a hundred happy voices all jabbering at once in delirious abandon.

The church basement was large, thank heavens, but still every corner was filled. Colorful print dresses were interspersed only occasionally with the more somber shirt and tie. It was a weekday, after all, and most of the farmers were in their fields, or had been until the rain started. Only their wives could afford the luxury of a day off. But even they had earned it. The array of supper dishes and cake plates and aluminum pots and pans of every shape and size confirmed that fact. Food was everywhere. The air was alive with the smell of it. These ladies hadn't simply popped out of bed that morning and dressed for church. Most of them had been up half the night preparing dishes they could be proud of. Dishes, they hoped, that would pucker their neighbors' hearts with envy.

Basically, they were showing off. But Lord, theirs was a vanity of which I fully approved.

It didn't take us long, with all hands chipping in, to arrange the food on tables along the basement wall.

It was a mouth-watering assortment, to be sure. Meats first, then came the casseroles and veggies, and after that the delicacies I loved the best. Homemade pickles, wilted lettuce swimming in sugar and bacon grease (hellish in cholesterol but heavenly on the palate), tiny ears of young corn dabbed with freshly churned butter, garden fresh radishes and peppers dipped in vinegar, and a dozen other trifles.

After that, as you greedily meandered down the line of tables, you came to the breads and biscuits: Freshly baked sourdough that had been tenderly raised—covered with a dishcloth and placed in the sun for warmth—transforming it from an unappetizing wad of pale dough to one of God's greatest gifts to man, next only to the sacred act of sex itself. Chunks of home-baked bread the size of concrete blocks that you pulled apart with your hands. Round slabs of cornbread baked in cast-iron skillets and sliced in triangles, pie-fashion. Muffins of every shape and flavor—apple, blueberry, carrot, gooseberry, hickory nut, pumpkin, zucchini, and some that were unrecognizable but delicious just the same.

After the muffins, as you neared the apex of this fattening runway, you came to the desserts. Pies of every flavor, with delicate designs carved into the crusts. An angel food cake standing a foot high if it was an inch and topped with strawberries from someone's garden. Freshly picked cherries buried in coconut and whipped cream, cookies piled high on platters, a dozen different kinds, and at the end my personal favorite: a peach cobbler, baked, I knew, by Mrs. Shanahan, who with those pot-roast-size hands of hers could pull culinary wonders from her oven.

Guilt over calories consumed would come later. For now, everyone dedicated themselves, heart and soul, to the business at hand. We milled around like cows on a hillside, chewing our cuds, eyes half-closed in delirious bliss, as if this were the sole purpose for our existence. To eat. We did it with unbridled enthusiasm, occasionally exclaiming over a particularly delightful discovery and calling out to ask who made it. When the culprit was found, it was usually a stocky housewife with sunburned cheeks and eyes that crinkled at the corners from squinting in a truck garden for hours on end beneath a blazing summer sun. Hearing the compliments, a blush of pride from all the praise accorded her would raise the pink glow of those sunburned cheeks to a happy, fiery red. Then, to ease herself humbly from the spotlight, *she* would cry out in praise of some delicacy or other, and in so doing, pass the torch to someone else.

It was all very civilized and Christian. These people were, after all, friends. Many of them had known each other, like Sam and I, since birth. They understood that praise, like butter, must be spread around. One brief moment of glory was enough for anyone, but once your moment ended, lend it to someone else. Otherwise, the next time praise was being flung about like candy at a parade, you might find none of it flying in your direction. They were friends, yes, but they were friends who never forgot a kindness *or* a slight.

After a time, the clatter of forks on plates diminished, and snippets of conversations could be heard that didn't always refer to the food at hand. The feeding frenzy was winding down.

I sat back, sandwiched as I was between Sam and Mrs. Shanahan, gorged like a tick about to pop. Casually, so as not to be unduly noticed, I loosened my belt a notch. Sam looked about as miserable as I did, although he was still chomping on a fistful of oatmeal cookies.

I tried not to puke watching him, and while I gave my glutted body a much-needed rest, I let my attention roam around the room as I studied the faces of my flock.

These were the people who worshipped in my church, who suffered through my sermons, who sometimes came to me with their problems. We seemed a cozy, friendly group, sitting there huddled together with our bellies full while the summer storm howled outside.

The farmers should be happy, I reflected, watching the rain slap against the little ground-level windows placed high along the basement walls. They had certainly needed this rain, even if I had not. But what the hey, rain or not, the annual basket dinner appeared to be a raging success. Perhaps the rain had brought us closer together, here in this crowded basement room, than we would have felt underneath the elms outside with the endless summer sky overhead.

Gradually, for lack of anything better to do and too stuffed to do it even if there had been, I tuned in to the voices around me.

Mrs. Shanahan's, of course, was the first to pierce my awareness. She leaned across me and Sam to speak to Aggie Snyder, who was one of the farm wives and who, at the moment, was about as pregnant as a human being can be. Mrs. Shanahan blithely ignored Sam and me as if we were a couple of fence posts someone had had the audacity to sink into the ground smack in front of her face.

"Lordy, Aggie, I feel as full as you look! And this girdle is cutting me in two. 'Comfortable support for a lovelier you,' the box said. *That's* a laugh!"

They come in boxes? I asked myself. *Like stereos?* In the meantime, Sam choked on a cookie.

Like Mrs. Shanahan, Aggie leaned over Sam and me as if we didn't exist. "I don't know why you bother wearing those silly things. I really don't. You have a lovely, full figure. If you're trying to catch a man," she teased, "it will take more than a girdle."

"Yes," Sam whispered in my ear, "a bazooka," causing us both to break into giggles.

Mrs. Shanahan cackled as happily as we did. "A *man?* I've *had* a man, and let me tell you, they ain't all they're cracked up to be. I married Mr. Shanahan fifty-seven years ago. He hung around for two months, bailed out one morning after breakfast, and I haven't seen him since. The laziest creature that ever walked the face of the earth! Wouldn't milk the cows 'cause he said it pained his knees. Wouldn't hang my new kitchen curtains 'cause he said it pained his *neck,* don't you know, reaching his arms way up over his head like that. That man had more pains than a window factory!"

She leaned in even closer to Aggie Snyder, pushing my back to the wall with her head a mere inch and a half from my lap. "A man, you say! What on earth would I do with a man?"

And what, I wondered as I studied those intricate blue waves that seemed to undulate across the top of her head with a life of their own, *would he possibly do with you?*

I gazed over at Sam to see him beet red, laughing, and still with a mouthful of cookies. He'd choke to death if he wasn't careful. I patted his knee in sympathy as I tried with every ounce of willpower I possessed, to tune this particular conversation out. It was obviously going nowhere. Surely I could find a more meaningful discussion to tap into.

My gaze skidded over the faces of two young women, both unmarried and less than beautiful, who appeared for some reason to be staring at Sam and me and whispering heatedly to each other while they did. When they saw my eyes land on them, they jerked up to ramrod-straight sitting positions, smoothed their skirts primly, and cast me two innocent smiles that positively reeked of longing. It seemed obviously incomprehensible and beyond their ken to find Sam and me, two young single men, still unattached at the ripe old age of twenty-eight.

One of them gave me a little finger waggle of greeting, accompanied by a rather suggestive wink. I chose to ignore that she also licked her lips in a manner usually seen in pornographic films. In fact, they both licked their lips. I nodded politely, first to one, then to the other, and as soon as that duty was fulfilled, I searched the room for better game. Finally I settled on Lucy Adams and her sister Blanche, who was visiting from Cincinnati.

Blanche was rolling something around inside her mouth, savoring the taste.

"What *is* this?" she said to Lucy. "It's rather chewy but quite delicious. I don't believe I've ever tasted anything quite like it."

Lucy patted her sister's knee. "Oh, do you like them? They're mountain oysters. Harry harvested them just the other day."

Blanche's eyebrows shot up in surprise. "Oysters? In the Midwest? How odd. But they're so *big*. Wherever does he find them?"

Lucy cocked her head back and gazed upon Blanche as if the woman had fallen out of a spaceship. "Where do you think he finds them, dear? On the ass end of a hog, of course. They're pig testicles. Didn't you know?"

It was apparent to me and to Lucy, and no doubt would have been equally apparent to the pig, had he been present, that Blanche most certainly did *not* know. Her face turned a rather unattractive green, and with an inward cluck of sympathy for the poor woman, I decided to move along.

Maggie Knowles caught my eye. She was dutifully listening to her husband, Gordon, as he expounded upon some subject or other, which more than explained the less than happy expression on her pretty but careworn face. Gordon Knowles was a man who caused unhappy facial expressions wherever he went. The man had tried his hand at a dozen different jobs in the two years I had known him, but his abrasive personality was not conducive to long-term employment. Their son Kyle was my nephew's best friend. Surprisingly enough, considering the fact that Gordon was his father, the boy had turned out to be a pleasantly typical teenage kid, albeit with the hauntingly serious eyes of a poet and a penchant for speaking in sentences of less than three words at a crack.

Mrs. Shanahan should be so frugal with her conversation.

Kyle attended my MYF meetings on Wednesday nights and, like Jesse, seemed reasonably interested in the topics we discussed at those meetings. The Methodist Youth Foundation was geared to teaching kids the lessons to be learned from studying the Bible by bringing those lessons to bear on the way they lived their everyday lives.

This year, for the first time, we also had our very own MYF campground. A permanent location, it was the result of two years' worth of hassles and wranglings with the Methodist Conference, instigated by me and me alone. Aside from certain advancements in my relationship with my good friend Sam, it was the greatest accomplishment of my young life. According to Sam, the first of many more accomplishments to come.

While Sam accepted the task of actually getting the campground up and running, it was for Kyle's sake that I offered the job of camp custodian to his father, Gordon. I didn't much enjoy the man's company, and Sam enjoyed it even less, but if I could make Kyle and Maggie's lives a bit easier by bringing a little extra income into their household, I thought the sacrifice worthwhile.

Gordon Knowles was talking about his new job now.

"And he wants ramps built up to the front door of the mess hall and one of the cabins. Don't you think that's a lot of trouble to go to for one gimpy kid in a wheelchair? If that two-bit campground isn't equipped for handicapped kids, then they shouldn't be allowed in. That's the way I see it. One kid on wheels and there I am breaking my back to build a couple of blasted wheelchair ramps!"

Maggie cast nervous glances at the people around her.

"Gordon, please—"

He ignored his wife and cocked a thumb at me, not bothering to see if I was watching. Perhaps he hoped I was.

"His Holiness over there thinks he can do anything he wants so long as he's paying me minimum wage to handle the dirty work for him. If we weren't so stretched for capital right now, I'd tell him where to stick his lousy ramps."

Maggie rested a trembling hand on her husband's arm. "Gordon, please. Let's talk about this at home. Someone will hear you." She seemed on the verge of tears. I wondered how much of this conversation I'd missed.

"Oh, hell, all right," he grumbled. "Go fetch me another slab of angel food cake. Maybe that'll cool me down."

Maggie flashed her husband a grateful smile and hurried off to fetch his cake. Gordon chose that moment to turn his scowling face in my direction. The scowl disappeared in an instant, replaced by a phony show of cheerful greeting. He nodded his head and winked. I nodded back but couldn't bring myself to return the blasted wink.

What a jerk. Him, I mean. Not me.

I traveled on.

As if guided by some outside force, my eyes came to rest on one of my favorite faces in Nine Mile: Golda Burrows.

"Sweet" is an overly used adjective when it comes to describing people, but every time Golda Burrows's impish little face came into view, "sweet" was the word that inevitably accompanied it in my mind. Slight and in her upper seventies, with a frazzled mop of curly hair dyed a most unnatural-looking black, this was the woman I would most enjoy being trapped in an elevator with, if you could find an elevator in Nine Mile, which you couldn't. She was a bit bent over with age and arthritis, but her mind was still a keen-edged blade. Her face, a crisscross mass of laugh lines and gullies and ankle-deep ravines, in no way detracted from the ever-present sparkle in those happy old eyes.

Golda Burrows, a spinster, had lived out her years in a tumbledown house one street over from my own. Her house looked as happy as she did, with concrete birdbaths, concrete ducks waddling across the lawn, and a weathered concrete fawn that rested forever beside the geraniums on her front porch. Tumbledown the house might be, but it was still a cheerful place to behold, not unlike Disneyland might look after lying fallow for twenty years.

Walking past her house on a summer evening, you might see a fuzzy face peering out through the curtains in the front window. That would be Lazarus, Golda's cat. His hair was as black as his owner's, making you wonder if perhaps she didn't Clairol the cat's hair every time she Claireled her own. Lazarus was so named because Golda had snatched him from beneath the wheels of a passing car when he was just a kitten, and in so doing, raised him from the dead, so to speak.

More often than not, the lively plink and tinkle of an untuned piano might accompany your footsteps as you strolled past her house. The melody, if you could figure it out, might be anything from Brahms to gospel to ragtime. Golda wasn't picky about her music. She enjoyed it all, and she played it all with an equal lack of skill, not being overly snooty, as she said, when it came to deciphering notes on a sheet of music. After all, her eyes weren't what they used to be, as the thick rimless spectacles that always sat perched on the brink of her nose attested.

Why she never married is anybody's guess. She must have been a vivacious, pretty girl in her youth. Mrs. Shanahan thought her a bit mad, but Mrs. Shanahan thought most people mad. She told me once, in one of those rare conversational moments when she was actually speaking *to* me, and not *at* me or *about* me, that Golda Burrows entertained the most peculiar habit of keeping a kitchen chair parked in her bedroom closet for the sole purpose of sitting there, with Lazarus on her lap, during thunderstorms. Lightning, Mrs. Shanahan said, scared the poor woman to death.

Golda didn't seem to be minding it at the moment, however. The storm had reached its zenith outside, with flashes and grumbles every few seconds. The rain had become an absolute downpour, causing the air in our basement hideaway to feel heavy with moisture, as if we were being forced to breathe through damp cotton.

But Golda Burrows paid no heed to the storm. It didn't appear to bother her at all. What did bother her, apparently, was the woman at her side. Esther Reames, another lady in her upper seventies, and one whom I would rather *die* than be trapped in an elevator with, was explaining to Golda how difficult it was to buy a birthday present for her dear baby. Her dear baby's name was Oscar. He was eighty-six years old.

"I just don't know what to do!" Esther exclaimed for the third time as Golda blandly stared at her with eyelids at half-mast and the dullest expression I had ever seen on a human face. Esther stuffed cheesecake into her mouth as she spoke. "His cholesterol is so high the doctor's taken him off sweets, so I can't buy him candy. He won't wear those newfangled clothes they sell nowadays. Says they make him look like an old fool. I thought maybe an exercise bike, but Lord, what if Oscar fell off the thing and broke his hip? Then where would we be? And liquor's out of the question, of course, what with his blood pressure being practically off the charts. Can't buy him a book either. The poor man can't see past his nose since they bungled his cataract operation last year. We should sue that idiot doctor, we really should."

Esther gave an exquisitely timed sigh. Martyr-like and pained.

"What I'd *like* to do is take Oscar on a trip somewhere, but his heart's too weak to stand all the hustle and bustle." As she said that, Esther Reames slapped her thigh in disgust, causing a chunk of cheesecake to flip from her fork to the floor, where it was immediately smashed flat by a marauding child in pigtails.

Esther glanced at the damp smudge on the floor before prattling on. "All he cares about is that infernal organ of his. He's forever playing with it in the parlor. It's his most prized possession."

Golda patted her hair. "I've never known a man whose organ *wasn't* his most prized possession."

Esther nervously twiddled the cameo at her breast. "Good grief, Golda. I'm talking about a Hammond."

"Ham and what?"

"*Organ,* Golda! Hammond *organ!*"

"Oh. Sorry." She didn't look sorry.

Esther's expression turned wily, which gave her face a remarkable resemblance to a ferret. "And what do *you* know about— well—men's organs? You've never married. You're an old maid."

If this was meant to put Golda in her place, it failed miserably. "I've never sat on a porkypine either, but I reckon I'd recognize one if I did."

Esther tossed that around in her head for a minute, obviously trying to see if it came up vulgar. By the disgusted look that finally settled on her face, I think she thought it did.

Esther gave herself a little shake, like someone trying to clear an Etch A Sketch. "Let's get back on track, dear. We're talking about my baby's birthday present."

"No, dear. *You're* talking about it. I'm just trying to eat."

"Well, excuse *me!*"

Golda blandly stared at the woman beside her for another couple of ticks, then daintily cleared her throat into a petite little fist. When she spoke, her voice was as innocent and tuneful as her piano wasn't.

"Look, Esther, it's actually quite simple. Why don't you just get the man what he really *needs*."

Esther gazed at her friend with considerable suspicion. She knew Golda Burrows as well as I did, and the good woman was appearing a bit too angelic under that curly thatch of blue-black hair. Esther knew it and I knew it. But she simply had to ask, of course. Anybody would.

"And what might that be?"

Golda laughed. "A funeral, dear. He's not fit for anything else. More cheesecake?"

Mrs. Shanahan drew the curtain on this delightful scene by barking in my ear. I jumped two feet straight up into the air. Sam only jumped one, since he was two chairs away from the woman and not quite so clearly in the line of fire.

I jiggled a finger in my ear. "Sorry, Mrs. Shanahan. Your dulcet tones snuck up on me. What did you say?"

Sam giggled at that, but Mrs. Shanahan didn't. "I said, where's Grace? Grace Nuggett? I've just realized she isn't here. She was supposed to bring the persimmon pudding. I hope she isn't ill."

Sam tossed in a few words—to prove his existence, I guess. "I love Grace's persimmon pudding."

"Oh, pudding, schmudding!" Mrs. Shanahan barked again. "Where's *Grace*?"

From the chapel overhead, the choir suddenly kicked in. Their song seemed to float to us from miles away, like a scratchy old recording, competing as it did with the raging storm outside and the continued roar of my jabbering congregation. The crowd in the basement was thinner now, I suddenly realized. Apparently the dozen or so members of the Methodist choir had filed out of the room right beneath my nose, and in my lethargic state, I hadn't even noticed.

Rather than hush up so as to better hear the hymn, the crowd spoke louder, effectively drowning out the choir entirely. At choir practice, we had imagined the hymns on the program drifting soothingly out to the congregation as they sat beneath the elms at the side of the church, a warm breeze softly rustling the leaves above our heads, an occasional bee humming past to pluck nectar from the redolent honeysuckle along the fence, all making us feel relaxed and pleasantly close to God. It had been beautiful to contemplate. And about as far as one could get from what was actually taking place. The hymn was barely audible behind this cacophony of happy, chortling voices. If God was here at all, he had taken a back seat to the gossip and cherry pie, and no bee would have survived in this room for more than three seconds flat.

Choir practice, it would seem, had been a total waste of time.

Grace Nuggett's unexplained absence was temporarily forgotten when Chester Goldstone and his wife, Thelma, wandered over to speak to me about the church camp.

Chester and Thelma Goldstone were Maggie Knowles's parents, Kyle's grandparents, and unhappily for them, I'm sure, Gordon's in-laws. They were perhaps the closest thing to wealth one could find in Nine Mile as the sole proprietors of Goldstone Jewelry and Goldstone Electronics, located twenty miles away in adjoining storefronts in Bloomfield, the county seat. She ran one, and he ran the other. It was a perfect arrangement for both, since Thelma enjoyed jewelry above all else and Chester could tinker with his electronic toys until the cows came home and never tire of it. Perhaps they were a bit of an oddity as well, considering they were the only Jewish couple in town. The nearest synagogue to Nine Mile was a sixty-mile drive west, so occasionally I would spot them from the pulpit as I delivered my Sunday sermon, sitting next to Maggie and Kyle and, very rarely, Gordon.

"God's God," Chester once told me. "He don't care whether we worship here or there, just so long as we worship, and if He don't care, then why should we? Besides," he added with a mischievous smirk, "that drive to the synagogue causes Thelma's hemorrhoids to swell up like weather balloons, but then, what doesn't?"

Chester Goldstone was a likeable soul, and a patient one, apparently, since he had spent a large portion of his life in the all-encompassing shadow of his wife, Thelma. She was a sturdily built woman with vibrant red hair (Hadassah red, Mrs. Shanahan called it) and a manner of speaking that inevitably set Mrs. Shanahan's false teeth on edge, or so she had informed me more than once.

Thelma Goldstone was one of those tiring women who rarely spoke of anything but their health. Or lack of it. I pitied the woman. After all, her only daughter had married Gordon Knowles. That was reason enough to feel sorry for her right there. I supposed it possible her health truly was in sad decline, although to look at her one would never know it—she was built like a boxcar.

What annoyed *me* most about the woman was the cloying way she had of wearing her religion on her sleeve. Not the Jewish religion per se, just plain old run-of-the-mill religion. Like Reverend Morton, Thelma Goldstone spoke of God as if He were a visiting relative who was staying with her for the summer in the back bedroom. She rarely opened her mouth without invoking His name, which even to a Methodist minister can be a trifle rankling at times. Her sole purpose in living, it would seem, was to die so she could ascend that Golden Staircase.

She also had the irritating habit of referring to her grandson Kyle as her "golden boy," a practice that must have sent the boy into paroxysms of mortification when he was present. Happily for him, at the moment he was elsewhere.

"Our golden boy is *so* looking forward to church camp, Reverend Lucas. We do hope this horrible rain won't set back the opening."

I noticed Sam staring bug-eyed at the diamond rings on Thelma's fat fingers and wondering if the woman had borrowed them from the store for the occasion or if they were really hers. At least that's what I *thought* he was thinking. What he *said* was, "Don't worry, Mrs. Goldstone. Brian won't let a little rain stop him."

"That's right," I said. "Even if the place turns into one giant mudhole, we'll still be open for business. You should be proud of your son-in-law," I lied. "I couldn't have done it without him."

Chester started to speak, but he wasn't quick enough. Thelma was out of the chute first, like a Brahma bull. "Yes, well, if you say so." She turned her attention to Sam, then back to me, then back to Sam. "Are

you two joined at the hip? I never seem to see you apart, don't you
know? I swear, one would think you're an old married couple."

Sam snickered, then glanced at me and had the good grace to snap
his mouth shut when he saw my reaction to what Thelma had said.

To make matters worse, Sam and I answered in unison,
unrehearsed but so perfectly timed it might as well have been.

"We're friends," we said, sitting up straighter and hopefully not
looking too guilty.

Thelma Goldstone once again studied first Sam, then me, then
Sam. She didn't seem convinced. "I see," she droned.

As if a jolt of electricity had passed between us, I sensed Sam
tensing up beside me, about to say God knows what. But it was Mrs.
Shanahan who rode in, guns blazing, to put Thelma in her place.

When Mrs. Shanahan cooed, she sounded like a dyspeptic old
pigeon coughing up a wad of rubber bands. She was cooing now. "I
love your hair, Thelma. It looks so *natural.*"

Mrs. Goldstone tore her attention from Sam and me and coolly
smiled down at Mrs. Shanahan. Oddly, the smile never quite reached
her eyes. "So does yours, dear. What a lovely shade of blue it is too."

Chester, perhaps sensing the opening salvos of World War III,
swooped in with impeccable timing to defray the situation. "It was nice
to see you folks. Thanks for inviting us. The chow was delicious."

"Yes," Thelma agreed without much enthusiasm. "I just hope it
doesn't make my ulcer act up. The doctor told me to stay a mile away
from spicy food, and whoever made that peach cobbler must have
dropped a box of cinnamon in it."

Mrs. Shanahan laid a hand to her cheek. "Oh, dear. That was mine."

Thelma lowered her gaze to Mrs. Shanahan's upturned face long
enough to say, "Was it?" And with that she was gone, pulling poor
Chester along behind her like a tow truck.

Mrs. Shanahan cackled happily. She did so enjoy life.

Sam and I burst out laughing, although we tried to be discreet
about it. Mrs. Shanahan wasn't weighted down with the burden of
discretion. Never was and never would be.

She cackled again. "That silly cow has been a boil on my butt for
thirty years. She has more doctors than I've got relatives. For someone
so all-fired ecstatic about the concept of going to heaven, she sure
keeps a lot of medical men busy trying to keep her alive. Now does that

make sense to you? It seems a bit obscene, if you ask me, what with all the starving people in the world dying left and right for lack of food, and all the crime and misery afoot, that one person should be so darned concerned about their own personal health. Especially when there's not a thing wrong with her to begin with that a good enema and three hours of nonstop sex wouldn't cure. That woman hangs on to every single word those money-grubbing doctors utter. They're not dumb. They can recognize a gold mine when they see one."

Mrs. Shanahan leaned in and tapped Sam and me both on the knee, her old eyes still shooting conflicting sparks of fury and laughter. "You mark my word, boys. Thelma Goldstone will single-handedly deplete Medicare's resources before she's finished, and even then they'll have to knock her over the head with a sledgehammer, pull the plug, and *shoot* the bitch to get rid of her!"

Sam laughed so hard he almost fell out of his chair. For a brief second, as if I were a bystander off to the side looking on, I saw myself staring aghast at my best friend and this odd, odd woman who were squeezed in on either side of me like bookends. I realized suddenly that the two of them were actually remarkably alike in their ability to laugh at some of the strangest things imaginable, while I, on the other hand, was not.

Sam referred to this inability of mine to see the funny side of life as merely another manifestation of PPS. Preacher Pomposity Syndrome. A mental illness, Sam said, which afflicted nine out of ten practicing ministers. I had, he explained, set myself up to save the souls of the world, but somewhere along the line, I had lost track of the actual bodies those souls were attached to. Those bodies, he explained, were continually doing such absurd things to themselves and each other that only a dolt wouldn't find them funny.

Put simply, Sam and Mrs. Shanahan could laugh at the drop of a hat, while all I could do was pity the poor fellow who dropped it.

Now, watching Sam wipe happy tears from his face on one side as Mrs. Shanahan still cackled beside me on the other, the two of them in their own private world, I found myself wishing, and not for the first time, that I could be more like them.

Before I could figure out how to go about doing that, Mrs. Shanahan turned to me with a look of nettled impatience. Safe to say, I would never understand this woman if I lived to be a hundred. Two seconds earlier, she had been howling with laughter. Now she glared at me as if I were a puppy who had piddled in her shoe.

"Well, Reverend?"

I noticed Sam staring at me too, with wide questioning eyes. Apparently I had piddled in his shoe too.

"What?"

My two bookends exchanged exasperated glances. *Men,* they seemed to say in silent unison, which I thought was strange considering the fact that Sam *was* one. He cringed when I glared at him, and since he still had a lapful of oatmeal cookies, he stuffed one in his mouth to take himself out of the running, leaving his aunt in charge of bringing me up to snuff on whatever she was suddenly irked about.

"It's Grace," Mrs. Shanahan snapped. "I'm worried about her. Don't you think you should find out what has happened to her? She should be here."

I glanced at those tiny basement windows and the rain still beating against them. The storm showed no sign of diminishing in the near future, and a sudden crack of thunder seemed to corroborate that fact.

"She might be sick," Mrs. Shanahan said.

Sam now seemed to know what was going on, so he threw in his two cents worth. "Or fallen," he said.

"Or maybe she forgot."

"Or maybe she doesn't have a ride."

"Or maybe she's dead," Mrs. Shanahan finished up, with what had to be the last possible option.

"But the rain...," I muttered.

"Then *phone* her, Reverend. Go up to your office and *phone* her."

"Yes, of course," I said. "I'll phone her. I can do that."

The two of them stared at me a moment longer, eyebrows high. Finally Mrs. Shanahan made a shooing motion with her fingertips. "Well? Run along!"

"Of course," I stammered. "I'll do that now, then."

So I did. As I hurried off toward the basement steps, I heard Mrs. Shanahan bark to Sam, "I've had hogs who were quicker on the uptake." Sam's laughter followed me up the stairs.

I kicked myself into second gear, hoping to make my escape before the flush rising in my body could reach my face. Lord, I hated that feeling, but of course, I could do nothing about it. It was something I simply had to live with.

And live with it, I had. My entire life.

Pretty teenage girls should blush. Twenty-eight year old Methodist ministers, on the whole, should not.

Chapter Two

IN THE vestibule, I found Jesse and Kyle sitting side by side on the steps leading up to the chapel, staring out through the church's main entrance at the pouring rain. Scattered around them on every step were paper plates piled high with food in varying stages of annihilation. By the satisfied expressions on their young faces, I knew they had eaten well and were at the moment merely taking a short digestive break before tackling those plates a second time.

Just looking at them made my stomach hurt.

Gazing down at the boys with their long legs sprawled across the steps, I realized they were both well beyond the last stages of childhood and were now on the brink of becoming men. Their shoulders were broadening, and the angles of their handsome faces no longer reflected the softness of children. Over the past year, they had shot up like weeds, and their bodies were in the process of filling out to match the sudden lengthening of bone. When he was a toddler, my nephew's hair had been a fiery red, his face a maelstrom of freckles. The freckles were disappearing now, much to his delight, and the hair had gone to strawberry blond. Only in the brightest sunlight did it still flare red. The summer sun had coaxed his skin to a radiant, ruddy gold, the color of weathered oak. Like myself and my brother—his father—Jesse's tan would get no deeper no matter how many hours he spent outside.

Kyle was darker skinned, his hair a deep chestnut, curly and thick atop his head. I suspected Kyle had the sort of hair women would happily kill for. In fact, even Mrs. Shanahan could barely keep her hands out of it whenever the boy was near. She petted him constantly, like a favorite Schnauzer. He wore his hair longer than Jesse's. The curls framed his face, and he constantly pushed them aside with an absentminded stroke of his hand.

But it was Kyle's eyes that first captured everyone. They stared up at me now, bright and wide, the tenderest eyes I have ever seen in a human face. The irises were so deeply brown they appeared almost black. Black and bottomless. Through them, it seemed, I could see deep inside the boy. It was like viewing the depths of the ocean through a glass-bottomed boat. All manner of miracles might be down there waiting to be discovered if one could only delve there long enough.

Both boys seemed as unaffected by their beauty as they were by the world around them. When together, they presented a calm front, and they were together almost constantly. They were the best of friends and had been so for the majority of their fifteen years. Only death, I suspected, could ever sunder a friendship such as theirs.

At their backs, the choir had broken into its second selection of the day, "Standing on the Promises," a hymn Jesse once told me he particularly enjoyed since it had a lively beat and was perhaps the only song in the hymnbook that could wake him up after one of my long, dry Sunday sermons. I had informed him at the time, and in no uncertain terms, that my sermons were never dry. Long maybe, but never dry. He had only laughed.

Now when I stand at the pulpit on Sunday mornings, doing what a preacher most dearly loves to do, namely preach, that tiny three-letter word is always tapping at the back of my skull like a persistent and unwelcome neighbor pecking at the back porch door. *Dry. Dry. Dry.*

"Hey, Uncle Brian! Sort of wet out there, huh?"

Wet. Wet. Wet.

Kyle smiled a shy greeting, looking, as he always did for some unknown reason, slightly embarrassed. Apparently the boy's self-esteem was in no better shape than my own. I wondered if his grandmother's "golden boy" label might not have something to do with that.

"Hello, boys. Where's your boom box?" I asked Kyle. The boy could rarely be seen without it. The strains of reggae, classic rock, sometimes even chamber music, constantly followed him around like the scent follows a rose. It was hard to imagine the one without the other. His tastes varied with his moods, and his moods apparently had an infinite range—from high opera to Dr. Dre and everything in between.

Kyle rolled his eyes, but Jesse did the talking.

"Mrs. Shanahan said if he brought it to church, she would stomp it to pieces and flush it down the toilet."

"Oh," I said. "She probably would too."

Kyle made a grim face. "That's what we thought."

To change the subject, I cast a caustic glance at the array of plates surrounding them on the steps. "Get your fill?"

Jesse grinned. "Working at it."

"Well, don't work at it so hard you make yourselves sick," I cautioned rather *dryly*. I tipped my imaginary hat in farewell and set off across the vestibule to the wing of the church that housed my office and the children's nursery.

Come tomorrow, the story of Grace Nuggett's murder would be on the lips of every person in Nine Mile. Today would be the time we would all look back on as *before*. *Before* Grace Nuggett's death seemingly opened the floodgates on murder after murder. I would remember this brief walk I took toward my office telephone, and I would recall, with an odd feeling of blind destiny guiding my way, that the only thing I was thinking of at the time was what a blessing it was the members of the Methodist choir didn't know the only people listening to their well-planned choral program were two teenage boys parked on the chapel steps. Perhaps even they weren't actually listening either. They were simply trapped between the gossiping horde of adults in the basement and the driving rain outside, like innocent bystanders caught in crossfire.

But as I said, those thoughts would come later. For now, life was merely routine.

I poked my head through the nursery door, meaning to give Peggy Nolan a smile and a howdy as I passed. One look inside changed my mind. A smile and a howdy wouldn't help the woman at all. What she needed was a whip and a chair and maybe a shark tank. Feeding half a dozen toddlers by herself and trying to keep the food on their plates and off the walls and out of her hair and shoes was not an undertaking that lent itself to accepting casual greetings from passing ministers. There was a slightly crazed look in the woman's eyes I thought it best not to have aimed in my direction. I slunk away and entered my office, closing the door behind me as quietly as possible.

This was my special place. My retreat. I came here to read and study and prepare my sermons and, more often than I cared to admit, to hide out. Books were scattered across every surface—some open, some closed, some marked with ragged slips of paper and others with hand-embroidered bookmarks given me by various ladies of the church at random times during the two years I had been their minister. There wasn't a woman in Nine Mile, it seemed, who couldn't embroider, knit, or macramé a bookmark at a moment's notice. It was always the perfect gift since most people enjoy reading and those who don't would rather die a lingering death than admit the fact.

The subject matter of my books ranged from theology (a lot of those) to mysteries (a lot of those as well), and from the Holy Bible (in four different versions) to a beginner's guide to gardening.

I discovered the telephone buried, like a hidden artifact, beneath a well-thumbed copy of *Archaeological Discoveries in Ancient American Cities*.

The moment I found it, it rang.

It didn't take me long to realize the voice on the other end belonged to my brother, Boyd. Or, more formally, Greene County Sheriff Boyd Lucas, Jesse's father, presently on his honeymoon in Nashville, Indiana, with his second wife, Susan, which explained why Jesse was spending the summer with me.

I couldn't have been more pleased. "Boyd! You're the last person I expected to hear from. How is the honeymoon going?"

He didn't sound nearly as pleased as I did. "You mean, how *was* the honeymoon going. It's over, dammit!"

I dropped into a chair. "My God, Boyd, you haven't been together a week! What did you do to the poor girl?"

A flash of lightning outside my office window made the telephone sizzle with static. Boyd's voice sizzled too. With impatience. "The marriage isn't over, you moron. Just the honeymoon. I was called back on business. We—"

"Business? What kind of business could be important enough to interrupt a man's honeymoon? Surely one of your deputies could have—"

"It's murder, Brian. If you'll shut up for a minute, I'll explain it to you."

"S-sorry," I stammered. "Who—who's the victim?"

Boyd sighed. "One of your flock, I'm afraid. Grace Nuggett."

"Oh, my God—"

"She was found this morning by her son, who came to drive her to your basket dinner at the church. It's a nice day for it."

"For what?" I asked. "Murder?"

"No. A basket dinner."

I gazed at the pouring rain through my office window. "Oh. Yes, I know. I've been told that more than once today. But forget the basket dinner. *What happened?*"

I could hear the rustle of turning pages. Boyd was checking his notes. "It seems Charlie Nuggett spoke to his mother last night, and she asked him to pick her up at ten o'clock this morning. Her arthritis was giving her trouble, and she didn't want to drive to the church. As far as we know, that's the last time anyone spoke to her. Charlie called again this morning to say he might be a few minutes late, but all he got was a message on Grace's answering machine. Number one."

I thought I had misunderstood. "Did you say 'number one'? What the heck does that mean?"

"We're not sure. But it leaves us with a very unsavory possibility."

I held up my hand as if Boyd were with me in the room and not miles away in....

"Wait a minute," I said. "Where are you?"

"I'm at Grace's farmhouse three miles out of town. You know where it is."

"Okay," I said. "But what did you mean by 'number one'? Are you saying that was the message on the answering machine?"

"That's right. Two words. Number one. Nothing else."

"But what the heck does it *mean*? Number one what?"

Boyd sighed again. "Well, unless I'm sorely mistaken, and I hope to hell I am, it means exactly what it says. This is number one. The first murder."

"The *first* murder! Do you mean to say there's going to be *more*?"

Boyd gave me his "patient voice," the one usually reserved for Jesse in times of exasperated fatherhood. "Yes, Brian. Judging by the evidence at hand, which isn't much, let me tell you, that's exactly what I mean to say. There's going to be more. We don't know if it's one more or, God forbid, a dozen more. Just more."

A thousand thoughts whirled inside my brain as I stared, unseeing, at the storm still raging outside my office window. None of those thoughts were particularly pleasant to contemplate. "So you're saying the murderer killed Grace and then recorded a message on her answering machine? Number one? That's all he said?"

"No," Boyd said. "It wasn't like that at all. Grace recorded the message herself. It's her voice."

"*What*? Is this some kind of sick joke, Boyd? You're really in Nashville, aren't you. You called to rattle my cage with this ridiculous story you and Susan dreamed up in a moment of boredom to make me look like a—"

"Bry, listen to me. First of all, while the honeymoon lasted there *were* no moments of boredom. And secondly, Grace Nuggett was coerced into putting that message on her machine. You can hear it in her voice. The woman was scared to death. As soon as the message was down on tape, or shortly after, she was killed. We found her faceup on her kitchen floor, right next to the phone. Someone had shoved a brand-new, bright yellow, freshly sharpened lead pencil, Ticonderoga Number Two, directly through her left eye and into her brain. She died instantly. The pencil was sticking out of her head like a goddamn flagpole."

I swallowed bile. "A *pencil*? The murder weapon was a *pencil*?"

"I need your help, Bry."

"C-certainly. But what can I do?"

"You can warn your congregation."

"But they'll panic."

"No. Not if you do it face-to-face. I've given this some thought. It's the only way. There's no TV or radio station in this county, and it will take us twenty-four hours to get something in the paper. A lot could happen in twenty-four hours. But right now, right at this minute, you have most of your congregation gathered under one roof. It's the perfect opportunity."

"But what should I say?"

"Tell them the truth. Tell them everything I've told you. But whatever you do, don't mention the murder weapon. Just tell them she was stabbed. If they ask for details, tell them you don't know. That pencil is a piece of evidence we've decided to keep to ourselves. Charlie was sworn to secrecy, the poor guy. It'll be a while before he can talk about it anyway. Outside of us, only the killer knows what the murder weapon was. The son of a bitch!"

"Then I should tell them about the message on the answering machine?"

"Yes. That will put them on their guard. We have no idea who the next victim is supposed to be. Don't worry, they won't panic. They may get madder than hell, but they won't panic. These aren't city people we're talking about here. They're country. They may be short on sophistication, but they're long on brains and common sense. They'll come together on this like they always do when there's trouble.

But we have to give them a fighting chance. I can't watch over everybody in the county. They have to be warned. Will you do it?"

I was suddenly assailed by an image of Grace Nuggett's lifeless body, lying on her kitchen floor in a pool of blood. That floor was tile, textured to look like brick, I remembered. The warm blood spilling from her body would have followed the path of least resistance, slowly spreading across the floor in straight, narrow lines inside the recessed areas between the bricks. Her mouth would be agape, her eyes open. One of them, at least. From the other, protruding upward....

I pinched the bridge of my nose as if to squeeze the image from my mind.

"Are you sure?" I asked. "Maybe there's some mistake."

"There's no mistake, Bry. I knew the woman as well as you did. And I saw the body myself. I examined it, for Christ's sake. It's her."

"No. I mean about the message. If someone wants to kill people, why would he give a warning like that? What possible reason—"

"Look, Bry, I don't have time to palaver this back and forth with you. We have a million things to do. We have to dust for fingerprints. We have to vacuum for trace evidence. Photographs need to be taken, the whole nine yards. As soon as you look at the circumstances calmly and unemotionally, you'll see I've come to the only rational conclusion possible. This is going to sound like a line from some silly movie, I know, but offhand I'd say we're dealing with a maniac. If you weren't a preacher, Bry, I would have said a *fucking* maniac, but since you *are* a preacher, I kept it clean. Now will you do what I've asked you to do or not? We're running out of time."

A maniac. In Nine Mile. It did sound like a line from some R-rated spoof of a horror movie. So why wasn't I laughing?

"I'm sorry, Boyd. Yes. Yes, of course. I'll do it right away."

"Good." With that, he hung up, and after a moment, so did I.

A maniac. Here.

Something had changed. The tempo of background sound was different. Then I realized the rain had eased up. And the lightning only came in intermittent bursts of light, dimmer now as the storm moved away. Soon the rain would stop altogether, the sun would come out from behind those black thunderheads, and it would be any other summer day. With heat and sunshine and warm gusts of wind.

And murder.

I pulled open my desk drawer and rummaged through mounds of assorted junk until I found a glass vial, sealed at both ends, with red letters printed along the side that said In Emergency Break Glass. Inside the vial rested a single match and one cigarette. I hadn't smoked in a year and a half, but suddenly I needed a cigarette so badly my fingers shook as I held the vial in my hand. But what would be the point? Half the tobacco had spilled out of the cigarette. This thing had, after all, been rolling around inside my desk drawer for over a year. Even if I could put the cigarette back together again, it would probably taste like dried donkey dung. My stomach felt none too stable as it was.

I tossed the vial back into the drawer and slammed it shut with a bang, my action more anger than willpower. Then I took a deep breath, closed my eyes, and prayed that Grace Nuggett's last living moments were something other than what I imagined them to be. Death, I knew, had come quickly. But what came before? Fear? Terror? Had she prayed, as I was praying now? Or did death take her too quickly for prayer? She was, I knew, a good Christian. A good mother to her son, Charlie. Regardless of the horrors inflicted on her body, I knew her soul, at least, was in safe hands. It would stay that way forever.

Thank you, God, for that much, but where were you earlier? Why don't you stop things like this from happening at all?

This was a question I had asked of Him before. If the answer was forthcoming, I've never heard it. That's when faith comes into the picture, of course. With a God who never makes His presence known, faith is really all we have. And I'd need it now, I thought, as I hauled myself to my feet.

I stood at the window staring out at the dwindling storm, gathering my courage for the task of presenting my congregation with a bit of local news they would be far from happy to hear.

First the rain, now this.

Today's basket dinner would be one they would not soon forget.

The whisper of footfalls on the carpet made me focus my eyes on the reflection in the glass in front of me. I saw the familiar outline of a man enter through the office door and close it softly behind him. I turned to see Sam crossing the room toward me.

He stopped mere inches away and brought his hand up to lay it on the side of my neck.

"What's wrong, Bry? What's happened?"

I tilted my head to feel his fingers on my cheek. He stroked me gently with his thumb for a moment before I forced myself to pull away.

A hurt look dimmed his eyes, but I was used to that. I had hurt Sam a lot lately.

"Not here," I said.

He simply nodded and stepped away to a respectable distance.

"I'm sorry," I said, and he nodded again.

I brushed my hand over his arm as I headed toward the door. "Come downstairs with me, Sam. I have news."

JESSE SAW us first. He looked first at Sam, then centered his attention on me. "Uncle Brian, what's wrong?"

Was my face that easy to read?

"That was your dad on the phone," I said. "He—"

Jesse nudged Kyle with his elbow. "Did he sound tired? Did he sound like he hadn't slept for days?"

"Jesse, please. This is no time for jokes. Something's happened."

His lecherous, lopsided grin instantly vanished.

"They didn't have a car wreck, did they? Is Susan, I mean—Mom—is she okay?"

"Jesse, nothing's happened to *them*. Your dad had to come back early, that's all. There's been a murder."

The boys' eyes opened wide, and so did Sam's. He tensed beside me.

Jesse swallowed with an audible gulp, but I jumped in before he could hit me with a barrage of questions. "Now, I want you and Kyle to help Peggy bring the kids down to the basement. I have to make an announcement, and I want everyone to hear it together. Will you do that for me?"

Thanks to Kyle, I didn't have to ask twice. Jesse obviously had a dozen questions he wanted answered, but before he could begin his inquisition, Kyle grabbed him by the front of his shirt and pulled him along down the passageway toward the nursery. I supposed with a father like Gordon Knowles, one learned to obey orders the first time they were given or suffer the consequences.

With the boys gone, only the choir remained. Before I could lay a foot on the bottom step leading up to the chapel, Sam tugged me gently to a stop.

"Is it Grace?" he asked. I simply nodded.

He nodded back, as if he expected as much. "What can I do, Bry?"

"Nothing," I said. "Just go on downstairs and wait with the others."

"All right," he said, the hurt look that had deadened his eyes earlier now mixed with concern. Without another word, he turned and headed for the basement.

I climbed the steps to the chapel. Sharon Nolting, the pianist, saw me first. I ran a finger across my throat, and she immediately stopped playing, dropping her hands obediently to her lap. It took the choir another stanza of "In the Garden" before they realized they were singing without accompaniment. Only then did they let their song fall away in tattered remnants to a final awkward silence.

"Will everyone please come down to the basement?" I said, my voice sounding far too loud in the suddenly silent church. "I have an announcement to make."

"How rude!" one of the ladies sputtered to the woman next to her, but they followed me readily enough, marching out single file and plunking their hymnals down on the pulpit beside the piano as they passed.

The animated chatter of happy voices in the basement was a bit harder to silence, but eventually I succeeded. I stood on the bottom step so as to be a head taller than everyone there—not that I wasn't already—and I watched as a hundred quizzical faces turned to gape at me. Many folks still held plates in one hand and plastic forks in the other.

Mrs. Shanahan read my expression as easily as Sam and Jesse had, and I knew she immediately realized something was wrong. With a troubled expression, Mrs. Shanahan scooted across two chairs and laid her large fist in Aggie Snyder's hand for comfort.

Aside from a few shushings of children, I soon had the room's undivided attention. I took a deep breath.

"I'm afraid I have some bad news," I announced, trying to find the proper range for my voice. "The sheriff phoned to tell me Grace Nuggett is dead."

A dozen people turned to look at someone else. The basement was now completely silent. I doubted it would stay that way much longer, and I was right.

"She's been murdered," I added with what I hope didn't sound like a theatrical flourish.

Even the children now stared up at me, slack-jawed and uneasy, as a collective gasp filled the room. Sam stood against the wall, holding his hand over his heart. Mrs. Shanahan's mouth formed a perfect O before she pressed her fingers to her lips and wiped it away. She brought Aggie's hand to her breast and held it close to her heart, rather like Sam had done with his own.

"But how?" someone asked. "Why?"

"I don't know why," I answered truthfully. "These things simply seem to happen sometimes."

"Not here they don't!" Paris Foster barked. He was a truculent old character of ninety-three who had only recently turned his farm over to his son, Amos. He stood before me now with a look of righteous indignation spread across his ancient, weathered face while one palsied arm rested consolingly about his wife's meager waist. They needed only a pitchfork poking up between them to complete the picture.

"I'm afraid they do now," I answered for lack of anything better to say. "But, please, let me—"

"How?" Mrs. Shanahan called out. "*How* was she murdered?"

I wiped my sweaty palms along the side of my trousers.

"She was stabbed," I said, trying once again to keep the image of Grace Nuggett's dead face from entering my mind.

"Oh, dear God," someone muttered.

I raised my hands above my head. "Please. You have to let me finish. There's more." They fell silent. What had only minutes before been a happy throng of gossiping neighbors was now nothing more than a sea of sad and angry faces. "Whoever killed her left a message on her answering machine. That message is the reason the sheriff asked me to tell you about the murder. The message said, 'number one.'"

Gordon Knowles popped up with a bloodlike smear of strawberry juice at the corner of his mouth. "Number one? What the hell is that supposed to mean?"

Maggie touched her husband's arm, leery perhaps, of what he might say next.

Jesse and Kyle stood beside them. As I studied my nephew's eager face and tried to think of what to say next, his hair caught a bright finger of sunlight that suddenly poked through the basement window above him. It made his hair look redder than it really was, shimmering with fire.

The storm, I knew, was over. The one outside, at least. But another storm seemed to be brewing before me in this basement room beneath the church, this room that had moments before seemed cozy but now felt claustrophobic.

I cleared my throat. My tongue was as dry as paper. "Boyd thinks the message means there will be another murder. Possibly more than one. That's what the message implies. He doesn't want to frighten people, and he certainly doesn't want you to panic, but he feels you should be made aware of what's going on. As a cautionary measure," I feebly ended.

Sharon Nolting, the church pianist, played her long fingers across her cheek in nervous flutters. "Is it just us?" she asked. "Those of us in the church? Or—or is it—"

I stared at her as I considered her question. Good Lord, that put a new twist on things. A twist I hadn't previously considered. *Was* it only the members of my congregation the murderer meant to come after? Surely not.

"No," I said, trying to soothe her fears as well as my own. "I believe my brother means to warn everyone in the township. There's no reason to think the murderer has singled us out. No reason at all. The sheriff wanted to start here because, well, there are so many of us gathered together in one place. With all of us spreading the news, the word will get around that much faster."

I hoped to God I was right.

"Poor Grace," someone said, someone in the back of the room. The person who said it was lost somewhere in that sea of concerned faces. It was like a voice that came from all or none of them. A sudden chill made me catch my breath as an unexpected thought slapped me across the face like an icy hand. The murderer could very well be here with us right now. Grace had been murdered sometime during the night or early morning. Hours ago. Her killer could be standing here among us, visible, but invisible too. Like that voice from somewhere in the back of the room. Faceless, but flesh and…

…blood. Moving slowly across a kitchen floor in straight, narrow rivulets, meeting itself at the junctions between those make-believe bricks, growing fatter until it overflows its tiny sluiceways, covering the floor neatly, brick by perfect brick, like a child at play slowly and deliberately crayoning in the spaces of a picture puzzle. Finally the blood stops moving. Perhaps a twitch of the body and the picture is still, silent. Complete. Grace Nuggett's lifeless form rests in a crimson pool, her head impaled by that innocent-looking yellow pencil. Above her, on the kitchen counter, a persimmon pudding cools on a metal rack, the cloying sweetness of its fragrance mixing with the musty, coppery smell of warm blood.

I shook myself.

No, it was impossible. The killer couldn't be here in front of me. I grew up in this town. I knew these people. None of them were capable of such a violent, senseless act. Murder, yes. Anyone is capable of murder under the proper circumstances. But not this. Not this.

A baby cried. Once again I saw only those anxious faces in front of me. Good faces. Kind faces. My friends. My congregation. The image of Grace's still body had retreated to some hidden corner of my mind, but I knew it would be back—at a time, no doubt, when I least wanted or expected it.

Suddenly everyone spoke at once, and to anyone who would listen. Outrage. Fear. Disbelief. All the emotions were there. But panic, as Boyd had predicted, didn't seem to be gaining much of a foothold. Perhaps living as close to the earth as these people did, they understood the futility of such a response. If anything, also as Boyd had predicted, they appeared to be coming together, uniting on a common front. All their lives, when things needed to be done, they simply went out and did them. This was no exception.

Paris Foster, stubborn as hell at the best of times, summed up the general reaction to my announcement when he stated matter-of-factly to a nine-year-old boy at his side, "I may be as old as Methuselah, but I can still shoot groundhogs when they come pestering around the corn, and if I can shoot groundhogs, then I can damn well shoot myself a dang murderer just as easy. Ain't no homicidal asshole gonna put the fear of God in me or my kin. I'll plug him, skin him, and fry him up for dinner with turnips and mashed p'taters!"

His wife rolled her eyes and nudged him to silence, but the boy at his side chucked the old man on the arm and cried, "You tell'em, Grandpa!"

Paris swelled up like a peacock as he tousled the boy's hair and grumbled, "You bet I'll tell 'em."

I yelled above their heads. "Now, we've got to help the sheriff all we can! I think Boyd's biggest fear is that people will be caught unaware. So until he can spread the word in a more conventional manner, it's up to us to help him out. Tell everyone you know. But don't scare them to death. Give them the facts and let them take whatever precautions they think need to be taken to protect their own. As long as we're alert and aware of the danger, we won't have any problems."

I hoped.

I gazed around the room and spotted Sam, now standing next to Mrs. Shanahan. When he felt my eyes fall on him, he smiled gently and gave me a wink. That old familiar tug of guilt and other torn emotions gave me a wrench of discomfort, but I pushed it to the background as I always did where Sam was concerned. Mrs. Shanahan noticed our little nonverbal exchange, which was no surprise, for she never missed anything. Especially where Sam and I were concerned. After all, Mrs. Shanahan was Sam's aunt, and she loved him more than she loved ragging on Thelma Goldstone, which is saying a lot. She was also the only soul in town who was privy to Sam's secret. And my own.

I gave them both a soft smile, then refocused my attention on the congregation. Feeling uncomfortably like a high school basketball coach giving a pep talk to his team, I added, "Let's wind up this basket dinner and do what the sheriff has asked us to do. We're a community. We've always done things as a community, and we'll get through this the same way."

Nods of agreement from a hundred determined faces bobbed up and down in front of me like those ridiculous bobblehead toy dogs in the back windows of cars. A few scattered comments—"You betcha, Reverend." "We've faced worse than this." "If the sheriff don't catch him, we will."—peppered the air. And one small voice in the back of the room cried out in frustration, "Who ate all the apple pie?" Some chuckles at that and then obedient silence as I bowed my head.

Together, we prayed for Grace Nuggett's soul and for the strength of her family to endure what had taken place.

Outside, the ancient elm trees in the churchyard dripped and sparkled as the sun once again beat down on them from a clean blue summer sky.

The storm was indeed over. At least one of them.

Chapter Three

AS QUICKLY as it began, so did the matter of Grace Nuggett's murder seem to fade into the background of everyday life. The residents of Nine Mile were shocked and saddened by what had happened, but that was not an uncommon occurrence. They had been shocked and saddened before. Perhaps because of their closeness to the land, they understood matters of life and death and disastrous misfortune a bit better than other people in other places. Farming is a matter of luck as much as anything. Good luck or bad luck. The fall of the cards. Crops wither or bloom. Livestock sickens or thrives beyond all expectation. Either it rains or it doesn't, and when it does, is it enough or too much? Floods, drought, disease, a failing economy. Anything can go wrong.

Why?

The fall of the cards.

Grace Nuggett's murder was no exception. The woman had simply been in the wrong place at the wrong time. The fact that Boyd, after two days of investigation, could discover no motive for her death served to convince people even further this was truly the case. Wrong place. Wrong time. Poor Grace.

They weren't being cold or heartless, simply realistic. In the face of *everything*, life must still go on. Cry out in grief, scream yourself hoarse in anger, kick the cat across the yard, but in the end, go on. There were chores to do, obligations to fulfill, meals to prepare, children to raise. Lives to live. In the midst of all this life, an occasional death must be expected and endured. Even murder must be accepted. For what other choice is there?

While Grace Nuggett's murder *seemed* to fade into the background of daily routine, in reality that was only an illusion. Her murder was certainly not forgotten. Not for a moment. Nor were the words on the good woman's answering machine.

Number one.

In death, Grace managed to accomplish what she might never have accomplished, or even wished to, during her lifetime. She made the front page of the *Bloomfield Evening World*, picture and all, although the picture would most *certainly* not have been to her liking. It was a grainy news photo of Grace's sheet-covered body being carried down the front steps of her neat white farmhouse on the outskirts of Nine Mile, with Deputy Morris Carter—looking hot, fat and flustered—at one end of the stretcher and Boyd, lips pursed in disbelief and, one might say, stunned determination, at the other end. The head end. This was made all too clearly apparent by the dark stain soaking through the sheet at Boyd's end of the stretcher. Grace's hand had fallen from beneath the sheet and could be seen trailing along beside her almost leisurely, as if casually skimming the surface of a lake from the side of a boat.

The headline beneath the photo was less than casual.

LOCAL RESIDENT BRUTALLY MURDERED

Nine Mile—Seventy-year-old Grace Nuggett was stabbed to death at about 6:00 a.m. yesterday in her farmhouse on Buck Creek Road, three miles south of this small farming community.

Grace Nuggett's body was discovered by her son, Charles Nuggett, owner and manager of the IGA store in Bloomfield.

Mrs. Nuggett was a prominent and respected member of the Nine Mile Methodist Church.

Sheriff Boyd Lucas is investigating the murder with the aid of other law enforcement agencies throughout the county.

"We've got a crazy here," Sheriff Lucas told this reporter. "Before she died, Mrs. Nuggett was coerced into recording a message on her answering machine. The message said, 'Number one.' We are assuming this means there is another murder yet to come. Possibly more than one. We want to warn the residents to please be on their guard but not to panic. We fully expect to have this son of a b—— in custody before any further tragedies occur."

Mrs. Nuggett died of a stab wound to the head, which penetrated the skull, piercing her brain. She died instantly.

Funeral arrangements are pending following an autopsy of the body and notification of relatives living outside the state.

Sam rattled the newspaper as he read the article aloud. The rumble and growl of my old Rambler made conversational exchanges little more than shouting matches, but Sam and I were accustomed to that. Mrs. Shanahan was not. The old lady's numerous chins were draped across the back of the front seat, her nose pointed forward like a bloodhound on the scent. This strategic position afforded her a commanding view of the speedometer, of which she seemed inordinately suspicious. It also placed her in a perfect position for catching every syllable uttered between Sam and me. It was like driving with a hungry, slavering vulture perched on one's shoulder.

I was not comfortable.

Mrs. Shanahan sniffed. "You need to do something about your brother's vocabulary, Reverend. The man talks like an atheistic heathen."

"That's redundant," I mumbled to the steering wheel.

"It most certainly is!" Mrs. Shanahan huffed, sparking the possibility in my mind it was *her* vocabulary that needed improvement, not Boyd's.

Sam giggled out the window.

"And besides," I added, "trapped as we are between murders past and murders yet to come, Boyd's inclination to flowery language would appear to be the least of our worries."

"I suppose you're right," Mrs. Shanahan reluctantly agreed, much to my surprise. Perhaps the woman was mellowing with age, like a very old, very large cheese.

The Rambler sputtered and popped and suffered a brief coronary fibrillation before it once again remembered what it was supposed to be doing. Highway 67 continued to roll beneath our wheels for a silent mile or so. Then Mrs. Shanahan laid one hand on my shoulder and the other on Sam's.

"How are you boys getting along?" she asked. "You seem— quiet."

Sam gave me a glance, then wiggled around to face the woman behind us. "We're fine, Auntie. Things are getting sorted out."

I watched in the rearview mirror as Mrs. Shanahan puckered her lips in pity, then reached up to pinch Sam's cheek. She even gave a gentle squeeze to my shoulder. "I worry about you, is all. I worry about you both. This is a very dangerous thing you are doing. If word gets out, they won't understand. You know that, don't you? No one will understand."

"You did," Sam said.

She snorted a laugh. "Well, I'm smarter than all these other yahoos."

"You are indeed," Sam said, and he turned back around to stare through the windshield at the miles of farmland rolling past on either side. His hand slid across the bench seat and patted my knee. "We appreciate it too, don't we, Brian?"

Mrs. Shanahan's glance drifted to me in the rearview mirror, such concern in her expression, I could only agree. Much as I hated to admit it, the agreement was genuine. "Yes," I said. "We do appreciate it."

"Well, just be careful," she harrumphed, straightening her back and patting her finger-waved hair as if to reassure herself it was still there. "I don't fancy seeing you two rode out of town on a rail."

"Don't fret." Sam grinned. "I'm sure they'd shoot us before they did that."

"Oh!" Mrs. Shanahan barked, although I thought I detected a wee smile in it. "Now *that* makes me feel a whole lot better!"

Mrs. Shanahan took another gander at the speedometer to reassure herself I wasn't speeding. "Is this thing safe?" she asked, abruptly changing the subject. Since no one answered, she let herself assume she was in good hands, or at least that's what I imagined she was doing.

Sam's hand was still on my knee, and the moment Mrs. Shanahan turned to gaze through the back window at the highway trailing behind us, I laid my hand over his.

He smiled at me then, and I smiled back. When Mrs. Shanahan turned to face front again, I returned my hand to the steering wheel. Sam left his where it was.

"Here's our turnoff," I announced. "Hold on to your mahungas. The road's a bit rough."

A generation ago, Sunset Lake did not exist. The area had been a lunar landscape of tortured earth and shattered hillsides. Back then not a hint of green could be seen anywhere. No water, no trees, no plant life at all. This once-beautiful parcel of countryside had been strip-mined for coal, leaving the verdant slopes and valleys a colorless jumble of churned up dirt and clay.

When the miners came, new valleys were gouged deep into what had once been ageless hills. What were once lush green valleys, abounding with flowers and streams and wildlife, suddenly became little more than heaps of slag, buried beneath the parings of those hills that had since the beginning of time sheltered and protected them.

As the coal ran out, the rumble and scream of heavy machinery lessened. Choking clouds of dust and diesel fumes gradually cleared, until eventually the air once again blew cleanly across the hills.

With man gone, nature eventually staged a comeback. Soon brushstrokes of green began to appear on this barren canvas. Seeds sprouted, pushing their arms upward through the clay toward the sun. Rains came and nourished them. Seasons passed, and every new spring found greater color, thicker and deeper vegetation. Trees appeared, small at first, weak and timid, but they slowly grew, becoming stronger and surer of themselves.

Water trickled down through the green grasses. Tiny rivulets came together to become streams. In the valleys the streams formed pools. The water gathered. Every year the pools became deeper, wider. Pools became ponds. Eventually, the ponds came together to form a lake, parts of it shallow, parts bottomless—where man's machinery had dug the deepest.

With water came wildlife. Cautiously at first, the animals returned, reclaiming the land. The once-heavy silence of barren landscape was replaced by the happy chatter of birds and the rustlings of small animals in the underbrush.

As if cast there by Merlin's hand, fish appeared beneath the surface of the lake. A dozen varieties: catfish, sunfish, bluegill. The word spread. Fishermen came. A rutted path was carved among the trees, leading from the highway. Man, with all his accoutrements, returned. But not to destroy. This time he came to enjoy what he had found.

Sunset Lake, as it was named, became a favored spot for swimmers and fishermen, hikers and campers. Families came to picnic on the grass. Soon enough the government intervened. Now Sunset

Lake was state-owned parkland, assuring the animals that lived there (although they knew nothing about it, I'm sure) that never again would man come here for any other reason than recreation. It took a score or more of years, but the sound of screaming machinery had finally been replaced by the gentler sounds of spinning reels and radios and human laughter.

Sunset Lake was at last a happy place.

The road we traveled had once been paved, after a fashion, but certainly not recently. The macadam surface was cratered and splintered by years of freezes and thaws. As the seasons changed, so did the road, and not for the better. Every screw in my old Rambler seemed to screech and unscrew itself a bit more with each jounce and jolt. Tools jangled in the trunk. The windows rattled inside the doors. The rearview mirror, I noticed, had tilted to reflect the tree limbs swiping past the passenger side of the car.

Mrs. Shanahan held a death grip on the front seat and moaned. When she spoke, she sounded as if she were being brutally pummeled by an overly zealous masseuse.

"Good Lord, Reverend, take some money from the church treasury and buy some shock absorbers for this piece of—"

Steering around the perimeter of what might have been the spot where a small meteor recently landed, I cheerfully interrupted her tirade. "Just sit back and enjoy the ride, Mrs. Shanahan, because the road's going to get a whole lot worse in a minute."

"That's hard to believe!" she wailed.

It was very unminister-like, I know, but listening to Sam's old aunt grunt and groan in the backseat made me a happy, happy man. Hearing her *oof* and *ow* at each new bump filled me with a zest for life I didn't know I possessed. Hardly a Christian attitude, I happily berated myself.

Sam gave me a sly look. "You're having way too much fun."

I grinned. "Hee hee."

As we bounced our way up to the crest of a hill, the muddy wheel tracks coming onto the road from what looked to be an uninterrupted expanse of forest showed me where our turnoff was. An unsuspecting motorist might never have known it was there at all.

I battled the Rambler off the main road, if one could call it that, and into a cave of dark foliage. Evergreen trees spread their limbs across this shadowy path and held hands overhead. The air was still and muggy from the recent rain. Even the birds were silent, or I presumed they were, since I could hear nothing over the groans and growls of Mrs. Shanahan and the rattle and bang of my battered car.

The road we had left seemed little more than an unpleasant dream when we contemplated the total nightmare that faced us now. No macadam here. Nothing but muddy ruts and holes the size of washtubs children might actually swim in if they had a lifeguard present to ensure their safety.

A particularly nasty gully suddenly opened up directly in front of me. When I hit it, three heads collided with the roof at the same moment. I imagined the engine simply tumbling out of the chassis and disappearing in a gurgle of mud, never to be seen again.

Sam clutched his stomach. "Kind of sorry I ate that frozen pizza for breakfast."

I patted his knee consolingly as soon as I found a decent stretch of road where I might dare take my hand off the steering wheel. "Want me to pull over so you can barf it up for the possums and chipmunks?"

"Shut up, Bry."

I gave him a salute and put both hands back on the wheel.

Mrs. Shanahan aimed a sausage-like finger at the windshield and what lay ahead. An uneasy quiver sounded in her voice. "I didn't know Sunset Lake was so *big*."

"That's not Sunset Lake," I said. "That's a pothole. The lake is farther along this damn road."

She tsked my language but continued to hold on for dear life. "I've been constipated for three days, Reverend, but I think you've solved *that* problem. Much obliged."

Sam laughed while I shot an uneasy glance through the rearview mirror to gauge if she was serious. I certainly hoped not.

At last, after a few more jerks and jounces, one of which nearly severed my tongue, civilization approached in the guise of a wooden sign stretching across the roadway. The sign read Methodist Youth Camp in letters carved in pine, and beneath that, in smaller letters, Founder—Rev. Brian M. Lucas.

"Fancy!" Mrs. Shanahan barked in my ear. "What does the M stand for? Modest?"

Sam came to my rescue. "It stands for Michael, Auntie. And don't rag him about that sign. It was my idea. Brian worked like a demon getting this campground started. You wouldn't believe the red tape he had to wade through to convince the Methodist Conference to lease this land from the state."

"I couldn't have done it without you," I stated truthfully, and I was pleased to see Sam blush for a change instead of me.

"Be that as it may, Bry, you persevered, and look what you have to show for it. A summer camp for kids." He turned back to Mrs. Shanahan. "It's his very own. That sign with his name on it—which he fought against every step of the way, I might add—will make sure he is remembered for it. In fact, his name wouldn't be on that sign at all if I hadn't sneaked around behind his back to convince Mr. Pendergrast to go ahead and carve Bry's name on the thing whether he wanted it there or not."

Mrs. Shanahan rubbed her aching kidneys when I drove the front wheels into a particularly deep abyss bisecting the path. "Lord, Sam, you do rattle on. Who's Mr. Pendergrast?"

"The shop teacher at Bloomfield High School. He's the one who carved the sign. And it didn't cost the Conference a blessed nickel."

I loved it when Sam came to my rescue. He always did it with such alacrity. I must admit, inwardly and only to myself, my name did look rather impressive up there on that slab of pine.

Now, if I could only convince the Methodist Conference to fork up the money necessary to pave over these blasted potholes.

As we passed beneath the sign, the trees opened up, relinquishing their handshakes overhead to let the sun come beating in. The lane was drier here, but not by much. Hopefully by August, when the kids began to arrive, the sun would have dried the ground and made the place navigable. A horde of kids was bad enough. A horde of *muddy* kids, happily tromping through every puddle in sight, was something I didn't want to think about. Suddenly there it was. Sunset Lake. A hush fell over the three of us as a panorama of cool green water opened up before us. Around the lake, newly built structures hugged the shoreline.

"My goodness," Mrs. Shanahan cooed, obviously surprised. "It's lovely."

Sam gave me a friendly punch on the arm, but when I turned to face him, I could see by the warmth in his eyes he would have preferred a different way to congratulate me if only we were alone.

"I should have told Mr. Pendergrast to carve your name in bigger letters. It's wonderful, Brian."

I turned back to the view. "It does look great, doesn't it?"

Sam grinned. "You know it does."

Dragging myself back to the logistics, I parked the Rambler in the only spot I could find where we wouldn't have to swim to get out of the car. Mrs. Shanahan wrestled her bulk out of the backseat and gratefully planted her feet on terra firma. She immediately began flapping her hands in front of her face.

"My goodness, these mosquitos are as big as buzzards! These woods are swarming with bugs."

Sam gave me a wink as we climbed from the car. Then he turned his attention to his aunt. "It's called nature, dear. There are supposed to be bugs here. Bugs and snakes and poison oak and trees to fall out of and lakes to almost drown in and cliffs to stumble off of and—"

Mrs. Shanahan wrinkled up her nose at the sight of her mud-splattered orthopedic shoes. "You make it sound delightful."

Ever the gentleman, Sam took the woman's arm, and together they navigated around a puddle the size of a two-bedroom house.

"I know." Sam smiled, surveying the ground ahead. "The kids will love it."

I gazed about with considerable pride. *Yes. I believe they will.*

The camp was built in a natural clearing at the edge of the lake. Six log buildings had been constructed in a semicircle facing the water. One larger, five smaller. The largest, two stories high and really quite impressive, contained the kitchen, mess hall, infirmary, registration office, storage areas for camping gear and recreational equipment, and upstairs, sleeping quarters for the staff and counselors.

Sam and I would have adjoining corner rooms at one end of the second floor. Mine, however, was the only room with a tiny veranda poking off the side of it. I did, after all, design the place. I could see no reason not to reap a few benefits along the way. I envisioned Sam and I enjoying many summer evenings sitting out there on my little veranda, discreetly of course, sipping iced tea and speaking of inconsequential things as we watched the sun dip behind the trees on the other side of the lake.

This would be an excellent opportunity for us to share a little time together without worrying about the cruelties of the world. The picture

I held in my mind of Grace Nuggett's body, sprawled across her kitchen floor with a bloody pencil sticking out of her head, was still too near for my liking. It would be nice not to worry about certain other sorts of malice for a while as well. Sam and I knew those intimately, even if we tried not to think about them. I looked forward to having those put on the back burner for a while too. Thankfully we had weeks of work ahead of us before the campground would be finished. After months of construction, the buildings were now standing, and they looked as perfect as I'd imagined when I drew up the plans, but a thousand things remained to be done before we could open for business and let in the kids. With eight weeks ahead of us to get them all done, it would be nice to spend some time alone with Sam.

For after all, we had our own business to attend to, as well as decisions to be made. That was the business that really scared me to death.

But first, the campground.

Mrs. Shanahan, our cook (a job she had begged me for from the beginning), flatly refused to climb a flight of stairs after slaving away in a hot kitchen all day cooking for a pack of miniature Daniel Boones (her words). So in deference to her age and her uncanny ability to always get what she wanted anyway, we had partitioned off a small area behind the kitchen as her private sleeping quarters. She acted as if she were doing us all a great favor by blessing us with her skillful presence, but I knew, as much as I hated admitting it, that she honestly did enjoy cooking and had been eagerly looking forward to these next two months of feeding Sam and me and the workers, then later cooking for the kids as well.

Mrs. Shanahan was blunt, opinionated, crass at times, and had a constant inner need to make my life miserable, which she usually managed to accomplish with alarming success, but deep down—and I would rather die on the cross than admit this to her face—she was a good, honest, hardworking soul who loved doing things for others no matter how much she pretended not to.

She was also the only resident of Nine Mile who knew and understood the secret Sam and I shared, and she had kept the secret for two years now. For that I owed her a lot. However, it still didn't alter the fact that she drove me crazy. I had no doubt her presence would make for a most interesting summer. If nothing else, we would eat well.

The smaller five buildings, two on one side of the main lodge and three on the other, were identical to one another in shape and size. These were the children's cabins, one-room log huts with bunk beds stacked three high along the walls that could sleep up to eighteen kids per lodge. Indoor plumbing in these smaller lodges was something the Methodist Conference flatly refused to spring for, so a string of Portosans, looking extremely blue and extremely out of place in this wilderness setting, were lined up in rows behind each lodge.

That, I knew, would be my next endeavor. Somehow I would raise the money for indoor plumbing in those cabins before the campground opened for a second season. A few bake sales by the ladies of the Nine Mile Methodist Church would get us started. After that I would think of something else, but the money *would* be raised.

Hiking trails had been laboriously cut around the perimeter of the lake, a distance of perhaps three miles from start to finish. It was a large lake. The trails wound in and around the pine trees that had grown so abundantly along the shoreline, up hills and down valleys, with plank footbridges spanning streams and ravines.

In front of the main lodge, the land sloped gently down to the edge of the lake. There, a wooden jetty jutted out over the water. Newly built, it still smelled of creosote and tar from the treated wood. Half a dozen sparkling new aluminum canoes were tied to one side of the pier, sitting motionless in the still water. On the other side, a buoyed line stretched out across the lake in a wide arc, sectioning off an area safe for swimming.

Past the buoyed line, its bright orange markers spaced seven feet apart, the lake suddenly bottomed out. No one knew how deep it was, but from the icy feel of the water when you swam a few feet past the rope, you would think it had no bottom at all. Perhaps it didn't. I sincerely hoped no child would get the idea into his curious little head to find out. A tall lifeguard stand at the end of the pier, which I was determined would be manned at all times during the daylight hours, made me feel a bit more secure in that regard.

The entire campground was bustling with activity as preparations continued for what I hoped would be a spectacular grand opening. The construction crew was gone, their work finished days ago. Now it was all up to me, Gordon Knowles, and three of the counselors—Jesse, Kyle, and Billy Simmons—to make things ready for the thundering mob of boys and girls who would soon be bussed in. The other counselors and the extra kitchen help would not arrive until opening day.

Sam waved a cheerful farewell and, with Mrs. Shanahan leading the way because she couldn't wait another minute, headed off toward the kitchen in the main hall. There, for the very first time, she would inspect the work and living space we had prepared for her. I prayed she would be happy with our labors. I didn't relish the idea of listening to her complain for the next eight weeks because her kitchen wasn't up to snuff.

I forced the woman from my mind and, feeling somewhat like a proud plantation owner, set off on a tour of my new domain.

I found Jesse and Kyle on the lawn beneath my little veranda, all but buried up to their necks in a mound of paddles, balls, nets, and life preservers. The sporting goods had arrived.

Billy Simmons, the swimming instructor, looking tanned and muscular and next to naked in his tiny flesh-colored Speedo, was crawling back and forth across the pier like a deranged snail. The hammer in his right hand and the bandage on his left foot provided sufficient clues to explain what he was doing. With every improperly driven nail he discovered, a most unchristian curse accompanied the downstroke of the hammer. If he was half as well versed in the art of diving and backstroke as he was in the gentle art of profanity, I figured the kids would be swimming like guppies in a matter of days. I could only hope their vocabularies would not be unduly broadened in the process.

Billy spotted me and waved the hammer in reckless greeting, barely missing bonking himself in the head. With that duty out of the way, he cheerfully returned to his crawling, searching, pounding, and swearing.

For a burgeoning church camp, in fact, the air seemed fairly thick with profanity. Gordon Knowles, over by the second lodge, added a splash of vocal color to the morning stillness when he stupidly stepped backward into a slab of wet cement he had just finished pouring. But his curses, unlike Billy's, were pale and puny endeavors, sadly flapping through the air with a total lack of poetic style and technique. Compared to Billy, he was a novice, poorly copying the master with plenty of passion but very little flair.

And unlike Billy, who obviously took pride in his ability to swear with theatrical abandon and didn't much care *who* heard him practice his art, Gordon Knowles was far too cowardly to stand up for his own work, choosing instead to look embarrassed and slam his mouth shut like a car trunk when he spotted me watching him.

Now how does one respect a man like that?

Gordon beckoned to me with bogus goodwill. "Morning, Padre! So, what'cha think?"

"About what?" I asked, trying to be polite but not really putting my heart in it. Gordon's presence was simply not conducive to heartfelt greetings. Besides, I hate being addressed as "padre." Makes me feel like Friar Tuck.

"The wheelchair ramp!" he groused, losing his good cheer quickly enough. "What do you think I've been working on for the past two days?"

"There's a footprint in it," I said.

"Well, yeah, but I can fix that. What do you think of the whole thing?"

I stepped back and studied his creation. "Looks a bit steep for a twenty-five degree angle. Are you sure you figured it correctly?"

Gordon pulled an unlit cigarette from behind his ear and popped it between his teeth with a flick of the wrist. It bobbed there as he spoke. "A twenty-five degree angle made it too long, Reverend. The damn thing would have gone from here to the other side of the lake. I shortened it, is all."

I rubbed the back of my neck. Stress. "You not only shortened it, you made it twice as steep. How is Larry Fitzsimmons supposed to maneuver his wheelchair up a ninety degree slope?"

"Let the other kids *push* him. They're here to exercise, aren't they?"

It was like talking to a rather ill-tempered tree, but I persevered. "When he tries to go down it, he'll look like Evel Knievel sailing off one of those two-hundred-foot ramps after he flies over a string of school buses. He'll kill himself."

Gordon casually removed his cement-covered shoe and dragged it through the grass. "Nah. Kids are resilient. He'll love it. Make him feel like a regular daredevil. One of the guys, instead of a cripple."

Stress? Hell, this was anger. "If I hear you talking like that after the children arrive, you'll be emptying porta-potties for the rest of the summer. Now, no more arguing. Extend that ramp out another two feet and do it today. And be sure the one to the mess hall is right too. We don't have time to be doing everything twice."

I left him there grumbling something I probably didn't want to hear. God, the man was impossible. If Jesse and Kyle weren't such close friends.... Speaking of Jesse and Kyle, I could see them now, laughing and yelling and hopping down the hillside toward the lake, excitedly following the movement of something on the ground between them.

"Uncle Brian!" Jesse screeched. "Come here! And bring an axe!"

An axe? Where would I get an axe? Then I remembered the fire extinguisher hanging outside the entryway to the main hall. I plucked the bright red fire axe from the glass case beside the extinguisher and went chasing after the boys, who now seemed to have their quarry, whatever it was, cornered against the pylons beneath the pier.

When I reached them and saw what they were poking at, a hundred disparate thoughts went tumbling through my head, and none of those thoughts were designed to lower a person's blood pressure.

This was food for stress at its keenest level.

The timber rattler, all three feet of him, looked considerably stressed out too. Stressed out, unamused, and all too eager to sink his inch-long fangs into anyone dumb enough or careless enough to get within his strike range. Happily so far no one had.

Billy Simmons hung his head over the side of the dock and whistled with appreciation. "That's a big one! Saw a snake like that kill a calf when I was a kid on the farm. Nothin' meaner than a pissed-off rattlesnake, and timber rattlers are meaner than most. Spiteful little bastards."

"Thank you, Marlin Perkins," I droned. "But what in the world are we going to do with it?"

Billy grinned down at me. With his tanned torso and long blond hair and 600-watt smile, he looked like a surfer who had spotted the greatest wave of his career.

"Well, Reverend, you might want to think about using that axe you're holding on to with such a powerful grip of death. Chop the fucker's head off. That oughta solve the problem."

Jesse bounced up and down in his excitement. "Do it now, Uncle Brian! He's getting ready to take off again!"

So with no time to sit down and fiddle around drawing up a spreadsheet on the various pros and cons of the situation, I simply went ahead and did it. The axe came down in a smooth, graceful arc, cleanly severing the rattler's head. Those ugly jaws continued to chomp up and down, on nothing, thank God, as the muscular body, fully six inches away, twisted and twirled and writhed around in frenzied contractions. The air fairly hummed with the rustling of the rattles at the end of its tail.

Slowly, that eerie sound abated. Looking at this creature now, still menacing even in death, it was easy to understand the snake as a symbol for evil. I had never seen anything look more inherently malevolent in my life.

"Stay away from the head," Billy warned from his perch overhead. "He can bite you just as easy dead as he can alive. Give him some time to die down. Back on the farm, I saw a coonhound pup get bit on the end of his nose when he went sniffing around the head of a chopped up rattlesnake. He was dead in twenty minutes. The pup, I mean. Took the damned snake a little longer."

I wiped the sweat from my eyes. With the bloody axe still hanging limply from my hand, I made a halfhearted attempt to lighten the mood. "That must have been quite a farm you lived on. Rattlesnakes from one end of the place to the other."

Billy blessed me with an innocent grin. "Yeah, Reverend. Thick as blisters on a bimbo's backside, as my grandpa used to say."

I nodded. "Colorful fellow."

Kyle studied the dying snake with reverence. "I wonder how many more there are around here? I'd hate to see an ugly mother like this get his choppers into one of the little kids." That, in a beautifully phrased nutshell, was one of those unpleasant thoughts I had harbored a few minutes earlier. Kyle was so in tune with my own reaction to this unexpected visitor, it didn't occur to me until later to be surprised at such a long speech coming from a boy who was usually so frugal with his dialogue. How many more rattlers *were* slithering around my newly built campground? And what, if any, action could we take to protect the children from them?

The answer was disturbingly obvious. Short of locking the kids inside their cabins, there was nothing we could do at all. We would simply have to trust to fate on this one. Fate, and a child's inherent common sense, which didn't make me feel a whole lot better. I could, at least, speak to Dr. Hill, the local GP (and also our county coroner), about acquiring some antivenin to be stocked in the infirmary. That would ease my mind considerably. Perhaps a few warning signs on the hiking trails along the lake would help as well.

Any further protection, I supposed, would be in the hands of God and Lady Luck, and in only one of those august entities did I harbor any faith at all.

"Get a shovel from the toolshed," I told the boys. "I'll bury this thing in the woods."

Rattlesnakes and murder. This special summer I had so meticulously planned was shaping up rather less than nicely. I wondered if faith and luck would be enough to get us through it at all.

THAT NIGHT, after the day workers had gone and Mrs. Shanahan hitched a ride back to Nine Mile with Billy Simmons, Sam and I strolled along the trail beside the lake in the moonlight. Aside from going back into town to preach on Sundays and to officiate at the Methodist Youth Foundation meetings on Thursday evenings, I had decided to stay at the campground full time, at least until it was up and running. I had taken a leave of absence from my day job as clerk in the County Courthouse, since preaching doesn't pay much, and I have to say I looked forward to the time away. Sam would stay too. At least in his free time away from his job at the Home Depot store in Bloomfield.

Neither of us loved our evil day jobs anyway. No. I'm afraid Sam and I loved—other things. That was our biggest problem. A blanket of stars twinkled in the sky, and the moon hung over our heads like a giant wrecking ball. Somewhere off in the distance, an owl hooted. The air smelled fresh and cool, the scent of pine and damp earth a balm after all the excitement of the day.

Sam slipped his hand into mine as we crossed a footbridge. The clatter of our footsteps on the wooden beams echoed like gunshots through the silent woods, and the owl immediately clammed up. When Sam's fingers gripped mine, and he pulled me to a stop, my heart began to patter. I knew what the patter meant, but I was trying to ignore it.

"Do you ever think of what we talked about?" Sam asked softly.

"Sam—"

"Just asking."

We stood leaning on the rail of the footbridge, looking out at the moonlight shimmering over the lake. I could feel Sam's disappointment breathing with a life of its own in the darkness beside me. While he didn't remove his hand from mine, nor did I give him any indication that I wished he would, I could still sense his need to speak. To hear. To converse back and forth. To make a plan. Something.

"It's hard, Sam. You know that."

He nudged closer, his voice teasing. "Is it?" he asked.

I turned to face him, studying his white teeth gleaming in the moonlight as he grinned at me. I slid my hands along his forearms, enjoying the feel of the hair there, the heat of his skin. He was wearing a T-shirt and cargo shorts, like me. When he stepped completely into my space, I felt our bare knees touch as his hands came up to rest on my chest. His warm breath brushed my face.

"You've been so patient," I said.

He shrugged. "No choice in the matter."

"Why's that?"

"You know why. Don't play coy with me now."

"Sam, neither of us is happy like this. Are we?"

Sam shrugged again. He laid his cool fingers to my cheek. "At this particular moment in time, I'm as happy as a dog with two dicks."

"Lovely expression."

He sighed, then turned his face up to the moon. I followed his gaze. I could see the Lady there. The Lady sitting at the dressing table brushing her hair. I had to remind myself it was only a trick of light and shadow on the cratered surface a bazillion miles away.

Sam's eyes found their way back to me. "I'm happy enough, Brian. As long as we can steal these occasional moments together, I can survive." He let the forest sounds intrude for a moment before his smile returned. "Remember the first time we made love?"

I closed my eyes, remembering. "We were sixteen. It was right here. We were camping out on the other side of the lake. Just the two of us. You—touched me, and I trembled."

"We did more than touch and tremble that night."

I smiled. "Yes. We did."

"Bry, I've loved you ever since, and you know it. God knows I've told you often enough. I wondered if you would ever return after college, and you did. You said you returned to be with me. Was that really true?"

"You know it was."

He dug his fingers through my hair, pushing it back off my forehead. "You need a haircut."

"I know."

He let his hand linger there, atop my head. "There are places we could live together," he said. "There are places we could even marry."

"Sam, we've been through this."

"All right," he said. "You're not ready. I understand. I'll wait. Happily."

"You shouldn't have to wait," I whispered, lifting my hand to cup his ear in my fingertips.

"But apparently I do," he whispered back. "We can never be ourselves in this town. In this state. You know it as well as I do. But someday you'll be ready to leave, to give this place up completely. Your job, the church, everything. I know you will, Bry. And when you're ready, we'll hotfoot it out of here and never look back."

I blinked back a tear and felt my mouth twist into a sad little smile. "You really believe that, don't you?"

He met my smile with one of his own. "With all my heart."

He suddenly swatted at a mosquito on his neck. "Auntie's bugs have returned. Can I sleep with you tonight?"

The question caught me off guard. I thought it had been understood we would indeed be sleeping together, at least while we were the only ones on the lake.

"Yes, Sam," I said. "All night."

"This is quite a treat. Usually we steal a moment here, a moment there. Discretion sucks."

"I'm sorry."

He hastily shook his head. "No. Don't say that. I understand why we have to be that way. I do."

He let the forest sounds return for the span of half a dozen heartbeats. He leaned in and touched his lips to mine. Gently. As he always did. Well, *almost* always.

His voice was that of a little boy, begging for a favor.

"Can we go to bed now?"

I laughed when his fingers brushed the front of my shorts.

"Yes," I said. "By all that's holy, yes."

Later, as we lay in each other's arms, staring out across the veranda of my new digs above the mess hall, I squeezed my eyes shut and concentrated on the scent and feel of Sam lying next to me. I could still taste him on my lips, still trembled at the memory of his body arching as I drew the come from him with my mouth.

"It's never old," he said in a hush of whispers.

"What's never old?" I asked, already knowing.

"Us," he said, smiling against my shoulder, nipping gently at my skin with his teeth. "The two of us. Together. Making love."

I smiled too. "No. It doesn't get old at all."

Sam cuddled closer. "I don't care what they say. This isn't wrong."

Again, I echoed his thoughts. "No, Sam. It isn't." I waited for the question I knew was coming. I knew because I had heard it before. A hundred times.

"Bry, how can you work in a church that thinks this is a sin? How can you?"

I cupped the back of his head in my hand and pulled him closer. "Please, Sam. Don't talk. Just let me hold you."

He relaxed against me, trying to hide the sadness in his voice. The sadness I had heard there so many times before. "All right," he breathed against me. "All right."

Hours later, as the sun rose over the lake, I woke to find Sam gone. I had known I would. It was his way of protecting us. No, not protecting us. Protecting me. From being discovered. From having our lives destroyed.

Feeling more alone than I had ever felt in my life, I lay in the splash of morning light, wishing Sam was still in my arms. Wishing his hands and mouth were still on me. Longing for the taste of him again. Soon, I could hear him moving around in the room next door, getting dressed. In a minute, he would rap at my door, and another day of lies would begin. Lies to the world around us, not to each other. Yet somewhere deep in the back of my mind, back where the guilt was blackest, I had begun to suspect even our truths were lies.

They had become a way of life, you see. Those lies. I could only wonder how long Sam would continue to abide us living them.

Chapter Four

OUR FIRST week at the campground went smoothly enough. No major disasters. No injuries to speak of. No additional snakes. What more could I ask for? We hadn't accomplished everything I had hoped we would, but we still had seven weeks ahead of us to get those things done.

The nights were spectacular, of course. Nights in Sam's arms. Nights where we could be ourselves. We made love with a desperation that tore at us both because we knew we had only a few days to be truly alone at night. By the second week, Mrs. Shanahan would be staying at the lodge as well. While her sleeping quarters were downstairs, and while she knew of our secret, still we would be forced to act with a bit of propriety, and at that particular moment in time, propriety seemed to be an awfully lot to ask of two humans who loved each other as much as Sam and I did.

Still, there was work to do. Our feelings would simply have to be put on hold yet again. I could only wonder when Sam would finally grow tired of it and walk away. God, what would I do if he did?

Even I didn't know the answer to that question.

My little workforce, with perhaps the exception of Gordon Knowles, did my bidding with good humor and a reasonable degree of competence. Mrs. Shanahan, ensconced in her kitchen downstairs, remained a painful thorn in my side, but the food she prepared for us more than made up for the wound.

On Sunday evening I invited my brother and his wife up to the lodge for dinner. While neither Boyd nor Susan knew the truth of my relationship with Sam, they did know we were lifelong friends, so his presence at the dinner party would be no surprise to them.

It was a beautiful night, balmy and clear. That endless sprinkling of stars spangled the darkness, and the wrecking ball moon, though pared down a bit now from full, still hung high and heavy in the sky. The reflections of moon and stars were mirrored in the lake, and those reflections rocked gently as a summer breeze stirred the water. The same breeze rustled the evergreens that graced the shoreline. Fireflies twinkled like tiny Christmas lights over the sloping lawn leading from the lodge down to the edge of the lake. The air smelled of pine from the trees and woodsmoke from the campfire blazing down by the edge of the water, where Jesse and Kyle were roasting hot dogs for their dinner. The sound of their laughter floated up to us, making my little dinner party seem a jollier affair than it really was.

Kyle had ridden in with Boyd and Susan after a weekend at home, at Gordon's insistence, doing chores around the house. They arrived late. It was almost 9:00 p.m. when Boyd's Bronco with the Greene County Sheriff Department emblem on the doors finally pulled up to the lodge, by which time Mrs. Shanahan was furious.

"Dinner is *ruined*!" she railed, shoving a tray of food at me. "You can pack it upstairs yourself! I'm not a waitress. Why you can't eat in the mess hall like normal people is beyond me. What the heck did you *build* it for if you didn't want to eat in it?" To ensure I hadn't missed the point, she said again, "Your dinner is *ruined*."

But it wasn't. Dinner was delicious. We had fared considerably better than the boys, with nary a hot dog on our menu. Mrs. Shanahan truly was a marvelous cook, and as far as I was concerned, the fact that she had toddled straight off to bed after preparing it made the meal ever more enjoyable. I loved her food. I even loved her ability to keep a secret. Her actual *presence* was another matter altogether.

We dined on the veranda, and I didn't know if it was the imposing flight of stairs leading up to the second floor of the lodge or anger at my brother's tardiness that had informed her decision to retire early. Whatever her reason, I for one appreciated it.

In truth, as we pushed our plates away and gave a collective sigh of fulfillment at the excellent meal we had consumed (rather voraciously, I might add), I was feeling appreciative about a great many things. The two bottles of good chablis Boyd and Susan had brought with them as a sort of lodge-warming present might have been a contributing factor to my expansive frame of mind. Alcohol and I were unfamiliar companions.

Rattlesnakes aside, I could not help feeling pride in what I had achieved here at the edge of this beautiful lake, and I eagerly looked forward to the opening of camp. Boyd and Susan were effusive in their praise of the place, which meant a great deal to me. Boyd's praise especially.

My brother was four years older than me. In childhood I had always looked up to him as my friend and protector, while he, I'm sure, looked down on me as a pest and a persistently annoying shadow he could never quite shake. But growing up had changed all that. He was still my closest friend, aside from Sam. In a sense, being county sheriff, he was still my protector as well. What had changed, I think, with the passing of years, was *his* perception of *me*. He no longer looked down on me as he had when we were children. Sometimes, and it never failed to please and amaze me when it happened, Boyd would seek out my opinion on matters that concerned his job and even his private life. Not as a minister or a brother, but as a friend. We shared a closeness now we had never known as children.

Ministers, I'm afraid, be they blood relatives or not, were a commodity Boyd had little use for. As he had, indeed, for religion in general.

But I was proud of Boyd. Proud of what he had accomplished with his life. When, two years earlier, Jesse's mother had died of cancer, sending Jesse into a state of depression we wondered if he would ever be able to pull himself out of, it was Boyd's strength and Boyd's love that brought the boy back. Perhaps it was Jesse's suffering that helped Boyd through his own pain as well. For Boyd was as surely crushed by Helen's death as Jesse was.

This was why I was so grateful that, during the course of another criminal investigation a few months ago, Boyd had found Susan.

Boyd was no slouch when it came to picking beautiful women. Like his first wife, Susan was a knockout. Her pale skin shimmered in the glow of the cranberry-scented candles burning on the table in front of her. Like Helen before her, Susan wore little makeup. She simply didn't need it.

As soon as we had finished eating, her hand, as if moving with a life and purpose all its own, sought out Boyd's, and there it stayed, nestled snugly in his great paw for most of the evening. It didn't seem to matter that their honeymoon had been suddenly interrupted by what Boyd called business and everybody else called murder. In fact, at the moment nothing seemed to matter much to either of them except that they were together.

They looked so blatantly happy sitting there that I longed to seek out Sam's hand as well. But of course, I couldn't. For the millionth time,

I felt an almost uncontrollable urge to share our secret with Boyd, but still something held me back. The fear of losing his respect, I suppose. Or worse, losing his love altogether. So I bit back the urge to confess and had to make do with Sam's foot nudging mine beneath the table.

It was Sam who finally steered my focus to a safer siding, if you want to call it that. Up to now, it had been a cozy evening. Sam's first words put a touch of chill in the air.

"Any progress on finding your murderer? Any new clues?" he asked, and all eyes turned to Boyd.

Boyd rolled his eyes and loosened his belt buckle at the same time. He had eaten a lot.

"We found no trace evidence at the murder scene whatsoever," he said, leaning back in his chair and reclaiming Susan's hand. "No hairs. No skin beneath Grace's fingernails. No fingerprints on the murder weapon. Absolutely no sign of any sort of struggle at all. Just Grace's body, peacefully lying there on the kitchen floor with that goddamn pencil sticking out of her head."

Susan paled but said nothing.

Boyd still wore his khaki uniform. It made him look handsome, competent, and businesslike. He also looked a trifle out of place as he sat there sipping wine in the candlelight. For comfort, he had removed his gun and holster before sitting down to dinner. They rested, an ominous reminder of the brutalities to be found in this world, on the floor beside his chair.

"Her hands were primly laid across her breast, and her nightgown and robe were carefully arranged around her as if the murderer was a compulsive neat freak or something. He did everything but comb her hair. Never saw anything like it in my life. Blood everywhere, but there she was, feet together, hands across her chest, face pointed straight up at the ceiling as if she were already laid out in a pretty little casket down at Spanner's Funeral Home. It gave me the creeps to look at her. I'm afraid we're dealing with a real looney tune." He tapped the side of his head. "Nuts."

Susan daintily ran a fingertip around the rim of her wine glass. "Maybe he was shocked by what he'd done and simply tried to give the woman some dignity in death. It's a small consolation, I know, but…."

Boyd gazed fondly at her and shrugged. "Who knows? Maybe he did. But that still doesn't alter the fact that we're dealing with a fucking fruitcake. Nobody in their right mind would murder an old woman by stabbing her in the eye with a pencil and then hitting that pencil with the palm of his hand to drive it into her brain."

This observation served to sober me considerably. "Good Lord," I said. "Is that what he did?"

Boyd gave a solemn nod. "Afraid so. Dr. Hill said that's the only way the pencil could have been so deeply embedded into the woman's head. It's a wonder it didn't break. He must have hit it just right. Maybe, ha-ha, he practiced on a watermelon before he got there."

Sam laughed, but I'm familiar with every sound he's ever made, and as laughs go, it was a pretty feeble shot. He took another sip of wine. That looked like a good idea, so I took one too. The wine felt cool going down, but it did absolutely nothing to remove the image of Grace's dead face that still lingered in my mind.

"And get this!" Boyd grunted like a man lifting a heavy weight. "The killer even helped himself to a slab of persimmon pudding before he left. Murder must be hungry work. It was a fairly healthy slab."

"How do you know Grace didn't eat it herself?" Sam asked.

Boyd's face was suddenly relaxed and smiling in the flickering candlelight. But for his words, the illusion was one of peaceful contemplation. Maybe the wine was calming him too. "Nah," he said. "We analyzed the contents of her stomach during the autopsy. No persimmon pudding there, I'm afraid. Nothing but the remains of her last night's dinner. Chicken and tapioca."

Sam blanched. "Jesus. Sorry I asked."

Boyd gave a good-natured snort. "Yeah, well, don't be sorry. I asked the same question. Couldn't believe somebody could kill a sweet little old lady like that and then sit down for a bite of dessert. Ate it with his hands too. Didn't use the silverware. That's how we know he did it after the murder. If Grace had given it to him before she realized what he was up to, it seems a reasonable assumption she would have given it to him on a plate and handed him a fork to eat it with. Nothing like that was found. Except for the blood, her kitchen was spotless."

"Do you think she knew him?" I asked. "Knew who her killer was?"

Boyd pulled his hand away from Susan's long enough to light a cigarette, then returned it when he had finished. He puffed out a cloud of smoke that drifted away toward the lake.

"If he's a local, she must have known him. Everybody knows everybody in these parts. You can't *start* a face in Greene County that a longtime resident like Grace Nuggett wouldn't recognize in a minute. She must have known him, and she must have let him in. There were no signs of forced entry. Nothing was stolen. Her purse was hanging on the back of the dining room chair, right there in front of God and everybody, with sixty-three dollars and change in it. Hadn't been touched. We still don't have the faintest clue as to why he killed her."

"And her son?" Sam asked, gently steering a moth away from a candle's flame. "Any possibility he had anything to do with it?"

Boyd flicked his ashes off the veranda and watched a spark or two fly off into the darkness. "Naturally, when we couldn't come up with another suspect, we halfheartedly concentrated on Charlie for a while. But Charlie Nuggett was having breakfast at home with his wife and kids at the time of the murder. No two ways around it. He didn't kill her, although he will inherit the farm now that his mother's dead. The father died years ago, and Grace never remarried, as you know. Charlie was the only heir. But I knew he didn't kill her anyway. If you'd seen his face when he spoke of finding his mother's body, you'd have known it too. The guy was in shock. I'm not sure he'll ever recover."

"Poor man," Susan muttered. She turned to me. "When is the funeral, Brian? Do you know?"

I looked in turn to Boyd. "Beats me," he said. "Whenever the coroner releases the body, I suppose. Will you deliver the service?"

I nodded. "Charlie's already contacted me about it. When the time comes, I'll be the one to do it."

A momentary hush settled around us. A night bird trilled somewhere off in the trees, and in our silence the air seemed suddenly to come alive with the sound of crickets, frogs, and another burst of laughter down by the boys' campfire.

I blinked hard, trying to stem the dizziness of consuming three glasses of wine. "That message on the machine," I mused, bringing our peaceful interlude of silence to a thudding halt. "I wish I knew what that was supposed to mean."

Boyd gazed at the burning tip of his cigarette for a moment before pulling himself together enough to answer. I couldn't help wondering what his thoughts were.

Nothing profound, it seemed.

"Shit in one hand," he said, "and wish in the other, and see which one fills up the fastest."

Susan jerked her hand away from Boyd's and chucked him on the arm with her tiny fist. He only smiled. I figured it would take some time for Susan to become accustomed to my brother's colorful manner of speaking.

She turned embarrassed eyes to me, managing to laugh and look flustered all at the same time, and she did it quite prettily. She really was an extremely attractive woman. "Brian, I'm sorry. Your brother's a heathen."

I reached across the table and patted Susan's hand. "Never fear," I said. "Mrs. Shanahan said the same thing about him this morning. You'll get used to it."

"No, no," Sam corrected. "Auntie said he was an *atheistic* heathen."

"That's redundant, isn't it?" Boyd asked, lighting another cigarette. Then—jokingly, I presume—he narrowed his eyes and gave me a growl. "And stop touching my wife's hand before I throw you over the railing."

I laughed and withdrew. Susan blushed. Sam grinned from ear to ear.

Boyd focused his attention on Sam. "Teach your friend some social skills, Sam. My brother's drunk, groping my wife, and pretty much ignoring you. That can't be good, can it?"

Sam's eyes flitted to me, and I could see a spark of uneasiness in them when he did. Sam had long been of the opinion that Boyd knew about us, but I had always pooh-poohed the idea. Now I wasn't so sure.

When in doubt, the best thing to do is punt. Changing the subject back to where it felt more comfortable seemed like punting to me, so that's what I did, much to Sam's relief. "Let me get this straight, Boyd. After a week of investigating, you've pretty much turned up bupkis. No suspect, no clues, no second murder, no nothing. Is that pretty much the result of your labors?"

Under the circumstances, I thought he appeared fairly amused by my statement. It was almost as if he knew exactly what I was doing. Still, he answered, and that rather surprised me.

"Couldn't have said it better myself. We've got nothing. To make matters worse, I'd like to admit maybe I was wrong in my original conclusion as to what that message on the answering machine meant, but unfortunately I still don't believe I was. There *will* be another murder. I know it. Call it a hunch if you want."

"A fairly unsettling one," I said.

Sam's foot nestled closer to mine beneath the table. "It certainly is."

Boyd continued. "As far as I know, aside from Dr. Hill, Charlie Nuggett, the police, and the four of us at this table, not to mention the murderer, no one knows about that goddamn pencil. I'm glad they don't. Somehow the inanity of that murder weapon is the most frightening aspect of Grace's death. It adds a real element of terror to what happened in that house. A *pencil*, for Christ's sake!"

He gave the table a solid *thump* with the heel of his hand, rattling the silverware and causing one of the candles to list alarmingly to the left. Sam straightened it.

"Maybe it was a weapon of opportunity," I conjectured. "Something the killer happened to grab on the spur of the moment."

Boyd wasn't buying it. "No. I think there's a message there somewhere. That pencil is supposed to mean something. Don't ask me what. If the killer needed a weapon of opportunity, why didn't he grab one of the kitchen knives that were hanging neatly on the wall not three feet from the body? Besides, we found no other pencils exactly like that in Grace's house, which would imply the murderer brought it there with him. Now what kind of deranged mind would set out to commit murder with nothing but a pencil in his arsenal? It's almost funny if you think about it. But then, it's not so funny either. That pencil was new. Freshly sharpened to a fine point. It was probably poking out of the killer's shirt pocket when he came to Grace's door. As innocuous as a pack of cigarettes." He leered angrily at the cigarette smoking in his hand. "If you want to call cigarettes innocuous. Anyway, it's something the average person would hardly notice. In the right hands, though, a pencil is as deadly as a butcher's knife. Poor Grace pretty well proved *that* point."

Boyd leaned forward, elbows on the table, engrossed in what he was saying, trying to make some sense of it in his mind. He was, I knew, a very good county sheriff. So good, in fact, that I could hardly imagine him being anything else. Neither, I suspected, could he.

A sardonic smile twisted the corners of his mouth. "Lord knows there's plenty of gossip going around about the murder. The Nine Mile gossip mill is doing its job well and with its usual lack of restraint. But there are a few facts they haven't picked up on yet. The pencil, for one. And the pudding. No one knows about that either. Nor do they know about the murderer's penchant for neatly laying out the body the way he did. This is all information only the killer is aware of. Maybe it will help us catch him, maybe it won't, but at the moment it's about all we have."

"Well," I said, "there's bound to be gossip. Murder isn't exactly a common occurrence in Greene County. It's not something the people here live with in the back of their minds. Not something they hear about so often it becomes an integral part of their everyday lives. If you were a cop in a big city, this would be any other case. Here, it's *the* case. *The* murder. Not just another grape in the bunch."

"I know," Boyd groused, pushing himself away from the table and stepping to the edge of the veranda. He leaned against the wooden railing and stared out across the lake, looking for—what? Inspiration? "It's really pissing me off. We've got to catch this guy before he kills again."

Susan crossed the veranda to wrap her arm around her husband's waist. She rested her head against his shoulder, and together they gazed out at the stars reflecting off the water.

Sam took the opportunity to graze his fingertips across the back of my hand, sending a shudder of desire shooting straight to my groin. He smiled and immediately pulled his hand away. I guess he figured his work was done. I smiled back at him.

I heard it then. Footsteps thumping up the staircase at the end of the veranda. *Heavy* footsteps.

"Someone's coming," Sam said.

At the same moment, Boyd and Susan turned toward the sound, and a second later Boyd gave a happy little cluck of laughter. "Carter! What the hell are you doing out here in the middle of the boondocks?"

A round, shiny head appeared above the railings. Deputy Morris Carter pulled himself up those last two steps as if he had conquered the summit of Mount Fuji. It was, for him, a long, arduous climb. Three hundred pounds of deputy sheriff is a lot of deputy sheriff to lug around, a heart attack waiting to happen. His face sparkled with beads of perspiration that caught the candlelight in a dozen teeny flecks of light, not unlike those lightning bugs flickering among the trees down by the lake.

Carter huffed and puffed and spouted and wheezed and finally spoke.

"Howdy, folks." He made a weary stab at doffing his cap at Susan, but in the long run, he never quite finished the motion. It was simply too much work. "Sorry to bother you, Sheriff. But you did tell me if anything came up to let you know about it."

He smiled happily at his boss, as if to say, "Well, here I am. How'd I do?"

The floorboards of my newly built veranda creaked beneath his feet, and the railing, too, gave an alarming *pop* when he leaned his bulk against it. I imagined the lot of us tumbling to the ground, twenty feet below, in a cloud of dust and plates and splintered timbers.

"Why didn't you phone?" Boyd asked. "You might have saved yourself a trip."

I spoke up. "No way, Boyd. The phones aren't in yet. Won't be hooked up until the end of the week."

Boyd waved his cell phone in my face. "Welcome to the twenty-first century, little brother." Then he waggled it in front of Carter. "Well? You lost another one, didn't you?"

Carter hung his head in shame.

"This one stolen too?" Boyd asked.

"Nope," Carter said, his eyes cast downward to his shoe tops. "I lost it fair and square."

Boyd sniffed. "At least you're admitting it."

To me, Boyd said, "Carter here has lost three cell phones this year. Two were stolen by traveling Hottentots, but this one he lost fair and square."

"Well, what do you know," I said.

Boyd narrowed his eyes at me. "Thanks for the insight, Bry." To Carter he added, "This cell phone is coming out of your pay, Morris. I warned you."

Carter shuffled his feet. "I know."

"You should be more careful."

Carter shuffled his feet some more. "I know, I know, I know."

"As long as you know. Now! What was it you drove all the way out here to the ass end of the world to tell me?"

"Let me catch my breath," Carter panted, burrowing his bulk more comfortably into the railing, causing another chorus of creaks and groans to stab the night. He pushed his cap back from his sweaty forehead, which caused his hair to stick up in damp, steely spikes.

Deputy Morris Carter held the unusual distinction of being one of Boyd's most and least favorite people, all at the same time. Lurking there behind the vacuous facade of this fat smiler was a man with the unbelievable ability to screw up nearly everything he set out to do. But he *was* likable, and pitiable too. Like a fat puppy, he was slaveringly eager to serve his master (Boyd) and loyal to the point of suffocation. I always imagined him to be a reincarnation of Barney Fife, grown obese and plucked from the television screen to be dropped unceremoniously into the middle of real life. It fed Boyd's sense of magnanimity, I think, to keep him around. There was history between them as well. They had been friends since childhood, same as Sam and I had. The synergy of their relationship had been the same even then. Boyd had been the handsome and charismatic leader, while Morris played the part of loyal but inept disciple. An unlikely duo, then as now.

Sam rose to greet the deputy. "Would you care for some dinner, Morris? You must be hungry after that long drive out here."

Carter sighed. "Oh, I am. I could darn near eat the shingles off your roof. But," and here he patted his belly, which spilled out over his belt buckle, "the sheriff went and put me on a diet. Have to lose a few pounds or he said he'd parcel me out for pandemoniums."

Sam looked as blank as I had ever seen him look. His face only came alive again when Boyd gave such a great honk of laughter that the frogs in the lake shut up.

"That's condominiums, Sam. Not pandemoniums. Once we get his weight down, we're going to start right in on polishing up his command of the English language. Carter needs a lot of work, as you can see."

Bright specks of color appeared on the deputy's chubby cheeks. A moment later his entire face flared into a wonderful shade of crimson. He didn't seem embarrassed, however, only happy to be the subject of conversation. *Any* conversation. A fat, wet puppy, thrilled by the attention he was getting. He did everything but wag his more than ample tail.

Morris Carter, I knew, drove my brother crazy. But he also made him smile. A lot.

Boyd was smiling now. "So what have you got?" he asked, not unkindly.

Carter plucked his shirt away from his damp chest and flapped it about to cool himself. The khaki cloth was soggy with perspiration.

"You tell me," he said. "You're the brains of the outfit. Check it out."

Carter handed Boyd a crumpled sheet of yellow notebook paper, the kind a child might carry to school. It had faint blue lines running across it and a ragged edge along the top where it had been torn from its binder. It, too, looked a bit soggy from being carried in Carter's damp fist.

Boyd moved closer to one of the candles on the table, spreading the paper out in front of him. His eyes narrowed for a moment, and then he emitted a soft curse under his breath.

He turned angry eyes to Carter. "What the hell is this? A riddle? What?"

"Turn it over," Carter said.

Boyd did. Even I could see what Boyd was looking at this time. Large print, written in what appeared to be sharp, angry jabs with a dull lead pencil.

The words read *#2. Just for you.* The downstroke of the capital *J* had been written with such force that it tore the paper.

"What the…?" Boyd flipped the sheet over and read the first side again. This time I moved closer and read it with him. As the words sloppily scrawled across that crumpled yellow paper slowly soaked into my consciousness, the sweet smell of the cranberry candles burning cheerfully between us seemed suddenly cloying. Sickening. My stomach rumbled with either nausea or fear. I wasn't sure which.

Sounds of nature once again intruded into the momentary silence. A mosquito hummed around my ear. A night bird chortled somewhere up in the eaves.

Boyd's eyes came up and locked onto mine.

"Like I said," he groaned, "a maniac."

Sam had seen the look of anger and dread on Boyd's face as clearly as I had. His next words sounded as if they had been wrenched up from the bottom of his feet. "There's been another murder."

Boyd's lack of denial was somehow more unnerving than anything he might have said in agreement. Only then did I realize Sam was right. I stared back at the paper in Boyd's hand, a chill of dread shooting up my spine.

By sheer will, Boyd snagged Carter's attention. "Where did you find this? And when?"

Carter wiped his brow with his hat. "In the patrol car. On the floor. Sort of stuffed up under the seat. I found it about an hour ago. I had just written a speeding ticket. Jimmy Carl again. Caught him flying down Route 67 outside of Bloomfield like the Huns were after him. Clocked him at eighty-five. Damn kids. Anyway, after I wrote the ticket and sent him on his way, I got back into the car, and right away I dropped my pen. So there I am scrambling around on the floorboard trying to find it, and I come up with *that*. God knows how long it's been there. I was in and out of the car all night. Had dinner at Max's diner in Nine Mile. Diet special. Three hundred calories. Some sort of packing material in tomato sauce. After that, I got a call to break up a domestic squabble over at the Roses' again, but naturally when they saw me coming, they quieted down on their own. Harvey Rose was drunk as usual. Clobbered his wife a couple of times for burning his fish sticks, the putz."

Boyd was impatiently tapping his toe. "Where else did you go?"

The look in Boyd's eyes stirred Carter to speak a little faster. "Let's see. After the Roses I went back to Bloomfield. Somebody had chucked a rock through the window at Miller's Feed Store. There was glass all over the street. Nothing was stolen, but old man Miller was pretty upset about it, so I talked to him a while trying to calm him down. Jeez, boss, there must have been fifty opportunities for somebody to toss that ball of paper into the car. Hell, maybe it wasn't even tonight. The damn thing might have been in the car for days."

Boyd wearily ran a hand across his face. "Let's hope not."

"Why?" Sam asked. "What does it say?"

"Here," Boyd said. "You figure it out."

Sam hesitated. "What about fingerprints?"

Boyd grunted. "Don't worry. If there *were* any prints on it, Carter's sweaty paws will have pretty well obliterated them."

Carter jumped. "Oh. Sorry, boss. I didn't think."

Boyd sighed. "I know. It's a chronic problem you've got."

I could tell Sam still didn't want to touch the paper. He left it lying on the table in the ring of candlelight. When a small gust of wind lifted the edge, he held it down with the tip of his fingernail.

After a silent moment, he looked up. His eyes found mine as he pushed a strand of pale hair from his forehead.

"Brian...."

"I know," I said.

"What?" Boyd asked. "What am I missing?"

I took a shuddering breath. "Nothing," I answered, pulling my gaze from Sam's. "It's just that it sounds so—so *biblical*. What kind of insanity are we dealing with here?"

I moved to Sam's side, and together we read the note again. The heavy pencil strokes more than clearly conveyed the anger with which it was written.

Another chill shot through me. The madness of the thing was almost palpable. I read the note aloud.

In this blood so divine a wondrous beauty I see. Do you see it too? Can you raise the nailed dead who themselves raise the dead? Are you that clever?

I longed to reach out and take Sam's hand. The fact that I couldn't made me ache inside.

Boyd turned away from us. He gripped the railing and stared out across the lake. "But what the hell does it *mean*?"

"This first line," I said, trying to keep my voice calm, "is a line from one of our hymns. 'The Old Rugged Cross.' Surely you remember it from Sunday School when we were kids."

Boyd turned into the light, his knuckles still white where he had gripped the bannister, his face incredulous, suspicious. "Yeah? So?"

My brother had hated Sunday school. I almost smiled, remembering. Then I stammered on. "And this... this second part obviously refers to Jesus raising the dead. But—"

Boyd's anger bubbled forth. Not at me, I knew, but at the circumstances. "What the hell are you trying to say, Bry? Are you trying to tell me this crazy son of a bitch has gone out and *crucified* somebody?"

"Well, no. Of course not. Nobody's *that* crazy."

"We hope." It was Susan, sounding small and childlike. Boyd looked at her, and I could see his anger temporarily drain away. He took a deep breath of the fragrant night air and once again ran his hand over his face, as if attempting to erase the reality of what he was hearing.

Susan stepped closer to him, and he folded her into his arms.

Perhaps feeling no one's eyes were on him at the moment, Deputy Carter wandered over to the table and plucked a wedge of boiled potato from a bowl. He hastily popped it into his mouth and poked it all the way in with a dainty movement of his finger. This was, it seemed, his way of facing the same reality Boyd was trying to erase. A defense mechanism, or perhaps it was simply the only way he could think. With a mouthful of food. I doubted he even realized he had done it.

"What's all this," he asked, still chewing, "about raising the dead who raise the dead? And is *who* that clever?"

"He's taunting us," Boyd said. "He thinks he's smarter than we are, so he's playing us like a fisherman plays a salmon. This guy has some serious emotional problems. I can't wait to get my hands on him. When I do, he'll have more than emotional problems to deal with. I'll shoot the son of a bitch stone cold dead."

I tried to lighten the mood. "That's not exactly out of the policeman's manual, is it?"

Boyd sniffed. "No, but it'll feel *so-o-o* good."

Carter, for once, made an intelligent observation. "You'll have to catch him first."

Boyd stepped away from Susan, angrily snatched the paper from the table, and read it again. He glared at it with an intensity designed to eke out every ounce of information he could glean from the damned thing. After a moment, he slumped. The paper, it seemed, had won, keeping its secrets to itself.

My brother gazed at me. "Help me, Bry. You're better versed in this biblical shit than I am."

I cringed at his choice of words but nodded understandingly anyway.

He continued. "I get the distinct impression this guy is trying to tell us who he just killed or who he's *about* to kill." He rattled the paper in front of my face. "Does any of this mean anything to you? Do you understand what he's hinting at? Who's the victim? What in God's name has this crazy bastard gone and done?"

I could tell him little. None of it made any sense to me either. Hymns. Crucifixions. Riddles. Was there an ounce of reason behind any of it?

All I could do was give my brother a sad, apologetic shrug.

He leaned in close and offered me a sardonic smile. "I think you're drunk, bro."

I couldn't see much sense in denying it. "Please don't tell the congregation."

Boyd swore himself to secrecy by making the sign of the cross over his heart like we had done as kids. He made one last perusal of the note in his hand, muttered, "Dammit," to no one in particular, and on that incomplete note of bewilderment and failure, not to mention impending doom, the evening ended. Or rather, it stumbled off into oblivion in a sort of self-disintegration, propelled along by its own aimless momentum.

The five of us said our good nights with little more than casual politeness, wandering apart, our thoughts elsewhere.

Chapter Five

ODDLY ENOUGH, less than an hour later, I found myself in the throes of a toe-curling orgasm, exploding endlessly with a shuddering sense of urgency and sensual abandon I had rarely experienced since puberty. Perhaps it was the wine, or the novelty of new surroundings, or simply the lush heat of Sam's lips surrounding me, the velvet warmth of his eager mouth feeding hungrily on my juices as I did everything but stuff a pillow down my throat to keep from crying out with a pleasure that was close to pain. Again and again, my back arched upward to meet his relentless urgings for more.

I did, I imagine, look somewhat akin to a slobbering fool, but God, who cared? Not me. And Sam was too busy to notice.

"I'm drowning," he finally muttered around me, his hair brushing my stomach, sending tendrils of excitement shooting across my skin like the fragile legs of water bugs skittering over the surface of the lake outside our window. Ripples of energy burned me in their wake. My heart hammered inside my chest as I struggled to catch my breath and relax my knotted muscles.

"God, Sam…."

I reached down to take his head between my hands. Caressing it, holding it still as he continued to taste me. He was trembling as I was, his mouth still sliding, still hungry.

"Stop," I managed to croak. "Please."

His movements slowed, but the pressure of his lips increased. The pain was exquisite. Wonderful. Impossible to endure. He seemed to swallow me whole. At that moment, his body tensed against mine. He pushed his face into me as he cried out softly. A sudden jet of heat sprayed across my shin. He pushed his swollen cock against me, over and over again, until finally his movements slowed. His orgasm ended. And still, he savored the juices I continued to leak into him. His hands were everywhere on my skin.

When we were both drained, I gently eased my softening cock from between his lips and fell back against the pillow.

He rested then, his cheek against my hip, his warm breath stirring the hair on my thigh. His hand, hot and moist now, like his mouth, slid up my stomach to caress my chest. He moved slightly, nestling his face into my pillow of pubic hair. The heaviness of my passion withdrew to settle softly against his chin. I could feel his smile.

"I'm sorry," I said. "You came without me."

His smile on my skin broadened. "Hardly. It was the taste of you that made it happen. Lord, I love it when you fill my mouth with come."

I buried my fingers in the softness of his hair. It shone golden in the moonlight streaming through the sliding door leading out to the veranda. I scooted down on the bed until I could lay my lips to that mass of blond hair, until his chest pressed against mine, the entire length of his delicious body lying cuddled up to me.

"I'm sorry," I said again.

Sam's voice was lazy against my skin, so light it barely stirred the air. I could hear both our hearts calming in the darkness. "What are you sorry for now?" he asked.

"I'm sorry I can't give you more than what I'm giving you."

His fingers spread across my chest. He tilted his head back to look at my face on the pillow beside his head. "I love you, Brian. Hopefully one day you'll realize you love me too."

I squeezed my eyes shut, wishing I hadn't heard those words. "I do love you, Sam. You know I do. It's just—"

"Hush," he said. "I understand. I do. If you are willing to go on living this lie we're living, then so am I. As long as I have you, I guess I can put up with about anything."

"It won't always be like this." The words sounded empty, even to me.

Sam gave his head a tiny shake. His fingers came up to stroke my lips. "Yes, it will," he said. "Until you make up your mind to be who you really are, then it will always be like this."

"But the church—" I said.

He hushed me again. "I know. The church. They'll never accept a gay minister. Hell, Brian, you and I both know in this small town they wouldn't accept a gay *human*. But let's not talk about it anymore. Let me enjoy this whole long night that I can be with you. Our nights together are few and far between. I don't want to miss a minute of this one."

I nodded, my fingers still buried in his hair. "All right. Just don't give up on me. I'll figure something out. I swear I will."

"All right," he said, but with little hope in the words. I could sense the emptiness in them as well as he could. But once again, I let them slide. I was getting good at that. Then Sam did something that made me love him all the more. Because he didn't want to quarrel, he let the subject go. It was the kindest thing he could have done, even if it made me feel guiltier than I already did.

His hands once again moved over my chest. His cock, sticky and flaccid against my leg, felt heavenly against my skin. He slid down the bed, lifting my arm so he could press his lips to my ribs. I could sense him inhaling the scent of me. The smell of our lovemaking filled the darkness. The heat of our skin. The fragrance of our two bodies, mingling into one.

Lightly, Sam's lashes brushed my flesh, sending another shudder through my overloaded nerve endings. I closed my eyes when he burrowed farther down the bed until his face was once again resting on my hip. I twisted my body until my soft cock lay against his cheek. When I had it where I wanted it, and where he wanted it too, I cradled his head in my hands to hold him in place. I curled myself into fetal position, still holding his face in my lap. His hands came up to grasp me from behind and pull me even closer.

Faintly, in the darkness, I could once again feel the movement of his smile on my skin. The gentle flutter of his lashes in my pubic hair.

His breath blew over me as his words drifted through the shadows. "I love you, Bry." His voice was languid. Tranquil. His tongue came out and licked the final drop of moisture seeping from my cock. "Hmm," he sighed. "The things I do for the church."

"Thank God I'm not a Catholic," I muttered back. "Celibacy and I would not get along."

He laughed.

I tried to bring some order to the tangled bedclothes but finally gave it up. I couldn't bear to pull far enough away from Sam to actually accomplish anything. The night was warm anyway.

The scented breeze wafting through the window smelled of pine and felt almost liquid against my heated skin. Luxurious. I languished alongside Sam's nakedness, letting the night air roam wherever it would across my body, feeling decadent and happy and full of love for the man beside me. I tried not to think of the words we had spoken, the promise I had still refused to give.

Curled into each other, I laid my face to the back of Sam's neck and held him close against me. His back felt warm and comforting beneath my hands.

The prayer came unbidden. Unforeseen. *Thank you, God, for Sam.*

I tried to relax, to let my mind go blank. I was tired. Aside from the tail end of it, this week had not been one I'd particularly enjoyed. Mrs. Shanahan's nettling voice always in the background. Gordon Knowles, stupidly building a wheelchair ramp at the angle of a ski slope. Nails in the pier. Rattlesnakes on the lawn. My brother speaking matter-of-factly over dinner about a pencil being pounded into an old woman's brain.

The note.

What did it mean, that note? What did it *imply*? *Was* the murderer from my church? If not, then why the reference to religion? *Had* he killed again? Was it only a matter of time before a second victim would be found?

In this blood so divine a wondrous beauty I see.

In the hymn, that line referred to the sacrifice of Jesus in surrendering His life for the sins of mankind. But in the insane note Deputy Morris Carter had delivered into my brother's hand, those words took on a completely different meaning. They implied… many things. None of them pleasant to contemplate. Enjoyment in killing, for one. A gut satisfaction in the spilling of blood. An almost Godlike power in deciding who would be the next to die. Godlike, and yet childlike too. A game.

Catch me if you can.

And what of the riddle?

Can you raise the nailed dead who themselves raise the dead? Are you that clever?

Are we? I wondered. Or I should say, *is Boyd?* What does it mean? *Can you raise the nailed dead who have raised the dead?* We had joked about it earlier, but what else could this person be referring to other than crucifixion? Did crucifixion always encompass the physical act of nailing a person to a wooden cross? No. It held other implications as well. Suffering. Pain. Yes. But not always that one horrible physical act. A person may be crucified in other ways than having nails driven through his hands and being left to die ten feet above the ground. It's a matter of semantics. The way a word is intended.

I hoped.

And the victims "who themselves raise the dead"? What the hell was *that* supposed to mean? No one can raise the dead. There are many acts of faith, but none of them as tangible as that. Not now. Not in this day and age. Jesus no longer walks here. Two millennia have passed since He did, and the ability to raise a soul from the grave, to once again breathe life into what is lifeless, passed with Him.

Sam's breathing grew deeper. He was sleeping soundly now. His hands on my skin had relaxed, fallen away.

I eased myself out of bed and rummaged around in the dark for my pajama bottoms. I found them at last in a heap at the foot of the bed, where Sam had tossed them. I slipped them on and quietly left the room, latching the door softly behind me.

I was wide-awake. Had, in fact, seldom felt less need of sleep in my life. The words from the note were like fingers in my brain that would not let me go. Fingers of pain too, coursed through my head from the wine I had consumed at dinner. I rarely drink, and my body was now reminding me of that fact in no uncertain terms. I needed a fistful of aspirin. With milk to wash them down.

The campground, I knew, was all but deserted. Sam asleep in the bedroom upstairs. Mrs. Shanahan, no doubt, snoring away like a lumberjack in her makeshift lodging behind the kitchen. Jesse and Kyle in sleeping bags down by the lake, adamantly refusing to lie beneath a roof on this, the first week of their summer adventure.

I wondered if the mosquitoes had yet reduced them to withered husks, tucked away in their sleeping bags like ancient, dusty slabs of papyrus cut into the shape of fifteen-year-old boys. Their campfire, I noticed as I gazed out across the lake, had dwindled down to a few glowing embers.

None of the other counselors would be spending their nights here until the camp officially opened. Only Sam and I, the boys, and Mrs. Shanahan were in residence.

Before murder became so prevalent in my mind, this was to have been a peaceful, relaxing interlude in my life. A delightful way to spend the summer and a chance, perhaps, to spend some much-needed quality time with Sam. In the process of doing all that, if I could eventually bring a few kids closer to God, then that would be a good thing too.

I found myself now with the first real opportunity to be alone here inside this lodge I had designed. I roamed from room to room, switching lights on and off as I went. It all looked remarkably well planned, sturdily and attractively constructed. Rustic but beautiful. Had I really drawn up the blueprints for this place myself?

Well, Sam had helped, of course. Sam helps me with everything. I could not survive without him. Nor would I want to.

Once again, I pushed away my guilt concerning Sam and concentrated on the lodge. I couldn't help feeling impressed by what had been accomplished here. Could pride such as I felt at that moment be considered a sin? I thought not. Pride was pride. Nothing more. It was welling up from me now like the orgasm I had experienced a few minutes earlier, in continuous waves, like a passion of the flesh.

My Methodist Youth Camp would be a great success. I just knew it. Assuming, of course, no one drowned in that bottomless lake, no children were gobbled up by a voracious herd of rattlesnakes, and Larry Fitzsimmons didn't sail off into oblivion after recklessly attempting to roll down a ninety-degree wheelchair ramp unassisted.

I would have to remember to check out the ramps first thing in the morning. God, there were a hundred things to check on. Oh, well. It would all get done. Somehow.

I navigated my way through the inky darkness of the mess hall toward the kitchen. After a few awkward seconds of fumbling around among a host of unfamiliar shadows, I finally found the light switch and flicked it on. The fluorescent lighting overhead blinded me for a moment, but my eyes soon adjusted. I pulled a jug of milk from one of the two industrial-size refrigerators that lined the wall and slugged down a quart of it before feeling satisfied.

I jumped at the sound of shuffling footsteps behind me.

"You're in *my* kitchen now, Reverend, and in *my* kitchen you're supposed to drink from a glass."

I turned to find Mrs. Shanahan standing imperiously in the doorway of her jerry-rigged bedroom, hands on hips, one slippered foot tapping impatiently on the floor. She was draped from neck to ankles in a moth-eaten bathrobe that might once have belonged to Martha Washington. Her head was swathed in yards and yards of pink toilet paper. I wondered if she bought that color purposely to match the faded remnants of her bathrobe. Surely not.

"And your kitchen," I said, "just happens to reside smack in the middle of my lodge, so I'll drink my milk from my *hat* if I choose to do so."

She shrugged and grunted. "Fair enough."

It was the easiest battle with her I had ever won.

"What," I asked, "is the purpose of all that stuff on your noggin? You look like a head-shot revolutionary."

She patted the paper bindings, making sure they were still in place. "It protects my hair," she announced, rather defensively I thought, "and keeps my waves in place."

I studied her like I might have studied a bizarre piece of statuary on a gallery floor. "Don't you worry about dying in your sleep and being hauled from the house like that for all the neighbors to see? I should think there'd be less disgrace involved being found with your hair a mess rather than with a head encased in two miles of toilet paper."

She flapped a fat hand at me and chuckled. "Oh hush! You don't know anything!"

She shuffled over to one of the tables and eased herself into a chair.

"Mind if I join you?" she asked. "It isn't every day I get to sit in my kitchen with a half-naked man."

I looked down at my sagging pajama bottoms and hitched them up a bit for modesty's sake. "How about some coffee?" I asked.

"Wonderful," she sighed. "My arthritis is kicking in. I can't sleep anyway. And I keep thinking about poor Grace."

"I know. It was a terrible thing to have happened. To live out so many years of her life and then come to the end of it like that. Not exactly a proper exit."

I filled the teakettle from the tap and placed it on the stove. It took a minute for me to figure out the workings of this monstrous twelve-burner range, which alone had cost the Methodist Conference a small fortune. I finally succeeded and sat down opposite Mrs. Shanahan to wait for the water to heat.

I cleared my throat. "Hope instant coffee's okay."

"Instant's fine."

It was rather cozy sitting there in that small puddle of light surrounded by so many miles of darkness. Even with Mrs. Shanahan for company, I couldn't help feeling snug and serene. The crickets outside were happily cricketing up a storm. The night was alive and thrumming with their song.

Mrs. Shanahan looked at peace as well. I decided to make the best of our unspoken truce.

"Dinner was excellent," I said. "Boyd and Susan asked me to relay their compliments to the chef."

She smiled a lazy, satisfied smile. "I haven't learned much in the eighty-four years I've lived on this planet, Reverend, but I did learn how to cook. It's about the only pleasure I have left. It's sad too, though. Most of the things I cook I can't eat anymore. One of the dubious benefits of a ripe old age."

I figured our truce could withstand a playful dig at Mrs. Shanahan's expense.

"You didn't seem particularly hindered by what you could and could not eat at the basket dinner. You pounded down the food quite handily, if I remember correctly."

She pooh-poohed me girlishly and hooted that happy cackle of hers, seemingly pleased by my teasing. For the briefest of moments, I caught a glimpse of the young woman she must once have been. It was an attractive, and rather astounding, revelation. I wondered vaguely why I had never seen it before.

"And you didn't?" She laughed. "I saw you loosening your belt when you thought nobody was watching!" Here she sighed, sadly, as if regretting a time in her life which was now lost to her forever. As indeed it was. "But you're right. I did make a pig of myself, and believe me when I tell you that I paid for it later. I think maybe I'm still recovering, in fact."

I clucked with sympathy and was rather surprised to realize my sympathy was earnestly given. Could it be possible I disliked this woman less than I had always thought I did? Or perhaps I was simply in that postsexual frame of mind that produces a contentment even Mrs. Shanahan's peckish bickering could not penetrate.

My question was doomed to remain unanswered because she chose that moment to throw me a curveball.

"I'm worried about Sam."

An empty second or two was filled with the sound of the teakettle hissing its way to a boil before I could think of anything to say.

"But why? Are you talking about the murderer?"

She cocked an eyebrow so high it disappeared beneath a layer of toilet paper. "No, Reverend. I'm talking about you. I didn't practically raise that boy after his parents were killed in a car crash to let him end up with his heart broken by you."

My own heart did an unhappy somersault. "That's a little harsh."

"Is it?" she asked.

"Yes," I said. "Trust me. I will never hurt Sam. Ever."

Her old eyes softened as she studied my face. "No," she said. "I don't suppose you will."

She threw her head back then, barking out a laugh. "Lordy, you're a charmer, Reverend. No wonder Sam is head over heels in love with you. I wish everybody else in this county felt about it the way I do."

"Yeah," I said, fighting back an old familiar sadness. "So do I."

Mrs. Shanahan splayed her large hands across the surface of the tabletop as if attempting to ease the arthritic pain in her fingers. "All right, Reverend. I'll not say another word. You know your secret is safe with me."

"Thank you," I said. "I know it is."

She let the darkness and the silence of the night settle in around us. "Don't you worry about the fact that we're stuck out here in this godforsaken wilderness, miles from the nearest doctor? What if something happens to someone? What if one of the workers, or, God forbid, one of the kids, when they get here—"

"Now wait," I said, amused. "This is hardly a godforsaken wilderness. If anything, God simply abounds in these hills. Nor are we stuck out here, as you so pleasantly put it. We have the car. We can get to town in less than an hour if the need arises."

Mrs. Shanahan cocked her head at me. A steely glint sparkled in her eyes. "Over miles of road that would shake the shit out of a constipated moose."

I grinned. "Beautifully put, my dear. You have the heart of a poet. Did anyone ever tell you that? Sometimes you sound so much like my brother I can hardly tell the two of you apart. But seriously—"

She waved down my objection before I could finish uttering it. "I wouldn't trust that pitiful excuse of a car of yours any farther than I could pick it up and throw it."

This wounded me to the core. "That car has never failed me yet."

She gave me a mischievous little smile. "Your face is getting red. I think maybe you should have your blood pressure checked. Elvira Potts used to flush up like that, and the next thing anybody knew, she was dead of a stroke. Massive. Killed her like a shot. In the produce aisle of the IGA store, it was, right in front of the bananas. And her only seventy-nine."

The woman was utterly impossible.

Fortunately, the teakettle chose that precise moment to spit up a rather angry sounding whistle. It was so perfectly timed, in fact, the thought crossed my mind that if this were a Bugs Bunny cartoon, that arrow of steam would have been shooting from my ears.

I pushed myself away from the table, grateful for something to do with my hands as I went about the mundane task of preparing us each a cup of instant coffee.

"Milk and sugar, please," she crooned sweetly at my back. "Put the milk in first and the sugar in last. Stir it twice. Oh, and I'd like a saucer under the cup. I'm not a truck driver."

I gritted my teeth and stretched my lips into a phony smile that felt as if it were thumbtacked to my face.

"Of course."

By the time the coffee was ready and I had dutifully delivered it to the table, rejoining Mrs. Shanahan there, I knew my little fit of petulance was under control. Not for the first time, however, or probably the last, did I contemplate this woman's unerring ability to make me react to her in a most unminister-like fashion. Perhaps more to the point was the question of why she always seemed to enjoy it so much when I did.

From some hidden cavern of strength, I dredged up a look of infinite patience and plastered it across my face, hoping it would stick. This was my "minister look," as Sam called it. He absolutely refused to let me aim it in his direction. "Don't take that tone of face with me!" he would rail, usually reducing us both to a couple of giggling idiots.

Mrs. Shanahan, of course, didn't know me as well as Sam did. I could haul out this "minister look," or any *other* look from my personal arsenal of facial expressions, with impunity. At least as long as I didn't pull it out too often. With repeated usage, it tended to lose its fizz.

My voice too, I hoped, sounded patient and reassuring. It was meant to go with the face. A package deal.

"Anyway," I said, "don't worry so much about what might or might not happen. This summer is no different than any other season of our lives. We're in God's hands. We have to trust Him to do what's best."

Her eyes bored into mine. "Did He do what was best for Grace?"

I stared right back. "That's really what's bothering you, isn't it? Grace's murder."

She smiled then, resigned, perhaps, to her own foolishness. If that's what it was.

"You see a lot with those big bedroom eyes of yours, Reverend. I think maybe you're seeing something about me that *I* didn't see. Maybe it *is* Grace's murder that's got me spooked. I keep hoping maybe the good Lord will turn back the clock, just this once, and let us all make believe it didn't happen. She was a wonderful woman, Reverend."

I nodded understandingly. I was in my element now. This is what a minister does best. He listens.

"I know," I said. "I know she was."

Mrs. Shanahan's old eyes, dim and pale now, opaque with age or possibly cataracts, looked through me as she spoke. Pleasant memories seemed to transport her somewhere else. A smile appeared, wrinkling the papery skin along her cheek. She blew a dainty breath across her coffee and tucked the cup beneath her chin.

"I thought of killing her myself, you know." She coughed up a chuckle that caused her tremendous breasts to quiver beneath the fabric of that beat-up old bathrobe. "Grace Nuggett was the only woman in Nine Mile who could bake a peach cobbler that came anywhere close to matching my own. That's why I never let her bring one to any of the basket dinners." She saw me now, registering my presence, squinting at the silliness of this ridiculous memory. "Got around it by telling her how much everyone loved her persimmon pudding. And she enjoyed baking a persimmon pudding about as much as she enjoyed washing her feet. There's nothing to it, you know. Easy as Jell-O. But she did it. For me. Never said a complaining word about it. She knew as well as I did the only reason I wanted her to bring that damned persimmon pudding was because I was jealous of her peach cobbler. Women are funny creatures, Reverend. God, they are *that*."

I tried to conjure up a reasonable argument to that last statement, but I couldn't seem to find one.

She leaned in close and pierced me with her stare. Without warning she changed the subject. You needed a road map to converse with the woman. "Do you think your brother's right? That this man is going to kill again?" For the first time in her life, she called me by my first name. "Are we in danger, Brian?"

I tried to soothe her fears by making light of what she had said. In the process, I also managed to avoid the question.

"How do you know it's a man? Everyone is always attaching masculine pronouns to this guy. For all we know, there may be an insane housewife out there who is willing to do murder to get her hands on Grace's recipe for persimmon pudding."

Carefully sipping her coffee, Mrs. Shanahan composed her face into a more businesslike expression. "Ain't likely, Reverend. Persimmon pudding was the only thing Grace couldn't cook for nuts. God knows I gave her ample opportunity to perfect the darn thing, but I guess maybe her heart just wasn't in it. When I took away her peach cobbler, I sort of knocked the wind out of her zest for baking."

I grinned and pointed my finger at the ceiling. "Could be she's up there right this minute serving God a big hot slice of that famous peach cobbler of hers. The one you wouldn't let her bake down here. I can almost smell it, can't you? I'll bet it's delicious."

She plunked her coffee cup down and glared at me. "You've got a vicious streak in you, Reverend, that one doesn't usually run across in a preacher. If God's been offered up a slab of Grace's peach cobbler, then I'm sure He's trying to think up a tender way to refuse it without hurting poor old Grace's feelings. He's waiting for mine, you see. I just *know* He is."

I gouged a little deeper. "This could be your atonement, you know. You could be cooking up persimmon puddings in Hell for the rest of eternity because of the way you treated poor Grace and her cobbler here on earth. Seems fitting too. Perhaps I'll have a word with my Boss about it first chance I get."

She smiled a bit too sweetly as she cast a glance upward, obviously to where a certain nephew of hers was lying sound asleep in my bed. "Please do, Reverend. I've got a few newsflashes to relate to the Man myself."

I laughed, raising my hands in submission. "Okay, okay, you win! My lips are sealed if yours are."

Her old head bobbed up and down. "Fair enough," she huffed.

Like a slap across the face, I suddenly realized how much I was enjoying this moronic little chat. Lord, I thought, I must be coming down with something. A dangerously high level of tolerance, perhaps.

Then another thought occurred to me. Mrs. Shanahan's opinions were always interesting, if not a bit bizarre. I wondered what she would make of this new development in Boyd's murder case.

"There's been a note. From the killer. Delivered to the police." I then relayed to her the circumstances of the note—what it said and how it was delivered.

"Morris Carter is a fool," she announced without preamble. "The biggest fool to ever walk around in a pair of pants. I'm surprised he had the brains to realize it *was* a note, and didn't toss it in the garbage with the rest of his candy wrappers."

I grinned. "Boyd put him on a diet."

She clucked. "That'll last."

"But forget about Carter," I said. "What do you think about the note? What do you think it means?"

She prompted me to recite the words again. When I had done so, she repeated the words aloud as if analyzing the way they tasted on her tongue.

She tapped her fingernails on the tabletop. "It's from 'The Old Rugged Cross.' Third verse, I think."

"Yes."

"Paraphrased, of course."

"Somewhat."

Then Mrs. Shanahan let a silence descend around us as she savored her coffee in petite sips and absently nodded her head up and down as if shaking her thoughts, stirring them around until the good ones floated to the top. She almost smiled, but not quite. She glanced down at her fingers, flexed them, then looked surprised they could still move.

"This fool is making a game of it, isn't he? He's having fun."

"I'm afraid he is."

"That's scary. It's someone from the church, isn't it?"

This was a jolt. "Good heavens!" I cried. "Why do you say *that*?"

"Too many references to religion, Reverend. He's got religion on the brain. It ain't healthy."

"Oh, come now. You can't—"

She had started shaking her head before I opened my mouth, as if she already knew she disagreed with what I was about to say.

"Don't get me wrong. Religion's a good thing. A wonderful thing. But sometimes people take it too much to heart. They see more in it than what's really there. It's a guideline for life, Reverend. But it's not the be-all end-all of existence. God didn't put us here with the expectation we would all be perfect. He's smarter than that."

"Well, yes, but—"

"When someone *tries* to be perfect, when someone *tries* to be a good Christian, then that's fine. That's the way it's supposed to be. But every once in a while you run across some clown who actually *believes* he's perfect. And when someone *believes* he's perfect, that person has some serious wiring problems in the old fuse box." She tapped the side of her head. "Religion can be a dangerous tool, Reverend. More wars have been fought over religion than anything else you can name. More people have died because of religion than cancer and traffic accidents and plain stupidity put together. They call it martyrdom. I call it lunacy."

I frowned. "You're being awfully hard on us."

"It's not *us*, Reverend. I'm not talking about *us*. I'm not talking about those of us who believe religion can create a better way of life. It most certainly can. I'm talking about the ones who twist religion into any shape they choose. The ones who use religion to do whatever the hell they want. There's plenty of them out there, believe me."

Once again, she tapped a finger against the side of her head. "It's a sickness, Reverend. Fanaticism. It's like drinking. Some people can handle it, and some people can't. Some people go overboard on everything they put their hands to. They have addictive personalities, if you want to call it that. Personally, I think they're just plain weak. But they can stir all that weakness around in their heads until it comes out strength, or they make themselves *believe* it's strength. Maybe it is. *Dangerous* strength. People will do practically anything if they've convinced themselves what they're doing is right."

"But why is he killing?"

She sadly shook her head. "Who knows? Whatever the reason, it's buried somewhere in that sick mind of his. If you ask me, it's just an excuse—religion. The man craves violence. That's what it boils down to. And he's using religion as an excuse to feed that craving."

I could think of no reason to dispute anything she said. "You're a wise old woman. You truly are. A little scary perhaps…."

She barked out a laugh that came from so deep within her it made me smile.

"I'm smart enough to know when I'm being diddled, Reverend."

"Excuse me?"

"Talk to me about Grace. Tell me what it is your brother's holding back."

"I don't know what you mean."

"Oh, I think you do. Why is it that with all the rumors flying around about Grace's murder, no one seems to know what the murder weapon was? Nothing was released in the papers about it. All they'll tell us is that the woman was stabbed."

Boyd had sworn me to secrecy on this. I had to wangle a way around it. "I assume she was stabbed with a knife. That's what people are usually stabbed with."

Mrs. Shanahan peered at me over the rim of her cup. She was nobody's fool, and I knew she knew I knew it. The satirical glint in her eyes told me as much.

"Then why didn't they come right out and *say* it was a knife instead of pussyfooting five miles around it? Why all the secrecy?"

I found myself wishing I had stayed in bed, cuddled up to Sam. "Because the truth is much worse than that. Ridiculous, in fact. So ridiculous I still can't believe it happened."

"But it wasn't a knife, was it?"

"No," I admitted. "It wasn't a knife."

Mrs. Shanahan pushed her cup away. It was empty. "All right, Reverend. I know you must have promised your brother not to tell anyone about the murder weapon, and I respect you for keeping your word. Let's drop it."

I tried not to breathe an audible sigh of relief. Mrs. Shanahan had an uncanny knack of acquiring information from people whether they wanted to give it out or not. Unfortunately, she also had an incredible gift for redistributing that information—with an uncommon lack of discretion. I was grateful to be let off the hook so easily.

I also felt certain if I did tell her all the circumstances of Grace's death, it would be information that sooner or later she would be sorry she knew. If only I could relinquish that knowledge myself.

I glanced at my wrist, but of course my watch wasn't there. It suddenly came as somewhat of a belated shock to me that, in fact, I was sitting there having this long conversation with Mrs. Shanahan in a baggy pair of wrinkled pajama bottoms and nothing else.

It seemed Mrs. Shanahan had an uncanny knack of reading people's minds as well.

"Don't worry, Reverend. There's nothing you could possibly have that I haven't seen before. Not *recently*, perhaps…."

She let the sentence trail away to a long, drawn-out sigh as if regretting the truth of the words. She then fished out a timepiece on a sturdy silver chain from the bottomless well of her cleavage, not unlike a shrimper hauling in his net.

"It's after two," she said. "If that's what you're wondering."

"Thanks."

We let the hush of approaching morning gather around us, content, it seemed, to let it come. Neither of us made a move to leave the kitchen or return to our beds. I thought of Sam sleeping peacefully upstairs and felt a tug at my heart to know he was safely there, seconds away.

"Who's it going to be?" I asked. "Who's the killer going to go after next, if he hasn't already? God forbid."

She began unwinding the toilet paper from around her head, wrapping it carefully about her hand as she went, apparently meaning to save it for later. The clips that held it in place, she absently dropped into a pocket of her robe, conjuring up half-forgotten memories of my grandmother.

When Boyd and I were small children, we had spent many happy hours on our grandmother's lap, going through her pockets and finding a myriad of delightful objects that made us squeal with each new discovery. We always asked her what she used them for. What was this, what was that? It wasn't until years later, with our grandmother long dead but still sorely missed, that we came to understand those funny little objects had no purpose whatsoever. She had simply stashed them in her pockets for us to find.

"He's trying to tell us, Reverend. That's plain enough. But I'll be pickled if I can figure it out."

"Nobody raises the dead," I said. "What the heck is he trying to say?"

Mrs. Shanahan gave a forward shove to the hair on top of her head, and like magic those flattened waves popped into crisp little ridges, like the furrows in a freshly plowed field. She gave them one more pat, for luck I guess, then twisted her pale lips into an odd, lopsided grin.

"The only creature I ever heard of being raised from the dead, aside from Jesus Himself, was Lazarus, and the only Lazarus I know in this day and age is that ugly black cat that belongs to Golda Burrows. But I don't think the murderer would stoop to slaughtering a cat, do you? Bit of an anticlimax after the number he did on Grace. Wouldn't make any sense at all, not that any of it *does*."

I drained the last drops of coffee from my cup. They tasted cold and bitter. "He doesn't say he wants to raise the dead. He said he intends to go after the person who *raises* the dead."

Mrs. Shanahan blinked. "You don't suppose he means Golda, do you? You know she's always pecking around about the way she raised that silly cat from the dead by yanking him out from underneath a car when he was a kitten. That's why she named the damned thing Lazarus, of course. The old twit."

"Seems a bit far-fetched," I said. "How many people could possibly know about that?"

"Everybody and his dog knows about it, Reverend. Golda Burrows talks about that infernal cat as if it were a man. Can't really blame her, I guess, since it's the closest thing to a man she's ever had, what with it being male and a carbon-based organism. It follows her around like a henpecked old man too. If it wasn't so blasted ugly, it would be cute. Sneaky, like all cats are, but cute. Never much cared for 'em myself. Too darned independent. Always seems to be a matter of dispute as to who's the pet and who's the master. Especially in Golda's case. She feeds the filthy thing on the dining room table. *That* ain't normal!"

A tiny alarm bell sounded somewhere in the back of my head. "We have to call her. See if she's all right."

Mrs. Shanahan gazed at me as if I were a glob of something that had fallen out of a tree and landed on her foot.

"At two o'clock in the morning?"

"Yes. I think we should."

"Where's your cell phone?" she asked.

"Upstairs."

"I'll get mine," she said. "It's closer."

She hustled off through the door to her sleeping quarters and was back a moment later with her tiny cell phone and her address book. She slid the phone across the table to me and leafed through the address book until she found what she was searching for. She slid the book to me as well, tapping her finger on the number we needed.

I punched in the numbers and listened to a phone ring somewhere miles away, off in the distant darkness. Golda Burrows's phone. It rang until Mrs. Shanahan's cell phone automatically ended the call without an answer.

I couldn't believe what I was about to do, but there was no way around it. I would simply have to drive back into town to see if she was all right. I could call Boyd, but if Mrs. Shanahan and I were chasing the wrong possum up the wrong tree, my brother would never let me hear the end of it. I'd rather drive all the way over there in the middle of the night than face my brother's ridicule.

"Care to go for a ride?" I asked.

A look of concern suddenly crossed her face. Or was it fear? "Do you think we should? What about Sam? What about the boys?"

"We'll leave them a note. If we're wrong, we'll be back before they know we're gone."

Mrs. Shanahan seemed reluctant to be moved from the security of her kitchen. "Your brother's the one who should be doing this. Not us. He's the county sheriff. He—"

"Why should we bother Boyd until we know for sure something's wrong?"

"Yes, but—"

"You said yourself you can't sleep."

I remembered Sam. The heat of his lips. The gentle prodding of his tongue leading me to orgasm. The words we had spoken later in the darkness. Once again I realized how content I was to know he was safe and sound in my bed, nestled among my sheets, leaving his heavenly scent on my pillow.

"I can go alone," I said. "I guess you're too old to be gallivanting across the state at this time of night."

Mrs. Shanahan blasted me with a look of pure disdain. Her jaw dropped open like a trapdoor.

It was almost too easy.

"A little drive," I insisted. "A little fresh air."

"A little murder," she stated without enthusiasm. "A little mayhem."

"Hopefully not," I said and meant it.

"Yes," she agreed, patting her hair one more time. "Hopefully not."

Chapter Six

THE PHYSICAL act of manhandling my old Rambler along those muddy miles of potholed roads, steering by the bouncing beams of a poorly aligned pair of headlights and guided, too, by Mrs. Shanahan's continual complaints and directions, helped me forget for a time what it was we had really set out to do. But by the time we reached the main highway and my threadbare tires began humming smoothly beneath our butts, those distractions were left behind.

My imagination, overly active at the best of times, popped out of the wings for a second curtain call. I could only hope and pray Mrs. Shanahan and I were wrong in thinking we had deciphered the cryptic message so cleverly hidden among the words of that damnable note.

The memory of Golda Burrows's laughter, forever exploding from that pixie-like face of hers, had at some point in the last few minutes reached out to take a death grip on my mind. I couldn't shake it. The sound of her laughter seemed to follow me down the highway, always there inside my head, where I was powerless to stop it. A great sadness fell over me to think that wonderful sound might now be reduced to simply that. A memory.

So while Mrs. Shanahan periodically dialed Golda's number and hugged the cell phone tightly to her ear, waiting for an answer that never came, I used the silence to pray. I prayed I was wrong. But the words of my prayer became continually jumbled, confused, and eventually lost altogether among those phantom echoes of girlish laughter in my head. Only one comprehensible sentence of my ill-fated prayer seemed to float to the surface and survive.

Please, God, don't let this happen.

For the tenth time, Mrs. Shanahan tucked her cell phone into her pocket. Her hand came out of the shadows beside me. Her fingers touched my arm with a gentleness one would not suspect she possessed.

"I don't like this, Reverend. There's still no answer."

"I know."

"But—I keep going over that note in my mind. It does make sense, in a way." Her voice sounded breathless, awed. "But why would he want to kill that crazy old woman? What possible reason could he have to—"

She fell immediately silent, as if her words had been yanked right out of her throat by invisible fingers, when we passed a battered, faded sign at the edge of the highway.

NINE MILE—Population: 327

The sign had not been changed or updated, I knew, since I was a boy. It had always announced the same number of souls living here: 327. Even so, I doubted the number was far from wrong. Nine Mile was not a town well known for its pattern of cosmopolitan growth. It survived, but did little else. No new businesses had settled here for more than a decade. Paint peeled from the sides of houses. Dogs yawned on dusty front steps. Weeds grew up from cracks in the sidewalks, and the weeds looked far healthier than the lawns around them. The only changes one might see in the faces of the people who walked those sidewalks came from age. There were few new faces.

The young ones, for the most part, equated adulthood with escape. No reason for them not to. This town held out little future for them. The handful of small businesses in Nine Mile could offer very few jobs. The town existed to service the farmers in the outlying areas. They came here to buy the few things they could not produce themselves, to pick up their mail, or to have a cold beer in the Oodle Inn after a long, hot day in the fields.

Or to worship.

Their children, upon graduation from high school, took off for the cities to find work. If they wanted to spend their lives doing anything other than farming, they had no option but to leave. Most never returned.

Nine Mile might be, as Sam always said, little more than a pimple on the butt of the planet, but it was still a happy, friendly town. Homey and content with its unchanging aura of familiarity. It did not presume to be anything it was not and gave the impression of being oddly proud of itself for that. A simple town populated with simple people, who understood the quirks and qualities of their neighbors in the same way a family knows its own strengths and weaknesses.

The Nine Mile Methodist Church, *my* church, was perhaps the only truly attractive structure standing. It was the town's heart, its core, or had always appeared so to me. Houses might tumble down around it, seedy with neglect, but the church itself was kept in pristine condition by the loyal members of its congregation. *My* congregation. They might not give three hoots how their own houses looked, but they took great pride in having a pretty church to attend every Sunday morning.

I could see the church now in the light of an approaching streetlamp. The white of its clapboard walls seemed to glow as if lit from within. The louvered steeple rising tall above the main entrance, with its tremendous iron bell silent now inside, stretched up into the darkness and disappeared where the light from the streetlamp couldn't reach. I caught a glimpse of the silver cross atop the steeple as it was silhouetted briefly against that gigantic moon hanging high up in the sky. Then it was gone—the church, the cross—left behind as we passed. And the sense of security I always gained by simply looking at that building passed with it. Fear reclaimed me in a heartbeat.

Mrs. Shanahan leaned forward in the seat and clutched the dashboard like a child who is eager to see what's up ahead.

The streets in Nine Mile are not named. That would be an extravagance in a place where every resident is familiar with each and every tree and stone. As we turned off the main highway that slashed its way through the middle of town, I thought of the shadowed stretch of pavement that now lay before us as "Golda's street." Nothing more. No other title was necessary. Golda Burrows's house stood at the very end of the street. The last house on the left.

Inside that house, I hoped, we would find nothing more than a peacefully sleeping, eccentric old woman with a very ugly black cat. I could imagine Golda's impish face smiling from her doorway as she peeked outside to see what manner of idiot would come pounding on her front door at three o'clock in the morning. I could almost hear her laugh at us, not unkindly, with pepperish squeals of delight when we announced, shamefaced, our reason for interrupting her much-needed beauty sleep. I could even imagine the words she would use.

"Dead, Reverend? Do I look dead to you? Well, maybe I *do*, but let me tell you I most certainly am *not*! *Am* I, Lazarus?" Again she would blast a peal of laughter out past our heads toward the sky.

I could picture our embarrassment, and I could picture Mrs. Shanahan's tirade as we humbly wended our long way back to Sunset Lake with our proverbial tails tucked between our legs.

Mrs. Shanahan would then share her own take on the matter. "That woman will never let us hear the end of this, Reverend. You mark my words, she won't. This story will be all over town in the time it takes to pluck a two-feathered chicken. We should have killed her ourselves and spared us the humiliation that's about to be rained down on our heads."

"Oh, come now," I might say. "It isn't as bad as all that."

"Not for you, maybe. But what about me? Out gallivanting across the township at three in the morning with a man young enough to be my son."

"Grandson."

"Don't be insulting!"

It might go on for days, this wrangling between Mrs. Shanahan and myself. Sam, of course, would relish every minute of it.

But then my old car bounced to a stop at the edge of Golda Burrows's front lawn, and all my pleasant imaginings bled away into the night, leaving me now with nothing to face but stark reality. Whatever that reality might prove to be.

The familiar sounds of my poor engine sizzling and popping and hissing as it gratefully began the weary process of cooling down did little to make me feel less apprehensive. It made the eerie silence of the night around us more noticeable, in fact. More threatening. It felt as if a heavy pall had been laid across the town.

Neither of us made a move to leave the car.

Standing as it did beneath the shadows of a towering sycamore tree that was probably older than Mrs. Shanahan and me put together, Golda's house could barely be seen. No lights shone inside or out. The house, the entire street, in fact, appeared lifeless.

"Smell her camellias?" Mrs. Shanahan whispered. I hadn't. Not until she said it. Then suddenly the night was awash with the cloying, sticky fragrance that always reminded me of high school proms and funerals and skinny maiden aunts who inevitably kept a spray of camellia blossoms floating in a bowl of water on their sideboards.

Their appeal had always been lost on me. The pungent stench that wafted from those waxy white heads was somehow vaguely reminiscent of small dead animals rotting in the underbrush.

As my eyes adjusted to the darkness, I took a closer look at the house. I could now see the fluorescent outline of a white concrete duck standing alone on the lawn. In the daylight, when Sam and I had sometimes passed this house on one of our evening strolls, with the strident tones of Golda's untuned piano playing like an ill-conceived soundtrack in the background, we would often have a good chuckle at the expense of that silly duck.

It had stood in the exact same spot for years. So long, in fact, that the grass was dead beneath it and most of its original paint had bled away with the seasons into the dirt. Golda Burrows, in her inimitable fashion, had resurrected the faded creature with a fresh coat of paint, right down to a bright orange beak and blue, bulbous eyes that somehow became, in the transformation, crossed. Consequently, it no longer simply looked like a concrete duck. Now it looked like a *stupid* concrete duck. Crossed eyes and all. Sam had dubbed it Wilbur.

Looking at that unfortunate duck now in the moonlight, with the dew glistening on its broad back, it appeared almost to be real, as if it might suddenly quack or walk away, or simply drop a casual load of concrete duck shit on the lawn.

This absurd thought, which I decided not to share with Mrs. Shanahan for reasons of self-preservation, served to rouse me from whatever state of mental hibernation I had fallen into. I hadn't driven these many miles in the dead of night to sit in a parked car and wait like a fool for a concrete duck to come to life.

"Well," I hissed, more to myself than Mrs. Shanahan, "let's get this over with."

"Lord," Mrs. Shanahan whispered. "My heart's doing flip-flops."

"So is mine."

As we eased ourselves quietly from the car, I realized my eyes had indeed adjusted well to the darkness. I could now see the outline of Golda's front door and windows. Even the pots of red geraniums and the concrete fawn dawdling idly on her front porch were visible in the shadows. Visible enough, at least, to distinguish what they were.

I could also see movement—movement from inside the house—as one of the curtains shifted at the window!

I smiled. Thank God, we had figured it all wrong. The note. Our suspicions. Everything. Golda Burrows must have heard the car pull up, and now she was peering through her living room window to see what the heck was going on. I began to say as much to Mrs. Shanahan, but then I spotted the tiny face pressed up against the glass. It wasn't Golda. It was Lazarus. The cat. As I watched, he pressed both forepaws high on the glass and, like a cat in season, screamed. That anguished, piercing cry made the tiny hairs on the back of my neck pop up like bread from a toaster.

Mrs. Shanahan stumbled to a stop beside me. "What was *that*?"

I pointed to the window. "Lazarus."

"Oh, God," she moaned, meaning what I wasn't sure.

Mrs. Shanahan gripped my arm, and together we traipsed across the dew-soaked grass and climbed the steps to Golda's front porch. Sidestepping the concrete fawn, I bent down to wag a friendly finger at Lazarus as he stared at us through the window.

Where his feet had pawed the glass, I saw heavy smears of some dark, viscid substance. Mud perhaps. But how could he get muddy feet inside the house? I looked closer. He arched his back against the glass, eager for a sympathetic pat. I could make out no discernable color in the darkness, but I nevertheless knew, as if by instinct, what that stuff was Lazarus had so carelessly smeared along the entire length of Golda Burrows's front window.

It was blood. I strongly suspected it wasn't his.

Lazarus screamed again. A long, plaintive wail that reverberated against the glass, bouncing back to echo through the dark, silent house like metal screeching angrily over metal. His head butted the window with a thud, causing the glass to rattle in the frame and leaving another smear of blood on its surface.

Then he was gone. Only the fluttering of the curtain showed he had ever been there at all.

A scratching noise immediately issued from the base of the front door. It was Lazarus again, frantic now, clawing at the wood to let us in. *Or to let himself out.*

Mrs. Shanahan's voice sounded frail and old. "He's scared to death, Reverend. But not of us. That's plain. He's scared of whatever it is that's inside that house with him. I think maybe he wants himself out more than he wants us in."

"Can't say I blame him," I croaked. "Should we knock?"

Mrs. Shanahan pushed me aside. "You *are* a fool. Who do you think's going to answer? The murderer or the cat?"

She was right, of course. Knocking was pointless. If Golda Burrows was alive inside that house and in any fit condition to make it to the door, the screaming of her beloved pet would have brought her running long before this.

Locked doors are a rarity in Nine Mile, so I was not surprised when Mrs. Shanahan simply twisted the knob and pushed the door open with her fingertips. With that, I guess, she figured her obligations to the night's activities were more than fulfilled. She stepped well back, making it crystal clear I would be the one who walked through that doorway first.

Before either of us could step inside, a flying ball of black fur went sailing out between our legs with a hiss, vaulting over the concrete fawn and disappearing into the night before I could do so much as gasp.

"Smart cat," Mrs. Shanahan muttered. "That's what *we* should be doing."

I groped around inside the door for a light switch and finally found it. With a fervent prayer for God knows what—guts, I suppose—I flicked on the overhead light in the living room. I immediately felt Mrs. Shanahan sway against me as she almost collapsed with the shock of what we saw there in the harsh, glaring light.

Golda Burrows was a dedicated disciple of the doily, doll, and foofaraw school of interior design. Milk-glass figurines. Fringed pillows. Pressed flowers in ornate frames. Old family portraits by the dozens, standing and hanging on every conceivable surface. Throw rugs upon throw rugs, seemingly scattered at random. And dolls. Dolls everywhere. All mail order by the look of them. Sitting on the furniture. Standing in the corners. Each in native costumes from a score of different countries.

The past was well represented here. So too was the present, in the guise of an immense Mediterranean-style console TV that dominated one corner of the room. It sat there looking smug and cocky and completely out of place, like a ball gown hanging on a rack of rags. The remote control for this twentieth-century monstrosity rested on the coffee table, inside a cranberry-colored vase with frilled edges and pewter handles any antiques dealer in the state would have given his mother's eyeteeth to acquire.

Golda Burrows had apparently found a comfortable niche for herself somewhere between this century and the last. The evidence of her long life could be seen all about the room. So could the evidence of her death.

Lazarus's bloody footprints were everywhere. Tiny crimson stencils plastered across the floor and furniture. Smears of blood, no longer red but a deep mulch brown, stained the curtains and the doilies on the arms of the sofa.

If Golda were to see the condition her living room was in, she would no doubt be thrown into a seizure of grand mal proportions. But of course she couldn't see it because she was dead. As dead as King Tut.

She sat arrow-straight, with her back to us, on a needlepoint-covered piano bench. One foot still pressed idly on the center pedal, as if she were frozen in time, as indeed she was. But her hands did not rest on the ivory keyboard as one might expect. Instead, they were stretched out in front of her, one at either side of the old upright piano, like someone praising Jesus. They had been nailed in place at about shoulder level with two blood-soaked metal spikes that had been hammered through her hands and into the wood.

The spikes were thick and square and headless—the kind you might see sticking out of an old railroad track. Rusted too, as if an old railroad track might be *exactly* where they had come from. Even without the grotesquely splayed-out hands they had so viciously pierced, those spikes would have been wicked, nasty-looking things.

The blows that had driven those spikes through Golda's hands had been delivered with such force, such violence, they'd splintered the wooden face of the piano from top to keyboard. Blood from the wounds had dribbled down her arms to stain the sleeves of her dress.

Another wash of blood extended down the back of her dress, beginning at the collar, to form a glistening crimson *V* that reached all the way to the bench and below, forming a puddle on the floor. Over this stain on the carpet, several feet of white electrical cord lay as if tossed out into the room from underneath the piano. Perhaps she had kicked it there during her death struggle.

This last collection of blood came from a wound to her scalp, where a vicious blow had torn the skin and collapsed the skull at the crown of her head.

Trancelike, I moved toward her. I could hear Mrs. Shanahan sobbing quietly behind me. I should have known she would not be the type to scream. She had seen too many horrible things in the long years she had lived on this planet to scream at the sight of one more. I doubted, though, she had ever seen anything quite like this.

"Call the police," I whispered.

"Yes" was all she said. All that needed to be said.

Mrs. Shanahan had left her cell phone in the car. She moved off into the kitchen, where apparently she knew a phone was located, making a wide berth around the area directly in front of Golda's piano. A moment later I could hear the ratchety sound of dialing on an old rotary phone. Golda must have owned the last one in town.

I took another step closer to Golda's body. I approached it in the same manner the boys had approached the rattlesnake by the lake: cautiously, as if afraid of what it might do.

As I neared her, I noticed the sickly-sweet smell of meat about to turn bad. I pulled the neck of my T-shirt over my nose and left it there. *She's been dead a while*, I thought. A few more hours, I knew, and the smell would have prevented us from entering the house.

Over Golda's shoulder, I could see the hymnbook where it rested on the little music stand built into the front of the piano. It was the same book we used at the church. Blue binding. Well-thumbed pages. Somehow I knew, even before I looked, to what page it would be turned. Page 216. "The Old Rugged Cross." The murderer had done exactly what he had threatened to do in the words of his note. He had performed a crucifixion. Ritualistic, sacrificial, and as bloody as any Old or New Testament crucifixion one could ever hope to witness. This woman, this good Christian woman, had died in a way that perhaps she might not regret. She had died like Jesus. Nailed and murdered and left to bleed.

I moved a bit closer in a roundabout fashion to where I could look upon her face. Her glasses had fallen from her nose and now rested on the age-yellowed ivory keys. Her eyes were open, her head thrust back, held there by the tension of her outstretched arms, as if she were gazing with those empty, clouded eyes at the photographs of family and friends arranged in rows across the top of the piano. A few had toppled over with the force of the blows that nailed the old woman's hands to the wood, but most were still standing.

Those faces, the faces of the people she had loved enough in life to wish to remember, looked down on her now and smiled. They continued to do the things in the photographs they had always done—

pose, smile, laugh—as if nothing at all had changed. For them, I supposed nothing *had* changed. They were dead, most of them, judging by the age of the photographs. As dead as Golda herself.

She had joined her friends at last.

Mrs. Shanahan showed herself at the kitchen door, looking pointedly at me and not at the body in front of me.

"They're on the way," she said through the handkerchief she held over her nose. She must have caught a whiff of poor Golda, as I had.

Her eyes fell upon a trail of Lazarus's bloody paw prints that snaked their way into the kitchen beneath her feet. She stepped quickly away from them.

"I think I'll wait outside, Reverend. I'm...." She didn't finish the sentence. She merely shook her head and left. A second later I heard the squeak of Golda's porch swing as Mrs. Shanahan lowered her bulk into it.

Night sounds once again pervaded my consciousness. Crickets. A dog barking on a distant street. A clock ticking somewhere off in the direction of Golda's bedroom. A long, anguished sigh that tore from deep within me before I was aware it was coming.

I closed my eyes and prayed. Prayed for the soul of the woman before me. Prayed for a world where things like this were allowed to happen. I even tried to pray for the murderer. For the forgiveness of his crimes. But somehow I could not quite force myself to form the words inside my head. They simply would not come.

I felt suddenly exhausted. Great sex, too much wine, a horrible murder, and the exhausting presence of Mrs. Shanahan, all packed together into one unforgettable evening, were enough, I supposed, to wear anyone out. All I wanted to do was sleep. I also had the nagging suspicion my legs were about to buckle beneath me. I looked around for a place to sit, decided it best not to disturb the evidence lest Boyd slaughter me as well, and walked outside to join Mrs. Shanahan on the porch.

She had switched the porch light on. The bugs had found it already, swirling around that globe of light like the components of some crazy cosmic storm around a distant moon, plunking themselves to death against the bulb in the process.

Mrs. Shanahan sat in its circle of light, her cheeks damp with tears, motionless on the swing. As I joined her there, a sound escaped her lips that might have been either a sob or a sigh. Or both.

Her voice was hushed. Reverent.

"How long has she been dead?"

I eased myself into the swing and laid my hands in my lap. Looking down at them, I remembered the spikes which pierced that other pair of hands inside the house.

"I don't know. A while, I guess."

She too looked down at my hands. "You're trembling."

I nodded. "I know."

"Did you pray for her, Brian?"

I attempted to force a smile to my lips. It was like working with hardened clay. "I tried to. It probably didn't make much sense, but maybe God was able to sort it out."

A silence settled over us, interrupted by the sound of bugs slapping the porch light over our heads.

Finally Mrs. Shanahan said, "I'm scared."

I reached out to take her hand, a simple thing that, before this night, I might never have imagined myself doing. Her skin felt papery and dry, like cool crepe.

"Perhaps you should go home," I said. "As soon as Boyd arrives, I'll drive you. There's nothing more you can do here. Me either, for that matter."

"No," she said. "Absolutely not. I don't want to go home. I want to go back to the lake. I'll feel safer there with you and Sam and the boys." She gazed around at the darkened houses lining the street. "All of a sudden I don't much care for this town anymore. It feels so—*evil*."

I followed her gaze. It seemed odd to look at my hometown from this new vantage point. This was the view of Nine Mile Golda Burrows saw as she sat on her porch swing of a summer evening, idly swinging back and forth and watching Lazarus, maybe, stalking sparrows in the camellia bushes. Here she could check out the movement of her neighbors. Say howdy to that nice young preacher and the preacher's friend as they strolled along the sidewalk on an evening constitutional.

Sitting here was like seeing Nine Mile for the first time. Or seeing it through another person's eyes. I knew exactly what Mrs. Shanahan meant. I felt it too. A sinister air of something ugly festering in the shadows. Something I had never sensed before. Something I would never have suspected could be there. Something waiting. Wicked and hungry and murderous.

A moth landed lightly on my leg. I flicked it gently away so as not to harm its delicate wings.

"I understand," I said softly. I did. All too well. I too wanted nothing more than to get back to the peace and serenity of my beautiful lake. To Sam. I hoped he was still asleep. I hoped he had not yet woken to find that ridiculous note I'd left pinned to the pillow beside his sleeping head, explaining that his old aunt and I had trundled off in search of a murder.

I was suddenly itching to be out of there. Back to Sam and the boys. To be sure they were safe.

I forced my mind away from that thought. Of course they were safe. They had to be.

The porch swing squeaked alarmingly as I heaved myself out of it and searched among the shadows in the yard for a frightened black cat.

"Seen Lazarus?" I asked.

"Nope," she said. "He's probably in Ohio by now."

At that moment the distant wail of sirens split the night. We could hear them approaching along the highway leading into town, and I could tell by the increased pitch of their screams when they turned onto Golda's street. Headlights suddenly stabbed their beams into the darkness as a line of police cars barreled up to the front of the house and slid to a stop, sprinkling my old Rambler with gravel. Flashing red and blue lights illuminated the branches of the sycamore in the front yard with an eerie strobe effect. The sirens wailed down to a strange, incomplete silence that was broken by the staccato sound of car doors creaking open and slamming shut.

Lights began to appear in windows along the street. Voices could be heard from other houses. Nervous questions asked. Soon faces too, familiar faces, could be seen converging upon us from every direction. Old men in hastily donned trousers, their bare feet looking slick and white beneath their cuffs. Wives and children in pajamas and bathrobes, rubbing sleep from their eyes and asking each other what in the Sam Hill was going on. Why the police? Why the sirens? What had happened?

Boyd mounted the steps to the porch with the same speed Lazarus had descended them. He was dressed in full uniform, but I knew by the crazy way his hair was poking up in twelve different directions we had roused him from his sleep.

He didn't seem to mind.

He took one look at Mrs. Shanahan, nervous and wide-eyed on the porch swing. Then he turned to study me, still standing on the lawn where I had been searching for the cat. Apparently I looked equally wide-eyed and nervous because Boyd instantly gave his head a sad little shake.

"Susan and I left you people back at the lake not three hours ago. What the hell are you doing here?"

It must have been a rhetorical question because he didn't give us time to answer.

"Where's the body?"

I aimed a trembling finger toward the front door and the horrors that lay within. I figured once he caught a glimpse of Golda Burrows sitting nailed to her piano, no other explanation would be necessary.

I was right.

He rushed toward the open door, and I heard him mutter a most Boyd-like curse as he daintily stepped across the threshold as if testing the thickness of ice on a frozen pond. Deputy Morris Carter and Deputy Willie Lawson trailed along right behind him, both appearing as reluctant to be there as I was. Deputy Carter, in fact, looked scared to death, like a man about to skydive for the first time and uncertain how well his parachute is packed.

Behind Boyd and his deputies came a state policeman, who graciously doffed his hat in Mrs. Shanahan's direction before disappearing inside the house. I didn't know the man from Adam, but assumed he had been in the general area when the call went out. This, I later learned, was exactly what had happened.

His name was Donald Allan Kramer, and it was his second week on the force. Later that night he would go home to tell his wife about the old lady he saw nailed to her Baldwin upright, and she would beg him to quit his job and go back to farming like his father wanted him to do. But he would only laugh at her. He loved his job already. He also loved snuff movies and film clips of the Nazi holocaust. Quite a guy, Boyd would say later. For now, however, I knew only that Kramer was a pleasant-appearing chap who had the good manners to doff his cap to frightened old ladies.

"Bovine!" Mrs. Shanahan barked, making me jump.

"I'm sorry?"

She flapped an accusatory finger at the crowd gathered out there in the shadows on Golda Burrows's front lawn, all eagerly straining to see what was going on inside the house.

Mrs. Shanahan *harrumphed* and proceeded to spit a rather unladylike glob of phlegm over the porch railing.

"I said bovine and I *meant* bovine! The usual collection of bovine old men and bovine old women with nothing better to do than mind somebody else's business! Golda liked her privacy. She did! The last thing she would have wanted is to wind up as a starring act in this circus your brother's got going here. You march in there and tell him to disperse this crowd right now, or I swear to the heavens I'll do it myself!"

She finished up this tirade with one more "Bovine!" aimed with a sort of general flourish at anyone who happened to be listening, which was just about everybody, I'm sure.

I thought Mrs. Shanahan looked a bit bovine herself at that moment, like an obstreperous old cow protecting her hillside. I suspected I might find myself in considerably worse shape than the woman inside the house if I ventured to say so, so I didn't. Based on the sanctimonious glint in Mrs. Shanahan's eyes, I thought it best not to tangle with her, so I did as she asked. Immediately and without reservation.

I found Boyd and the other three officers standing around Golda Burrows's living room in the same trancelike state I had experienced a few minutes earlier. There was something truly breathtaking and awe-inspiring in the sight of that poor old woman nailed to her piano. It was a sight that bred humility.

I cleared my throat, feeling like an interloper.

"Boyd," I said. "There's quite a crowd gathering outside, and Mrs. Shanahan thinks...."

Boyd leaned forward to take a closer look at one of Golda's hands. "Mrs. Shanahan is quite right," he said. "Carter, take care of it."

Deputy Carter probably wouldn't have jumped much higher if he had shot himself in the foot. "Uh. Take care of what exactly?"

"The crowd, dipshit. Get rid of them. There could be evidence out there. I don't want it trampled into the mud."

Carter cast an uneasy glance through the front door. "Um, how do I do that, sir?"

Boyd jerked himself upright and glared at his deputy. "Short of shooting them, I don't much care *how* you do it. Just do it. And put up the barricades. The crime-scene tape is in the trunk of my car. Do it and do it now."

Carter got up a little momentum and eventually moved his 300 pounds out the front door to do as he was told. Soon I could hear him wheedling with the citizenry to please step back. Please go home. Please let the police do their jobs without a bunch of nosy parkers getting in the way and screwing things up.

I quickly realized that last wheedle didn't come from Carter. It came from Mrs. Shanahan, who was *helping* Carter and apparently doing a damn fine job of it. I could hear the crowd unhappily mumbling now from a greater distance away.

Boyd didn't look like his mood would be improving anytime in the near future, so I thought it best to get my own request out of the way as soon as possible.

"I'm leaving, Boyd. Mrs. Shanahan wants to get back to the lake so she can be with Sam and the boys. So if you don't need me…."

Boyd rounded on me with the stunned look of a man who has been asked to surrender his last viable organ to science when he's pretty sure he hasn't finished using it yet.

"But I *do* need you, Bry. Stick around. We have to talk."

I resisted the impulse to shuffle my feet. "But the boys…."

Boyd turned to Lawson. "Get outside and help Carter put up the barricades. When you're through with that, tell Carter to drive Mrs. Shanahan back to the lake and stay there until I tell him he can leave. He's a bigger pain in the ass than you are when it comes to investigating crime scenes, so this way he'll be doing something useful. Tell him Mrs. Shanahan will cook him up some breakfast. That'll give him a little incentive. Now go."

Lawson went.

I, of course, stayed. Not that I had much choice in the matter. When my brother took charge of a situation, *any* situation, he did so with enthusiasm and unbridled bossiness. Admittedly, he always got things done. But he didn't make many friends in the process.

Chapter Seven

I RELUCTANTLY admitted it might prove fascinating to watch my brother work. I had always loved mysteries. An untidy stack of crime novels piled to the height of a ten-year-old child dominated one corner of my office at the church. Unfortunately, *reading* about a dead body and *looking* at one were two entirely different matters. Oddly enough, though, my interest in the whodunit aspect of this case was less than it was in any of those pleasantly distracting books I so enjoyed because personally I didn't give a rat's rear end who was killing these old women. I wanted it to stop. *Now.*

Boyd, I knew, felt the same. This wasn't a game to him; it was his job. Boyd loved police work, but not for the same reasons Officer Kramer loved it. Boyd received no vicarious thrill in witnessing the misery of others. The only thrill he might receive came from the elimination of those miseries. He was a good man, and whether he chose to admit it or not, a Christian man.

At the moment, however, there should have been a Handle with Care sign plastered to his forehead. The brutality of this second murder had put my brother in a dangerous mood.

Kramer found this to be true when he made the mistake of parking his hat on top of that monster of a TV. The nonchalant way in which he did it, as if he had tossed his hat down as a prelude to sharing a spot of tea with the deceased, caused me to dislike the man in an instant. That simple act of flinging his hat so carelessly among the figurines and photographs on Golda's Panasonic and then stepping back, arms crossed, as if waiting for something interesting to unfold, made me want to casually walk up to patrolman Donald Allan Kramer and introduce his snoot to the knuckles of my fist.

Boyd apparently felt a similar urge, but for different reasons.

"Pick up that hat!" he growled. "You're disturbing the crime scene! Don't they teach you people anything?"

"Sorry, Sheriff."

Kramer didn't look sorry. He looked amused.

But Boyd wasn't finished with him yet. "What the hell are you doing here anyway? These murders are under the jurisdiction of the sheriff's department, and I've been given the go-ahead to investigate them. You state people have nothing to do with it."

Kramer screwed his lip into an unpleasant smirk. "Thought you might like some professional help. Your staff seems a mite, shall we say, incompetent?"

He aimed that ugly smirk in my direction as if expecting me to agree with him. When I didn't, he simply redirected it back to Boyd.

Boyd, God bless him, returned it with a pretty good smirk of his own. When he spoke, his voice was an ominous rumble, as if thunder and lightning were booming and flashing somewhere deep inside his chest.

"Listen, you jackass. I'm the closest thing this county has to a homicide detective. It's my job. It's what they pay me for. You understand what I'm saying? I'm the one in charge. And as my first order of business, I'm telling you to get the hell out! Go nail a speeder or something. Just remove your simpering, ugly face from my sight, or I may be forced to rearrange it and make it uglier, if that's humanly possible. And try not to disturb any more evidence as you fumblefuck your way out the door."

Amused even more, happy as a clam as a matter of fact, Kramer calmly retrieved his hat and reparked it on the top of his elongated head. The man took a few obstinate seconds to position the hat with a slight rakish tilt to the left, then sauntered out the door with a "Ta-ta, girls."

"Asshole," Boyd muttered to the late Miss Burrows, who didn't seem at all offended by my brother's choice of words. She merely continued to stare blandly at the bank of photographs on top of the piano to which she was nailed, infinitely patient and seemingly without any interest whatsoever in the proceedings around her.

For some bizarre reason, I kept expecting her to strike a discordant chord and begin another verse of "The Old Rugged Cross." I had the good sense to shake that crazy thought from my head immediately. Golda's piano playing days were definitely over.

"What evidence are you talking about?" I asked after Kramer was good and gone.

Boyd shrugged, and while he was shrugging, he took a blasé swipe at his silver sheriff's badge, cleaning it of imaginary flecks of dust. "Beats the hell out of me," he said. "Sounded pretty good though, didn't it?"

I smiled as our gazes bumped into each other. "Sounded great."

He threw his voice out into the night with the force of a shotgun blast. "Willie! When you're finished with that barricade, bring in the photo and fingerprint kits! We've got work to do!" He bent down once again to study the spikes that pierced the old woman's hands.

My stomach rumbled like Mount Vesuvius. "Maybe I should...?"

Without looking up, he said, "Yes, Brian. Now that we're alone, maybe you should... tell me what the hell you're doing here?"

Before I could begin, Mrs. Shanahan poked her head through the front door and glanced uneasily around, not unlike a cautious turtle inspecting a slab of freeway before attempting to cross it. I noticed that even now she refused to aim her eyes at anything but the floor and walls.

"Reverend, I'll be going now. I'll tell Sam you'll be back when you get back. That all right with you?"

I nodded. "That's fine. Boyd?"

My brother still didn't bother looking up from his examination of those nasty spikes. "Yes, Mrs. Shanahan, you go ahead. I'll probably be out to the lake later today to talk to you. Don't forget to tell Carter to stay with you people until somebody relieves him."

This apparently struck one of the many raw nerves Mrs. Shanahan appeared to be abundantly blessed with, all of a sudden.

"No offense, Sheriff, but that fat fool couldn't guard his mother's cookies. I already informed him, and now I'm informing you, that we're stopping by my house on the way to the lake to pick up my 16-gauge rabbit splatter. If you'd like to express any arguments about that, you can just put them in a letter and stuff it up your—"

Boyd waved his hands in the air like a man trying to flag down a speeding bus that was about to run him over. "No, no, no. You go right ahead and do that. Try not to kill anyone who isn't trying to kill you first."

Mrs. Shanahan bobbed her head up and down, once, as if to say, "Well, good. I'm glad there isn't going to be any arguing about it!" Then she mumbled something about poor Golda and what a terrible way it was for the silly woman to exit this vale of tears, and then she was gone, bellowing orders at Carter even as the sound of her retreating footsteps thudded down the front porch steps.

Boyd leaked most of the air out of his lungs in what could only have been a sigh of relief.

"Now, then," he said to me. "Tell me why you're here."

I told him how Mrs. Shanahan and I, over a cup of coffee in the kitchen of the lodge, had doodled with the words in the murderer's note and finally came up with what we thought might be a reasonable explanation as to what the killer was hinting at.

"Which was?"

So then I told him about Lazarus, Golda's cat, and how the ugly creature had acquired that name.

"It was the only explanation that made any sense at all," I finished up.

Boyd stared at me with his eyebrows arched high on his forehead as if waiting for more, so I kept talking.

"Actually, Mrs. Shanahan figured it out first. Once we thought we knew what the note meant, we didn't have much choice but to drive out here and see if Golda was all right." I tilted my head in the dead woman's direction without really looking at her. I figured I had looked at her enough already. "As you can see, she most certainly was not."

Boyd dryly agreed. "Yeah, I noticed." His eyes swept the room. "What we have here is about fifty-thousand cat prints in dried blood, but no cat. So where is he?"

"I'm afraid he took off for parts unknown the minute we opened the front door. He had blood all over him, poor chap. Must have been rolling in it."

Boyd gave an uncharitable grunt. "Probably lapping it up like cream." He shivered. "I don't like cats. What I like is witnesses. I don't suppose you happened to see any of *those* lurking around when you arrived, covered with blood and hightailing it for the moors."

"Sorry," I said. "The street was deserted. After all, it was three o'clock in the morning. The murderer must have been long gone by then."

Boyd flicked an eyebrow up in sardonic agreement. "I knew one little witness would be too much to hope for."

"But you have a witness."

Boyd broke off his visual examination of the bloody mass of blackly tinted curls at the back of Golda Burrows's head long enough to stare at me with renewed interest. "*What?*"

"I said you have a witness."

"Who?"

"Lazarus."

"Who the hell is Lazarus?"

I indicated the uninterested woman sitting in front of him at the piano. "Her cat. Remember?"

Boyd blinked a couple of times, then stuck his fists on his hips in an unconscious parody of Mrs. Shanahan in one of her peevish moments. "Oh, of course. The cat. Well, thank God for that. For a minute there I thought I might have to muddle through this investigation without the benefit of eyewitnesses."

He touched the side of Golda's head with the tip of his finger and pushed. Like a statue tilted on its pedestal, Golda's entire body moved with it. One didn't have to be a heart surgeon to realize she was stiff with rigor mortis. My stomach rumbled again when I saw how firmly she was nailed to the piano. I wondered if Boyd would consider it to be disturbing the evidence if I were to puke all over the living room.

"For your information, Bry," he said, pulling his finger back and wiping it absentmindedly on the seat of his trousers, "it's been my experience that four-legged witnesses aren't worth much more than a bucket of squirrel shit. Neither, I might add, are some two-legged witnesses I've seen. But the four-legged types are definitely a bust. Total waste of time, believe me. Unless, of course, you're an expert at cross-examining cats." He glanced at me hopefully. "You aren't, are you?"

I decided to take a gander at my shoelaces. "No, of course not."

Boyd nodded, as if he had expected as much all along. "Very well, then. Let's forget about the cat, shall we, and try to concentrate on the human aspect of what has taken place. What did you do after you discovered the body?"

The chitchat was over. I braced myself for some serious questioning. "Mrs. Shanahan went into the kitchen to call the police and I—I prayed."

He stuck a finger in his ear and dug out a pound of imaginary earwax. "Excuse me? You did *what?*"

I hoped this wouldn't lead to a familiar argument. "You heard me. I prayed."

"A bit late for prayer, wasn't it?"

This conversational path was looking uncomfortably familiar indeed. I tried not to put on my high hat, then thought, *to hell with it.* That's what high hats are for.

"It's never too late for prayer, Boyd. I've told you that before."

"Yes, Bry, I know. Hundreds of times. But right now let's try to keep our minds on the business at hand, shall we? We'll discuss your all-consuming faith and my all-consuming lack of it at some later date."

"Good," I said and meant it. Boyd, like Mrs. Shanahan, could infuriate a fire hydrant if he really set his mind to it.

"What did you do then, little brother?"

I stopped to think. "Well," I said, "I guess that's about all I did. I joined Mrs. Shanahan on the porch—she was pretty upset by then—and we waited for you to arrive."

"Didn't happen to see the cat while you were out there, did you?"

"I thought you wanted me to forget about the cat."

The sight of Golda's body appeared to be the only thing keeping Boyd's smile from reaching its full potential. "It just occurred to me it might prove interesting to test the residue of blood that's still on Lazarus's feet. You never know. He could have scratched the killer. We might conceivably find a trace of the killer's skin on one of his claws. It's a long shot, of course—"

"I should think it would be!"

"Yes, well, I suppose you're right. Better stick to the human element. If you want to call what somebody did to this poor woman 'human.'"

I sadly shook my head. "No," I said. "I would never presume to call it that."

Boyd stared at me for a moment, then asked, "So Sam is still with you at the lake?"

"Yes."

"You two have certainly become close lately."

I had no idea what he was getting at, and I wasn't entirely sure I wanted to know. "Sam and I have always been close. You know that, Boyd."

Boyd continued to stare at me. Finally he said, "Yes," and simply turned away.

He squatted down on his haunches and peered beneath the piano bench, first at the floor, then upward to the bottom of the bench. I hoped he wasn't going to tell me her rear end was nailed to the bench in the same way her hands were nailed to the piano. All he said was "Hmm."

I couldn't seem to stop myself from saying what I was about to say. "About Sam," I began.

But Boyd waved me to silence. He was studying Golda's slippered foot. "Still on the pedal," he mumbled to himself. "Strange."

I pushed Sam from my mind, and my impromptu confession as well. "That couldn't be natural, could it?" I asked. "Her foot."

Boyd knew what I meant. "No. She couldn't have died as calmly as all that. Her foot was positioned on the pedal after death. He's a theatrical son of a bitch, whoever he is." As if to accentuate his opinion, Boyd whistled a couple of bars from *H.M.S. Pinafore* as his eyes trailed from Golda's foot to the electrical cord coiled under the piano bench. He followed the length of the cord until he satisfied himself it belonged to the light perched over the music rack on the front of the piano. "Not unlike the way he posed Grace Nuggett after he killed her, is it?"

"But why?" I asked. "Why does he do that?"

"Why does a fruitcake have nuts?"

"Uh—"

"Forget it, Bry. Rhetorical question."

"Oh, of course."

"Look at this," he said, pushing himself to his feet and indicating the spikes protruding from the backs of Golda's hands. "Look how violently these spikes have been driven into the wood. It took some work to do that. Split the damn piano from top to bottom. What the hell did he do it with? That cat didn't happen to be carrying a hammer when he sailed out the front door, did he?"

I refused to answer that for fear it might be rhetorical as well.

Boyd simply nodded. "I didn't think so. Which means the murderer took it with him when he left. Unless we find it somewhere on the premises."

A sudden thought caused my vision to blur. "You don't suppose he used a hammer to…?"

Boyd glanced at me, then back to the body. "To what? Strike the death blow? Yes, I suppose he did. The same hammer, no doubt, that he used to nail her hands to the piano."

He motioned me closer. "Look at this. See that?"

This was as close as I had been to Golda's body. As I peered at the wound on the top of the woman's head, now only inches from my face, I realized I could smell the blood. A musty, feral smell. It was the smell of a slaughtered deer strapped to the fender of a hunter's car. The smell of violent death.

I wasn't sure what it was Boyd wanted me to see, and I knew I couldn't remain this close to the body for many more seconds before something would be disgorged. That something would most likely be my dinner from the night before, if it was still hanging around in a disgorgeable location.

Desperately I said, "Tell me what I'm supposed to be looking at, Boyd."

He pointed to the head wound.

"So?" I said. "I don't—"

"Bry, look closer."

Then I saw it. Two cuts extending out from the center of the wound. One to either side, the vertical cut longer than the horizontal, forming a perfect cross. The cuts were ragged, as if gouged into the woman's scalp with a blunt blade or—*the claw end of a hammer*.

"My God."

"Bry, whoever this asshole is, he's got it beautifully orchestrated. He's having fun with it. Giving us hints all over the place. Either that, or he figures we're so stupid we have to be hit over the head like Golda here before we can figure it out."

"But figure *what* out?"

Boyd looked a bit nonplussed by the directness of my question. "Well, there I'm afraid you have me. I don't know what the hell it is we're supposed to be figuring out. Wish I did. It would make things a lot easier. Any ideas?"

Before I could do so much as hazard an ignorant guess, Deputy Willie Lawson came strolling through the front door with all manner of equipment in his hands and tucked up under his arms.

"Got everything?" Boyd chirped. He began plucking the items from Willie's hands and placing them in a neat and orderly fashion on the floor just inside the front door. "What about the crowd? Are they dispersed?"

Willie had a slow way of talking that made you want to reach down his throat and pull the words out by hand to speed them up. "They're about as dispersed as they're ever likely to get. And that's only because Mrs. Shanahan told them she was going after her shotgun if they didn't skedaddle. You oughta hire that woman for crowd control, Sheriff. She could send the faces on Mount Rushmore scrambling over the rocks to the other side. Got a way about her. Scares hell out of most everybody."

"Scares hell out of *me*, I know that," Boyd mumbled as he checked the camera for film. "Let's get going with the pictures, Willie. Don't touch anything. Remember the golden rule. That goes for you too, Bry. Don't touch anything until photos are taken and sketches and measurements are made of any evidence we happen to find. Okay, Willie, let's take some pictures."

Under Boyd's direction, Willie concentrated on the body first. Full shots from every conceivable angle. Then close-ups of the hands and head. Golda Burrows flashed to life in the split second that every flashbulb went off, but immediately afterward she returned to being as stone-cold dead as she had been the moment before. The phantom echo of her girlish laughter was still rattling around somewhere inside my head. Wherever she happened to be at the moment, I had a sneaking suspicion she was probably enjoying all this hoopla no less than she had enjoyed everything else that had happened to her in the many years of her long and happy life. I wondered if she could be staring down at us from on high and giggling at the solemn expressions on our weary faces. It would be like her to do exactly that. She had always found humor in the strangest places.

The screen door slammed.

Dr. Elmer Otis Hill was another person capable of finding humor where little humor actually existed. Sprightly, bald, and in his seventies, he had single-handedly delivered most of the babies in Nine Mile during the past forty years. Everyone breathing life in this room he had just entered, Boyd, Willie, and me, were all here due to his prolific workmanship. Not that we remembered anything about it. I doubted Dr. Hill remembered much about it either, considering the sheer number of babies he had slapped into screaming life over the past four decades.

He groaned, dropping his black bag on the floor next to Boyd's array of cases and boxes. "I've been a doctor for nigh on as long as I can remember, and I've never yet seen a baby or a death come at a decent, respectable hour. Why the hell *is* that?"

Willie and Boyd were too engrossed in what they were doing to answer, so Dr. Hill settled his bifocal gaze on me for an explanation of this phenomenon.

"Well, Doc," I said, deciding to take a stab at it. "I guess it's a conspiracy by someone in control of the situation to keep you from getting a good night's sleep. Can't think of any other reason."

Dr. Hill bounced across the room in two long strides and pumped my hand up and down for a good ten seconds, all smiles and friendly pawings, like a lonely old dog whose master has finally come out to play.

"Good to see you, Reverend. How cynically enterprising of you to ferret out the truth of the matter. It's exactly what I've suspected all along. Up until now, I've been the only one smart enough to figure it out."

By my calculation, Dr. Hill had now been inside the house for no less than two minutes, and he had as yet not bothered to glance in the direction of the body. Was he so immune to the sight of death that it no longer held any interest for him? Even a death such as this one? But I quickly realized it had nothing to do with indifference. Dr. Hill apparently knew the golden rule as well as Boyd did, and he understood that any examination of the body could only come after Boyd was finished taking his pictures and measuring his measurements. Dr. Hill, in his way, was as professional as Boyd. One just had to look at him a bit more closely to see it.

He was an infrequent addition to my congregation, but I liked the man nevertheless. Always had. After all, a much younger version of Dr. Hill, and one with more hair than he had now on top of the old braincase, had seen me through half a dozen childhood illnesses and injuries with gentle humor and a tender touch that had endeared him to me forever. He treated children in the same way he treated adults: with amused tolerance. This was the backbone of his bedside manner, and it seemed to work for him very well.

As if being a skilled and busy GP were not enough to fill his days, he also served as the county coroner, working out of a remodeled Victorian house on the outskirts of Bloomfield, the basement of which was the County Morgue. The ground floor contained his suite of medical offices and examination rooms for the *living* patients, and above those, on the second floor, were the living quarters where he resided with his wife, Gladys, and their five cats. Spare parts from the morgue below, he swore up and down, were not fed to the cats as it was popularly believed by most of the children in the area, and not a small number of adults as well. Gladys, he once assured me, shopped for her meat at the IGA store like everyone else.

He gazed around now with the air of a man who has lost something more than the hair on his head.

"Where's Lazarus? He's usually right here, hitting me up for one of these." With that, he dug a tiny tin of cat treats from his mysterious black bag, rattling the treats purposely in an attempt to coax Lazarus out of hiding.

But Lazarus, it would seem, was having no part of it. He had suffered a far too upsetting evening to be lured out of the shadows by anything as mundane as a cat treat. Wherever he lay hidden, he stayed there long enough for Dr. Hill to finally shake his head and toss the tin of cat treats back in the bag.

By this time, Boyd and Willie had produced, by way of their instant camera, a generous collection of snapshots I felt no inclination whatsoever to browse through. Their photography session was winding down, and Willie had already begun to unpack the fingerprint equipment. Police work, I decided then and there, could be as dull and plodding as it was, less frequently, exciting.

"Willie," Boyd directed. "Don't forget my brother. Get his prints before you start on the furniture."

Boyd smiled at my shocked expression, but before he could explain, Dr. Hill patted me consolingly on the shoulder. "Not to worry, young man. I seriously doubt if your brother considers you a suspect. He needs your fingerprints for elimination purposes. Isn't that right, Sheriff?"

"Right as rain. Don't worry about the victim's prints, Willie. We'll get them later at the morgue, after the blood has been cleaned from her hands."

Willie gave an efficient little nod and proceeded to transfer my prints onto a fingerprint card he pulled from his shirt pocket. Afterward, he plucked a paper towel from his other pocket and handed it to me.

"When you're finished with that," he said, "toss it in the box there."

I did as he asked at the same moment Boyd turned to Dr. Hill. "Okay, Doc. She's all yours. Hasn't been touched. Not by us, anyway."

Dr. Hill faced, at last, the body of Golda Burrows. He stared at her from halfway across the room as if feeling it unnecessary to approach any closer. Later, Boyd would explain to me that Dr. Hill liked to get the overall picture settled comfortably in his mind before he went after the particulars in a case of death, be it natural, accidental, or a matter of murder, self-inflicted or otherwise.

The doctor ran a lazy hand across his freckled scalp as if checking for a sudden regrowth of hair. If he found any, he didn't mention it.

"Jesus God!" he hissed under his breath. "Felonious homicide if ever I saw it."

Boyd clucked. "Brilliant, Doc. What gave it away? The dent in her head or the spikes in her hands?"

"Piss off, Sheriff. You do your job and I'll do mine." But his words were delivered in a friendly manner, like a ball player jokingly insulting a teammate in the locker room.

As if shaking himself awake, Dr. Hill finally approached the body and began his examination. Like Boyd, he too pressed a finger to the side of Golda's head and pushed.

I turned away.

Dr. Hill's voice was soothingly calm. Apparently that air of calm was such a major component of his bedside manner, he even practiced it on corpses.

"Rigor complete. She's been dead a while. Between six and twelve hours. Maybe more. She's about to turn ripe."

Snippets of conversation hovered around me as I stared out into the night, past the porch light where the bugs continued to beat themselves to death against the bulb. If a crowd of nosy citizens were still gathered somewhere on the unlit street, I couldn't see them.

"I can give you a better guesstimate, Sheriff, after the autopsy. But six to twelve hours is about right."

Rustling sounds.

Boyd's voice. Businesslike. Matter-of-fact. "No ligature marks."

Dr. Hill agreeing. "No. And no signs of a struggle. The wound to the head was the killing blow. Judging by the lack of facial expression, I'd say she died instantly. Wouldn't you?"

Boyd grunted a curse. "Yeah. Somewhere between the chorus and the bridge."

"What? Oh." Dr. Hill coughed up a cynical laugh. "The hymnbook. Yes, I suppose she was playing a hymn when the killer sneaked up behind her. Or maybe she knew he was there. Either way he caught her by surprise. I've heard her play, you know. She wasn't good, but Lord, she wasn't *this* bad."

Boyd. Deceptively calm. "Notice which hymn she was playing?"

"Yes." Nothing more. If Dr. Hill thought anything about the particular title on page 216 of that hymnal, he had apparently decided to keep it to himself. Perhaps he figured that was Boyd's domain. The body, and the body alone, was his.

I imagined him leaning in to peer closely at the head wound.

"There are cuts here," he said. "They radiate out from the point of impact. Not made by the initial blow."

"He did it later," Boyd said.

"You're absolutely right, Sheriff. The cut marks were administered postmortem, after the body had already stopped pumping blood. They're clean and almost bloodless. The blow itself produced a quarter-sized indentation in the skull. Perfectly circular. But not deep. Maybe only half an inch or so."

"But deep enough to kill her?" Boyd asked.

"Oh, yes. More than deep enough. She was an old woman. Well into her seventies. At that age the skeleton becomes fragile. The bones, including the skull, lose strength. Become brittle. Easily snapped. Or perforated. This blow might only have caused a bad concussion in one of you young men, but it was more than enough to kill Miss Burrows here."

A groan and a loud pop startled me into looking back at the murder scene, half expecting to see the doctor illustrating his words on poor Golda's body. Dr. Hill had merely straightened and was massaging his back, and I stifled a nervous laugh.

"She was not a strong woman to begin with," Dr. Hill continued. "I've been treating her for years for heart trouble. She's had two small heart attacks in the past, and there might have been more we didn't know about. She was an easy kill, Sheriff."

"So tell me, Doc, this circular indentation you spoke of, could it have been caused by the business end of a hammer?"

"Oh, yes. I'm sure of it. That's the first thing I thought of. If I were to venture a guess, the claw end of the same hammer was used to gouge out the flesh that forms the cross that intersects the wound." He sadly shook his head. "A vicious thing to do. In all my many years of practicing medicine, I thought the murder of Grace Nuggett was the worst thing I had ever seen." His eyes wandered to Golda's old hands, so brutally pierced by spikes. "I'm afraid I'll have to revise that opinion."

I swiveled away again, leaned against the doorway, and let the predawn breeze cool my face. The air carried with it the funereal fragrance of camellia blossoms, as if the conversation behind me wasn't doing enough to remind me of death.

My mind flashed on Sam, snug in my arms, his lips moving against my chest as he whispered words of love in the darkness. I squeezed my eyes shut at the memory, trying to lock it in place. Dr. Hill's droning voice battered its way through anyway.

"No facial expression. No signs of a struggle. Not a great amount of blood coming from the wounds in her hands. It's obvious she was first struck in the head, dying instantly. Then, postmortem, her hands were nailed to the front of the piano, and the additional wounds were administered to the scalp. What the hell for, I don't even want to know."

A long silence ensued wherein I imagined Dr. Hill once again rubbing a palm across his bare scalp in stunned contemplation of the violence he saw before him.

Willie gently scooted me aside so he could powder the doorknob for prints. For lack of anything better to do, I tucked my hands into my trouser pockets and turned to watch as the powwow between my brother and Dr. Hill continued.

"Let's get her down," the doctor said.

"Yeah, I guess there's not much more we can do with her like this."

"These spikes have no head on them, but they're considerably wider at the top than they are at the points. If we pull her hands away it will mean a bit more tearing of the flesh."

"Can't be helped, Doc. It's either that or dismantle the whole goddamn piano."

"Did you get all the photographs you need? Have the spikes been dusted for prints, or is that feasible?"

"Naw. They're soaked in blood. No legible prints could have survived the piercing of her hands. Let's tear her loose and get it over with. I want to lay her down. She looks so damned—so damned *obscene* like this."

"Okay, Sheriff. Grab a wing. Don't let her fall."

I decided to take a walk.

There were small clots of people off in the distance, palavering back and forth in hushed tones about the tragedy that had come to their very own street. But those people were standing on their own lawns now, not Golda's. As I waded through the dew-soaked grass of Golda's side yard, I saw the deputies had indeed erected a formidable barricade. It extended along the outer perimeters of the entire yard. Front, sides, and back. A deceptively festive yellow ribbon was tied from shrub to fencepost to tree, encircling all of Golda's property. That yellow ribbon flapped playfully in the breeze. On it was printed at two-foot intervals in bold black letters: Police Line—Do Not Cross.

The sky had lightened with the approaching dawn, causing the stars to slowly begin their process of fading away in the wake of another passing night. The fat moon now hung low in the western sky, as if luring the sun to rise on the opposite horizon. By the smell and feel of the breeze that swayed the camellia blossoms alongside the house, I doubted if we would be seeing much of Mr. Sun this day. The air was sodden and heavy with the mushroomy stink of muddy swampland and soggy leaves.

It smelled like rain, in fact. A lot of it.

Lazarus was still nowhere to be found. Or if he was, he remained in no mood to *be* found. I checked for him beneath the camellia bushes, behind a stack of old flower pots on the back porch, and even on the outer windowsills where I had sometimes seen him napping on sunny mornings when his mistress was alive.

I wondered who would take care of him, now that his only contact with the human world was gone. I doubted if he could ever adopt another human who would love him as much as Golda had, if he could find anyone to adopt him at all. He certainly wasn't show cat material. His long suit was personality, not looks. And at the moment, I knew, covered with his mistress's blood, he looked like a feline from hell.

Poor thing. Poor homeless thing. Or so I thought.

It wasn't until hours later, as I steered my weary way back to the lodge on Sunset Lake in the midst of a cloudburst so intense it was like driving underwater, that I realized Lazarus *had* found a home. Mine.

Little did he know he was almost orphaned twice in the same night when he calmly crawled from beneath the Rambler's front seat and casually plopped himself down in my lap to take a much-needed snooze. He frightened me so badly I nearly chewed up and swallowed two hundred yards of barbed wire fence in my surprise.

Judging by his contented purr as he nestled his head against my stomach after a minute or two of concentrated kneading to render it into a shape more comfortably rumpled, Lazarus considered himself adopted and home at last.

I regained control of the car and laid my hand alongside his whiskers, accepting his presence with no more thought than I would have given to acquiring a new pair of socks. Lazarus reciprocated by giving me a proprietary lick across the palm, and with that metaphorical handshake sealing the deal, he fell into a fast and fearless sleep.

Chapter Eight

IT WAS approaching eight in the morning when I finally arrived back at the lake. Golda Burrows, her hands now free of those bloody spikes that had so viciously pierced them, had been hauled off to the morgue under the watchful eyes of Dr. Hill and my brother. I had stayed out of their way during the remainder of the investigation at the house, asking no questions and seeking no truths. Boyd, in turn, asked no further questions of me, convinced, I suppose, that if I knew anything, I would volunteer the information without being grilled.

By the time I reached the lane leading up to the lodge, the cloudburst had ended, but the sky continued to dribble sporadic moisture onto my windshield. Those stretches of road leading up to the campground, which had been boggy the day before, were now a morass.

Lazarus had panicked miles back at the first spine-jarring bump in the winding, muddy lane leading to Sunset Lake, steadfastly refusing to act like anything but a raving lunatic from that point on. As I bounced through the first in a long line of inundated potholes, rattling the Rambler to its core and splashing muddy water all the way up to the tip of the antenna, Lazarus popped awake, dug his claws into my lap, and with a war whoop that sent shivers galloping up my neck, proceeded to fling himself about the interior of the car in a frenzy of horrified energy that, if properly harnessed, could have lit up every building from here to Chicago. At one point he went so far as to hang upside down from the roof by his claws until a pothole dislodged him, screaming, from his roost.

When I finally reached the lodge and sloshed to a stop next to Morris Carter's patrol car, I don't know which of us was more grateful, Lazarus or me. The moment I opened the car door, he catapulted across my legs and, tail high, made a beeline for the nearest shelter, which happened to be the porch leading into the main lodge. Once there, Lazarus gave a prissy shake of his head to let the world know he didn't like the rain one bit, and then he began the odious task of cleaning the base of his tail. Odious to me, at least. Oddly enough, to him it seemed a rather enjoyable and relaxing experience.

Not once did he condescend to look back and see if I was following or not. It was enough, apparently, that *he* had found safety and comfort and a reasonably dry place to lick his… wounds. I could fend for myself. Or die in the mud. It mattered not a whit to him.

Sam showed up as I leaped and skidded my clumsy way across the slippery lawn. Before I could do so much as lift a finger in greeting, Lazarus took it upon himself once again to seek comfort ahead of me. He emitted a plaintive little squeak and, as if starved for affection and unaccustomed to the dastardly treatment he had suffered at my ungentlemanly hands, arched his back and collapsed with a pitiful *thump* onto Sam's booted foot. There he lay like a gutshot possum.

Predictably, Sam scooped the old con artist into his arms and *oohed* and *aahed* his way back into the lodge with him. I began to wonder if perhaps Lazarus hadn't murdered his mistress and nailed the unfortunate woman to her antique upright as a way of garnering a little attention for himself. Obviously he would stop at nothing to further his own ends.

"Don't worry about me," I called out to the empty doorway. "I'm perfectly all right! Be along in a minute."

I kicked off my muddy shoes, squeegeed some of the rainwater out of my hair, and padded through the lodge to the kitchen, where I found Sam already heating a pan of milk over the stove. Not for me, but for the cat.

Sam gave me a stern look while giving Lazarus a gentle stroking, much the same way he had stroked me the night before. "This animal is scared to death. What did you do to him?"

"Well," I said. "Let me think. First I tied him to the bumper of my car and dragged his sorry ass down the highway at sixty miles an hour in the pouring rain, but when that didn't seem to upset him as much as I had hoped it would, I took his tongue and tried to wrap it around the…."

Sam smiled in spite of himself, but then his face grew serious. "Auntie told me what happened. Was it honestly as awful as she said it was, or did she exaggerate the situation? She tends to do that sometimes."

Lazarus cast a suspicious glance in my direction as I dropped wearily into a chair. One would think he had never seen me before in his life. "For once, there is no possible way your aunt could have even minutely exaggerated the situation. It was every bit as horrible as I'm sure she said it was."

"I'm sorry," Sam muttered, placing a dish of warm milk in front of Lazarus, who was staring up at him now with an expression of martyr-like patience and obsequious devotion. The scoundrel.

Sam scooped me into his arms and pressed his cheek to mine. "Thank God you're back," he whispered, drawing me close.

I eased myself out of his arms, uncomfortably aware of the open doors and open windows all around us, where anyone might appear at any moment. He stepped back with a familiar hurt on his face that made me want to cry. But as I knew he would, he resolutely wiped it away as quickly as it had come. He knew the rules as well as I did.

"Where's Carter?" I asked. "He was supposed to be guarding you people until I returned."

Sam gave an uncharitable chuckle. "Whose bright idea was *that?* Yours?"

I resisted the impulse to squirm beneath his gaze. "Boyd's, actually. He thought you and the boys and your aunt needed protection, stranded out here all alone."

Sam slid his finger along my cheek with a grin, then quickly pulled his hand away. "How stupid do I look? You just didn't want to have to worry about us while you were off playing cops and robbers with your brother. The boys are probably safer out here than they would be in town. Especially now. Auntie brought a cannon with her, you know. Heaven help the fool who takes it into his head to criticize her muffins."

I preferred not to think of Mrs. Shanahan wielding a 16-gauge shotgun anywhere near the general vicinity of my loved ones. "So where *is* Carter?"

"He's out with the boys. Auntie threw them out of the lodge an hour ago. She was tired of feeding them, I expect."

"Where is *she?*"

"She toddled off to bed. Something we should be doing about now." He cast a sexy leer that sent a shiver up my spine. A *good* shiver.

"We can't," I said. Sadly.

He nodded just as sadly. "I know."

Lazarus had by now finished his bowl of warm milk and curled himself into a comfortable crescent, mouth to tail like a shrimp, on one of the dining room chairs. He had, I thought, wasted precious little time mourning the untimely demise of his previous owner. I leaned forward to study him more closely.

He really was a remarkably hideous animal. His coal-black coat appeared dangerously sparse in several locations, as if someone had taken sandpaper to him. His overall shape seemed to be slightly out of whack for some obscure reason I could not quite put my finger on. He simply was not a handsome cat. Never was and never would be.

He opened his eyes and flicked his tail to let me know he didn't appreciate being gaped at by *anyone,* be they newly adopted humans or not.

"I guess he plans to keep us."

Sam smiled. "I think he's cute."

"Hmm," I hummed. "Not two hours ago our cute new pet was covered with the blood of one of the sweetest ladies in Nine Mile."

Sam ran a soothing hand over Lazarus's side. The cat's motor kicked in with the sound of a lawn mower starting up on a summer day. He rolled onto his back, presenting his stomach to Sam rather like a king offering his ring to a peasant for the obligatory kiss. And there on his breast, for all the world to see, was a muddy smear of red.

Sam yanked his hand away. "Holy shit! Is that…?"

I took a closer look. "Yes. I'm afraid it is. I think Lazarus should be given some time to clean himself up before we start pawing him with affection. What do you say?"

Shuddering, Sam turned away. He moved to the window that looked out on the roadway leading up to camp. The rain had settled into a healthy, persistent drizzle that looked as if it might go on forever. Ark weather. There could be little outside work done until it stopped. Camp was scheduled to open in a few weeks. Our time was running out. I remembered the promise I had made to Chester and Thelma Goldstone about the camp opening on schedule regardless of how much it rained. For the first time I found myself wondering if I would be able to keep that promise.

I moved to the window and laid my hand on Sam's back. He leaned into me, but made no overt gesture of affection, which saddened me because I knew he really wanted to.

The day was gray outside. Gray and wet. Over the peppering of raindrops against the glass, I heard the sudden rumble of an automobile revving and clawing its way up the muddy lane.

"Gordon's here," Sam said.

I groaned. "Wonderful."

Hooking an apple from a basket by the window, I gave Sam a sullen peck on the cheek and a not so sullen (and entirely unclergy-like) squeeze on the ass before starting for the only place I could think of on the spur of the moment where I could be alone. My veranda.

I needed time to think. Something about the murder scene bothered me. I could neither put my finger on it, nor shake the feeling I was missing an important clue that should have been blatantly obvious to anyone with two eyes and a brain. Or was I simply playing cops as Sam suggested?

Before stepping through the kitchen door, I turned back one last time. "Do me a favor, Sam. Send Gordon home. There's nothing he can accomplish here until the rain stops, and the last thing I feel like doing is listening to him swagger and boast and complain all day. Get rid of him. Please. I'll love you forever."

Sam turned from the window and gazed at me. "I thought you would love me forever anyway."

"Sam," I softly said.

Then he nodded. "All right. I'll tell him."

I ducked through the doorway and headed for the stairs. Behind me, I heard Sam speaking to Lazarus in a tone that was both gentle and kind. "Welcome home, kiddo."

I took the stairs three at a time, munching on my apple and wondering what sort of night Sam and I could expect to share when this day was over. Another one like last night would be nice, if we could manage to not entertain another murder in the middle of it.

Rain pelted the fiberglass roof over the veranda. It sounded like a bucket of ball bearings being poured into a cardboard box. It was noisy as hell, but comforting too. Lulling. Like being all wrapped up and snug in a blanket of sound.

I plopped myself down on one of the canvas lounge chairs and looked out at the lake. A mist of splattering raindrops, like fog, covered the water to a height of five or six inches, making the lake look muted and blurred. Nearer to shore, I was surprised to see Jesse and Kyle sitting in the rain, their bare legs dangling over the side of the pier, seemingly searching for something in the water. The mystery was solved when Deputy Morris Carter—clad only in a pair of very large boxer shorts pulled low by the drag of the water to expose the crack of his more than ample rear end—breached from the water with the force of a whale exploding through the surf. Three voices howled with laughter as Carter back-paddled with all the grace of a floundering cow toward the pier. Right before Carter reached them, the two boys sprang to their feet and cannonballed into the lake, one on either side of the poor man, causing them all to disappear completely from the face of the earth in a gushing fount of water. A few seconds later, *three* whales breached, one large and two small, honking and spouting and spitting up large quantities of my lake into the air, which with the rain was wet enough already.

I wondered if perhaps this wasn't the most fun Deputy Carter had had since he left grade school. I posted a note on the refrigerator door inside my head to remind myself to ask Carter up to the lodge sometime for dinner. The boys would like that, and so, I suspected, would Morris. I doubted the man had many friends. But not, I thought, watching him cavort in the water like a six-year-old with my nephew and my nephew's best chum, for any lack of a fun-loving spirit.

I glimpsed movement from the corner of my eye. A tiny black face, all curious eyes and ears, peered around the leg of my chair as if checking out the terrain. Apparently Lazarus found the sound of raindrops on fiberglass as comforting as I did. He crawled up into the gap between my outstretched legs, rested his chin on my knee, and stared out across the lake, wondering, I suppose, what all the hubbub was about down there.

"I wish you'd make up your mind," I said. "I hate having my emotions toyed with. Are we friends or are we enemies? Which is it going to be?"

Lazarus looked up at the sound of my voice, gave a long, trembling yawn, and dropped his chin back onto my knee. This meant, I gathered, that he would have to think about it and get back to me. While Lazarus pondered our blossoming relationship, or lack thereof, I hooked my fingers behind my head and prepared to do some serious pondering of my own. As horrific a scene as had confronted Mrs. Shanahan and me when we flicked on the light in Golda Burrows's living room, something else continued to bother me about it. Aside from the carnage and the blood and the brutality of what we saw, something was out of place. Something that didn't quite make sense. But what was it? *What is wrong with this picture? What doesn't belong?*

A glimmer of insight almost reached me before it was plucked from my head by the sound of footsteps climbing the stairs from the lawn. Hurried footsteps. Someone running to get out of the rain.

Lazarus hissed, tensing in my lap as if preparing to spring away, then decided it was too much work. When Gordon Knowles's head became visible over the landing, Lazarus studied him for a moment, then tucked his head beneath my leg and went back to sleep. He was too worn out from the night's adventures to be bothered by another human being.

Gordon hastily ducked under the roof, shook himself off, and looked at me as if he thought I might be trying to hide from him. A perceptive man.

The first thing I noticed were the scratches on his cheek.

"Soggy as a hooker's crotch," he sputtered, raking the baseball cap off his head and beating it against the railing to dry it off. He hung it on the newel post and eyed me with a little more suspicion before saying, "I hear you had a bit of excitement last night. Care to tell me what happened?"

"Why should I? Do you know anything about it?"

He plastered an innocent expression across his face and pointed a wet thumb in his own direction. "Me? What makes you think that?"

I shrugged. "No reason. Just thought I'd ask. My brother is experiencing an awkward shortage of suspects, I'm afraid. It would be nice if I could present him with one. Make his job a lot easier."

Gordon Knowles spat up a couple of uneasy chuckles that petered out and died before they really came to life. "Sorry I can't help you out, Padre."

After that, I thought, he looked at me with more suspicion than he had before. He plunked himself down on the foot of my lounge chair in a companionable sort of way I didn't care for at all. Lazarus growled ominously. He didn't care for it either.

"Seriously, Reverend. I thought you might want to talk about it. Get it off your chest, you know. So the sheriff doesn't have any suspects, huh? No clues? No witnesses?"

"No reason to tell me if he did," I answered, once again studying the scratches that extended down the side of Gordon's face from ear to chin. They weren't deep, nor especially nasty, but they certainly were curious. I wondered if, given the proper set of circumstances and the proper motivation, Lazarus might not be able to inflict marks like that.

"Have a fight with Maggie?" I asked, hoping to sound casual and buddy-buddy and all the while trying to ignore the thudding of my heart inside my chest.

He immediately knew what I meant. "Oh, these?" He patted his wounded cheek and grinned. "Yes, Padre, as a matter of fact I did. She came after me with a pot-roast fork. The big kind. Two prongs. Foot and a half long." He seemed to find it quite amusing. "Women, huh? I'm lucky she didn't skewer my brains." He cast me a wily look. "I suppose one of these days when one of the young heifers at the church gets her paws into you, you'll know what I mean."

I didn't like what he said and I didn't like the way he smirked when he said it, as if Gordon Knowles had some sort of inside knowledge that convinced him I wasn't exactly marriage material. Not for a woman, at least. I ignored that thought. I simply wouldn't allow myself to go there. Instead, I slapped a mosquito that was foolish enough to get himself all tangled up in the forest of hair on my forearm. "So what did you fight about?"

Gordon appeared appalled, as if I had blown my nose on my sleeve. "Come on, Padre. I'm the one asking questions. If you want to worm your way into my private life, you'll have to go through Maggie, 'cause I ain't talking."

The rain suddenly pelted the roof with a series of metallic clicks. A shriek out on the water caused Gordon to stare across the lake. I followed his gaze and spotted Deputy Carter and the boys dashing toward the nearest cabin. Morris Carter, running along the edge of the water in a pair of wet, sagging underwear, was a primordial sight if ever I had seen one, conjuring up visions of fat little cave dwellers tromping through the forest, clad in the skins of whatever unlucky creature they had managed to club and consume for dinner.

Oddly enough, the rain wasn't merely splattering the ground now. It was bouncing. Strange. Then I realized it wasn't rain I was seeing, but hail. Smears of white began to form across the hillside where the tiny balls of ice had bounced into patterns on the grass. They would be gone, I knew, in a matter of minutes, melted into the mud. But for now those little drifts of ice were lovely and curious to look at. A summer blizzard to be briefly enjoyed and forever remembered.

Gordon was less charitable than I when confronted with the sight of Morris Carter galloping through the hail in his dripping underwear.

"Lord have mercy! If that don't make you want to run right out and join Weight Watchers, I don't know what would."

Disliking Gordon as I did, his facetious remark prompted me to defend Deputy Carter with more alacrity than I might otherwise have done. "He's here at Boyd's request," I said. "He's been guarding the people here at the lake. *Including* your son."

Gordon seemed honestly surprised. "Guarding them from what?"

I folded my arms across my chest and cocked my head to one side in disbelief. "Don't you understand what's going on? Someone is killing people. Greene County isn't a safe place to be right now. If you had seen what this person did to that wonderful old woman last night—"

"What?" Gordon all but pounced. "What did he do?"

"Forget it, Gordon. If you want answers about last night, you'll have to get them from Boyd. He'll be here later. You can question him yourself."

"The sheriff is coming here?"

"Yes," I said, not altogether surprised this bit of news served to make Gordon as jumpy as a sick cat. "He said he would be here as soon as Dr. Hill finished with the autopsy of the victim."

Gordon narrowed his eyes and studied me, nervous but trying not to show it. Any residual humor that might have been left on his face after seeing Carter in his underwear was gone now. "She was stabbed, wasn't she? Stabbed like the other one. The Nuggett woman." After he spoke he gazed back at the cabin the boys and Deputy Carter had ducked into to get away from the hail. His eyes were troubled.

"No," I said, wondering if I should. "She was not stabbed."

Gordon jerked himself to his feet and leaned wearily against the railing, looking out at the lake, thinking thoughts I would have given a hundred dollars to know.

His back was wide and strong, his hips narrow beneath the gray work pants he wore. He was a powerful man. Powerful enough, I imagined, to—

"Did they find the murder weapon, Reverend? Do they know what he used to kill her?"

Did I detect a tremble in those long legs? A tension in the slope of those broad shoulders?

I hesitated perhaps a second too long. To Gordon it was answer enough. I knew that by the way he hung his head for the briefest of moments. He turned to me then with a kinder look on his face than I had ever seen planted there before. Kinder and sadder.

"I guess your brother's sworn you to secrecy, huh? They do that with murder investigations, don't they? Keep little tidbits of information set aside only the murderer would know about? Keep them from the public?"

"Sometimes."

"But you know what those secrets are, don't you? You found the body. You saw what happened inside that house."

"I wish I hadn't," I said truthfully. "I wish I hadn't seen any of it."

Gordon stared down at his strong hands. "Don't you ever wonder, Padre, how sometimes people turn out the way they do? How they take it into their heads to do things that—that hurt other people."

For the first time, I gave Gordon a genuine smile, sympathetic and understanding. This was a side of him I had never seen, a side perhaps only Maggie really knew. A side I almost liked. "Yes, Gordon. These past few weeks, I've thought about that a lot. We all have, I suppose. But with all the thinking and pondering, I haven't come up with any answers. Have you?"

He removed his hat from the newel post and twisted it in his hands as he spoke. He gazed at Lazarus, asleep in my lap. "Only that maybe sometimes people are born bad. With black hearts. As black as that cat. Maybe some people don't feel things the way other people do."

I couldn't stop myself from wondering if he was speaking about himself. "Like remorse?"

He slowly nodded. "Yeah. Guilt. Remorse. Whatever you want to call it. Some people just don't have it in themselves to feel those things, do they?"

"There's a word for it," I said. "A word the police use for a person like that. They're called sociopaths. They think only of themselves. They'll do anything it takes to get what they want, but show no regret for the actions they take to get it. It's a sickness. A very dangerous sickness."

He turned away then, staring back out across the lake. The hail had stopped. So had the rain. For the moment. The veranda was deathly quiet without the rain and hail beating on the fiberglass roof. I had not noticed when the noise ended and the silence began, but suddenly that silence was deafening.

"But what is it he wants?" Gordon asked. "Why do you suppose he's doing it?"

"You mean killing?"

"Yes. Killing."

I cupped my hand behind Lazarus's head and stroked his neck. "I don't know. It makes no sense to me. Only he would know the answer to that question. And if he's truly sick, then maybe *he* doesn't even know."

Gordon's words sounded far away, as if coming to me through his mind and not his lips. "How do you help a person like that, Reverend? What can you do to make them well again?"

I sighed. "Nothing, Gordon. There's nothing you can do. I don't think they *can* be made well again. It's like a cancer of the mind. Half the time doctors can't cure cancer of the body, and they have something tangible there to work with. How can they ever really treat something like that in the mind?"

"Psychiatrists do it all the time."

"Yes," I said. "They do. But not this. This is inborn, I think. These murders are not simply acted out. They're planned. They don't appear to be the acts of someone who doesn't know what he's doing. He's taunting the police. It's a game to him. He's enjoying it."

Gordon pulled his hat snug atop his head. "I refuse to believe that."

I studied the man before me. Something in his stance, in his manner, frightened me.

"Gordon, do you—"

"I'm taking the day off, Padre. I've got things to do. Keep an eye on my boy for me, will you? Keep him safe."

"Yes. Yes, of course."

He gave me a weak smile, muttered, "Thanks," and took off down the stairs. Lazarus and I watched him go, neither of us, I suspected, any wiser than before the conversation began.

BOYD ARRIVED as the lot of us were sitting down to lunch. He was not in the gentlest of moods.

The hail had stopped and the rain had settled in with a dogged persistence that seemed to imply it meant to stay a while. Sam cringed in mock horror at his aunt's venomous countenance when Boyd stomped into the mess hall, soaked to the skin and wearing an extremely filthy pair of boots that left a trail of muddy footprints on her sparkling new floor. I glanced around quickly for the woman's shotgun, didn't see it, and figured for the moment, at least, we wouldn't be forced to cope with another murder.

"Hi, Pop!" Jesse yelled, french fries poking from his mouth at various odd angles. "What do you say?"

Boyd stood before us, dripping. "I say that bloody cow path is a bloody hazard to life and limb!"

Kyle elbowed Jesse in the ribs and whispered, "Blimey! How bloody British!" Which sent them both into sputtering gales of laughter.

Boyd spotted Morris Carter, fully dressed now and looking rosy-cheeked and happy. He too had a mouthful of french fries, and a newly built cheeseburger poised directly in front of his florid cherub's face. The meticulous construction of this six-inch-high gastronomical horror had taken Morris forever. He had carefully selected and precisely applied, layer by layer, every condiment known to man, and now that the moment had come when Morris could appreciate all that labor, Boyd plucked it from his hands without so much as a how-do-you-do. When Boyd spread his mouth wide and chomped into Morris's cheeseburger as if it were his own, poor Morris looked as if someone had shot his favorite dog.

"How's the diet coming?" Boyd asked around a mouthful of his deputy's sandwich. Morris blinked back what might have been tears, reluctantly plucked a dill pickle from a jar on the table, and gave a stricken sigh. "Fine, sir. Just fine." He continued to mourn Boyd's energetic attack on his burger with a brave show of stoicism, but it didn't fool me.

When I could stand it no longer, I held out a platter of raw vegetables. "Here, Morris. Have a carrot with your pickle." Morris took one with all the enthusiasm of a man accepting a summons.

Mrs. Shanahan pushed herself away from the table and said, "Sit yourself down, Sheriff. Might as well be comfortable while you're eating. Pour yourself a glass of iced tea. I'm sure you'll excuse me while I drag my eighty-six-year-old bones over here and mop up some of the muck you've managed to track from one end of the building to the other."

"Okay," Boyd said around another mouthful of Morris's burger. "Don't mind if I do."

For an intelligent man, my brother could sometimes be mind-bogglingly obtuse. I didn't see it, but I imagined a little puff of steam shooting up from the top of Mrs. Shanahan's blue, finger-waved head as she stalked off in search of a mop.

One could not help but admire the nonchalant way Boyd accepted this flurry of activity and resentment his mere entrance into the mess hall had spawned. Oh, to be more like him.

Gradually the room settled back into a semblance of normality. What resentment remained after Boyd's intrusion on everyone's sensibilities was hidden beneath a cloak of forced courtesy and teeth-grinding politeness. Even Mrs. Shanahan, after petulantly flinging the dirtied mop through the back door with a crash, conceded to playing the game, much to my surprise.

"Well, Sheriff?" she asked. "What have you learned?"

Boyd opened his mouth to answer, then froze, staring across the mess hall to the doorway leading into the kitchen. Finally he spoke. "Is that who I think it is?"

I looked where Boyd was staring and saw a familiar black face peeking around the edge of the door, six feet above the floor.

I smiled. "None other."

Boyd plucked a french fry or two from Jesse's plate as he and Lazarus continued to study each other.

"Tall, isn't he," Boyd observed.

"No, sir, Sheriff," Kyle informed him. "Lazarus is just an average-sized cat. But he's standing on a cupboard, you see, and when he looks around the door like that while he's standing on that cupboard in the other room, it makes him look like he's as tall as you are, which he isn't. He's just an average-sized cat, like I said."

Kyle apparently realized everyone was gawking at him as if he had beamed himself through a wall from some other dimension, and he ducked his head. "But, uh, I guess you already figured that out on your own, huh?"

Nearing hysteria, Jesse spat a mouthful of food back onto his plate before he choked on it. This in turn elicited a groan from Sam and a look of severe disapproval from Mrs. Shanahan.

Kyle turned a marvelous shade of red, one usually unique to sports cars and Christmas ornaments, and this made everyone laugh, including Boyd.

"Yes, son," he said, with a patient smile stuck on his handsome face. "As a matter of fact, I did figure that out on my own."

Mrs. Shanahan looked to be in a decidedly better frame of mind. She had apparently decided to forgive Boyd for dragging thirty square feet of mud into the mess hall with him. Morris was still sadly eyeing the desecrated remains of his burger, however. Not much forgiveness on *his* face.

"Well?" Mrs. Shanahan asked again.

Boyd gazed at her with a vacant expression. "Well, what? Oh! What have I learned. Well, let's see. Where should I begin?"

Even Jesse could not tolerate his father's obtuseness any longer. "Begin anywhere you like, Dad. Just begin!"

Boyd nodded. "Sage advice, son. I'll do that." So he did. Between bites.

"The murder weapon was indeed a hammer, like I told you, Bry. Autopsy confirmed it. Of course, we never found the damn thing. God knows where it is. The blow forced bone fragments into the woman's brain. That's actually what killed her. She died in less time than it takes to tell about it."

Mrs. Shanahan carefully laid her fork alongside her plate, no doubt suffering from a sudden loss of appetite. I couldn't say I blamed her.

I glanced at the boys. Jesse was still eating, but Kyle was sitting wide-eyed, the food on his plate forgotten, as he soaked up every word my brother uttered. I wondered if the boys should be listening to this. Kyle's boom box was sitting on the table next to him. Although it was turned down low, I recognized an aria from *Aida*. The boy certainly had varied taste in music. The plaintive song seemed to fit the subject of murder quite nicely.

Boyd went on.

"A very interesting autopsy. Even Dr. Hill said so. The spikes in the hands were old railroad spikes. Could have been picked up anywhere. Consequently nothing much could be learned from them.

More's the pity. Golda Burrows died instantly, like I said. Somebody walked up behind her while she was pecking away at her piano and drove that hammer into the top of her head like he was pounding a nail. Bam! One blow. Murder in an instant. Just like Grace Nuggett, he didn't make her suffer. I'll give the bastard that much. But, Lord, what he did to Golda Burrows afterward!"

Boyd was warming up now. His hands began to move through the air for emphasis, a habit of his since childhood.

"Just to satisfy an irrational need to prove some obscure point concerning crucifixion, the murderer nailed the woman's hands to the front of her upright piano—constructed, by the way, by the Baldwin Piano Company circa 1930—causing massive tissue damage to her hands and all but destroying the piano in the process. It's a marvel the entire neighborhood didn't hear the racket. But they didn't. Not one soul heard a blessed thing." Boyd shook his head as if he still couldn't believe it. "Incredible. Must be a bunch of morons living on that street. *Deaf* morons."

I began to feel a great deal of sympathy for Boyd. "How can that be?"

Boyd gave a grunt of disgust. "Who knows?"

"Excuse me, Mrs. Shanahan," Morris asked Mrs. Shanahan, "could you pass me another one of those delicious pickles?"

"Certainly, Morris."

Mrs. Shanahan offered him a sympathetic smile as well, and he accepted both the smile and the pickle with martyred humility. Poor man.

Like a molting snakeskin, Mrs. Shanahan's smile slid away as she turned back to Boyd in exasperation. "So the neighbors never heard her playing?"

"Oh, yes," Boyd said. "They heard the piano music, all right. It seems Golda Burrows played nearly every evening for an hour or so. Drove the neighbors nuts. From what I gathered, she wasn't too picky when it came to choosing notes. If she couldn't hit them, she played along without them. Made some fairly botched up recitals, I understand. She seemed to have been especially wound up on the evening of her murder. Played for almost *two* hours. Made the neighbors twice as happy."

"Let me guess," I said. "'The Old Rugged Cross.'"

Boyd shrugged. "Among other selections, I presume. If the woman had spent two hours playing the same song over and over, I'm guessing someone would have shot her before she could get herself murdered. No, it seemed to be Golda's regular set of assorted butchered hymns. As one man put it, 'People with tin ears shouldn't own pianos, and if they *do* own pianos, they shouldn't live in town, and if they *do* live in town, they oughta just play the goddamn radio and give everybody else a break.' Unquote."

"Quaint," I said.

"Quite," Boyd agreed.

Morris looked a little stupefied. "What's with all the *Q*-words?"

"Oh, for the Lord's sake, Morris!" Mrs. Shanahan snapped, banging the pickle jar down in front of him. "Shut up and keep eating. That's what you're good at."

She rounded on my brother again. "That would be Hector Scanlon," she offered Boyd as a sort of side dish. "Impossible man. Complains about the least little noise. Maybe *he* killed her. God knows he's threatened to kill everybody on that street at one time or another."

Boyd appeared decidedly disappointed when he replied, "No, we checked the old geezer out. I don't doubt he's a raving lunatic, but I don't think he's done anything with it yet. Give him time." Any humor implicit in Boyd's observation was lost on Mrs. Shanahan, who merely nodded, accepting Boyd's words as the truth, the whole truth, and nothing but the truth. I had a feeling she would be keeping a weather eye on the unfortunate Hector Scanlon when she returned to town. Heaven help the man.

Boyd went on. "Traces of blood were found in the trap beneath the kitchen sink. The killer washed his hands after finishing his handiwork. But the blood belonged to the victim. Not much good to us, I'm afraid. If the killer dried his hands, he did it on his own clothing. There were a million latent fingerprints in that house. We probably found a sample from everyone in town. The only prints we found in blood, unfortunately, came from that damn cat that keeps staring at me from the pantry." Boyd turned to me. "How the hell did he get *here* anyway?"

I told him.

He laughed. "So all the time you were searching for the little black bastard, he was hiding underneath the seat of your car."

"Afraid so."

"Sneaky devil."

I shifted the conversation away from Lazarus, who had leapt to the floor and was now sitting in the middle of the kitchen doorway licking his butt. Cats. "Did Dr. Hill establish a solid time of death?"

"Yes," Boyd said, tearing his gaze from the cat as I had done. "Dr. Hill's estimate at the crime scene was six to twelve hours. But he later recanted that. The house was closed up. Doors and windows shut tight. That made it hotter than hell in there. As everyone knows, warm temperatures tend to accelerate the appearance and disappearance of rigor."

"Oh, yeah, Pop." Jesse smiled. "Everyone knows that."

Kyle hastily swallowed a mouthful of food. "I didn't."

"I was being facetious," Jesse responded under his breath.

Boyd dragged a french fry back and forth through a puddle of ketchup on his plate. "Anywho, because of the heat factor inside that house, it's almost impossible to estimate a precise time of death. We'll say nine o'clock with a three hour plus or minus possibility of error. That, Dr. Hill decided, would be a forensically sound estimate."

Sam chimed into the conversation. "Did she have any visitors? Did any of the neighbors see anyone come or go from the house?"

Boyd finally poked that ketchup-soaked fry into his mouth, thank God. I was tired of watching him play with it.

He nodded. "As a matter of fact, they did. Several. At about five fifteen, or thereabouts, Golda Burrows made her first appearance of the evening. She stepped out onto her porch with a plate of cookies for a group of children who were playing at the edge of her yard. Toll House cookies, or so I've been told. She passed the cookies out to the kids and asked them to play somewhere else because they were scaring her cat."

You mean *my* cat, I thought. Lazarus and I made eye contact, and I swear he knew what I was thinking.

Boyd continued. "Her bribery worked. The children left. Then at five thirty, almost on the dot as near as we can figure it, Golda sat down at her piano and started playing. Esther Reames, a neighbor, stopped by and spoke with her for a few minutes and promised to come back later for tea after Golda had finished playing. As Esther put it to me later, it would have been impossible to enjoy her tea while Golda was ham-handedly slaughtering all those hymns. So she did what she said she would do and went back around six. Before reaching the house, however, she heard Golda still pounding away at her piano and decided to hell with it. If she wanted a cup of tea, she'd have one at home. So she didn't even knock on Golda's door. Just did an about-face and headed back to her own house. As she did so, she saw Chester Goldstone drive up to Golda's property, park the car, and go inside."

Kyle's reaction to this was less than sedate. "Grandpa? What was Grandpa doing there?"

Boyd quickly calmed the boy. "Hear me out, son. It's not as bad as it sounds. It was almost dark then, and since there aren't any streetlights on that street, Esther Reames, who it would seem has a healthy curiosity about the goings-on among her neighbors—"

Here Mrs. Shanahan *harrumphed* and flicked a crumb from her lap. "That cake needs a little more icing, Sheriff."

To my surprise, Boyd smiled at the interruption. "You're right, of course. The woman's a snoop. Better? So she dawdles around her front yard for a while, and it's lucky for us she did. She told me Chester Goldstone remained inside Golda's house for no more than three or four minutes. He had promised, Esther knew, to deliver some jewelry to Golda that needed cleaning while on his way home from work that day. Apparently Chester fulfilled that promise. After Chester Goldstone drove away—in a leisurely sort of fashion with obviously nothing to hide, since he waved to Esther as he passed—Esther once again heard the piano being played in Golda's living room, and deciding it was maybe too late for tea now anyway, toddled off into her house and popped a beer. Has one every night, she said. Drinks it through a straw. Told me it was good for the kidneys that way."

Boyd gazed a bit too innocently around the table, as if trying not to laugh out loud.

Mrs. Shanahan had no such compunction. She brayed like a jackass. "Kidneys, my foot! The woman's an alcoholic. Pure and simple."

At that, Boyd's laugh bubbled to the surface like a frog coming up for air. He spoke to Mrs. Shanahan in the same tone of voice, and with the same hope of success, that a scientist might use to explain the theory of relativity to an Oldsmobile. "One beer doesn't make her an alcoholic, dear."

Mrs. Shanahan's eyebrows climbed up toward her hairline. "It does in my book, *dear.*"

And *that* was *that.*

Boyd sighed. Not unhappily, I thought.

"Well, anyway, it now puts us at a few minutes past six. Golda's had a couple of visitors, but she's still alive at this time and still playing her blasted piano. She continues to play it for almost another hour. Half a dozen neighbors testified to that, but as to what time she *stopped* playing, no one could be exactly certain. A couple of people noted that as the hour grew late, her playing improved dramatically. Became, in fact, flawless."

"That's odd," Sam said. He had heard Golda play too.

Boyd shrugged. "With all that practice, she had to improve sooner or later. But let's move on. Other cars were heard on the street that night, but no one paid much attention to them. It was totally dark by then, of course. People were inside their houses, where they were supposed to be. Watching TV. Eating dinner. Getting ready for bed." He cast a conspiratorial eye at Mrs. Shanahan. "Or drinking themselves into oblivion."

Morris's sandwich was only a fond memory by now. Boyd pushed away his plate. "Then there's the matter of the cord," he said.

I slammed my hand down on the table, causing everyone to jump. "That's it! I knew something didn't make sense, but I couldn't figure out what it was. It was the electric cord."

"What cord?" Sam asked.

"The white cord that went to the light over the music stand on the piano," I explained. "It wasn't stained with blood. It was lying on top of the bloody carpet, but there wasn't a drop of blood on the cord itself."

"That's right," Boyd said. "But don't get too excited. There's a simple explanation for it. This guy likes to pose his victims. When he placed Golda's foot on the pedal below the piano he must have disturbed the cord, dragging it over the pool of blood. We dusted it for prints, but it was clean, dammit." Taking a deep breath, he finished up with, "And that's about all we know."

A thoughtful silence settled down around us, but it was short-lived.

"Did you talk to Grandpa?" Kyle asked. "What did he say?"

Boyd gave the boy a friendly wink. "Yep. Freely admitted he was there. We found the little bag of jewelry right where he said he left it. Cheap stuff, really. Nothing much anyone would go out of their way to steal. Your grandfather said he did little more than drop off the jewelry and run. Said he does that sort of thing for Thelma's customers quite frequently. Especially the older customers. They don't drive. He does. It's a small town. Blah blah blah. Nice man, your grandpa."

Mrs. Shanahan blessed Boyd with a sympathetic cluck. "So what you've got, Sheriff, is a whole lot of nothing."

Boyd didn't have much choice but to agree with her. "That pretty well sums it up. We don't know who killed Golda Burrows, or why. We only know how. I'm afraid the same goes for Grace Nuggett."

"What about a connection between the two women?" I asked. "Anything?"

Boyd didn't seem to mind being grilled by a pack of ignorant laymen. Perhaps it helped him think things through.

"If there's a connection, outside the fact that both women are members of your congregation, Bry, then we sure haven't been able to scratch it to the surface." A tiny trench formed between his eyes. That was Boyd's pensive look. "As a matter of fact, I've about come to the conclusion we aren't dealing with motives here. There *is* no connection between the two women because there doesn't *need* to be. We're dealing with a nutcase. An honest-to-God madman. The victims were probably picked at random. There's nothing in either woman's past to remotely justify what happened to them. No hint of scandal. Nothing. Death by murder was the only thing to ever bring them into the public eye at all. Not the sort of recognition they would have hankered for, I'm sure."

Mrs. Shanahan came to one of her on-the-spot decisions. "Well, I'm staying right here in the tulies, Sheriff, until you get this lunatic put away."

This was news to me. "Are you sure?" I asked. "Dr. Hill released Grace's body to the family. The funeral is tomorrow. I'm delivering the eulogy. This is a small town. People will talk if you don't show up."

"Let 'em talk," she snapped. "It's what they do best."

Sam laid a hand on his aunt's arm. "I'm going too, Auntie. So are Kyle and Jesse. You'll be here at the lake all alone."

Mrs. Shanahan cocked her head to the side and took a good long look around the lodge as if taking soundings of all the empty rooms. She quickly came to a different on-the-spot decision.

"Maybe you're right, Reverend. I'd prefer to be in yelling distance of *somebody*. I'll go." Then, attempting to salvage whatever remained of her stubborn Irish pride, she added, "If it doesn't rain."

The wind chose that moment to buffet the lodge with a gust that rattled the wooden shingles overhead and whistled around the eaves and gables. The pines along the lake rustled and shook.

The sky darkened. Rain that had previously peppered the windows now slapped against the glass in cleansing sheets with an angry hissing sound. No longer soothing. No longer a pleasant backdrop for lunchtime conversation, even if that conversation did pertain to murder. Now, instead of accompanying our voices, the rain controlled them, forcing us to speak louder and a little breathlessly to be heard above the racket outside.

A flash of lightning made us hunker down in our seats, and less than a heartbeat later, a crash of thunder, like a boulder of sound, boomed across our heads and jerked us to our feet. A chair overturned. Mrs. Shanahan gasped. Sam took a step toward me, then as quickly reined himself in.

Lazarus sailed across the mess hall, his tail bushed out to three times its normal size. As if the devil himself were hot on his trail with a pitchfork and a flaming torch, the terrified creature flew up the stairs to the second floor, a yowling blur of black.

FORTY MINUTES later Boyd was gone, returned to his investigation, and the storm had carried its fury over the horizon. Thank God. I, for one, had had enough. Sam and I stepped outside to see what damage had been done by this latest onslaught from Mother Nature.

Impossibly, the campground was muddier than before, churned up, littered now with branches torn from trees as if in its madness the wind had tried to rip the hair out of its own head. The forest surrounding us was sodden. Exhausted. Limp.

Wherever Lazarus had hidden himself, he stayed there unseen by human eyes until well into the following day. He would not be seen again, in fact, until after Grace Nuggett's funeral the following morning.

Later, far into the night, I awoke beside Sam and wondered if Lazarus, secure in his hiding place, was thinking of Golda. Of his mistress's death. Did her passing mean anything to him at all? Or was murder simply another of those inscrutable acts of cruelty that humans sometimes inflicted upon each other and upon the animal kingdom with a seemingly equal lack of restraint or discretion?

Perhaps to a wise old cat like Lazarus, it was business as usual and little more.

When Sam's hand came out of the darkness and slid across my stomach, I suddenly realized I was not the only one lying awake. His body followed his hand until he lay snug against me, his face on my chest. While he played lazy circles over my belly, he spoke in whispers, his breath warm on my skin.

"Don't worry," he said. "Your brother will figure it out."

I pressed my lips to his hair. "I know."

His hand moved slowly south, finally brushing my groin. I trembled as my cock lengthened quickly in his hand. He smiled against my skin.

Turning his head just enough to press his lips to my chest, he scooted down in the bed, all the while sliding his kiss downward. When his mouth touched my nest of pubic hair, he lifted the weight of my erection and laid it across his face, inhaling my scent.

"This is where I want to die," he muttered softly. "Right here. Like this."

When he took me into his mouth, I quietly gasped. The boys were just down the hall.

"I love you, Sam," I murmured, opening my legs to his prodding.

"I know," he said around me. "I've always known."

"One day," I breathed, "I'll make it right between us. We'll come out of hiding. I promise."

He nodded, and the movement of his head made me tremble again. My cock lay deep in his mouth. His hands were all over me.

"Turn," I gasped. "Turn over."

He released me then and reached out to the nightstand drawer to retrieve a jar of lube from the mess inside.

Moments later, he was ready for me. He lay on his stomach as I crouched behind him. Taking his hips in my hands, I lifted him to his knees.

"Oh, yes," he said in a rush of hunger. His words were barely audible, but the passion in them was unmistakable. "Fuck me, Brian. Make me yours."

"You're already mine," I said, my voice a tremor of longing. And as I slid the length of my oiled cock deep inside him, he buried his face in my pillow and whimpered softly.

I pressed my lips to the back of his neck and circled his heated body with my arms as I forged a path through him. In and out. Over and over again.

I reached beneath him and cradled his cock in my fist. Gently I stroked it, in time with the movements of my own cock plowing through him. His hands came up behind him and pulled me closer, pulled me deeper. The instant before I came, I froze in place, buried deep in his core. He shuddered beneath me, waiting for my next lunge, but I held my place, not moving at all.

"Oh God," he softly cried out, and a moment later his juices filled my hand. I stroked him lovingly as he came, milking every drop, relishing his insides spasming around my swollen cock. Savoring the scrape of his leg hair against my own, the warmth of his broad, smooth back against my chest. When he was finished coming, I once again began the gentle rocking motion that eased my cock in and out of his tight heat.

When it was my turn to come, he twisted his head around to find my mouth with his own. With our lips bound together, I buried my seed deep inside him, both of us bucking at the sensation of my release.

Later, as we sprawled in a sweep of moonlight on the bed, drained and happy and content, Sam laid his hand to my cheek and snuggled his face into the crook of my neck as I held him tight against me.

"I will make it right," I whispered softly. "I promise, Sam." But he was already asleep. Prayerless, wondering if I had lied to the man who loved me, I soon fell asleep as well.

Chapter Nine

"…AND THERE, with the eternal blessing of God, shall her soul reside forever."

I gripped the edge of the pulpit and finished our communal prayer with a silent amen. Silent, because nothing less than an inappropriate shout could have been heard at that moment above the rumble of sighs, the rustle of shifting skirts, the clearing of throats, and the shuffling of feet that suddenly filled the crowded church as my congregation, never ones to miss a cue, rose from their pews.

Funerals were a popular pastime with the residents of Nine Mile, and like solidly rehearsed dancers, the residents knew every step, kick, and grind of a funeral's choreography as well as they knew their own children's names. Consequently, they knew precisely when to sit, when to stand, when to pray, and when to leave, with little or no direction from me. They also knew when it was time for the grand finale. The final viewing. They wouldn't have missed it for the world.

Today the church was SRO. I had a hit on my hands.

First came the mourners, who had stood like a regiment of stiff tin soldiers along the back wall of the chapel throughout the entire ceremony. Saintly men, one and all, or so they considered themselves, since they had made the gallant gesture of surrendering their pews to the women.

They were farmers for the most part, for that is what this country breeds in the greatest abundance, all of them looking hot and uncomfortable, their large, sweaty hands leaving damp smudges on the hats they held clenched. They lumbered down one side of the center aisle, single file, made a quick and somber inspection of the body, then humbly and self-consciously lumbered up the aisle's other side and out the door with an all but audible sigh of relief. More than of few of them, I suspected, had unwittingly carried into the church a plug of chewing tobacco moistly tucked inside their cheek, and the saliva had been flowing for more than an hour with nowhere to graciously discard it. Those few had the look of desperate men indeed.

When the standing crowd was depleted, the line of advancing mourners was augmented by fresh new recruits from the last pew. Then the pew before that. In this way, the church gradually emptied, from back to front, like marbles dribbling from a box.

Grace Nuggett accepted these various displays of grief and sundry expressions of farewell from friends and loved ones (and not a few of the simply curious) in a regal and congenial silence, not unlike the manner in which she might have accepted them in life.

This was without a doubt the largest gathering of citizens I had seen come together inside my little church. It seemed the entire county had turned out for Grace's bon voyage party. If only I had planned a bake sale around it, I ruminated, my happy young campers might have been squatting over indoor plumbing before poor Grace was cold in the ground.

The line of mourners continued on, slower now since most of those who had yet to view the body were women. Being women, they were more inclined to give Grace's powdered face a thorough perusal for any and all signs of the violence that had killed her. The fact that Grace's reading glasses were perched uselessly on the end of her cold, pale nose did little to discourage this type of examination. It made those viewing the body, in fact, more determined to discover what it was we were trying to hide behind those spectacles.

In all my reading, I have yet to stumble across the name of the fool whose decision it was to label women "the gentle sex." Whatever his name, he apparently had never observed those women at a funeral for one of their murdered cronies. If he had, I felt certain he would have revised his opinion forthwith.

The ladies of Nine Mile, almost every one of them, be they young, old, or in-between, gave Grace's face a once-over that made Jackie Spanner, the undertaker, cringe. Jackie always managed to appear a few weeks deader than his latest client anyway. Pale as a ghost, he loitered behind the piano, looking as hot and uncomfortable as any of the farmers. He seemed to be waiting for one of those crazy old ladies who had wrapped themselves up in sweaters and shawls on this, the muggiest day of the year, to reach into the casket and pluck from behind Grace's lifeless eyelid the ball of waxed cotton that was meant to give shape and substance to the spot where her ruined, butchered eyeball had once resided, so as to take a good long gander at the damage firsthand.

The belligerent expression on Jackie Spanner's tired, cadaverous face seemed to say, "Sweet Jehoshaphat, ladies, maybe you would have preferred we left the pencil *in*!"

Sam, I was pleased to note, was one of the few who barely glanced at the body. He seemed to be gazing more closely at me, which I rather liked.

Mrs. Shanahan, on the other hand, snuggling up behind Sam and peering over her nephew's shoulder in her eagerness to see, did everything but pry open the dead woman's mouth and check the condition of Grace's bridgework. I thought too that she gave considerably more attention than was necessary to Grace's damaged eye. Mrs. Shanahan then peeked surreptitiously beneath the closed half of the casket lid that covered Grace's legs, hoping, I suppose, to see the woman's recipe card for peach cobbler down there somewhere, tucked among the folds, about to be buried in the dirt for all eternity, which is exactly where Mrs. Shanahan would love to see that recipe card end up, I'm sure.

The line of mourners had come to a grinding halt, what with Mrs. Shanahan's minute inspection of the corpse, so I cleared my throat and sternly peered down at her from my lofty position of authority in the pulpit. Mrs. Shanahan, never one to be cowed by authority, shot me a look in return that would have killed a weaker man, then grudgingly moved along.

Now that the line was in motion again, the mourners from the front two pews filed forward, more tearful than the rest and with more sincerity in their grief. For these were the faces of Grace Nuggett's family.

Her son, Charlie, still looked to be in a state of shock. He had, after all, been the one to discover his mother's body as the murderer had left it. Neatly laid out in a pool of blood on the kitchen floor, that pencil we had all heard so much about still protruding from the gentle woman's face, where moments before a compassionate hazel eye had been located, undamaged and full of life. Seeing everything. Seeing the murderer. *Her* murderer.

Now, but for the support of his wife's arm, Charlie Nuggett might have simply collapsed to the floor like a puppet whose strings have been cut. His children, two teenage boys and a girl of eight or nine, trailed along behind their parents with tears sparkling their cheeks, grieving as much at the sight of this tearful stranger wearing the skin of their father as for the dead grandmother in the casket. The death of grandmothers was a thing to be expected after all. But the sudden loss of their father's strength and their father's smile was not. It scared them mightily.

Behind Charlie Nuggett's children came a woman who had created quite a stir when she arrived for the funeral. Her name, I later learned, was Faith Thompkins, and she was Grace Nuggett's twin sister, just flown in from Ganonoque, Ontario, where she ran a chicken ranch with her third husband, Ray. Faith still resembled her sister closely enough to set several hearts skipping in stunned amazement when she stepped out of Charlie's Wagoneer in front of the church. Introductions were quickly made, apologies proffered, and condolences extended. Now the woman appeared exhausted by the scrutiny, as if she harbored no greater desire in life than to exit this town as quickly as possible and whiz right back to her Canadian husband and their six thousand Rhode Island Reds.

Boyd, looking inscrutable and mysterious, stood at the back of the chapel during the funeral, studying the crowd. Now as the last of the mourners filed out the door, he came forward with Jackie Spanner, and the three of us approached the casket. Ours would be the last faces Grace Nuggett would ever see in this world, if she were capable of such a thing, which she most certainly was not.

Jackie reached in and removed Grace's reading glasses, tucking them casually into a pocket of his black suit to be given later to her son, along with Jackie's standard parting patter about the sad but inescapable loss of loved ones. He then brushed a speck of lint from the bodice of Grace's dress and reached up to close the coffin lid, sealing the woman into a snug cocoon of satin darkness.

"Fetch the pallbearers, Reverend."

The six pallbearers waited in the vestibule, all but one of them tugging at their collars and praying they wouldn't drop the casket or pass out from the heat or trip over their own feet or do anything else equally stupid or humiliating.

That one calm exception was Chester Goldstone. Perhaps his serenity stemmed from the simple fact that he was the only person among them who was accustomed to wearing a suit. He had worn one to work at his electronics store every day of the week for more years than even he might care to remember. The others in the group of pallbearers were more used to loose bib overalls and baseball caps, a trickle of sweat on their brown necks a more familiar sensation than the strangling woolen tie their wives had so painstakingly fastened about their throats that morning. Chester Goldstone was probably the only man among them, believe it or not, who could tie a tie without spousal assistance.

Theirs was a simple life.

Grace at last was ready to go. A blanket spray of white carnations had lain across the foot of the casket since Grace's arrival at the church the evening before, carefully secured in place with little wire hooks. The pallbearers, trying not to grunt or break into a sweat, picked up the heavy coffin and carried it out into the sultry summer morning. As I followed along behind them, I heard car doors slamming and umbrellas popping. The umbrellas were all black and all compliments of Spanner's Funeral Home. It said so on the handles.

A line of automobiles stood outside the church entrance, their engines sputtering to life and steam spitting from their exhaust pipes into the moisture-laden air. Headlights blinked on, one after the other. A small confusion erupted among the mourners as to who would ride with whom, but with the appearance of the pallbearers lugging Grace's bronze casket down the front steps of the church, everyone seemed to suddenly understand where they should go, not that it really mattered as long as we all ended up in the same place—namely, the cemetery.

The first car in line was a spanking new Cadillac hearse. Then came two black limousines, also from Spanner's Funeral Home, for Grace's closest relatives. After those came a string of privately owned automobiles, all freshly scrubbed and still glistening with the evidence of the last little rainstorm. The cloudbursts were coming now, it seemed, every hour on the hour. Some with lightning, some without, but each one more unsettling to me than the last, because with each new storm came the ever-increasing possibility that the road to my campground would be so flooded *nothing* could get through. That, friends and neighbors, would mean an end, or at least a postponement, to everything I had worked for over the past two years. Even in the midst of murder, I was stubbornly determined to see my summer camp open for business on schedule.

I quickly scanned the line of funeral cars for the familiar sight of my old Rambler. It wasn't hard to find. Seven cars back, it stood out like a turd in a box of doughnuts. Sam, God bless him, showed no sign of embarrassment at being stuck behind the wheel of the ugliest car in the procession. Mrs. Shanahan, however, sitting beside him in the tattered front seat, did. She did not look happy at all with the seating arrangements. It was either that, or someone had shoveled a pound of wet gravel down the back of her girdle. I suspected it was only her devotion to Sam that kept her in her place.

I was none too pleased with the seating arrangements myself. I could think of nothing to endear me to the idea of a long, slow ride in a funeral caravan with the likes of Sam's aunt, unless of course it was actually Sam's aunt's funeral and she was laid out in a box with her lips sewn shut, in which case I might have enjoyed it rather more. Sadly, this was not the case.

While I cast an apologetic glance skyward, pleading forgiveness for that thought, Sam simultaneously cast an apologetic glance at me. I immediately understood why. My choices were obvious. I could either ride in the backseat like a toddler, or if I preferred to drive, Sam could sit in the back, and I could have Mrs. Shanahan all to myself in the front seat. Needless to say, I wasn't thrilled with either option.

I was about to shrug my shoulders in a manner meant to show what a good sport I could be in the face of adversity, when a hand came to a tremulous rest on my arm, effectively hauling me to a stop ten feet from the car.

I was not surprised to see the hand belonged to Maggie Knowles.

"Please, Reverend, I need to talk to you."

"Certainly," I said.

During the funeral, as I stood at the pulpit gazing out upon the congregation while delivering what Jesse would no doubt later describe as a *dry* and uninspired eulogy, my eyes had been drawn repeatedly to the look of fear on Maggie Knowles's face. She had been seated three pews back, next to her parents, Chester and Thelma Goldstone. Her husband, it would seem, had better things to do than attend an old lady's funeral.

As I rattled on about the marvelous qualities of the good woman lying dead before us, Thelma Goldstone had impatiently worried a thick gold rope about her neck. Chester sat next to her with a bland expression and an apparent total lack of interest in his surroundings. But Maggie? Maggie looked as if she might suddenly run screaming from the chapel were it not for the fear that kept her glued to her seat. Her eyes were the eyes of an injured, frightened rabbit. Hunted. And haunting.

Watching her now, as icy raindrops began to pelt the back of my neck, causing me to shiver despite the oppressive heat of the day, I saw she had been crying as well. Like turtles, we both ducked our heads from the rain.

"Certainly," I said again, taking her arm and leading her toward the car. "Ride with us to the cemetery. There's plenty of room. We can talk on the way."

Maggie glanced back at the pallbearers as they wangled and coaxed the coffin into the back of the hearse. She seemed to be wondering what her father would say if he should see her speaking to me like this. I couldn't imagine why. I had no idea where her mother might have gone. She was nowhere in sight. Cruel experience had taught me "nowhere in sight" was always an excellent place for Thelma Goldstone to be.

Maggie came to a decision. "All right. But I need to speak to you *alone*."

I gave her hand a reassuring pat, one of my specialties, and led her to the car. "After the graveside ceremony. I promise. Come along now. Let's get out of the rain."

Maggie meekly let herself be shepherded into the backseat of the Rambler, where we were surprised to find her mother already ensconced like the Queen of England inside the royal carriage.

The tense tilt of Mrs. Shanahan's shoulders told me she was more than ready to claw her way over the dashboard and through the windshield should a sudden escape from Thelma's customary health-oriented monologue be deemed necessary.

Sam amused himself by casting me a few glances, innocent and doe-eyed, in the rearview mirror as the funeral cortege began to snake its way through town toward Highway 67.

If Maggie had any intention of confiding in me during this long, dull drive to the cemetery, her mother saw to it she didn't get the opportunity by droning endlessly on about the sad condition of her bowels. Then she forged onward about the shocking incompetence of the tag team of doctors whose unhappy lot it was to keep those bowels in motion. By the time we pulled beneath the arched gateway of

Heavenly Ridge Cemetery, I found myself feeling more sorry for the doctors than I did for Thelma.

From the front seat, Mrs. Shanahan fumed, rigid and silent. A large, unpleasant stone. Sam mugged for me one last time in the rearview mirror before the car grumbled to a halt and Thelma Goldstone's endless oratory finally petered out—through no fault of its own, but because her audience was spewing forth from the car like lava shot from a volcano, quickly and with little care where it ended up, its sole purpose merely to escape.

The graveside service was a damp and hurried affair, my words made almost indistinguishable by the drumming of rain on the tent that had been erected over the grave. Midway through the final prayer, a sudden burst of wind unhooked a corner of the tent, sending it flapping about our heads, scattering hats and lifting hairdos and causing everyone to scramble about with nervous giggles in search of a reasonably dry location. Many tried opening their umbrellas inside the confined space, whapping neighbors in the head and creating even more confusion. My carefully prepared closing prayer, indeed my entire train of thought, was washed away in the mayhem. The few who were actually listening to me showed signs of needing a road map to follow where I was trying to lead, my incoherency having apparently reached a strata I had not yet aspired to.

Sam stood among the crowd, watching me closely, his wet hair plastered to the side of his face and tears streaming down his cheeks. Not tears of grief, mind you, but tears of stifled laughter. Most inappropriate, I remember thinking, as the blood positively *flowed* to my face in mortification. I finally had the good sense to give it all up as hopelessly lost and stammered an embarrassed amen.

Even Grace's relatives seemed relieved the prayer had finally ended. The usual handshaking and cheek kissing that accompanies the close of such ceremonies failed to materialize. Someone at the back of the crowd shouted, "Way to go, Reverend!" and everyone popped their umbrellas and hightailed it for the nearest car, grateful for the chance to dry off and blow the unsettling smell of a freshly dug grave (or perhaps the stench of my ill-fated closing prayer) from their nostrils and their minds. Their muddy shoes they would contend with later.

The caravan of cars broke apart, some pulling ahead of each other or falling behind as they all hurried away from the graveyard, destroying the reptilian illusion of a slow-moving train they had displayed when they arrived. Now they appeared to be more like a demolition derby of bumper cars, with everybody trying to get ahead of everybody else.

I shooed Sam and his aunt out of the tent and back to the car so as to be alone with Maggie Knowles. Thelma Goldstone, thankfully, had rediscovered her husband and departed with him.

Sam, still holding his stomach and trembling with laughter but trying not to show it, gave me a sympathetic nod as he shuffled off to the car, his auntie in tow. Mrs. Shanahan, of course, had come alive with curiosity. Her interest in what Maggie Knowles and I might conceivably need to talk about in such privacy that we were forced to do so inside a flapping tent in the middle of a storm-ravaged cemetery made the angles of her body, like radar, point off in a hundred different directions at once. Poor Sam had to all but drag her back to the car.

Maggie and I faced each other amid the chaotic sounds of rain and wind and whipping canvas, as well as the squeaky winch that slowly lowered Grace Nuggett's coffin into the mud.

At thirty-six, Maggie Knowles's beauty was quickly becoming a thing of the past. But her goodness was not. Nor, I feared, was her fragility.

She came right to the point.

"I'm afraid Gordon is having an affair."

I had expected to hear a dozen different declarations, but this was certainly not one of them. It required a great deal of concentration and most of my meager supply of willpower not to say, "Huh? Gordon *who*?"

If Maggie registered any surprise at my less than intelligent response, she didn't show it.

"He's hardly ever home anymore, Reverend. He comes in late at night and leaves early in the morning. The only time I can be sure of where he is, is when he's working for you. He is, isn't he? Working for you?"

I rested a comforting hand on her shoulder as lightning crackled overhead. "Of course he is. You know that. He brings his paycheck home, doesn't he?"

"Yes."

"Well, then?"

She seemed to suddenly deflate, to lose momentum, as if unsure now whether to continue this discussion or not. A wet curl slid from beneath her scarf and dangled limply between her eyes. A drop of rain formed at the end of it, and as I watched, the drop shimmered and fell, tickling her nose. She shivered and wiped it impatiently away.

"You don't like my husband, do you, Reverend?"

I opened my mouth to say—what?

Happily she didn't give me a chance to grope around too long.

"You don't have to answer that. Most people don't like him, I suppose. But he can be a good man when he wants to be. I'm afraid none of us has given him much reason to *be* a good man lately. My parents hate him. They always have. And lately I've been worried about my parents, Reverend, so I suppose I haven't shown Gordon as much attention as I should."

"Maggie," I said, trying not to sound as if I were preaching, which is a difficult thing for a preacher to do. But I had rarely seen anyone who needed a dose of confidence as badly as she did. "You shouldn't blame yourself. Gordon isn't a child. So what if you haven't shown him as much attention as you think you should? He isn't showing you much attention either, I gather, if he's staying out all night and rarely coming home. All blame doesn't automatically come home to roost on your shoulders, you know."

"I know," she muttered, still trying to poke that wayward strand of hair up under her scarf, but it was clear she didn't "know" at all.

What, I wondered, did she really expect from me? Somehow a few encouraging words and a minister-like pat on the back didn't seem sufficient. Surely I could do better than that. She obviously needed more. Needed it badly.

I remembered what Gordon had told me on the veranda the day before and decided to take the bull by the horns.

"Is that what you fought about?"

Her show of surprise was genuine. It had to be. That gentle face simply wasn't built for deception.

"Who?" she asked.

"You and Gordon."

It seemed a matter of some concern for her to set the record straight. "We never fight, Reverend. Never. Gordon may blow off steam once in a while, but he has never raised a hand to me or Kyle."

"What about the pot-roast fork?"

She looked at me the same way she might have looked at a two-headed cow.

"The *what*?"

I wondered if it could be healthy for her to disassociate herself with happenings from the past. Especially such a recent past. What was it? Yesterday?

"What about the scratches on your husband's face?"

Her eyes opened wide. "Do you think *I* put them there? He said he got them working for you, clearing brush along a hiking trail." A dawning realization lit her face. "So he lied about that too."

I gave her a lopsided grin, then immediately thought better of it and guiltily wiped it away. "He told me you did it to him with the pot-roast fork. Said he was lucky you didn't skewer his brains."

"He'll be lucky if I *don't*!" she stated with considerable heat.

I thought it best to head the conversation off into a slightly different direction. I appeared to be instilling more confidence into the woman than I had originally intended.

"Um—why are you worried about your parents?"

Maggie sighed, letting the sudden burst of anger drain out of her as quickly as it had rushed in.

"My father is ill, Reverend. We can't get him to a doctor, but mother's convinced he has the beginnings of Alzheimer's. She says he does some of the screwiest things sometimes, wanders off in the middle of the night, loses stuff, then at other times he is just as normal and sweet as always."

"Perhaps I could help convince him to see a doctor. He likes me. Or at least I think he does."

Maggie reached out to touch my cheek. Regardless of the small disparity in our ages, the touch of her fingers against my face reminded me of nothing more than a motherly pat, as I'm sure it was intended. Even so, as if my head were on wires, I quickly glanced toward the car to see if Sam had witnessed it. Sometimes one feels guilty about the oddest things.

Maggie's smile faded. In an instant, the look of fear I had noticed in the church was back.

"There's something else, Reverend. Something I haven't told you." Maggie continued to stare out at the cemetery as she spoke, as if she thought the dismal panorama outside the whipping tent flap a perfect background for what she was about to say.

"My mother's a willful woman, Reverend. She has always kept Daddy under her thumb. He hasn't had a happy life, I'm afraid. But now she's done more than make Daddy miserable. She's set out to hurt Kyle. Not intentionally maybe, but—"

"Kyle? But how? Why? I thought Kyle was her 'Golden Boy.'"

Maggie spat out a rather uncharitable chuckle. "Oh God, if I hear her say that one more time, I'll kill her. Kyle positively dies inside when she talks that way in front of him. But that is what's so funny, Reverend. She does love Kyle. But apparently she hates Gordon more."

"You lost me, Maggie. What does Gordon have to—"

"She's cut us out of her and Daddy's will. Me, actually. Cut *me* out of the will. It's my punishment for marrying Gordon, you see. First she finagled Daddy into giving her power of attorney. He's wonderful with electronics, but she always had more business sense than him. So she convinced Daddy it would be best to give her complete control over the family money. No one at the bank in Bloomfield would dare defy her. Nor, apparently, will Daddy, although it's broken his heart that she did what she did. It's a great deal of money, you know. I have no idea who she intends to leave it to, but it certainly isn't us. To tell you the truth, Reverend, I don't really care. Not for me. I have the life I chose for myself. I have a husband I love. Life isn't always smooth sailing with someone like Gordon, but..."

She let this sentence fade away into unfinished oblivion, as if permitting me to end it any way I saw fit.

"...but how could she do this to Kyle? We can offer him very little, I'm afraid. But someday, someday far off, an inheritance might have made all the difference in the world to him. The difference of a happy, carefree life, compared to the kind of life Gordon and I are living. We're happy enough, Reverend, don't get me wrong. But there's no security. And not much hope for improvement."

The winch lowering Grace Nuggett's coffin into the ground gave a metallic *click* and fell silent.

"Does Gordon know about the will?"

She flapped her hands at her sides as if to indicate she was sick of the entire situation. "No. I haven't told him. I should, I suppose. But then he started staying away from the house for such long periods of time, and I didn't want to make a bad situation worse by telling him my mother has cut us off without a penny. We always counted on that money, Reverend. We counted on it for Kyle."

Maggie crossed her arms and looked sadly at the hole Grace had disappeared into. "Everything seemed to happen at once. The will. Gordon. The murders. One would almost think they were connected, but of course they aren't. They can't be."

Before I could ask her how she knew that for a fact, Jackie Spanner, standing over by the winch with his hands on his skinny hips and gazing down into the open grave where the coffin had just descended, caused Maggie and me to jump by shouting, "Jesus H. Christmas! What the hell is that?"

He had removed the blanket spray of white carnations before final interment, and there, taped to the top of Grace's $3900 Sunset Bronze Sky Casket with the Soft Almond Velvet Interior and optional Cover Lock (which seemed a bit excessive in my opinion), sat a business-size envelope addressed in yellow marker to none other than my brother, the illustrious Greene County Sheriff. In those exact words, no less. "Illustrious" being underlined three times.

Boyd and Morris Carter were deep in conversation over by the squad car, where Carter had parked the thing astride a puddle the size of Lake Huron, thus requiring either wings or some fancy footwork to gain access to it without splattering one's freshly laundered uniform, which Boyd seemed to be explaining to Morris at that moment with the aid of a prodding index finger and an endless outpouring of profanity.

I figured my brother had more important matters to worry about now than the condition of his uniform.

"Boyd!" I yelled over the wind and peppering rain. "I think you'd better see this!"

Boyd's index finger gave his deputy's chest a final emphatic poke before he sloshed his way back to the tent, grumbling to himself and shaking his head as he came. His face grew as stormy as the sky when he saw what we were pointing at, but all he said was "Get her out of here."

I apologetically ushered Maggie back to the Rambler and motioned for Sam to go ahead without me. I would catch up to him later at the church. I rather enjoyed ignoring Mrs. Shanahan's frantic gesturing to find out what was going on. As Sam drove away, the old lady had her nose smashed against the side window, her eyes beseeching me to toss her at least a crumb of information as to what all the hubbub was about. I smiled and twiddled my fingers at her in a fawning farewell and was more than gratified to see a rather large and unattractive artery bulge across her forehead in anger. Sometimes life could indeed be worth living.

I returned to the gathering at the edge of Grace's grave and found Boyd already issuing a spate of orders at the little throng of peons around him.

"Carter, get Willie on the honker and tell him to set up a perimeter around the church. Maybe this cheesedick left his picture ID laying around when he posted my mail. Jackie, reverse the winch and let's get this casket out of the ground, and don't touch the damn thing unless you have to. We're going to powder it for prints, or try to anyway, if it isn't too frigging wet. And for Christ's sake, would somebody please nail down this goddamn flapping tent? It's driving me crazy!"

Boyd grasped the envelope by one corner, tucked it beneath his jacket, and moved into a more sheltered area of the tent, well away from the wind and rain. There he pulled the envelope out and carefully slit it open with a penknife.

"Guard this," he said, handing the envelope to me. The rain had already caused the yellow letters to run. I obediently slipped the envelope under my suit jacket to protect it from any further damage until Morris Carter could return from the squad car with an evidence bag.

"This cocky son of a bitch," Boyd mumbled, unfolding a yellow sheet of notebook paper identical to the paper on which the previous note was written. "He's beginning to get on my nerves."

I listened to the rain tap ragtime on the canvas above our heads while Boyd read and reread the note. Finally, with a sigh, he handed it to me.

"Careful," he said. "Fingerprints."

I held it by the corner between thumb and forefinger and read it quickly through. Once again, the murderer had printed his taunting letter with sharp, angry jabs of a lead pencil.

What do I have to do, Sheriff? Publish a list of prospective victims in the Evening World*? You are missing one bright and shining clue that binds the*

murders together. Murders past, murders present,
murders yet to come. Clarity of thinking might lead you to
#3 in time to save the poor woman from a most
unpleasant fate, but alas, I fear it will not. Your stupidity
will kill her dead. Eventually, I suppose, her stench will
lead you to her. Cock your head to the side, Sheriff. Listen
closely. Above the rain. You can hear her screaming now.

Boyd plucked a tulip from an arrangement in the corner and
twirled it absentmindedly between his fingers as he watched me tilt my
head as if taking the murderer's last sentences as a literal command.
Oddly enough, above the wind, above the hammering rain, I thought I
could almost hear it. A scream for mercy, a scream of pain, and a
scream cut suddenly silent, trailing upward into the storm-blackened
sky like a banshee's dwindling cry.

Considering the worried look on Boyd's face, I suspected he
could hear it too.

That night was a warm one, the heat almost tropical. A strong
wind swept across the lake, carrying the threat of more rain in its wake.
The honeysuckle, freshened by the recent downpour, laid a heavy
fragrance on the air, a fragrance of such intensity I could almost feel it,
like silken sheets pulled across my body. Or the heat of Sam's sleep-
warmed chest, where I had kissed him softly minutes before, then
slipped away to leave him napping, naked and beautiful, on the bed.

The evening was so muggy I wore only cargo shorts. My favorite
pair. They had been with me since college and washed so many times
(and accidentally bleached twice) the khaki had turned to eggshell. The
camouflage pattern was now so faded as to be little more than a
memory. The shorts were baggy and soft and comfortable, and with the
night air on my bare belly and the easy sway of my genitals beneath the
loose fabric, made me feel nakedly decadent and free of restraint. Like
a faun. A tall, skinny faun.

I managed through sheer willpower to push the disturbing events
of the day from my mind. The funeral. The killer's second note.
Maggie's tears as she stood in the rain at the grave site. This moment,
this one moment, as I trod the cool grass on the hillside leading down

to the lake, barefoot, while the wind tore through my hair as if blowing away unpleasant memories, was the first true contentment I had experienced during the long hot hours since dawn.

I could not know who the third victim would be, and I refused to think about it. It was enough for me to know the small family of humans I had gathered around me on this hot summer night were safely tucked away out here in the woods, away from town, away from harm. Mrs. Shanahan. The boys. Dearest Sam. The five of us would see the morning come. We would go about our business for yet another day, doing all the silly, inconsequential things that occupied us. Later, after we had accomplished either a little or a lot, we would return to our beds. All snug and safe and untouched by the evil surrounding us.

But someone out there would not. I said a quick, silent prayer of thanks that those closest to me would remain close to me for yet another day. I did not pray for the victim's safety because I knew in my heart it was too late for that. The words in the note had convinced me the murder had already taken place. I would pray for the living tonight. Not the dead. The dead were in God's hands. Only the living were still in mine.

I felt restless. I needed to speak to the boys for a while, or listen to them speak between themselves. I needed their youthful enthusiasm and their happy banter to cleanse my mind, to bury my fears.

I also needed to lay aside my worries about Sam for a while. The future that lay before us. If we had one at all.

I longed for Sam even now. I ached to see his mouth gape wide in a silent scream at that wonderful moment when his body opened up to me completely. I longed for the instant when his nectar gushed forth to fill the air with the scent of man, of desire, of love. Nowhere on this planet was there a person I desired more. One would think having that love returned would be enough, but it wasn't. I wanted more. I wanted the world to know how we felt about each other. I wanted to walk down the street holding Sam's hand. I wanted to feel him lean into me in a crowd of souls and not be afraid to brush his lips across my ear and tell me how much he loved me. And for me to do the same. I knew Sam wanted all that as well. Sometimes I think he wanted it more than I.

But those things could never happen. Not here. Not in Greene County. Not in Nine Mile. How long would Sam wait for me to decide between my love for my church and my love for him? Was my position as preacher in this one-horse town, a position I truly loved, really more important than the fact that I was also truly loved by him? That I just as hungrily loved him back?

When would I decide which mattered the most? Us or me? The church or Sam?

I closed my eyes and let the wind cool my fevered thoughts as I approached the lake. The grass was cool and damp beneath my toes, my footsteps silent.

The boys' campfire had burned low, casting little light on the surrounding area. The moonlight, however, told me everything I needed to know. The boys were asleep. They were huddled together in one sleeping bag. The other bag was draped across a low bush at the water's edge. The boys were constantly jumping in and out of the lake, and the sleeping bag must have gotten wet at some point during the evening. They were tucked together inside the other bag, not for warmth, but for protection from mosquitoes. Without it they would have been eaten alive.

In his sleep, Jesse had come to rest a hand on Kyle's shoulder. They looked so peaceful and innocent lying there in the moonlight—Jesse on his stomach, Kyle on his back—that I spun on my heel and headed back to the lodge, stepping softly so as not to disturb them.

Mrs. Shanahan was sawing logs in her little nook behind the kitchen, and I found Sam no longer asleep in the bed upstairs, but sitting at my desk in the office, browsing the Internet.

Sam wore only a rumpled pair of boxer shorts. His blond hair was ruffled from sleep, his eyes heavy and sexy as hell. He smiled as I walked through the door.

"When I left," I said, "you were asleep in the bed."

"Yeah," he answered. "The big, lonely bed. When I woke and you weren't in it with me, I came looking for you. Did you see the boys?"

"Yep. They're sleeping."

He nodded. "Long day. They're probably tired."

I grinned. "They're conked out side by side in the same sleeping bag."

"Are they?"

"Yes. I think the other one must have gotten wet."

Sam reached out and hooked a finger in my belt loop, pulling me near. He gave my bare stomach a lingering kiss. "Did you wake them?"

His mouth felt heavenly on my skin. "No. I let them sleep."

"Good."

Sam gazed up into my face as if he were about to say something. I waited, pushing the hair from his forehead.

"What?" I asked.

He gave a tiny shake to his head and said, "Nothing."

"Come to bed, Sam," I said. "I want to hold you."

Ignoring my comment, he laid his hand on the fly of my faded cargo pants and said, "I love these."

I laughed. "Me too. So many pockets."

"That's not exactly what I meant," he said, again leaning in to brush his lips against my stomach. "There's some sort of psychic connection between these pants and your libido. Don't tell me you haven't noticed it."

"What a whimsical notion," I said, and at the same time, I felt something stir beneath Sam's hand. He felt it too.

"Uh-oh," he said. "There's something alive in there. Alive and trying to get out."

"Another whimsical notion."

Sam gazed up at me with a look of angelic innocence, but at the same time, there was a glimmer in his eyes that wasn't innocent at all. "Let's just see," he said. "Shall we?"

His eyes bore into mine as he grasped my zipper tab with his slim, elegant fingers and began slowly sliding it downward.

"The bedroom," I said, breath catching in my chest.

"No," he said. "Here."

I gasped as those damn cargo pants—they had always been too big—slid down my legs to crumple at my feet.

Sam's eyes opened wide. "No underwear?" he asked.

"Didn't think I'd need any."

"You're right. You don't."

Still sitting in the desk chair, Sam slipped his hand around to the back of my thigh and pulled me closer. He plucked at my pubic hair with his teeth, coaxing me to step even nearer, which I did.

He sighed, running his tongue along the length of my cock, which had been pointing due north for the last minute or so. He kissed me below the corona, his eyes still centered on my face.

"Oh God," I said, my voice an octave lower than usual. Sam moved his hands across my body. I could feel his breath on me. My legs were weak.

His voice, huskier now as well, was a hush in the silent night. "I love you, Reverend Lucas."

As the first tremble of desire coursed through my body, I replied, "Show me."

And he did.

Dear Reader,
By now, your Cock must be HARD.
So is mine. I have 8" Cock
I can Fuck you.
How big is your Cock?
7' 8" ... 10" ?
I like to Suck your Cock.

How does your CUM Taste?

Sweet, Bitter, Salty?

Mine tastes Salty.

Chapter Ten

I AWOKE the next morning with Boyd's final words to me in the cemetery still running through my head.

"They're giving me forty-eight hours to sew this case up, or they've threatened to call in the big boys. Maybe they're right. About all I've been able to show them is a whole lot of nothing. I'm standing around with my thumb up my ass, spinning like a top, while the body count keeps climbing."

"Don't worry," I said, doing my best to ignore the crystal clear image conjured up by my brother's words. "You'll catch him."

But did I really believe that? Now, this morning, I wasn't so sure. I harbored a great deal of respect for Boyd's ability to do his job, but shouldn't he be getting around to *doing* that job before too many more lives were lost? Was my brother outmatched? How could he find a murderer with so damn few clues? Perhaps Boyd should give this one to the "big boys," and let them handle it.

My brother had never been one to succumb to outside pressure. "Fuck 'em," he'd say, with his usual lack of finesse. And fuck 'em he would. One way or another, he would go down fighting. No matter how big a fool he made of himself in the process, he would never give up.

I rubbed the sleep from my eyes and groped across the bed. Sam was gone. Down in the kitchen with his aunt, no doubt, worrying this latest note to death. Trying to aid Boyd in his game of "catch the killer." It was a countywide pastime, this race to identify the murderer before he could kill again.

Boyd, I knew, was out beating the bushes this very minute, playing his own version of the game, searching for the killer's latest victim as promised in that last infuriating note.

I wished him luck for his sake as well as everyone else's. It had to stop. These murders seemed to be the purest form of evil. Something for the movies, not real life. Certainly not here. Not in my hometown. It was all so incomprehensible.

Whispered voices on the veranda made me sit up in bed, instantly alert. My heart gave a stutter of fear before I remembered Sam was no longer lying naked in the bed beside me. Immediately following that stutter of fear came the old familiar guilt for making Sam and me live this way. But there was nothing I could do about it now.

I swung my feet to the floor and grabbed a pair of trousers from the back of the chair.

The sun should have been well up in the sky by now, but if it was, I couldn't see it behind the bank of dark clouds hovering overhead. Not much greeted me as I stepped out onto the veranda, buttoning my pants. Nothing but that threatening sky, which had grown all too familiar in the past several days, and two wide-eyed, innocent faces gazing up at me from the top of the stairway.

Innocence notwithstanding, those faces were as bleak and dismal as the sky. Jesse and Kyle sat forlornly, hunched over like two little old men on the top step. Jesse's arm was draped across Kyle's shoulder. They gave the impression of having been there for quite a little while.

Jesse immediately withdrew his arm from Kyle's shoulder as I approached. I gave them my best smile, all the while longing for a toothbrush to wash away the taste of sleep.

"Morning, boys. I guess you've been waiting for me to wake up."

Brilliant deduction, Holmes.

Jesse cleared his throat, formally, like a child who is called upon to recite.

"Kyle needs to talk to you, Uncle Brian."

Jesse gently nudged the boy, but Kyle didn't need to be nudged. He was more than ready to talk. And talk he did. His hands flew in angry punctuation as the words came tripping from his mouth.

"What's happening? Why does everybody suddenly think my dad has something to do with the murders? Is your brother going to arrest him? Dad didn't kill anybody! He *couldn't* kill anybody! Is that what Mom and Pop are fighting about all the time?"

Poor Kyle. It wasn't enough his voice had been recently wracked with the ravages of puberty. Now it sounded as if he might have been crying as well. His eyes snapped and flared and sparkled with a light much brighter than the one offered up by that dull, leaden sky above our heads. It was as if strobe lights were flashing inside the boy's head, intermittently visible behind those wide, frightened eyes.

I shunned the chair at the end of the veranda in favor of a more personal approach. I sat down, cross-legged, on the deck before him, close enough that our knees almost touched. As I settled in with a few creaks and groans as befitted the fact I had just crawled out of bed, Jesse once again laid his arm over Kyle's shoulder. Jesse's hands, I noticed, were strong and brown like his father's. Like mine. He would soon be a man. A good man, I had no doubt. A good man and a good friend.

I reached out to give Kyle a comforting pat on the leg, feeling both impotent and deceitful as I did so. I sincerely hoped the sins of the father would not be visited upon this fine young boy in front of me.

With that thought came the realization that I wasn't as certain of Gordon Knowles's innocence as his son was. But let's be honest, I berated myself, were those suspicions based on any actual evidence, or were they simply based on the fact I didn't like the guy? Since hard evidence was a commodity I was a bit shy of at the moment, I had to admit it might be my personal dislike for Gordon Knowles, and little else, that prompted me to think of him as a murderer. I suddenly realized I *did* think of him that way. At some point during the night, as I slept in Sam's arms, the idea had crystallized in my mind, and now, regardless of my complete lack of proof, the conviction was firmly embedded.

What impudence! I began to feel small indeed. Nothing like the innocence of youth and one's own petty prejudices to bring that out in a man.

I gave in to the always-risky business of opening my mouth to speak before giving my brain sufficient time to figure out what it was I wanted to say. This time, luckily enough, it seemed to work fairly well.

"I don't know where you're getting your information, Kyle, but I can assure you if your father is a suspect in the killings, then this is the first I've heard about it." On the face of it, this was true enough. *My* suspicions and *Boyd's* suspicions likely held little resemblance to each other. Or so I hoped, for this boy's sake.

A tear slid over the arch of Kyle's long lower lash and splattered his shirt. "It was Mrs. Shanahan. I heard her talking to Sam. She said…." But the thought was too much for him. He sniffled and fell silent.

I should have known. Although little Sam's aunt might say could hold much interest for me, I would dearly love to hear why she would be foolish enough to say such things about Gordon Knowles within earshot of his son. Regardless of what I might believe in the matter, I certainly gave myself credit for having more sense than that.

"She's playing amateur sleuth, Kyle. And she doesn't know what she's talking about." To myself I added, *never has and never will*, but that was not something the boys needed to hear. "Kyle, if your mom and dad are having problems at home, perhaps it's a good thing you are staying here for a while. It'll give them time to work it out on their own."

My words sounded hollow even to me. God alone knew how they sounded to Kyle. Was that all my religious training had taught me, to string a bunch of useless words together that probably would have been as comforting to a horse as they were to this unhappy boy?

I pinched the bridge of my nose. I could tell already this would not be one of my better days. Self-flagellation first thing in the morning is never a good sign.

Jesse, to my surprise, came in with a little supporting ground fire. He dragged Kyle closer and said, "That's wight, wabbit. They'll work it out. Parents are weird. One minute they're bashing each other's brains in and screaming loud enough to wilt the houseplants, and the next thing you know they're slipping you a couple of bucks for a movie so as to get you out of the house long enough for them to play a few rounds of hide-the-salami in the back bedroom, while the cat watches from the dresser drawer where he was trying to cop a few *z*'s before these two morons started banging the bed against the wall with such happy abandon that the pictures are crashing to the floor and all the neighbors have come running outside to see who's killing who and wondering why the shingles are falling off the roof of that house across the—"

I coughed. "Thank you, Jesse. That was most descriptive. Your father must be very proud. Taught you everything he knows, I see."

Jesse beamed. "Yeah. I'm a chip off the old block, ain't I?"

"Yes," I droned, rubbing the back of my neck. "I'm afraid you are."

I noticed a smile fanning out across Kyle's face as he wiped the tears from his cheek with the back of his hand. It dawned on me maybe Jesse wasn't quite the fool he sometimes made himself out to be. In the space of ten seconds, he had done more to ease Kyle's fears than I had. And he managed to make the boy smile on top of it. There were lessons to be learned here, if only I knew what they were.

Jesse was not yet finished being a chip off the old block.

"These old bones tell me it's gonna rain today like a cow pissing on a flat rock." He scanned the sky for a little meteorological corroboration. "What do you think, Uncle Brian?" Strangely enough, I couldn't. Think, that is. That damned cow with the golden waterfall gushing from her backside filled my mind—except at the corners, where snippets of other images still lingered. A yellow pencil. Ticonderoga number two. A bronze casket, newly stripped of flowers, sliding into the sodden earth. Eyeglasses taken from a cold face and slipped into an undertaker's jacket. Lazarus. His paws smeared with blood. Sam's heated breath, rustling the hair on my stomach as my heart slowly hammered itself back to a normal rhythm. Fragments of death, and life, that had now become such integral parts of my consciousness I wondered if they would be with me to my dying day. Some I hoped I would never lose; others I would rather live without.

At least, thanks to Jesse, Kyle's fears seemed to be eased for the moment.

"Have you boys had breakfast?"

Jesse grinned. "One breakfast, yes. But what about second breakfast?"

Kyle giggled, his eyes still bright from recent tears.

I groaned. "*Lord of the Rings*? You're quoting *Lord of the Rings*?"

Jesse looked at me as wide-eyed as a squirrel that has stumbled across a bag of almonds. "You've seen it, Uncle Brian?"

"Seen it? No. I read it."

Jesse's eyes opened even wider. "You mean it was a book or something before it was a movie?"

I gave my nephew what I hoped was a withering glare. "Yes, son. It was a book or something. Three books, actually. For your information, masterpieces aren't generally created in Hollywood. They end up there later, for better or worse."

Jesse eyed me with wonder. "And you read this book?"

"Several times. I didn't just fall off the literary turnip truck, you know. Unlike others I might name."

"I'll be damned" was all he said as he pulled Kyle up by the shirt collar and dragged him down the stairs.

With a sigh of exasperation, I had turned to go back into the bedroom when I heard Kyle speaking softly beneath the veranda.

"You've read the trilogy how many times?"

Jesse laughed. "Four. Working on the fifth."

Kyle sounded a bit confused. "So what was the point of all that?"

"No point. I like to get Uncle Brian's goat once in a while. He's so cute when he gets riled. Even Sam says so."

I watched them head toward the lake, arms around each other's waists, their laughter ringing sharply in the morning air.

I blinked a couple of times as I watched them go and finally turned away to prepare myself for the day.

My nephew thinks I'm cute, I thought, shaking my head. So much for the role-model hype. *Apparently Sam thinks so too*. Although I rather wished he hadn't voiced that opinion to the boys. It might start them wondering about things.

I tried not to smile as I considered how to best approach Sam about it, knowing full well I never would. I would rather find myself mud wrestling with a bikini-clad Mrs. Shanahan in nothing but Speedos and a sombrero.

After all, being cute isn't such a bad thing. Even for a Methodist minister.

THIRTY MINUTES later I entered the kitchen to find a scene of total chaos and destruction. There were only three participants in the unholy riot taking place, but it seemed three was a sufficient number to wreak havoc on my once pristine kitchen.

Pans and cooking utensils were scattered across the soapy floor. A curtain had been torn from one of the windows and now lay in a rumpled, soggy mass by the door to the walk-in freezer. Sam sat at a table with his head on his arms, laughing, while Mrs. Shanahan, soaked to the gills, stood over the sink bellowing like a bull as she manhandled a screeching Lazarus back into the soapy water from which he was desperately and angrily attempting to escape. His furious yowls curled the hair at the back of my neck.

Sam, upon seeing me, tried to explain the situation but was unable to create so much as one understandable word through his breathless laughter. Tears streamed down his face, and snot dripped from his nose. Finally he gave a helpless shrug and dropped his head back onto his arms. His whole body continued to shake with uncontrollable mirth. He was a happy, happy man.

Mrs. Shanahan, on the other hand, wasn't happy at all. She shot me such a glare of indignation I decided on the spot to forego breakfast and did an about-face and left the room.

I was obviously the innocent bystander in this conflagration, and we all know what happens to innocent bystanders.

As I crossed the dining hall, I heard one last plea for help from a screaming Lazarus before I exited the lodge, thankful to have escaped so easily.

I wished Lazarus luck. In Mrs. Shanahan he was pitted against a mighty foe.

Outside, I took a deep breath of crisp morning air and looked around for a friendly face.

Kyle and Jesse were stomping the boxes in which all our athletic equipment had arrived, making a manageable pile to be carried off to the trash. Billy Simmons, once again looking naked from a distance since he wore only a tiny pair of beige swim trunks, was painting the lifeguard tower white. Most of the paint, however, seemed to have landed on him instead. With his deep tan blotched with smears of white, he might have been the vitiligo poster boy of the year.

He gave me a cheerful wave with his paintbrush, lost control of the thing, and dropped it on his foot. The F-word sailed up from the lakeshore, shot over my head, and dissipated into the hills beyond, no doubt giving much of the wildlife fodder for thought. I really had to do something about the boy's vocabulary before the children arrived, or I would have parents taking potshots at me through my kitchen window with their hunting rifles. Church camp, indeed.

At the second cabin, Gordon Knowles was mixing cement in a metal bucket, obviously preparing to elongate the wheelchair ramp I had complained about more than a week ago. By the unhappy tilt of his head when he saw me, I was surprised not to hear the F-word, with an "er" attached at the end, once again echo across the hills.

For company, I chose the more forthright and appealing of the two and headed straight for Billy Simmons.

I stood a moment surveying his work. "Shouldn't you be starting at the top and working your way down instead of starting at the bottom and working your way up?"

He stepped back, rubbed his freshly painted foot against the calf of his other leg, thus spreading the paint around even more, and studied the fifteen-foot tower before him.

"I guess it might have been easier that way," he admitted.

I nodded. "Easier and neater."

He shrugged and gave me a goofy grin. "Oh, well. Live and learn."

"And paint," I commanded. "We open in a month."

"Yes, massah," he said with a salute and immediately went back to work.

After two brushstrokes he stopped, looked sheepishly at me, then stared pointedly at Jesse and Kyle, who were carting the flattened boxes toward the back of the lodge.

I followed his gaze. "What is it, Billy?"

Whatever it was, he seemed to be struggling to get the words out. A reticent Billy Simmons was not something I had ever expected to see. It caused me to look once again up the hillside and watch the boys disappear with their burdens to the rear of the lodge.

"Uh, Reverend, I don't want to stick my nose in where it doesn't belong, but—"

"But what, Billy? Out with it."

He scratched his head with his paintbrush hand, leaving a smear of white in his sun-bleached hair. At this rate it would take a gallon of kerosene to get him clean.

"It's just—well—I think maybe you should have a talk with your nephew over there."

I looked up the hill, but the boys were gone, hidden behind the lodge.

"About what?" I asked.

Billy took a halfhearted swipe at the tower with his paintbrush. I could see the blood rising to his face. The boy was mortally embarrassed about something, but I didn't have the vaguest idea what it was.

"Geez, Reverend. I don't know. Spiritual stuff, maybe. Whatever it takes."

I gazed once again up the hill and saw Jesse and Kyle, laughing as they returned for another load.

"Whatever it takes to do what?" I asked. "Can you be a little more specific? I'm afraid you've lost me. Has Jesse done something wrong?"

Billy's cheek bulged out with a wandering tongue as he considered the question. "Depends on how you look at it, I guess."

"How you look at *what*, for heaven's sake?" Beneath his tan Billy's face was now a deep, glowing terra-cotta red. He looked like someone who would dearly love a hole to crawl into.

He dipped his brush into the paint and went back to work. "Just keep your eyes open, Reverend. You'll see."

"I wish you'd tell me what's bothering you, Billy. I can't do much about it if I don't know what it is."

"I've said enough. Too much, maybe. I don't usually poke around in other people's business. Just thought maybe you should know."

"Know *what*? You haven't told me *anything*!"

"Good," he said. "I hate squealers."

He pointedly turned his back to me and recommenced dragging his paintbrush over the lifeguard tower as if our conversation had never taken place. For all intents and purposes, it hadn't, since I didn't have the least notion what the hell we had discussed. All I could do was stare at a perfect white handprint on Billy's naked back and wonder two things. How had he painted a perfect handprint in the middle of his back, and why did I suddenly feel so apprehensive?

I turned away, once again watching Jesse and Kyle climb the hill toward the lodge, laden with boxes, laughing and bumping shoulders as they playfully attempted to dislodge the other's load.

The two had been friends since they were old enough to *make* friends. I could not remember one argument between the two that had ever threatened the solidity of that friendship, which was more than I could say for most of the adults I knew, who seemed to thrive in a cloud of spats, feuds, and unforgiven betrayals, imagined or not, by those professing to be closest to them.

The young are purer of heart. It's a simple fact. And in my eyes, Jesse and Kyle were two of the purest. They both did well in school, attended church regularly, and had never been in any trouble whatsoever.

So what was Billy Simmons driving at?

These thoughts were driven from my head by a streak of black shooting across the hillside. It took me a moment to realize it wasn't the largest rat I had ever seen, but Lazarus, ears flat in anger, still soaking wet from his unwanted bath.

He took one look at me, hissed, spat, and gave me the kitty finger (as we've all seen these creatures do even without the benefit of proper digits), before scooting up the nearest pine tree to lick his wounds and plot revenge. He stretched himself out along a limb with his skinny black tail dangling down, dripping water and flipping back and forth in agitation. A low growl emanated from his throat as he watched me through slitted eyes. He was obviously rethinking the wisdom of his recent adoption. Golda had never subjected him to such torture. Not once.

I heard the sound of an automobile approaching down the rutted lane, and soon a van from the phone company appeared through the trees, bouncing to a muddy stop by the lodge's front porch. I waved as a young man stepped from the van in phone-company garb. He turned, hands on hips, to study the lane he had traversed, shaking his head and mumbling to himself.

As I came up to him, he stooped and peered beneath the van.

"Everything still intact?" I asked.

"Looks like it," he said. "I thought maybe I'd left body parts from old Betsy here scattered along the last two miles of that goddamn obstacle course you call a road."

"It is a bit rough," I said.

He stood up and studied me with all the trust of a man who has a gun held to his head.

"A bit rough? Driving across the Andes on rims would be a bit rough. But there, of course, you wouldn't need scuba gear and pontoons to get through the pits and potholes."

I chuckled in a commiserating sort of way, but it didn't seem to appease him much.

The van was splattered with mud from the running boards to the roof. The young man was standing in six inches of water, but he didn't seem to have noticed it yet, and I thought it best not to draw it to his attention. He was in a bad enough mood already.

"I can see why you need a phone," he said. "Once you get here, you have to wait for a drought to get the hell back out."

I laughed. "Well, it isn't quite that bad."

"No?" he asked, as he flung open the back doors of the van, then pulled out his equipment. He draped a coil of phone wire around his neck and stuffed several other items under his arms. Only then did he realize he was standing in a puddle. He looked down at his feet, then back at me, then down at his feet again. He let out a long, martyred sigh and stomped off toward the lodge, dragging his telephone wire behind him through the mud.

"A little water never hurt anybody!" I yelled after him. "You're not going to melt, you know!"

I thought I detected a sudden tension in his retreating back, but he didn't respond. He just kept walking.

Unfriendly fellow.

AN HOUR later our phones were connected, the unhappy phone man gone, and Mrs. Shanahan, like a fat Navy bos'n's mate, was angrily shoving a mop across the floor in an effort to obliterate his tracks. The Band-Aids needed after her recent battle with Lazarus ran up her arms like hash marks, furthering the impression.

I heard her mumble something about dirty cats and muddy boots before she once again hurled the filthy mop through the back door and plopped herself down at the kitchen table with a cup of coffee to, like Lazarus, lick her wounds.

Sam, on a coffee break of his own, placed a box of doughnuts before her like a nurse doling out blood pressure meds and eased himself into a chair. The kitchen was once again spic and span. Mrs. Shanahan had not been idle while I was outside.

I was about to commend her on her enterprise when our brand-new phones, one in my bedroom, one in my office, and one that hung on the kitchen wall, all came to life at once, causing the three of us to jump.

"That didn't take long," Sam said, plucking a doughnut from the box.

I picked up on the second ring.

Boyd was never one for pleasantries, and he didn't bother with them now. "Your car was seen in Bloomfield last night. Would you care to explain that?"

"My car?"

"Yes, bro. Your piece of shit Rambler. It was spotted at three in the morning by one of my deputies. What were you doing there?"

"I *wasn't* there. What's this all about?"

"Who stayed with you at the campground last night?"

"Mrs. Shanahan, Jesse, and Kyle. Oh, and I think Sam stayed over because it was late when he finished work and he didn't want to risk the lane in the dark." Surely I wouldn't burn in hell for one small lie. "Billy Simmons might have camped out with the boys down by the lake. I'm not sure. He was here this morning when I woke up."

"Well, find out."

"You mean *now*? Look, I'm sure there's been some sort of mistake. My car hasn't been moved since I returned from the funeral."

"There's no mistaking that heap of yours, Brian, and I want to know what it was doing in Bloomfield at three in the morning. If you didn't take it out, someone else did."

"That's impossible."

"Are you sure?"

"Well…."

Sam and his aunt were giving me quizzical looks, practically vibrating in their seats with curiosity.

"Where are you, Boyd? I'll call you right back."

"I just left the church, heading for the office. So call me on my cell."

"Did you find anything at the church? Any idea who left the note on the casket?"

"No. Your fucking church was as clueless as I was."

I winced. When frustrated, Boyd would inevitably strike out, not physically, but with words. With me, he always aimed that acerbic tongue at religion. Knowing Boyd was, aside from his short fuse, a good person at heart, I had learned to endure it. I often wondered how he would react if, under a poor guise of wit, I should attack the law in the same way he attacked my faith. But I sensed this was not the proper time to find out.

"I'll call you right back," I said again and hung up the phone.

"What was that all about?" Sam asked.

"Boyd wants to know if anyone took the car out last night."

"Like who?"

"I'm not sure. You gassed up after the funeral, right?"

Sam batted his eyelashes and nodded. "At my master's bidding, yes. Filled her right up to the top."

Around a mouthful of doughnut, Mrs. Shanahan muttered, "Good Lord, Sam, show a little independence."

Sam, in a rare moment of gay abandon, slapped his aunt's arm and simpered, "Oh, Auntie, I can't. You've never seen him naked in the moonlight."

"Praise Allah," Mrs. Shanahan said, focusing her attention back on her doughnut.

Ignoring them both, I stalked out of the lodge and down the hillside to where the Rambler was parked. I climbed inside and turned the key in the ignition. As usual, the gas gauge was a bit slow on the uptake. I gave it a few seconds to give me a reading, but it barely budged.

The tank was nearly empty.

Chapter Eleven

ALL I could learn about the disappearance and *re*appearance of my beloved Rambler was that Gordon Knowles could not believe anyone would steal it. Billy Simmons, who had *not* spent the night at the campground, could not believe anyone would stoop to driving it. Kyle crawled out of his cone of silence long enough to inform me it should be in a plexiglass booth in the Smithsonian with a sign that read Dorkmobile, circa 1960. Jesse had simply shaken his head and giggled. I had no idea what *that* meant, other than the fact it was less than complimentary to my car.

Needless to say, any idea as to how the Rambler came to be seen in Bloomfield on the night in question was a matter of purest conjecture. If Boyd wanted an answer to the riddle, he would have to ferret it out for himself. My powers of interrogation were obviously insufficient to the task.

Morris Carter saw the car parked in the business section of that town, across from the County courthouse, at 2:45 a.m. as he was making his rounds. Later, at 3:15, the car was gone. But for the missing gasoline, I might have concluded Morris was mistaken. The man was not known for his eagle-eyed perception. The empty tank, however, could not be explained away so easily.

I could not comprehend how my car, not the quietest of machines, to put it charitably, could have been driven away under our noses without waking everyone within a two-mile radius. Could someone not connected to the campground have taken it? Who would do such a thing, and what would they have been doing at the campground in the middle of the night to begin with? Kids on a joyride surely would not have gone to the trouble of returning the car to the place they had stolen it.

I rang Boyd back to explain all this to him, and he informed me if indeed someone had taken the car, then he intended to find out who the culprit was.

"But why?" I asked. "What is so all-fired important about my car turning up in Bloomfield in the middle of the night?"

"Because," he growled, "the third victim was found this morning. In Bloomfield."

"*What?*"

"I believe you heard me, little brother." Boyd's voice had a dangerous edge to it.

"Surely you don't think *I* had anything to do with it."

"Oh, don't be stupid."

I took a deep breath to calm myself. "God help us all," I finally said.

Boyd huffed into the phone. "He hasn't been much help so far."

I sighed. Here we go again. "I suppose not."

"I need you here, Bry. Your presence has been requested."

"By whom?"

"By the husband of the victim. Chester Goldstone."

My heart bucked inside my chest. "It's Kyle's *grandmother* who's been murdered?"

"I'm afraid so."

I heard laughter outside and cast my gaze through the window of my office, where down by the lake, Jesse and Kyle were scooping water from the canoes after our last cloudburst the day before. Kyle's father was sitting on the stoop in front of Cabin #2, smoking a cigarette. I had no idea what he had been doing, but whatever it was, he was certainly not chomping at the bit to begin anything else. As I watched, I saw him look up and study the boys in the canoe, as if wondering how they could possibly be so young and yet so industrious at such an early hour of the morning.

"Gordon and Kyle are both here. Should I tell them?"

"No."

"I'll need a ride into town. My car is low on gas. I'll have Sam bring me in."

"No," Boyd said. "Have Gordon do it. He must have driven in to get to work. Get a ride with him. I want to talk to him anyway. But don't tell him about the murder. Don't say anything to the boy either. His parents should do that."

I remembered Thelma Goldstone at the basket dinner and then later in our car during the funeral procession for Grace Nuggett. She had not been a likable woman. I guiltily realized I would not miss her nearly as much as I already missed the other two victims. I wondered if her husband would find her absence a trial. Somehow I could not imagine it.

Then I wondered if that was an unchristian thought. Not really caring. Just wondering.

Maggie Knowles would grieve, of course. Kyle's mother, I suspected, would take it hard. Yet I recalled Maggie's words to me after the funeral. According to Maggie, Thelma Goldstone had taken Maggie out of her will as punishment for marrying Gordon. Did Gordon know this? Maggie said not, but could she be mistaken? Gordon, who lied to me about the scratches on his face, might not be above taking matters into his own hands if he had found out about the will from someone else. Chester, perhaps. A lot of money was at stake. But would he go so far as to commit murder because of it? And even if he did, what possible connection could there be to the *other* two killings? Obviously, all the crimes were connected. The notes alone proved that. I doubted if Gordon Knowles had even a passing acquaintance with either Grace Nuggett or Golda Burrows.

I continued to study Gordon through the window.

I had almost forgotten the phone in my hand until Boyd's voice brought me back.

"I'll send Morris out there until you return. He's like a pig on ice at a murder scene anyway."

"Thank you, Boyd. Where shall Gordon and I meet you? At your office?"

"No. Goldstone Jewelry. Meet me there."

"Is that where…?"

"You guessed it."

"Has the body been taken away?"

"No. It'll be hours before we remove it. We haven't processed the crime scene yet."

"Great," I said.

Boyd chuckled. "Don't worry, Bry. If you can survive the sight of Golda Burrows nailed to her piano, you can survive this. Although it isn't pretty. Remember not to say anything to Gordon about why you need him to take you into town. I'd like to surprise him."

"Is he a suspect?"

"Who has a better motive?"

"What motive is that?" I asked. Did Boyd already know about the will?

My brother apparently was not referring to the will at all.

"Gordon had Thelma Goldstone for a mother-in-law. Why *wouldn't* he want to kill her? I would."

WITH GORDON Knowles at the wheel of his rusty and battered F-100 pickup, it proved to be an uncomfortable ride from Sunset Lake to Bloomfield. Thirty excruciating miles of evasions on my part and a mixture of forced camaraderie and hostile silences on his. When I told him I needed supplies for my office, he agreed readily enough to drive me into town, an offer I suspected had more to do with getting out of a few hours work than any sense of community spirit. Although I didn't like the man, I felt guilty blindsiding him. I tried to control my growing anger at Boyd for putting me in this position. It would have been so much simpler and more forthright if I could have simply told Gordon the truth.

Aside from what the boys had accomplished, I doubted there would be much work done at the campground today, other than what Sam could get done. I had confided the truth to Sam about Thelma Goldstone before conning a ride from Gordon. He promised to watch over the boys and his aunt until Deputy Carter arrived. By the sarcastic moue on his face when I told him Carter was on the way, I suspected Sam would stay to watch over everyone anyway. His faith in Morris's abilities as a law enforcement officer, I'm afraid, was not much better than mine.

Heaven alone knew how long Boyd would keep me at the crime scene, and after that I would have to visit Maggie. She was the one who would be most in need of comfort and spiritual guidance. She did not appear to be a strong woman, and her life had not been easy. Despite the matter of the will, I suspected she would take her mother's death hard.

A nagging fear had been settling in, and now I gave it free rein to let itself be known. It did so with uncommon clarity.

Three disparate women. One living in Bloomfield, the county seat, one in Nine Mile, a tiny town of less than 300 souls, and one living in the countryside between the other two. Until their deaths, the only time these three women ever came together under one roof, as far as anyone knew, was to worship. I had seen each of their faces from the pulpit as I preached. They did not sit together, but they were there. God brought them together in life. A murderer brought them together in death. In our minds, they would always be together now. Three women, slain.

Why? What was the motive?

I glanced across the pickup's wide bench seat at Gordon sitting there hunched over the wheel, glowering through the windshield at the road ahead.

Was I sitting next to the person who had murdered these three old women? Boyd suspected him, obviously, or else why had I been asked to perform this charade? Did we *want* Gordon Knowles to be the killer? He was not a pleasant man, but was that reason enough for us to label him a murderer?

I studied the scratches along his cheek. Had someone fought back? Did Lazarus get a couple of licks in while trying to protect his mistress? Why did Gordon lie about those scratches? Maggie said there had been no argument between her and her husband. She had not tried to skewer him with a meat fork, as Gordon had laughingly told me. If the scratches came from some sort of innocent accident, why didn't Gordon say so? What was the point of lying?

Gordon's words dragged me away from my thoughts.

"Why so jumpy, Padre?"

"What? I'm not jumpy."

"You kidding? You're like a cat at a dog show."

I tried to laugh, but it sounded unconvincing even to me. "I have a lot on my mind, I guess. Opening the campground. These terrible murders."

"Yeah, they're a pisser, all right. The campground will work itself out, I reckon. But the murders. Now that's something to worry about. Interesting, though."

"*Interesting*? You find them *interesting*?"

He watched the road. "That's not what I said. You're putting words in my mouth. But you have to admit it's a hell of a puzzle. What's the point of it?"

"The point?"

"Yeah. Those two old women had nothing in common. Where's the motive?"

It surprised me to realize Gordon had been having the same thoughts as I, although he did not yet know of the third victim—unless he was the one who killed her.

"There must be a connection somewhere," I said. "You don't kill people for no reason."

"Seems to me that's exactly what the killer is doing. They weren't raped, were they?"

"Good heavens, no! They were old. Old women. If rape was the motive, don't you think the killer would seek out younger prey?"

Gordon grunted at my shock. "The Boston Strangler didn't. So unless the killer had some unresolved sexual issues—"

I laughed. "You've given this some thought, haven't you?"

"Who *isn't* thinking about it?" he snapped, tearing his eyes from the road for a moment to glare at me. Our gazes locked for a couple of ticks before he turned back to the highway.

We were nearing Bloomfield now. My mouth disconnected from my brain before I could stop it.

"Where did you really get those scratches, Gordon? Maggie said the two of you never had a fight."

I was thrown against the dash as Gordon slammed on the brakes. With screeching tires, the old pickup quickly bounced to a stop at the side of the highway. He switched off the ignition and twisted around in his seat to face me, his manner both threatening and extremely amused.

"You've been talking to my wife behind my back, Padre. Why the hell would you want to do a thing like that?"

"That's not the way it was," I tried to explain, wondering for a fleeting moment how fast I could get out of the vehicle if the situation should turn violent. "She came to me. Over spiritual matters."

"*Spiritual* matters?"

"That's right. It had nothing to do with you," I lied. It dawned on me for the first time it might be possible I was wrong in thinking Gordon was the killer, and maybe Maggie was right. Maybe the man *was* having an affair. A sin, to be sure, but it didn't hold a candle to murder. It dawned on me also I might have lost myself a camp custodian, which, in the grand scheme of things, didn't really seem to be an overriding issue.

His eyes narrowed as he studied me, then slowly opened wider as the truth hit him. "You think I'm the killer."

"Don't be—"

"My God, you do," he said. "You think I murdered those women."

If you discounted Boyd's phone call informing me another body had been found, I then experienced my first truly surprising moment of the day as Gordon Knowles lolled his head back onto the headrest and laughed. It wasn't a gentle snicker either. It was an honest-to-God belly laugh.

He finally calmed himself long enough to sputter, "You'd better stick to preaching, Padre, and leave the police work to your brother."

He wiped a happy tear from his face as rain began to pepper the windshield. More rain. Great. Even murder couldn't stop my mind from flashing on my sodden campground and wondering if we would ever be able to open on time.

"What was my motive?" Gordon asked, drawing me back from my own selfish thoughts. "We were talking about motives. So what was mine?"

"I don't know. It was just a theory."

"You're a piss-poor liar, Reverend."

"I know," I said. "It's a failing of mine."

He leaned forward and rested his forehead on the steering wheel. A wide smile spread once again across his face.

"So where *did* you get the scratches?" I asked.

He turned his head and studied me again, not without amusement. He ignored the question.

"So where are we really going? Are you carting me off to jail?"

"No. Boyd wants to see you."

"Why didn't you just tell me that? Why all the secrecy and subterfuge?"

Subterfuge wasn't a word I would have credited Gordon with knowing, which showed how far my prejudice against this man had taken me.

My brother would kill me, but I had no choice. "There's been another murder, Gordon. It's Thelma. Your mother-in-law. They found her this morning."

For a long moment, the cab was filled with the rattle of raindrops hitting the roof. No other sound could be heard. Then Gordon found his voice. "Where?"

"In her store."

He gazed through the windshield at the quickening rain. "Maggie—"

"Yes," I said, tempering the truth with a lie that seemed to make sense under the circumstances. "Boyd wants you there to tell her about her mother. She'll be distraught. Her husband should be with her." For all I knew this might be true.

"Shit," he said softly, turning the ignition and slamming the truck into gear. He checked for oncoming traffic before pulling back onto the highway with spinning wheels, tossing a spray of mud up behind us.

We barreled down the hill into Bloomfield like a fighter jet swooping down on a carrier's flight deck, and we weren't the first to arrive.

The town square was packed with people. Citizens had poured from the courthouse and neighboring businesses, milling around the courthouse lawn and sidewalks to get a better view of the activity in front of Goldstone Jewelry. One industrious young man had found a vantage point atop the old cannon by the courthouse steps. He sat, hat in hand, straddling the cannon like a bronco rider.

The last time I had seen this many faces here was during the annual Covered Bridge Festival in the fall. Those had been happy faces. These were not. There were a few umbrellas scattered around, but not many. Most of these people stood in the rain, impervious to the weather. Water dripped from the bills of baseball caps and cowboy hats. Women sheltered their heads under purses or newspapers, all eyes directed at the storefront where one of Boyd's deputies was stringing crime scene tape across the entryway.

The only sound to be heard was the patter of falling rain. The crowd was silent. The sirens of the three police cars parked at odd angles along the street had been turned off long ago.

Gordon double-parked the pickup in the middle of Main Street, fear of a ticket, I guessed, not high on his list of worries at the moment. Spotting us, Deputy Lawson motioned us inside through the store's front door.

As we stooped under the yellow tape stretched across the doorway, he said, "The sheriff's expecting you. Careful of the blood."

I took a deep breath and stepped in out of the rain, my overriding emotion one of anger. Anger at being here. Anger at the sheer wickedness of it all.

My first glimpse of Thelma Goldstone's body knocked the anger right out of me. It was quickly replaced by fear. Fear for the people I loved. Fear for their safety. As the death count continued to grow, I suddenly realized how impossible a task it would be to protect them all. Sam, the boys, my congregation.

For these three women, death had come calling in the night, while others slept. It had come on stealthy feet under the cover of darkness. This idyllic stretch of real estate we all called home, this little piece of America's Heartland, with its small towns and quaint farms, was idyllic no longer. The violence of the rest of the world had finally crept in, like a cancer, the roots of which had at long last reached us. We could no longer feel secluded or safe as we went about the simple business of living our lives.

Goodness still thrived here, but evil, too, had now found a foothold. That first glimpse of Thelma Goldstone brought the presence of evil crashing down upon me like an avalanche of cold, sharp stone.

In contrast to the gloomy, wet sky outside, fluorescent lighting built into the ceiling tiles brought a stark clarity to every drop of blood and shard of broken glass. Like rubies and diamonds, the blood and glass lay scattered across the floor. The glass came from a shattered display case, one of many lined up on either side of the room, all undamaged but for the one. Like jewels, the shattered pieces of that one caught the light, shimmering across the floor. On closer inspection, I realized there *were* jewels there as well. *Actual* jewels. Precious and semiprecious. Diamonds and amethysts and amber. Green emeralds and tiny circles of gold. Stones of every hue, all sparkling like a spray of colored lights. In their midst, Thelma Goldstone's thick body lay sprawled, one heavy leg twisted beneath the other, arms outstretched, her eyes, opened wide in death, staring unseeing into the lights above.

Her throat had been torn open by a large sliver of glass that still protruded from it, bloody and sharp. Her throat had been gashed with such violence a spray of blood had flown across the floor and up the glass front of one of the undamaged display cases eight feet away. Her mouth was open in an obscene parody of fear. A handful of gold chains had been viciously stuffed between those silently screaming lips with such force her dentures had been shattered; a portion of them now lay on the floor beside her head like a ghastly brooch of pearls, broken and smeared with blood.

She was clad in a blood-soaked raincoat, but beneath it, where it had fallen open about her legs, a yellow nightgown with small daisies in the print could be glimpsed. Rain boots covered her feet, and she had rollers in her hair, a few of which had come loose and now dangled from curly ropes of red. Hadassah red, I remembered Mrs. Shanahan calling it jokingly. In the midst of this mayhem, I suddenly recalled an old episode of *I Love Lucy*. When Lucy and Ricky's apartment caught fire, Lucy stormed inside to grab a gallon of henna from the closet. Only after the henna was safely outside did Lucy run back to retrieve the baby.

I marveled at the inanity of this recollection here in the presence of murder and wondered if perhaps there might not be something wrong with me.

My brother gave me a curious look, as if wondering the same thing, but then he quickly turned to Gordon standing beside me.

I too glanced at Gordon. His eyes wide, he stared down at the corpse of a woman whom he had probably detested in life, but there was no smirk of satisfaction on his face, no twist of gleeful revenge on his lips. He was obviously as shocked as I was. As we all were. Gordon's hand came up to absentmindedly wipe the rain from his face. The hand trembled. Finally he tore his gaze away from this pitiable creature at our feet and met my brother's gaze.

"My God," he said.

We were startled by a cry of anguish behind us, and I spun to see Maggie Knowles struggling with the deputy at the door.

"Let me in!" she cried, trying to tear herself from the deputy's arms.

Willie was trying to be forceful, yet gentle. "No, ma'am. It's best you don't." He shot a pleading look to Boyd for help.

Quietly, Boyd spoke to Gordon. "Go to your wife," he said. "Take her home. Don't let her see her mother like this."

Gordon stared at my brother for a moment as if waiting for Boyd's words to sink in. Then, with a final glance at the bloodied woman on the floor, he turned away. As he passed through the door, Maggie tore herself away from the deputy and ran to her husband, burying her face against his chest. Gordon folded her in his arms with shushing noises and led her away. I spotted a woman across the street wiping tears from her eyes with a bright red bandana.

Boyd watched them go with a look of infinite sadness on his face before turning his eyes to me. Behind the two rows of waist-high display cabinets arranged along the length of the store was a walking space between the cases and the wall. Boyd pointed to the one on my left.

"I need you in the back, Bry. Come around that way. Don't cross the crime scene." Not until then did I hear the sobbing at the back of the store. It was coming from a small office in the rear.

I followed where Boyd's finger told me to walk, joining him on the other side.

Beyond a louvered door propped open with a tall stack of catalogs and old phone books, I saw Chester Goldstone slumped behind a cluttered desk in an office messier than my own. Piles of tiny gift boxes and reams of old receipts and correspondence covered every surface. A dozen rolls of assorted wrapping paper, in colors and designs for every occasion, leaned against the walls. In one corner of the room stood an old safe as tall as a man. Its doors were covered, like a refrigerator, with Post-it notes and photographs and magnetic odds and ends, all dusty and hanging rather askew. I concluded Thelma Goldstone was not particularly fastidious or artistic when it came to decorating anything other than herself.

I silently chided myself for this uncharitable thought and turned my attention to Chester Goldstone, sitting at the desk with his head in his hands.

Like Thelma, he too wore a raincoat. It hung oddly about his neck because the buttons had been misaligned, the garment obviously donned in haste. His white hair lay in disarray, and the collar of his pajama shirt peeked out from the top of his raincoat.

His hands were bloody.

"Are you hurt?" I asked.

He slowly lifted his head to look at me. He took a small intake of breath, as if surprised to find me there. Then he spread his hands out before him and studied them.

"I suppose I am," he said in a voice gravelly with grief.

I saw a long gash across the palm of his right hand and immediately pulled a handkerchief from my back pocket to wrap around the wound.

I glanced at Boyd, who was silently watching us from across the room.

Turning back to Chester, I asked gently, "How did you cut yourself?" While waiting for an answer, I knotted the handkerchief as best I could around his hand.

Chester removed his glasses, dropping them on the desk. He wearily squeezed the bridge of his nose. "The glass," he said, his voice flat and emotionless. "In her neck. I thought I could pull it out. Maybe help her. It wouldn't budge. It was too firmly... too firmly... embedded." He shook his head at that thought and stared at his hand. "All I managed to do was cut myself. I was too late to help her anyway. She was dead. I knew that from the beginning...."

His words trailed away, and he fell silent.

Awkwardly with his wrapped hand, he pulled the sleeve of his raincoat up and checked his wristwatch, which prompted me to check mine. I was fairly astounded to see it was still so early in the day. Not yet nine thirty in the morning.

Like a man talking in his sleep, Chester said, "Thelma and I should be opening up."

With my hand resting on Chester's shoulder, I turned my eyes to Boyd. My brother was staring intently at the old man, his expression a mixture of pity and confusion.

"Call a paramedic," he said to Willie.

"Right, boss," the deputy said. Taking the roundabout way through the store, Willie stepped outside the front door, probably to get a clear signal on his cell phone.

Boyd crossed the office and perched on the corner of the desk. I stepped back out of the way and noticed blood on my hand where it had touched Chester's coat. My brother noticed it too. We both examined the older man's back, where a large red smear had stained his raincoat.

Softly, my brother asked, "What time did you get here, Chester? Did you and Thelma come together?"

Chester knit his brow, considering the question.

"No. We were home. I heard Thelma's car starting up. That's what woke me."

"What time was that?"

Chester adjusted the handkerchief I had tied around his wounded hand, as if wondering how it had gotten there. "I'm not sure. Late. Maybe two or two thirty in the morning."

"Why did Thelma leave the house?"

"I don't know."

"Did she get a phone call? Is that why she left?"

"I don't know."

Boyd sighed. "Okay, Chester. I know this is hard for you, but try to remember. You followed her in your car, right?"

Chester looked up at Boyd, obviously confused. "Did I?"

"Both cars are out front, sir. They didn't get there by themselves."

"Well, then, yes. I suppose I did. It seems so long ago."

"Did you follow her right away? As soon as she left the house?"

"No. I—I waited."

"Waited for what?"

"I'm not sure."

"How long did you wait?"

"Not long. Maybe fifteen minutes. Might have been thirty."

"Then you followed her?"

"Yes."

"How did you know she was coming here?"

Chester gazed at Boyd with an expression of gentle patience, like a teacher confronting a rather slow student. "Where else would she have gone?"

Boyd smiled down at the old man, also with gentle patience. "And she was here?"

"Yes. Her car was parked on the street, and the front door was open."

"Were the lights on?"

"You mean the car lights?"

"No, I mean inside the store."

Chester thought about this for a second. "No. The store was dark."

"Did you notice any other cars on the street?"

"N-no."

"So you parked your car and got out. What did you do then?"

"I came inside."

"Did you turn on the lights?"

"Yes. The switch is by the door."

"Was your wife already dead?"

"No. She was alive."

"She was unharmed?"

Chester shook his head. "No. She was on the floor like she is now." He cast his gaze through the doorway. "But she was hurt. There was blood everywhere. I thought she had fallen. Fallen into a display case. I saw the glass in her neck. I tried to pull it out."

"That's when you cut your hand," Boyd said.

"Yes. Maybe I killed her by trying to remove the broken glass. Maybe if I had left her alone she would still be alive."

"No, Chester. She was already dying. There was nothing you could have done."

"The glass was so sharp. It was covered with blood. I couldn't get a grip on it. I tried, but I couldn't get it out. She was watching me. She was awake. But then—she just died."

The old man's eyes were dry and vacant. They gazed up at Boyd. Questioning. Innocent. Like a child.

"The chains," he said. "The gold chains. In her mouth. Did you see them? Are they still there?"

"Yes," Boyd said softly. "They're still there."

"How could that happen?" Chester asked. "How could a fall cause that?"

Boyd ignored the question. "What did you do then, Chester? How did you get the blood on your back?"

"My back?"

"Yes. There's blood all over your back. Did she reach out to you? Did she put her arms around you as she died?"

"She never moved. I don't think she could."

"Then how—?"

"The lights went out," Chester said, as if suddenly remembering. "The store lights. They went out."

"You mean someone turned them off?"

"They must have. One minute they were on, and then it was dark. I heard footsteps coming at me, and then everything faded away. Someone hit me, I think. Here."

He raised his hand to the back of his head.

I reached out and tenderly parted his white hair. There was a cut there, long but not deep. It had bled only a little.

"Someone conked him," I said to Boyd.

Boyd rose from the desk and studied the wound while Chester sat obediently still.

We heard a siren in the distance. The paramedics were arriving.

Boyd resumed his questioning. "You said everything faded away. Were you knocked out?"

"I—I'm not sure."

"What's the next thing you remember after hearing the footsteps?"

"I—I was here. At the desk. I phoned the police. I phoned you."

"Your call came in at 8:05 a.m. You said you arrived here at some time around three. We're missing five hours. You woke up on the floor, didn't you? Someone hit you, knocked you out, and you woke up beside your wife on the floor. That's how you got the blood on your back."

Chester Goldstone appeared to be a man who had somehow lost his grip on reality. I suspected he was going into shock. He looked down at the pajamas beneath his coat.

"I'm not dressed," he said. "It's past opening time, and I'm not dressed."

Two paramedics came bustling into the office after taking the circuitous route around the display cabinets as I had done, directed by the deputy outside.

Boyd patted Chester on the shoulder and stepped aside to give the paramedics room to work.

"Don't worry," Boyd said kindly. "You don't have to open today. Let these men take care of you now. We can talk again later. I'm sorry, Chester. I'm sorry for your loss."

Chester stared up at him, bemused. "My loss?"

Confirming my earlier suspicions, one of the paramedics told the other, "He's in shock."

The other paramedic, a young man who looked to be no more than a couple of years out of high school, still seemed stunned by what he had seen in the other room.

"Who the hell *wouldn't* be in shock?" he mumbled to no one in particular.

AFTER SUBMITTING to a brief examination, Chester Goldstone flatly refused to be hauled out on a stretcher, so the two paramedics, one on either side, walked him out to the ambulance.

When they were gone and the siren was wailing off into the distance, Boyd turned to me and asked, "Do you think he killed her?"

It was the last question I expected to hear. "Who? Chester?"

"Yeah. Chester. Or Gordon. Either one."

I thought about it. The old man had been stunned, practically robbed of his reason, by either the sight of his wife's murdered body or the blow he had received to his head. Gordon had been shocked all the way down to his socks by what he had seen in the other room. A person couldn't fake that sort of reaction, could they? Well, I supposed a person could, but Gordon's reaction certainly seemed genuine to me.

"Geez, Boyd," I finally said. "I'm not so sure it was either one of them. Did you see their faces?"

"Yeah, I saw 'em."

"So which one of them do *you* think did it?"

He didn't answer. Instead, he took the conversation and flipped it over on its head. "Who took your car out last night?"

I tried not to stammer. "I don't know. No one admitted to it. It must have been someone who wasn't with us at the campground. Somebody else. A stranger. Kids joyriding, maybe."

Boyd gave me a sidelong glance. "That's pretty lame."

I had to agree with him. "I know."

He hooked a thumb toward the front door. "Scram."

"What?"

"You heard me. Beat it. I've got a crime scene to process."

This was too much. "What the hell did you bring me out here for, Boyd?"

"I thought your particular brand of services might be needed, but I guess I was wrong. Also, I wanted Gordon's reaction. Since one isn't of use right now, and I successfully got the other one, you can go."

I felt my neck flush red with anger. "Go where? I'm stranded. Gordon took off in his truck, and my car is sitting back at the campground."

Boyd raised an eyebrow. "What's your point?"

I clapped my wrists together and thrust them in his face. "You're right. I killed her. I killed them all. Cuff me and take me in. Do it now before I kill Mrs. Shanahan too. She should have been first anyway."

Smiling, Boyd walked up to me and, cupping my face in his hands, gave me a big sloppy kiss right on the lips.

I stumbled backward, stunned. "Are you nuts? What the hell was *that* for?"

He pinched my cheek. "Cuteness, little brother. That was for cuteness. Being wronged and summarily dismissed seems to bring it out in you. I find it very appealing, this cuteness of yours. Now go home. I really do have work to do. Unless you'd like to help?"

The last thing I wanted to do was spend the rest of my day in the same room as poor Thelma.

I studied Boyd with a growing suspicion. "You seem awfully chipper all of a sudden."

He grinned. "Why not? I just eliminated a suspect."

"Who? Me?"

"No," he said with a wicked leer. "You're still on my list."

The horrified expression on my face must have been quite satisfying to him. He laughed. "I'm kidding, Bry."

"Who, then?"

"Never mind. Just run along. Ask one of my deputies to drive you home. Preferably Morris."

"Is he here? I thought you told him to take a can of gas out to the lake."

"I told him to wait."

"Your whole purpose in ordering me here was to deliver Gordon, wasn't it?"

"Yes," he said, "and you did it admirably. Now go."

Wounded, I went.

Chapter Twelve

AFTER THE third murder, the evil seemed to stop. As did the rain. We left a sodden, soggy June behind and moved into a sweltering, cloudless July. Temperatures soared. This was the sort of summer I remembered from my childhood. Lazy, hot days. Sultry nights. The whine of insects seemingly always within earshot.

With the campground nearing completion at last, Sam and I were becoming warier about stealing away behind my locked bedroom door, but still we slept together when we dared. There were too many eyes at the lake these days. The boys. Billy Simmons, who sometimes stayed over, sleeping in one of the cabins. I thought it strange he didn't spend his nights with the boys down at the lake. Maybe he was averse to being eaten alive by mosquitoes. Gordon Knowles seemed to be around a lot more lately too. Working long days and staying late to finish up this task or the other.

Sam and I were always on tenterhooks anyway, fearful our secret would be revealed. That fear, I knew, was bothering Sam these days more than it bothered me. In fact I could sense words on the verge of being spoken by Sam. Words I didn't want to hear. Words I was *afraid* to hear.

But apparently not tonight.

I positioned myself closer to the bedside lamp and tried to concentrate on the book I was reading, or pretending to. Trying to read over Sam's head, which he had rested on my chest, and trying not to shiver at the sensation of his warm breath stirring the meager scattering of hair there was no easy matter. His furry leg pressed against mine was hard to ignore as well.

In actuality, I had no idea what I was reading. It might have been a cookbook or *Les Misérables* or the daily stock quotes. For at the same time I was pretending to read, Sam was stroking, almost casually, but insistently too, a rather blood-glutted portion of my anatomy.

"I miss feeling you inside me," Sam murmured, the movement of his lips tickling my chest. "We don't make love as often as we used to."

"It's hard," I said.

"You're telling me." He nipped at my nipple.

"You know what I mean."

"Are you catching a cold, Bry? Your voice is getting hoarse."

"It's not a cold, you scoundrel. You know exactly what it is."

"Ah," he said. "Something to do with sex, then."

"Yes."

He changed the subject, but he didn't change it much. "I love the way you feel in my hand," he said.

"I love the way I feel in your hand too," I answered. "Uh, speaking of which…."

"Yes?"

"Your hand."

I felt his erection press against the side of my leg, and when it did, he gave a long tremor of desire beside me.

"What about my hand, Bry?" His stroking did not lessen one iota. Nor did the insistent rhythm of his thumb with every upward stroke, prodding my glans.

His smile on my skin, however, did widen.

His thumb did a final slide across my slit, and I knew the battle was lost. I tried not to gasp as I spoke. "Never mind." I shuddered, feeling my hips rise up off the bed. "Too late."

"Oh, goody," Sam said around a smile, sliding his face down along the heat of my stomach. The moment I felt his breath on my cock, I came. The orgasm was quick and powerful.

Sam giggled as my come splattered across his face. "Houston, we have a launch." Once those words were out, he tucked my spurting cock into his mouth and finished me off good and proper.

As he pulled me into his arms and continued to drain me of my juices, I mumbled an insincere apology for drenching him in come. At long last he released my emptied cock and stared up at me, his come-soaked face shimmering in the moonlight. "If you ever apologize for that again," he said, "I'll break both your arms."

I grinned at him, wiping a particularly thick gout of semen from his nose, where it dangled like a bungee cord. "Sorry I spoke," I said.

The humor left his face as quickly as it had come. "I guess I should go back to my room now."

"Not like that, I hope."

He failed to smile at that. "I don't know how much longer I can live like this, Bry. I—I think... I think after we get your campground going, I may bow out for a while."

My heart thudded like a hammer striking an anvil. "What do you mean, bow out?"

He sat up on the edge of the bed and grabbed a towel from the nightstand. Wiping his face, he turned to stare through the sliding door leading out to the veranda. It seemed odd now to see a blanket of stars, where before there had been only clouds and rain. The lightning bugs were dancing on the long lawn sloping down to the lake, and in the distance, as always, we could see the boys' campfire burning merrily by the water.

Somehow I knew the beauty of the view was lost on Sam. I could see it in his saddened eyes.

"I'm tired of living a lie, Bry. I want to be yours completely. I want you to be mine. I don't want to be ashamed of how we feel about each other. I want to be... happy."

I sat up on the bed and pulled him into my arms. "I want all those things too, Sam. I do."

He shook his head. "No. We'll never have them here, and you know it. We have to get away from the narrow-minded people in this county. We have to move. We have to start a new life somewhere else. Somewhere we can be accepted for who we are."

I slumped against him, listening to our two hearts stutter in the darkness. "My church...," I said weakly. "It isn't as easy as all that, just packing up and moving. People rely on me. I have obligations."

Sam gently eased me to arm's length and gazed at me in the moonlight. "I rely on you too. I'm an obligation too."

"I know."

I sucked in a long, shuddering breath and pulled him back into my arms, burying my face in the crook of his neck. His arms did not circle me in return. He made no effort to hug me back, and this hurt worst of all.

"I need more time, Sam. Please. Don't back away from me. It would break my heart."

"It would break mine too," he said softly, and only then did his arms come up to pull me close. He squeezed me tight, as if hanging on for dear life. I felt moisture on my cheek and knew it was a tear. Sam's tear.

"Give me a little more time," I pleaded. "Just through the summer."

"And what will happen then?" he asked gently, as if wondering out loud.

I spoke the only words I could speak. I spoke the truth. "I don't know, Sam. I don't know what will happen then."

He nodded, as if agreeing to a business deal. "All right." He kissed me gently on the mouth and eased himself from my arms. "I'm not threatening to leave because I don't love you. You know that, don't you?"

"I know."

"All right, then. Good night, Bry."

He quickly pulled his robe on and slipped through my bedroom door. A moment later the door to his room down the hall clicked open and then closed.

I fell back onto the bed and stared up into the darkness overhead. I heard a shout of laughter down by the lake. Somehow that innocent sound filled me with sadness.

I closed my eyes and tried to sleep.

BY JULY the murder investigation appeared to have ground to a halt. In desperation, Boyd finally brought the state police in, but they didn't make much more headway than he had.

Chester Goldstone never quite recovered from the shock of finding his wife's murdered body. The two stores on the town square, Goldstone Jewelry and Goldstone Electronics, remained closed. Three weeks after the murder, For Sale signs went up in both storefront windows.

Kyle and his father continued to work for me at the campground. The boy, always quiet anyway, seemed fairly unaffected by it all. He and Jesse remained the best of friends, and I still saw them laughing and roughhousing as they worked. If they discussed the murders, and they must have, they kept their conclusions to themselves.

If there had been a change in Gordon, it was only enough to make him surlier than usual. I stayed out of his way as much as I could. I was sure he had never forgiven me for my suspicion of him, but Boyd, apparently, could find no evidence against the man. Gordon was home in bed with his wife at the time of Thelma's murder. Maggie swore to it, and Boyd believed her. I still harbored doubts of his innocence, but I had to admit there was no sound reasoning behind those doubts.

Boyd, sometimes accompanied by Susan and sometimes alone, had taken to spending a lot of time with us at the lake, when his duties as county sheriff permitted. He was a great help to me. Boyd had always been good with his hands, but I couldn't help wondering if his frequent visits had more to do with keeping an eye on Gordon than any sense of obligation to help me get my campground open on time.

When not helping me, Boyd spent much of his time with the boys. Jesse and Kyle still preferred camping out down by the lake's edge to quartering themselves in one of the cabins. Boyd sometimes stayed with them late into the night, roasting hot dogs or talking around the campfire. Occasionally Sam and I joined them. There, under the stars, Kyle seemed to truly come alive. His shyness disappeared. It was an amazing metamorphosis. I wondered if it was the darkness or the distance from his father that gave the boy this new sense of freedom. Whatever the reason, he had changed immensely. He was more open. Happier.

Boyd, on the other hand, grew oddly withdrawn at these times, saying little, apparently content to merely listen to the conversation and study the faces around him.

More than once on these nights, I caught my brother staring morosely into the crackling fire, lost to everything around him. The unsolved murders still troubled him deeply. He was not accustomed to failure. Sometimes it took a playful punch on the arm from Jesse to bring him back. Then Boyd would once again contentedly watch the faces around him, giving us as much of himself as he could, but I knew his mind was still elsewhere. Revisiting the bodies. Rehashing the notes. Striving every moment to see a killer's face. A face that was always just out of focus, beyond his reach. Striving, too, to see the face of the next victim, if there was to be one. Or had the killings stopped? The possibility that it might be over, I imagined, frightened Boyd more than anything else. For if the murders truly ended, might they *never* be solved?

Sunday mornings now found Boyd firmly ensconced—rigid, miserable, and sweating buckets—in the third pew of the Nine Mile Methodist Church, dragged there by his new wife. He stared straight ahead during every prayer, refusing to bow his head. He glowered at me through every sermon. As pleased as I was to see him there, it was most disconcerting. Boyd and religion were oil and water, or a more apt metaphor might be fire and gunpowder. They simply did not go well together. An explosive mixture.

On the few Sundays when he was not present (Sundays when I was probably as relieved as he was), it was because of duties pertaining to law and order. Since the murders, the few crimes we had seen in Greene County seemed rather paltry and anemic things compared to what had come before. Secretly, and only half-jokingly, I suspected Boyd of committing some of these crimes himself to get out of going to church. In truth I was beginning to seek excuses myself for not standing behind the pulpit on Sunday mornings. Somehow I knew my presence in the lovely old church I had worshipped in since childhood was destroying any chance I might ever have of being truly happy. With Sam. I spent whole days refusing to think of it. Whole days turning my back on the truth—the truth of my feelings toward Sam and my fear of losing him.

Sam watched me during those sweltering weeks of July, waiting for me to choose the life I wanted. I know he did. I also knew his heart was as torn as mine. Still I could not bring myself to make the decision that needed to be made. I wasn't ready yet. It was as simple as that.

So I let my day-to-day life continue. The mysteries of it. The unspoken commitments. The needs of my heart. The fear in the eyes of people around me. For always in the background of Greene County life hovered the unsolved murders of three old women.

The matter of who drove my car from the campground into Bloomfield on the night of Thelma Goldstone's death remained a mystery as well. I doubted now we would ever know the reason behind it. Boyd never mentioned it again, and I often wondered why.

No one had yet discovered a connection between the three victims. Grace Nuggett, Golda Burrows, and Thelma Goldstone remained enigmas. Why they, of all the people in the township, had been chosen to die such ghastly deaths remained as inexplicable as it had from the beginning. I had pretty much convinced myself our first assumption was correct. The crimes had been committed by a madman, and there *was* no purpose other than bloodlust. They were simply three insane acts of cruelty perpetrated against three defenseless old women.

During the busy weeks after the third murder, as I worked to prepare the campground and my time was taken up with so many other duties and worries, something nagged at me. It was always there in the back of my mind. Billy Simmons's cryptic words to me as he stood on the jetty that day back in June kept returning to haunt me. It was not with any sense of foreboding that I remembered his words. It was merely curiosity. I could not begin to imagine what the boy was referring to when he told me I should have a few words of a spiritual nature with Jesse. A spiritual nature pertaining to *what*?

There had been no opportunity for Jesse or Kyle to have done anything wrong. They were always at the lake working. Neither of the boys had his driver's license yet, so they could not go anywhere unless someone drove them. What had Billy Simmons been hinting at?

I believe what bothered me most about his insinuations, if that was what they were, was related to the nature of Billy Simmons himself. This was a boy without a subtle bone in his body. He was not a person to *insinuate* anything. If he had something to say, he came right out and said it, usually with the vocabulary of a war-hardened Marine instead of a sixteen-year-old kid from the sticks. There was nothing sneaky about him. Nothing underhanded. He wore his honesty like a tattoo emblazoned across his forehead. He was a good kid, but he didn't beat around the bush about anything.

So why this sudden reticence to speak plainly about his misgivings concerning the boys?

One day as July was winding down, when our previous conversation had come back to nag me for the hundredth time, I confronted him with it, or tried to.

He was taking a break, sprawled on his back in the grass at the side of the lodge, soaking up the sun. It was a pointless undertaking. He was already as brown as a nut. His work uniform, that same pair of beige Speedos I had seen him in all summer, had taken a beating. At least now, with their splotches of paint and creosote, they stood out against his tan, and he no longer appeared naked from a distance.

His body was lean and hard, with a fine sprinkling of blond hair down his long legs, and his hair had been streaked by the sun. He was a good-looking kid. A displaced surfer dude who would have looked more at home on a California beach than in a Midwest cornfield. He lay there with his arms behind his head, watching me approach.

He had a southern lilt to his voice at the best of times, but at that moment he decided to go with a nineteenth-century negro patois. "Oh

Lawd, massah. Don't whup me. I'se jest ressin dese ole bones fo' a minute." Political correctness obviously wasn't in his vocabulary.

"Cute," I said, plopping myself down in the grass beside him. "Mrs. Shanahan will have lunch ready soon. You hungry?"

"I'm always hungry," he said, dropping the slave routine.

Billy Simmons had grown up with seven or eight siblings on a small farm outside Nine Mile. The house they lived in was a tiny four-room shack that had never seen a coat of paint. Half the shingles were gone from the roof, and it had been that way for as long as anybody could remember. Tar paper covered broken window panes, and three or four mangy dogs were always sprawled around the front yard among the flotsam and jetsam of old tires, a broken and rusty wring washer, and a couple of derelict automobiles that would never see the open highway again. The yard was bordered by a fence patched with stray boards gathered from God-knows-where, and it leaned in every direction except straight up.

Billy's mother had died from weariness several years earlier. His father, always one to hug a bottle, was abusive and shiftless and lived and drank on the welfare money he glommed from the county every month. The children saw little of it. The family lived in a state of perpetual need, which was why most of them eventually ended up on the wrong side of the law.

But Billy had always been different. He kept himself clean. He did reasonably well in school. And before the hair had sprouted on his body, he went out and found work. Odd jobs, mostly. Enough to help keep his brothers and sisters fed, or at least the ones who had not already left home on the road to either jail or oblivion.

I never once heard Billy speak ill of his father. This alone told me all I needed to know about the boy. He was a good soul. A bit rough around the edges, perhaps, but how could he not be?

When the campground opened, Billy Simmons would be our swimming instructor and lifeguard. At my insistence he had taken CPR classes from Dr. Hill, and he had worked like a dog for me, doing everything I asked him to do to prepare the camp for opening. He was earning minimum wage, so it wasn't all being done out of the goodness of his heart, but he never complained. I had never seen him be anything but cheerful and accommodating. Yet he stayed pretty much to himself, working alone, and like now, resting alone.

Billy was old enough to drive. He owned an old '57 Chevy he loved more than life itself. He drove it to work every day down our potholed lane at a speed roughly equivalent to that of a box turtle taking an afternoon stroll, sparing the car as many jolts and bounces as he could. In the evening he drove away at the same maddeningly slow pace. He occasionally spent his nights here, but not often, and he would not begin to do so regularly until the campground opened.

I dropped onto my back beside him and tucked my hands beneath my head as he had. Together we stared up at the sapphire sky.

"So tell me about this rattlesnake farm you grew up on," I said.

Billy tensed immediately. What I had meant as lighthearted banter, he apparently saw as prying. I hadn't been on the grass more than five seconds, and I had already put the boy on the defensive. Until that moment I never realized what an embarrassment his home life must have been to him. I wanted to rip my tongue out with a pair of tongs and toss it to the cat.

"Billy, I didn't mean...."

He thawed a little. "Sore subject, Reverend. Sorry. Every time somebody brings it up, it's like picking at a scab. Maybe if I wasn't so damned sensitive about it, the wound would heal. You reckon?"

I flashed him a sympathetic smile. "It might."

He smiled back, forgiveness already a done deal. "I'll work on it."

We fell into a companionable enough silence as I rummaged through my brain for a topic of conversation that might prove to be a little less invasive to the boy.

"How's your summer going?"

"Great," he said, gently shooing away a bee that had come a little too close for comfort. "This is the best job I ever had."

"You like it here, huh?"

"I love it. If I wasn't here, I'd be working for the farmers, putting up hay or digging fence holes or stringing barbed wire. This is a hell of a lot better than that. Food's better too. That old lady surely knows how to cook."

I had to agree with him. In the kitchen, Mrs. Shanahan was a marvel, despite being a holy terror everywhere else.

Billy rattled on, not waiting for me to keep up. "I'm going to drag the buoys in closer to the shore today, Reverend. They're too far out. Too close to the deep water. This old stripper pit drops off like the gates of hell about six feet past the boundary you've set up for swimming. Doesn't give a lifeguard much time if anybody crosses the rope and gets in trouble."

"It'll make the swimming area smaller," I said.

"Yeah. That's the whole idea. The kids'll be closer together. Easier to watch."

"I think you're probably right. Their safety is in your hands, so do what you think is best."

"I intend to," he said.

I smiled. A clear, sudden image of the man Billy would soon become popped into my head. A hardworking man. Loyal. Protective of those close to him. As profane as the worst sinner and as sweet as a saint. A good man—and quite possibly a nudist since I had yet to see him wear anything close to resembling a pair of long pants or a shirt.

My heart climbed into my throat when, down by the water, I saw Jesse balance himself atop the tall lifeguard tower and dive into the lake. It was a pretty good dive. Kyle, waiting on the rungs below him, then climbed up and stood poised for a good five seconds at the edge of the lifeguard chair before losing his equilibrium and sailing awkwardly off into space, hitting the water in a belly flop that sent a plume of water shooting twenty feet into the air and making *me* hurt.

Their laughter told me Kyle had survived.

"You don't hang out with the boys much," I said.

Billy cast me a leery look before answering. "Well, you know. They're younger than me. We don't have a lot in common."

I doubted if their one year difference in age could have that big an impact. "Is that really the reason? Did you boys argue?"

"Argue?"

"Yeah. Did you fight about something? If you tell me what it is, maybe we can get it straightened out."

Billy was looking uncomfortable again. He rolled over onto his stomach and began plucking blades of grass from the ground, laying each one neatly in a little pile in front of him. A moment later he impatiently flicked them away and raised himself up on one elbow to gaze down at the lake, where the boys were once again climbing the tower.

I thought I detected a sense of longing in his gaze.

"They don't need anybody else, do they, Reverend? Look at them."

I looked. Kyle's second dive was better than the first. Only by landing on his head on the pier could it have been any worse. Thankfully he managed to hit the lake. His legs and arms flailed in four different directions like a man tossed unwillingly from a plane, but this time when he landed, it wasn't a belly flop. Not quite.

Jesse applauded, then went into his own dive. Like an Olympian, he sprang gracefully from the tower, his slim young body barely ruffling the water as he went in.

Billy cleared his throat. "What's the point of all this, Reverend? What are you getting at?"

"I'm not getting at anything, Billy. I was just curious why you boys never hang out together."

Subterfuge was never my long suit. Sam would have laughed at my attempting it. Billy, too, seemed to sense my ineptness.

"You're wondering why I said what I said awhile back, aren't you?"

Now it was I who felt uncomfortable, and Billy knew it. He gazed over at me and grinned.

"You're not very good at this, are you, Reverend? Make a lousy spy, you would."

I had to laugh. The boy was absolutely right.

"So why did you say it?" I asked. "Why did you tell me the boys needed spiritual guidance? It doesn't sound like something you would say to anyone."

Billy thought about that for a second. "It really doesn't, does it?"

"Nope."

"Well, then, let's just rack it up to me sticking my nose in where it doesn't belong and leave it at that. I got no quarrel with those two. They're good kids. They've always been nice to me. Never tried to...."

"Never tried to what?"

"Never tried to nothing."

"Never tried to be friends?"

Billy dropped back down and stared at the sky again. "Sure, Reverend. That's what I meant. I'm sorry I said what I said. It wasn't any of my business, and it sure as hell wasn't my place to say anything. Who the hell am I to judge somebody else? I've got enough mice in my own corncrib."

I sighed. "I still don't know what you're talking about, Billy."

"I know you don't," he said. "Someday you will, I guess, but when you do it won't have come from me. Can we drop it now?"

"I don't even know what we're dropping."

"Good."

I figured I had done about as much damage as I could, and this had gone about as far as it could go without Billy's temper kicking in. I certainly didn't want to lose my lifeguard. I still hadn't the vaguest idea what he had been referring to back in June, and it was beginning to look like I never would.

Sam had told me to stay out of it. It was between Billy and the boys, he'd said, and anything I tried to do would probably make it worse. As usual Sam was right.

I patted Billy on the arm before hauling myself to my feet.

"If you ever want to talk," I said, "you know where to find me."

"I'm not the one who needs to talk, Reverend. You're barking up the wrong tree."

"Then I'm sorry," I said.

Billy gazed up at me, squinting against the sun. "You don't have to apologize. You're just doing your job, being a preacher and all. But I don't think being a preacher is going to help you on this one. Praying doesn't solve everything."

"It can help."

"Yeah, but it can't change people. Not really."

"There you're wrong," I said.

He politely dismissed me by once again rolling onto his stomach and resting his head on his arms.

"We'll see," he said.

WITH AN excellent dinner digesting in our bellies, Sam and I sipped Cokes and languidly watched the stars twinkling above our heads. It had been another long hard day of work, but now, as evening set in, my veranda was fulfilling its purpose admirably.

This was exactly how I had envisioned us enjoying it when we drew up the plans so many months ago. Well, almost.

I lolled back in my lawn chair with my feet propped up on the railing, while Sam sat rather stiffly beside me, stroking Lazarus, who had crawled up into his lap for a nap.

My heart felt like a stone inside my chest.

"You're thinking of leaving," I said softly. "You're wondering how to tell me."

Sam turned to study me in the moonlight. We had left the porch light off to prevent prying eyes from watching us in our quiet time together.

"No," he said. "I'm not. I shouldn't have said what I said to you the other night. I shouldn't have given you an ultimatum. Or given you a deadline."

"I gave myself the deadline, Sam. You didn't set it. I did."

"You mean to stick to it? You'll make a decision about us by summer's end?"

"I don't have a choice," I said. "You aren't happy. I'm not either, I guess. All this sneaking around is beginning to fray my good humor."

He blessed me with a lazy smile. "Well, we wouldn't want to fray your good humor. It's one of the things I love most about you. That and your dick."

I frowned and giggled at the same time. "Hush. Someone might hear."

"That's the problem in a nutshell, Brian. There's always someone around who might hear, or get the wrong idea, or feel appalled, or disapprove. We shouldn't have to hide the way we feel about each other. It's not a religious thing either. It's a *human* thing. I'm tired of living a lie. We shouldn't have to do it. It isn't right."

"No, Sam, it isn't."

We fell silent, letting the night sounds move in. Lazarus purred on Sam's lap. Crickets cricketed in the grass. Off in the trees, a night bird trilled. Down by the lake I heard voices once again, Jesse and Kyle talking in their tent.

"We used to camp out like that, Bry. Remember?"

I smiled. "I do indeed. We used to sleep together quite innocently at one time, if I remember correctly."

Sam laughed. "When we were kids, yeah. Even the first stirrings of puberty didn't wreck things."

"No," I said, whispering now, still afraid of being overheard. "It was those second and third stirrings of puberty that did it. God, you were beautiful. Still are."

He snickered. "You mean studly me?"

"Yes," I said, gazing into his face, loving the lines of it. "Studly you. Friendship turned to love in about two heartbeats the first time I saw you naked. I'll never forget that moment."

"Still, you couldn't make the first move, Bry. I had to be the one to dredge up the courage for that."

I patted my chest, as if to still my thundering heart for his benefit. "I still thank you for it with every breath I take. We were meant to love each other, I think."

"Yes," Sam said. "Openly."

I sighed a deep sigh and turned away to stare out into the night, at the moon hovering overhead, at the lightning bugs blinking little points of light across the lawn sweeping down to the lake. "Openly, yes, Sam. I'm sorry I haven't given you that."

"I can wait," he said. "Let's get through this summer. Let's do that. Then we'll see what life has in store for us. All right?"

"Thank you, Sam. Yes. All right."

I sprang to my feet. "I'm going to go talk to the boys."

"Are you crazy? They're asleep."

"No, they're not. I heard them talking."

"No, Brian. Stay here. Stay here with me."

"Why?"

"Just because."

"Don't be silly. I'll only be gone a minute."

"Brian…."

"What?"

Sam looked uncomfortable. "Yell out first. Let them know you're coming."

I laughed. "Why? What do you think they're doing down there?"

He merely gazed at me. Wide-eyed and innocent.

"Sam?"

"Never mind," he said. "Do what you think is best."

I pecked him on the cheek and took off down the stairs. Before I reached the bottom step, he hissed to me over the railing. "On second thought, get back here. You *never* know what's best. Get back here."

"But, Sam—"

"Rub my neck."

"What?"

"My neck hurts. Rub it."

"Good Lord."

I dragged myself back up to the veranda. Positioning myself behind his chair put us both deep in the shadows. Feeling safe there from prying eyes, I began massaging his neck.

"Where does it hurt?"

He let his head fall forward, obviously enjoying the feel of my hands. Sam's skin was warm velvet. I stopped kneading long enough to brush a mosquito from my ear. Sam took the opportunity to squeeze the hand that still rested on his neck.

"Brian, we need to talk. Sit down."

"What about your neck?"

His gift for subterfuge was apparently keener than mine. "It's fine now. Sit."

I sat, repositioning my long legs on the railing, Sam's hand still clutching mine across the gap between us.

"What is it?" I asked.

"I love you," he said.

This I already knew. "I love you too, Sam. Is that what you dragged me back up the stairs to tell me? Is there a history of bipolarism in your family?"

I applied pressure to my temples where I thought I detected the embryo of a headache. Again, I heard faint voices down by the lake.

Apparently, Sam heard them too. "Don't bother the boys tonight, Bry. They've been working hard. Let them rest."

"I don't understand."

Sam sighed. "I know you don't."

These were practically the same words Billy Simmons had used that afternoon on the lawn. It was beginning to look like everyone knew something I didn't.

"Sam, we've never had secrets between us. At least I don't think we have."

"This isn't between us."

"Is it between the boys? Is that who it's between?"

"No."

"You're lying."

"Bry, we look at things differently."

"What things?"

"All sorts of things."

My headache was now an established fact. "Lord, Sam, just come out with it. What exactly are you trying to say?"

I looked at Lazarus, lying on his back in perfect contentment as Sam idly rubbed his stomach. A horrible thought struck me.

"Does this have anything to do with the murders?"

Sam's hand stopped moving over the black fur. He hesitated a couple of seconds too long. "No, Bry, of course not."

Did I detect a note of uncertainty in his response, or did I merely imagine it?

I felt a sudden desperate need to speak to the boys. Not about work, not about how their summer was going, and not to have my mood lightened by their easy friendship. Jesse was like a son to me, and I knew Sam felt the same. If there was something troubling Jesse, or if he and Kyle had gotten themselves into any sort of mischief, then I wanted to know about it. I wanted to help them. This summer had brought Jesse and me close enough I felt we could be open with each other. If anything was bothering him, I felt sure he would tell me. Maybe even before he told his father. I was a safer harbor for the boy. Boyd tended to go a little overboard when handing out parental suggestions and ultimatums. Mine was a gentler ear.

"I'm going down there," I said matter-of-factly.

Resigned, Sam glared at me. "Fine, but…."

"But what?"

He shook his head. "Nothing."

Once again, before I reached the bottom step, Sam called out to me. This time his voice had an edge of panic to it.

"Brian, come here!"

I stopped in midstride, already rolling my eyes. "What?"

"Help me to the bed," he said. "I'm feeling funny."

"Funny ha ha, or funny insane?"

"Just get up here!"

For the second time I dragged myself up the stairs. When I reached the veranda, he said, "Take the cat."

I lifted Lazarus from his lap, eliciting a growl of annoyance from the creature, and placed him quickly on the deck before he decided to bring his claws into action.

"Help me up," Sam said. "Take me to the bed."

Fingers of fear gripped my stomach. "What's wrong?"

"I'm not sure."

I hoisted him to his feet.

"What hurts?" I asked.

"My foot."

"Your *foot*?"

"Both feet actually. I think they're asleep."

"You scare me to death because your *feet* went to sleep?"

"Oh, hush. Help me to the bed. Don't trip over the cat."

He tried to walk and stumbled. I quickly scooped him into my arms like a child and immediately felt a guidewire snap in my back.

"Oh, shit."

"What a thing for a preacher to say."

"I have to put you down, Sam. Something popped in my back."

I grunted as I lowered him to his useless feet, and we leaned on each other for a minute.

"Ouch," we both said.

I tried to straighten but couldn't quite manage it. "I think you've gained some weight, Sam."

"Blow me."

"Don't be crass," I said. "Help me to the bed."

"You're supposed to be helping *me*."

I groaned. "The tide has shifted."

The ridiculousness of the situation did not go unnoticed by either of us. I was immensely grateful there was no one there to witness it.

"I can feel my feet again," Sam said.

"Oh, good."

I was unable to stand erect. I stood there stooped over like a man with an anchor dangling from his neck.

Sam giggled. His giggles became laughter.

"Look at us," he sputtered.

I tried to chuckle like a good sport, but the first chuckle brought a spasm of pain that killed it deader than a Christmas goose. I couldn't breathe. I couldn't move. And I certainly couldn't chuckle.

"Poor man," Sam cooed, trying hard to wipe the grin from his face. "Let's get you to bed."

"Don't bother," I grunted. "I'll stand right here and sleep on my feet like a horse."

"Nope. Ain't gonna happen." Sam tugged me across the veranda and through the bedroom door, ignoring my whimpers of protest. When we reached the side of the bed, he simply pushed me over like a tree that had been sawn nearly through and is ready to topple anyway. I landed on my stomach with a crash and a moan.

Sam pulled off my pants and shirt, tugged down my underwear, and flung them all across the room. He then stripped and crawled into the bed beside me. With his warm body pressed against me, he began massaging my back. After a few minutes, his hand burrowed between my legs and discovered something hard beneath me.

I felt it too. I had for some minutes now.

"I guess you'll live," Sam said, flipping me over on my back.

"Ouch! Part of me, at least."

"Yes." Sam smiled. "It's the best part too."

"Thanks a lot."

Sam did a one-eighty on the bed and took me into his mouth. Without grunting too much, I managed somehow to do the same for him.

Hours later, I pulled myself from sleep with the realization I still hadn't spoken with Jesse or Kyle. I suspected Sam had arranged that quite nicely.

BY THE next morning, my back had not improved. I stood under a steaming shower for as long as I dared without incurring the wrath of everyone else who might desire a little hot water, but it didn't help. I had definitely pulled a muscle, and by the feel of it, one of the strategic ones. One that held everything else together. I envisioned it dangling loose beside my spine like a telephone wire ripped from the pole, sparks of pain shooting out the end of it like electricity.

I was physically incapable of walking without resembling a tall, skinny question mark, as Mrs. Shanahan cheerfully pointed out when I grunted and shuffled my way into the kitchen.

I told her to shut up in a most unminister-like way, but I might as well have been telling the sun to stop shining. She could no more shut up than I could stand erect.

"This is what he'll be like when he's old," she happily informed Sam, who was sitting at the kitchen table nursing a cup of tea. "Stooped, crabby, and miserable to be around."

Sam hummed as he pulled the tea bag from his cup and dropped it in the saucer. "I love him anyway," he said, eyeing me fondly. "He has talents you know nothing about."

Mrs. Shanahan looked unimpressed as she studied my hobbling gait, like a veterinarian about to tell the farmer his cow should be shot. "If you say so, Sam."

"I'm in the room," I groused, not a little chagrined they would continue to talk about me as if I weren't present.

Mrs. Shanahan tossed a muffin on a plate and shoved it in my direction. "Yes, we heard you coming down the stairs for the last ten minutes. I don't know which of us is in worse shape. You, Reverend, are bent over like a pretzel, and I feel like I swallowed a bag of cats. I've been eating like a hog, living day and night in this kitchen." She slapped my wrist. "Save some of that bacon for me."

Mrs. Shanahan flopped herself down at the table like a two-hundred-pound sack of eighty-year-old Idaho potatoes while I, thirty-two and supposedly at the peak of my virility, lowered myself by painful increments into a chair opposite her.

She studied me without much sympathy.

Sam pushed me the marmalade. "Poor baby."

His aunt sipped her coffee. "I don't know whether to call a doctor or a drama critic."

I vowed on the spot to never again waste an ounce of empathy over the woman's arthritis, or any other "itis" she happened to contract anytime in the near future. Let her suffer. The simple act of lifting my arm to read my wristwatch caused me to stifle a groan. My tattered muscle must have been connected to every moving part, the one coil that kept the whole clock functioning. Without it I could barely tick.

"The delivery truck should be here soon. Where is everyone?"

Sam answered. "Jesse and Kyle had some work to do out on the hiking trail. Billy had a dental appointment, and Gordon hasn't shown up yet."

"Great. Mrs. Shanahan, how would you feel about unloading seventy-six mattresses from a truck when it gets here?"

She didn't bat an eye. "Not good."

"That's what I thought. I'd better go find the boys."

I knew I would never be able to climb *into* the truck, let alone unload it. This was a job for younger and healthier backs than mine.

"Brian," Sam said. "It took you twenty minutes to get your pants on. It'll take you three weeks to walk around the lake. You can barely cross a room. I'll go find the boys for you."

Mrs. Shanahan harrumphed. "Yes, Reverend, the last thing we need is to find your crippled body lying dead out by the lake in a bed of pine needles and possum poop."

"A lovely image," I said. "But I can do it myself. If I'm not back by Thursday, call the rescue squad."

"Right after the caterers and the band," Mrs. Shanahan deadpanned, causing Sam to squirt tea through his nose.

I figured any show of compassion from these two would be about as likely as Boyd saying grace, so I left. I would have stormed out, but I was physically incapable of mustering the speed required for that sort of exit. I made do with a haughty but pathetic shuffle out the door and let it go at that. It was the best I could do under the circumstances.

Walking helped. By the time I reached the far side of the lake, I could stand erect, or pretty close to it. The pain had lessened, and if I avoided sudden moves, I could function without the humiliating grunts and groans Sam and Mrs. Shanahan seemed to find so amusing.

It was another hot July morning. The sky was robin's egg blue, and the breeze that skimmed across the lake and through the trees was redolent with pine and wild honeysuckle.

The trail we had cleared to encircle the lake was lined with railroad ties and meandered through the hills, up and over rises, circumventing the larger trees, for we had not wanted to sacrifice even one in the building of it. Four footbridges were built at different points along the trail, where streams had cut deep gorges down the hillsides as they poured their waters into the lake.

The bridges, all four of them, had survived the recent rains, but the trail had washed out in a few places. The boys were out here somewhere attempting to fix it. I had already found evidence of their work. I spotted drag marks on the hillsides where railroad ties had been laboriously hauled back into place after washing away in the water that must have sluiced down the slopes during the rainstorms. I also discovered places where new soil and gravel had been shoveled over erosion scars.

The boys had accomplished a lot. They must have been working long before I crawled out of bed like a slacker, complaining about my back. That realization gave me a twinge or two of guilt.

The lakeshore was teeming with life. Squirrels chattered in the treetops. Chipmunks scampered across the path or stood in the leaves and underbrush, watching me pass, as curious about me as I was about them. A blue jay dove past my head, protecting a nest somewhere nearby, his angry squawks urging me along.

In the distance, as I passed the halfway point of the trail, I heard music issuing forth from Kyle's ever-present boom box. The boys were somewhere up ahead, hidden from view by a bend in the trail. Kyle must have woken in an oldies state of mind. I recognized the music as early Beatles.

When I rounded the bend, I spotted their clothing scattered across a log, shoes and socks placed neatly on the ground. As I drew nearer, I saw them sitting in a bed of pine needles at the edge of the water. They were naked from swimming and were drying themselves in the sun before redonning their clothes.

I started to yell out, but instead I drew back behind the foliage, shocked, when I saw Kyle reach out to brush his hand through Jesse's red hair. They sat with their backs to me, their feet in the water. In the morning sun, the untanned skin at their hips gleamed white against their brown backs.

As I watched, Jesse pulled Kyle toward him, and their lips came together in a long, gentle kiss. When they lay back on the ground, I could see they were both aroused. Kyle's lips moved down Jesse's neck to his chest and lingered there for a moment before traveling on along the flat expanse of Jesse's stomach. Kyle took Jesse's young manhood into his mouth, and I heard my nephew moan. Kyle twisted his body around, and Jesse burrowed his face into Kyle's stomach. His hands stroked the length of Kyle's long legs, pulling the boy closer to him. Kyle gasped as Jesse too enveloped him with his mouth.

My first reaction was to stop them. My second reaction, the wiser of the two, was to simply back away. The scene I had witnessed was no awkward, spur of the moment act of sexual experimentation between two young boys with raging hormones and no other outlet in which to give them rein. There had been nothing awkward or fumbling about it. Theirs was an act of practiced love. And they were *not* boys. They were young men. The beauty and symmetry of their leanly muscled bodies told me that much. The passion in their actions told me they knew what they were doing. It had seemed almost a natural act.

With my heart hammering inside my chest and my face burning red, I quietly retraced my steps down the hill. Sam had known about this, or at the least suspected. Billy Simmons, too, must have suspected. What about Boyd? Did my brother know? Did this explain those late nights sitting around the campfire? I couldn't believe that. Boyd was no prude, but this would have been too much for him to know and not act upon. He would have separated the boys. He would have gone ballistic, making a bad situation worse. Or would he? Did I know my brother as well as I thought I did?

I tried to rationalize what I had seen. After all, they were fifteen years old. They seemed mere children to us, but in some cultures, I knew, they would have been considered adults. I remembered myself at that age. Could I have done the same thing? Unquestionably. Sex was on my mind every waking moment, as it is with all teenage boys, but somehow my desires had not matured as quickly as theirs. Looking back now on the nights when Sam and I had spent time together as teenagers, I could recognize longings I had shunted aside. Longings I hadn't been ready to act upon, and *wouldn't* act upon until after Sam's and my sixteenth birthdays. Only then did the true nature of our relationship become apparent to both of us. Only then did we begin to truly love each other, and act upon that love as adults do. With touch, with hunger, with passion.

But the world was a more aware place now. Young minds matured faster. Kyle and Jesse had simply been prescient enough to know where their longings were taking them a year sooner than Sam and I had known when we were teenagers.

Kyle and Jesse were still good kids, I told myself. If they were gay, and considering what I had seen, I could think of no reason to believe they were not, we would have to learn to live with it—as they would.

It would not be easy for them, I knew. Like Sam and I, already they were finding it difficult, I suspected, having to hide their feelings for each other, sneaking away for moments alone when they could be themselves and explore their feelings. In the cities their gayness would have been better accepted. But here in Greene County, it was a curse that would forever leave them open to ridicule and contempt. As it would for Sam and me if word leaked out about our relationship.

I needed to think how to handle this. Should I tell Boyd? Should I tell *anyone*? I knew I would have to talk to the boys. That could not be avoided. But what would I say to them? What *could* I say to them? Should I tell them I truly understood because Sam and I were living the same life they were? Was I ready to divulge the secret Sam and I had been living with for years, if only to them?

Deep down inside I was amazed to find a spark of relief. This had nothing to do with the murders, as I had asked Sam last night on the veranda. This had nothing to do with death, yet everything to do with life and how the boys would be forced to live theirs. As Sam and I were forced to live our own.

I hated that Jesse should have to experience what Sam and I lived with every day of our lives. I hated that, like us, he would be forced to hold back from being himself. Hold back from enjoying the relationship he shared with Kyle.

Yet their happiness depended on it. I knew this beyond all doubt.

When it came to judging, I could turn a blind eye to my own desires. God knows I had done it long enough. Seeing the same predilection in Jesse and Kyle, did I now think of it as a sin? My training had taught me I should. But did I truly believe it? No. My own life had proven that to me. The happiness I gleaned from my life with Sam, despite all the sneaking around, had shown me beyond all doubt that leading the life of a gay man was not a sin. It was the life I was born to live. The life we were both born to live, Sam and I. What I had witnessed at the edge of the lake had been no random, faceless act of carnal lust, anonymous and cold. Like Sam and me, the boys had known each other their whole lives. I recalled the tender way Kyle had run his hand over Jesse's hair. When they kissed it had shocked me, but what had shocked me more? The kiss, or the gentle sweetness of it? There was love in that kiss. Enough love to make me slink away like an intruder when I witnessed it. Slink away as I should have done. As I was still doing.

I thought of all the times I had seen the boys together since we arrived at the lake, their arms about each other's shoulders, huddling close around their campfire, or sleeping peacefully in the same sleeping bag. That last thought made the blush burn more deeply on my face. How could I have been so dense as to not see the truth long before this? Sam had seen it. Why else had he tried to stop me from going down to the lake last night to talk to the boys? Had he feared I would witness the same sort of thing I had finally witnessed today? I didn't doubt it for a minute. I wondered how long Sam had known. Even Billy Simmons had shown a keener perception than my own, for obviously this was what he had alluded to in our cryptic discussion of the boys.

Lord, how could I have been so blind? As I retraced my steps back into the lodge, I felt like the biggest fool on two legs.

I found Sam and his aunt still in the kitchen. Mrs. Shanahan was mixing a meat loaf in a huge bowl, and Sam was chopping onions for her at the table, obviously killing time until the truck with the mattresses arrived.

Mrs. Shanahan took one look at me and said, "He knows."

"Knows what?" I asked, feigning an innocence I didn't feel.

Sam watched as I crossed the kitchen, pulled out a chair beside him, and eased myself into it.

"You look like you've seen a ghost," he said.

I turned to Mrs. Shanahan. "What did you mean when you said 'he knows'?"

She shrugged with a smug expression on her face and continued to knead the great ball of meat and bread crumbs and whatever else she had thrown into the bowl to create a meat loaf. Her forehead glistened with perspiration from the work. I could feel the heat of a warming oven on my aching back. It felt good.

Sam rested his hand on my arm. The air was pungent with the smell of onions, and there were tears in Sam's eyes from chopping them.

"We both know, Brian."

"About Jesse and Kyle?"

"Yes."

"*How* do you know?"

"We just know. How did *you* find out?"

"I saw them."

"Oh Lord," Mrs. Shanahan muttered. "Your brother's going to kill us all. You, me, Sam, and those poor boys."

I couldn't believe what I was hearing. "Aren't either of you shocked? Doesn't this bother you?"

Mrs. Shanahan grabbed Sam's plate and scraped the chopped onions into the bowl in front of her. "Sometimes it's just human nature. Surely you ought to realize that, Reverend. You of all people. You and Sam."

"Well, of *course* I realize it. But you're all right with it?"

She stopped kneading the meat and gazed down her spectacles at me. "What choice do we have? About the same choice as those two sweet boys, I expect. Which isn't much of a choice at all as far as I can see."

I glared at each of them in turn. "When were you going to let me in on your little secret? And I still want to know how you knew."

Sam dabbed at his eyes with a paper napkin. "We just knew, Brian. It was little things mostly. The way they looked at each other when they thought no one was watching. The helpful things they did for each other. I believe they really love each other, Bry. I truly do."

"But Sam...."

Mrs. Shanahan joined us at the table, dropping into the chair as if weariness and old age had suddenly overtaken her.

"Don't get all preachy on us, Reverend. We need to figure out what to do without those boys getting hurt. They're not sinning, Reverend. You of all people ought to know that. They're just young."

Sam smiled at me when I reached out and took the old lady's hand. "If I live to be a hundred, Elvie, you'll never cease to amaze me."

She gave me a happy grunt. "If you live to be a hundred, that would make me a hundred and fifty. Ain't likely to happen. Not in this world."

"No. No, I guess it isn't."

"What were they doing when you saw them?" Sam asked.

"You don't want to know."

We sat silently for a few moments, pondering that, each of us staring blindly into our own thoughts.

"What about Boyd?" I finally asked. "Should we tell him?"

"Brian," Sam said, "don't you think Jesse should be the one to do that? In his own time? When he's ready?"

"I suppose."

He aimed a sympathetic smile in my direction. "There's really nothing we can do, Bry. It will have to work itself out on its own. Try looking on the bright side."

It was my turn to grunt. "There's a bright side?"

"Yes, there is," he said. "Some kids go through hell adjusting to the realization they are different from other kids. The dawning awareness of their homosexuality practically destroys them. They don't know how to cope."

I flashed on the boys, naked arms and legs entwined beside the lake. The sounds of their lovemaking floating up to me in the morning air.

"Those two seem to be coping quite well," Sam added.

I couldn't disagree with that. "To say the least. No sexual confusion there, thank you very much."

Mrs. Shanahan eyed me shrewdly. "What bothers you most? You're thinking the Bible says it's a sin, aren't you? Well don't forget, the Bible also said Methuselah lived to be nine hundred years old. I gotta tell you, Reverend, I'm taking *that* with a grain of salt."

"I know," I said. "No, I don't think it's a sin. How can I?" I reached out and took Sam's hand. "I—I fear for them, that's all. Fear for the life they'll have to lead because of this. The same kind of lives Sam and I have had to live."

Mrs. Shanahan reached out and took *my* hand, joining the three of us together. "Reverend, the Methodist Church put a ban on gay ministers last year. What did you think of that?"

"Well, I—"

"I'll tell you what you thought. You thought it smacked more of prejudice than religion, didn't you? Admit it."

"It did seem a bit mean-spirited, but that isn't really the—"

"Mean-spirited, my fanny! It was out-and-out prejudice, and you know it. What are all the holier-than-thous so afraid of anyway? Do they think it's going to rub off on them? Pompous twits."

I caught Sam nodding his head in agreement. When I stared at him, he stopped, gazing innocently up at the ceiling instead, although he didn't look particularly guilty about it.

"Yet you still stand there in the pulpit of an organization that would boot you out on your ear if they knew the truth."

"Y-yes. I guess I do."

I cast guilty eyes at Sam, but he quickly turned away, leaving me to deal with the old lady on my own. Mrs. Shanahan wasn't finished with me yet. "Who wrote the Bible, Reverend?"

"Men did. Men wrote it."

"And who picked through their writings, choosing a scroll here and tossing out another one there, until they came up with what they thought would be an appropriate philosophy to foist on the ignorant masses?"

"The Church," I said. "The Holy Roman Church."

Mrs. Shanahan bobbed her head up and down. Once. With emphasis. "Exactly. A bunch of dried-up old hypocrites who took it upon themselves to tell everyone else how to live their lives. Don't tell me they weren't fooling around with each other in the naves and apses. People need sex, young people anyway, and most of them are going to get it one way or another. It's human nature. Human nature can't be a sin, can it? No matter who a person finds himself attracted to."

"Well, no. Unless it's evil. Unless it hurts someone else."

"And just who are those boys hurting? You?"

"Of course not."

"Reverend, it's the world that will be hurting them if this gets out. When they're older they'll be able to handle that, I reckon. They don't have much choice in the matter. Like you two don't. But right now it's up to us to protect those boys as best we can. The people you need to talk to about this are the boys themselves."

"What exactly would you have me tell them?"

Mrs. Shanahan barked out a little note of exasperation. "Use your head, Reverend! Tell them to hold back. Tell them to be more circumspect. Tell them you understand their feelings, but they have to be more careful in acting on those feelings or their whole world is going to come crashing down around them. We can't change them, Reverend. It can't be programmed out of people. Only the more extreme fundamentalists are dumb enough to try that. The best we can do is protect them until they reach an age where they can protect themselves. Can you imagine what Gordon Knowles would do if he found out about this? He would kill that boy. I honestly reckon he would kill him."

This was an aspect of it I had not considered. Jesse was not the only one involved here. Kyle too was at risk. Boyd would likely throw a fit and make Jesse wish he were dead, but Gordon might go one step further. He would consider his son's difference a reflection on himself, and Kyle would be made to suffer for it. I suspected it would be physical suffering. Gordon would beat him to within an inch of his life. I could not allow that to happen.

"You and Sam have talked about this before."

Sam's eyes were soft and kind. "We've talked about it all summer, Bry. We saw what was happening long before you did. We can't change the boys, nor do I think we should try. But we do have to help them. The first thing we have to tell them is to be more careful. That could have been anybody today, seeing what they were doing. They need to know how lucky they are it was only you."

Mrs. Shanahan astounded me even further by saying, "I never understood what was so god-awful about two people with the same body parts loving each other anyway. You two manage to remain decent people in the face of it. Aside from the sex, which I must admit I've never quite figured out the logistics of, it seems to make more sense to me than a man and a woman. Two men would have more in common. Heck, they'd be able to swap clothes if wash day came along and they were behind on their laundry."

This caused Sam to snort with mirth, but he didn't interrupt.

"Lordy, Reverend, it makes all the sense in the world to me. More sense than murder at any rate."

That made me jump in my chair. "You're comparing homosexuality to murder?"

"Well, you seem to think it's a sin."

"I never said that. But—they're so young. They haven't grown up yet. They don't understand the risk they're taking."

Sam finally chipped in to stun us all. "I had sex when I was fifteen. I'm sure we all did." He leaned in to whisper to me, "That was before you and I dipped our quills in the ink, Bry."

Mrs. Shanahan looked down her nose at Sam as if seeing him for the first time. "Well, *I* certainly didn't have sex when I was fifteen."

"Neither did I," I said. Not for want of trying, I failed to mention. I was thirsting for Sam long before I hit fifteen. I think it started at twelve. "Neither did I," I said again.

Sam seemed to wilt in his chair. "Oh."

His aunt and I continued to stare at him.

"Admittedly it wasn't my finest hour," Sam stammered, trying to recoup his losses.

"Judging by the look on your boyfriend's face," his aunt said drily, "neither is this."

Sam simply brushed it all away as if shooing flies from a bowl of potato salad. "Well, that's neither here nor there."

Mrs. Shanahan gawked at him for a second, blinked, and then turned back to me, obviously groping for something good to say. She snagged something out of the blue and lobbed it in my direction like a water balloon. "We won't have to worry about teenage pregnancy!"

I ignored the old woman and continued to stare at Sam. He seemed to be avoiding my gaze.

Much to his relief, I imagine, the delivery truck arrived, the driver blasting his horn as he lurched to a stop outside the lodge.

"Mattresses are here," Sam chirped happily, staring gratefully through the kitchen window.

"Thank God for that," Mrs. Shanahan snapped. "This tension is killing me."

The truck driver, a man over sixty with approximately the same number of unneeded pounds hanging over his belt buckle, looked none too pleased to see me hobbling toward him, both hands on my back to keep it from disintegrating beneath me.

"*You* gonna unload this truck?" The way he said it made it obvious he didn't think I was up to the task. "I'm just the driver. I don't unload."

Sam joined me, but the driver still looked unconvinced. "Blast your horn again," I told him. "There'll be someone along in a minute."

He did as I asked, and sure enough, moments later Jesse and Kyle came racing along the foot trail toward the lodge. They were fully dressed now, and they both carried shovels over their shoulders. Their faces were flushed with the exertion of trying to run with the added weight down the uneven trail. I imagined their faces were flushed with other exertions as well, but this wasn't the time to mention it.

I gave them a wave and watched as they approached. Once on the lawn, they tossed the shovels aside and headed straight for the truck. Two minutes later they were trundling mattresses, stacked high on a dolly, up the hillside toward the cabins, beaming happily and bantering back and forth as they always did. Two happy kids.

Two happy kids with a secret.

Or so they thought.

It was a secret I dreaded confronting them with. I feared it would change our relationship forever. With Jesse, especially, the closeness we felt for each other, a closeness that had grown so strong during these summer months of working and living together, was something I didn't want to jeopardize.

If I had known another death was in the wings, waiting to pop out and stun us all, I might have worried about it a little less.

Chapter Thirteen

IN TIMES of crisis, time still manages to pass. But it doesn't always heal. Maggie Knowles had not coped well with her mother's death, the manner of which would have been difficult for any daughter to understand or put behind her. Especially here.

In Greene County, death rarely came with such violence and wanton cruelty. We knew death was always upon us, hovering overhead, waiting for an opportunity to swoop down and carry us away. But we were accustomed to death arriving gently in the night, padding softly on silent feet. It was merely another turn on the road of life. Another path we and our loved ones were destined to take one day. It came with still, cooling bodies, one moment awake and the next asleep. It did not leave us bloodied and savaged, with our silently screaming mouths agape in horror. Life was simply given up, and rightly so, like a debt come due at last. Not wrenched from our bodies by thieving, angry hands.

Murder was not an everyday occurrence for us. Until Grace Nuggett turned up dead with a pencil in her eye and a piece of persimmon pudding missing, the total number of homicides committed in Greene County over the past twenty years was… one.

In 1983, two brothers, Chester and Lester Swaby, lived together on a forty-acre scratch farm outside Nine Mile. Tiny plots of land such as theirs were called scratch farms because the only way for a family to turn a living from forty measly acres was to peck and scratch around like chickens in the dirt. It was a hand-to-mouth existence. Scratch farmers could live on what they grew, barely, but there was seldom any money for anything else.

Lester Swaby, the younger of the two brothers, took it into his head one summer day to take the egg money, fourteen dollars and change, and buy himself a hooker. But there were no hookers in Greene County, or none he knew of. Certainly none were listed in the yellow pages. He had checked. So Lester started up the family tractor (the only other vehicle on the farm was an ancient Ford pickup, which at that moment was up on blocks out behind the barn) and took off for the biggest nearby city, sixty miles away. The tractor, an old Case with front wheels set wide apart, was more ancient than the pickup and had a top speed of sixteen miles per hour. It took him five hours to get there.

Lester, not enrolled in Mensa at the time, nor would he ever be, picked up a drag queen by mistake. The fourteen dollars and change had been demanded up front, so Lester had no choice but to make the best of a bad situation (*caveat emptor* was not a principle he was familiar with until that moment) and proceeded to do what he came to the big city to do, after which he started up the old tractor and headed for home, smiling all the way.

That drag queen had known a few tricks Lester had never dreamed of.

He survived the trip home, but the tractor didn't. It blew a head gasket fifty yards from his front gate and shot up a cloud of smoke like the Hiroshima bomb. Chester, waiting on the porch for the past twelve hours wondering where the hell Lester and the egg money had gone, saw the smoke and came running. He was carrying the family shotgun, which he had been holding in his lap all the while he was waiting on the porch.

When Lester told Chester he had gone to the city to buy a hooker, Chester wondered why he hadn't thought of it first. Chester wasn't a member of Mensa either.

When Lester told Chester the hooker had turned out to be a guy named Clarence in a dress, Chester understood. He too had learned over the years to do the best he could do with what resources the Good Lord provided.

Chester forgave Lester for stealing the egg money. He forgave him for having sex with a female impersonator named Clarence. But the fact that his brother had blown up the tractor doing it pissed him off mightily. He took aim and blew Lester off the tractor seat with a shot to the head, which not only knocked the smile off Lester's face, but also broke a previously clean record, as far as homicides went, with the Greene County Sheriff's Department.

Some two decades later, the statistics had changed again with the deaths of Grace, Golda, and Thelma. It had been a good run while it lasted.

I thought of the Swaby brothers while I watched Maggie Knowles's hands tremble as she sliced the cake. The cake was chocolate with brown coconut icing. She had placed it before me when I first entered the room. Unbidden, she had poured me a glass of tea, and as we talked her eyes kept sliding back to the cake.

Four times she asked me if I would care for some. Three times I politely declined. The fourth time she asked, I said yes. It had finally dawned on me that she needed something to do. Something mundane. Something safe. Something that proved to her life was still normal.

So I finally accepted the blasted cake and watched her as she sliced it with those pale, trembling hands.

She seemed to be a woman adrift. Unanchored. Floating straight up into the sky while her life unraveled below her. She had lost the hold she thought she had on her life, perhaps a precarious hold to begin with. Ten minutes into my visit, I began to fear for her reason. I had seen nervous breakdowns before. During my childhood and teenage years, my mother had suffered two. Maggie Knowles showed all the symptoms.

Maggie was a woman of faith, as my mother had been. But faith, I knew, sometimes simply exacerbated the problem. How could God let these things happen? Where was He when we needed His protection? Why did He forsake us?

Financial worries had caused my mother's first breakdown, and the accidental death of my oldest brother, Gary, the second. While Boyd and I had taken Gary's death hard, his loss had almost destroyed our mother. At such times God made an easy target for blame.

"You haven't been to church lately," I said. "By the way, this cake is delicious." It was.

She nodded a little thank-you in regards to the cake and said, "I'm sorry, Reverend. People make such a fuss over me when I go out, trying to console me, I suppose. Staring at me when they think I'm not looking. Sometimes I'm able to put mother's death behind me for minutes at a time, but then someone will say something that brings it all back. I wish they would leave me alone. It's like all those prayerful sympathy cards one receives in the mail. They're meant to comfort you, but all they end up doing is torturing you more. I finally stopped reading them. Cruel things. I have a box of them in the closet, still unopened."

"They're meant to help."

"I know. But they *don't* help. They make things worse."

"How are you and Gordon getting along?"

We were sitting at her dining room table. She smiled, reaching out to pluck a cake crumb from its polished surface. "He's been wonderful."

"No more late nights?" I asked.

"No, he's staying home now. I'm afraid I was being silly when I told you he might be having an affair. It was just something married couples go through, I guess." She tried to laugh. "Jealousy rears its ugly head once in a while."

"But he *was* staying out late. Where was he going? Did he say?"

"Just driving around, he said. Thinking. He probably needed to get away from me. I can be pretty annoying at times."

"Oh, I—"

"Who did it, Reverend?"

"What?"

"Who killed my mother?"

"We're not sure yet. You know that," I added gently. "Boyd is working on it every day. So are the state police. They'll find out sooner or later. It takes time."

"But it's been *weeks*!"

"I know. I'm sorry."

"Did you see her? That night. Did you see her?"

"Yes. I saw her."

"You saw what they did to her."

"Yes."

She began rapping the side of the cake with the blade of the carving knife she still held in her hand. "How could anyone do that? Gordon said the killer crammed gold chains into her mouth like spaghetti after he cut her throat."

Harder and harder, she kept tapping the knife against the frosting on the cake, until I reached out and gently pulled the utensil from her hand, carefully laying it across my empty plate.

"Gordon should never have told you that," I said.

Her eyes remained glued to the knife. "But it's true, isn't it?"

"Yes, it's true. But she was already dying, Maggie. She couldn't have suffered much. It all happened so quickly." I wondered if that was true. I certainly hoped so.

"Why was she there?"

"What do you mean?"

"Why was she in the store at that hour? What made her go there?"

"Maggie, these questions you're asking me, you already know the answers as well as I do. Boyd learned through phone records that someone called her. The call was made from the store. What was said to get her there we have no way of knowing."

"How did this person get into the store?"

"We don't know that either. They must have had a key. Your mother had a dozen keys to the front door of the jewelry store lying around the house. One of them could easily have been stolen."

Maggie finally tore her eyes from the knife and gazed through the dining room window instead. "Mother was always careless about things like that. She could hold on to a dollar bill until George Washington squirted tears, but she was forever losing earrings and checkbooks and gloves. It drove my father crazy."

Maggie smiled at this memory but only for a moment.

"Why didn't she wake my father to go with her? Why would she go out alone so late at night?"

"We don't know. I'm sorry. The police are doing the best they can. You have to give them time."

She propped her elbows on the table and rested her chin on her fists. She studied me like a piece of artwork in a museum. Her eyes were bright and probing.

"Your brother still thinks Gordon had something to do with it, doesn't he? Why did he ask me where Gordon was that night?"

"Maggie, my brother asked *me* where I was that night. He asked everyone. That's what police do. They ask questions. Sometimes they ask questions we don't want to hear. But he believed you when you told him Gordon was with you. He told me so."

"My husband would never harm anyone, Reverend. He can be gruff sometimes. It's hard for him right now, jobs being so scarce, but one way or another he's always looked after us, me and Kyle. He's always taken care of us, and I know he always will. He's a good man, no matter what your brother thinks."

"Maggie, I'll say it again. Your husband is not a suspect." I had that queasy feeling one gets inside when telling a lie, but I believed as far as my brother was concerned, I was speaking the truth. My own feelings on the matter were not so clear-cut. I suspected once again my dislike for Gordon Knowles had a lot to do with it.

"It must be hard for you," I said. "Not having Kyle with you this summer. I can't tell you how much he's helped me with the campground."

She smiled. "I do miss him, but he stops in now and then when he can get away. He's growing up. He must have shot up a foot this past year. I guess it's part of being a mother, watching them grow up and leave the nest. Not much a mother can do about it except be happy when they turn out to be good people. Kyle is good people. He's a tender soul."

"He's a fine young man. You should be proud."

"I am. He's already talking about attending the university after graduation."

"That's always been Jesse's intention too."

"I know. Kyle told me. They want to attend together. They're inseparable, those two."

Images popped into my head I didn't want to see. I tried to push them away.

"It will be expensive," she went on. "My father will help us now that my mother is… gone."

Her eyes took on a faraway cast, like someone remembering past hurts. I reached out and laid my hand on her arm.

"I'm sure your mother would have helped too. Kyle was her Golden Boy."

Again Maggie smiled, but this time it was underscored with more than a little impatience. "Kyle hated it when she called him that. Just hated it. But I don't believe she *would* have helped us pay for Kyle's schooling. She hated Gordon so much she would have done anything to hurt him. Even if it hurt Kyle as well. Or me. My mother was not a kind woman, Reverend. I loved her, and I suppose she loved me, or she wouldn't have hated Gordon so much. But she wouldn't have lifted a finger to make my life any easier. Or Kyle's. Not as long as Gordon was still in the picture."

"Surely your father would have helped with the tuition, even if your mother was still alive."

"My father? My father is weak. He's sweet and kind and everything my mother wasn't. But he wouldn't have helped us. My mother would have never allowed it. She controlled the money. She always did. She pulled my poor father along like a dog on a leash, and he let her do it. I never understood that. I never will."

"Relationships are funny things, Maggie. We can never understand the dynamics between two people who love each other."

She looked at me. "There was no love in that marriage. I think my parents hated each other. I never remember a loving word passing between the two of them. Not even when I was a child. The only thing my mother loved was money and the control it afforded her in running other people's lives. How my father let himself be trapped in her net, I'll never know. But once he was trapped, he was too weak to get out. Now he's free, and I'm happy for him. I'm sorry for my mother's death, but I'm happy for my father. It should have happened sooner."

"Maggie!"

She shot me a guilty look. But in her eyes there was a coolness that told me she believed every word she'd said.

"I'm not happy for the way she died, Reverend. No one should have to die like that. But for my father, and for us, our lives will be better. One way or another she would have taken the money with her to the grave if my father had died first. She would have given it to charity before she let Gordon get his hands on a penny of it. Depriving Gordon would have meant depriving Kyle and me as well, but she wouldn't have cared about that. It would have been a final act of control for her. She cared about herself, Reverend. No one else. For all her talk of sickness, I think she believed she would live forever. She had to. How else could she have kept pulling the strings, controlling all her little puppets, making us dance when she wanted us to, and dropping us in a corner when she was finished playing? She enjoyed controlling us. It was a game to her. That's all it ever was."

"Maggie, I'm sure you don't mean these things you're saying. You're upset. You have every right to be."

It was as if I hadn't spoken.

"Now the game is over," she said, "and Mother lost."

I wasn't so sure about that. It seemed to me Thelma Goldstone was still very much in the game. At least in her daughter's eyes. I sipped my tea and mentally groped for a way to shift the conversation to a less upsetting track.

"What does Kyle intend to study at the university? What does he want to do?"

She adjusted a bloom in a spray of wildflowers that adorned the dining room table. "Oh, you know these kids and their computers. Kyle's a computer nut. Your nephew too. They would be in Kyle's room for hours and hours fiddling around online."

I doubted if all their time was spent online, but I didn't say so. Maggie had enough problems.

"Anyway, that's what he wants to do. Computer graphics, I think he called it. Jesse too."

I had never spoken to Jesse about what he wanted to do with his life, but I was not surprised to learn he too wanted to work with computers. My brother had given him one for his tenth birthday, and like all kids today, it quickly became second nature to him. The only thing I could do with a computer was type. Jesse could make the thing come alive.

I thought of the long hours the boys spent together, learning their computers, roaming the net, and playing their video games. All the while, puberty was kicking in. Was this when they began experimenting with each other as well? Was this when they became aware computers were not the only passion they shared? Did Jesse's fingers one day leave the keyboard and reach out to stroke Kyle's cheek? Is that how it began? A hesitant touch. A sudden intake of breath. A tentative kiss. Then nervous fumblings as their clothes were shed and they came together, truly came together, for the first time. Did that first delicate brush of each other's skin seem a wonder to them?

As it had with Sam and I?

I remembered their naked bodies at the edge of the lake with the sun beating down on them. Their passion for each other was the same passion Sam and I felt. I had seen it in the hungry, gentle way their bodies meshed. Their love, I suspected, had been a long time coming. After all, like Sam and I, they had all of society telling them it was wrong. But they found each other anyway. Perhaps they had no choice. Again like Sam and I, from boyhood they had watched their bodies grow strong. Watched each other become young men. When they were ready, when their desires had reached a point where they could no longer be ignored, they had taken that final step. Their first time in each other's arms must have seemed a natural progression to them. Natural and amazing.

"Reverend?"

I pulled myself out of my reverie. "Yes, Maggie. What is it?"

She took my hand. "Pray with me. Pray with me for my mother's soul. And we'll pray for the boys too. Pray that they have a happy life. Jesse and Kyle both."

I was touched. "Thank you, Maggie."

We bowed our heads.

THE DAY after my visit with Maggie Knowles, I decided to speak to the boys. A week had passed since I stumbled upon them at the water's edge, and I had postponed this confrontation long enough. I waited until the day's work at the campground was finished and Gordon and Billy had left for home. Even Sam was gone, off to take care of business in town. He had promised to be back before bedtime.

Mrs. Shanahan, knowing full well what I was about to do, had ordered the boys to report to the mess hall for dinner at seven. Their constant diet of Spam and hot dogs grilled over the campfire down by the lake, she told them, would eventually either stunt their growth or render them insane, so it was time they had a decent meal. She meant to give them one, she said, if it meant cramming it down their throats with a wooden spoon. Jesse and Kyle had meekly accepted her "invitation."

July evenings are long. At five o'clock the sun still burned hot in the sky. We had spent the day painting the five small cabins a rather bilious green that would have been an eyesore in town but, tucked in here among the trees on the hillside, made the cabins look merely rustic. While waiting for their dinner to cook, the boys dove into the lake to wash away the paint and grime from their bodies. I donned my trunks and joined them on the pier.

The water felt glorious after our long hours of sweating in the heat with paintbrushes in hand, and before long we were splashing and laughing and horsing around like three kids instead of two kids and a preacher. Jesse tried to lure me to the top of the lifeguard tower to teach me how to dive, but I told him I was still having a bit of trouble with my back. It was a lie, of course. I simply didn't want to break my neck.

Later, clean and dripping from our swim, the three of us stretched out on the pier with our heads together like three spokes on a wheel and let the waning sun dry our bodies.

The boys' faces were beaming with tired happiness. They had done a good day's work, and they knew it. The swim had refreshed them, and I was sure I would never find a better opportunity to confront them with what I knew. Mrs. Shanahan, I suspected, was casting surreptitious glances through the kitchen window, wondering how I was getting along with what I intended to do.

Earlier, Sam had wagged a finger in my face. "Stifle the PPS, Brian. The Preacher Pomposity Syndrome isn't going to help you with this one. Talk to the boys like a friend, not a Methodist minister."

"I *am* their friend," I said defensively.

"I know you are. Just make sure *they* know it. Don't preach."

I nuzzled my face into the little hollow at the base of his throat and tasted his skin with my tongue. "Yes, sir."

We had been standing in the kitchen. Mrs. Shanahan came out of nowhere and bopped me on the head with a spatula. "Stop that. Listen to my nephew and stop chewing on him."

I touched my scalp. My fingers came away greasy. "I wish you would beat me with clean utensils."

"It's always something with you. Besides, I didn't have time to look for one."

"Are you going to tell them about us?" Sam asked.

This was the question I had been asking myself for days. "I don't know," I said truthfully.

He stood before me, ignoring his aunt, and straightened the collar on my shirt. When he was satisfied, he pushed my hair off my forehead as well. "I'll leave that up to you. Your only job is to let them know… let them know, um…."

He turned to Mrs. Shanahan. "Let them know what, Auntie?"

Mrs. Shanahan mumbled something about morons I didn't quite catch; then she said more clearly, "Tell them we understand, Reverend. Tell them to be more careful. Tell them they're young and have their whole lives ahead of them. Tell them you love them. Tell them you're worried about their welfare. Tell them how their lives will be much more difficult than they are now if word leaks out. Tell them they're still in high school, for God's sake. Tell them you don't want them to be ridiculed by their friends and their lives made a living hell. Tell them to keep their pump handles in their pants and out of each other's mouths in broad daylight!"

Both Sam and I looked stunned.

Mrs. Shanahan backpedaled. "Maybe you should leave that last part out."

"That might be best," I said drily.

"Definitely," Sam agreed. "Did you say *pump handles*?"

"So off you go, then," Mrs. Shanahan said, ignoring Sam and pushing me toward the door like a coach sending her worst player out onto the field. "Give 'em hell, Reverend. But be nice about it."

So here I was now, wondering how to begin. I studied their innocent young faces. They were both such handsome kids. The whites of their eyes were so clear with youth and good health there was a tinge of blue in the white. Their skin was unlined with worry—worry being a trial they had yet to face in their lives. They smelled of the lake water, heady and sweet, that glistened on their strong, lean bodies. We lay in a circle, bellies down, our chins resting on our arms. Kyle and Jesse's elbows touched, but they apparently felt no awkwardness about it since they made no effort to hide it from me.

The innocence they exuded, I knew, was an illusion. They had perhaps gone beyond the innocent stage, as far as sex was concerned, long ago. But innocence does not always pertain to sex. They had both experienced loss as well. Jesse, his mother. Kyle, his grandmother. They had both suffered through the long summer, watching the body count grow at the hands of a killer. Younger than some, they had learned about death. Now they needed to learn about life. About living in this world. Treading softly, staying happy by following one's own path, but remaining a part of the whole. Not making oneself a target for the weakness and shallowness of others played a big part in that. Not opening oneself up to pain until one is mature enough to accept it played a part too. Perhaps most important was the ability to ignore the pettiness of those who mocked difference. Especially when you were the one who was different.

I braced myself with a short, silent prayer for guidance and waded in.

"Boys. About the other day. The day the mattresses came."

I thought I detected a flash of fear leap into Jesse's eye, but Kyle stared at me undaunted, as if he knew what was coming, almost daring me to proceed.

"I saw you by the water. I saw you… making love."

Jesse buried his face in his arms and muttered, "Oh God."

Kyle's eyes narrowed, but he said nothing. He reached out and placed his arm across the nape of Jesse's neck. "Shhh," he said. "It'll be all right."

I too reached out and patted Jesse's arm. "Kyle's right. I'm not here to read you the riot act or make you feel ashamed. I understand it. I do. How long has it been going on?"

Jesse merely shook his head, continuing to hide his face.

Kyle gave me a level stare. His voice was firm. "About a year. We love each other, Reverend. Nothing you say is going to make us stop loving each other."

I reached out to touch Kyle's arm as well, but he pulled away. "That is not my intent. Sam and I just feel—"

Jesse jerked his head up. Tears were in his eyes. "Sam knows?"

"Sam knew before I did."

"How? How did he know?"

"I'm not sure," I said. "You'll have to ask him that question. But he doesn't think badly of you for it. Believe me. None of us do."

Jesse's eyes opened even wider. "*None* of us do? Who *else* knows?"

"Mrs. Shanahan."

Jesse wiped a tear from his cheek with the back of his hand. "Jesus. Did she see us too? Did she see us naked?"

"No, Jesse. That was only me. But it could have been anyone. Do you realize how stupid it was for the two of you to do that? Anyone might have happened along."

Jesse's voice cracked with emotion. "We're sorry, Uncle Brian. We didn't think."

"Maybe we didn't think," Kyle interrupted, his voice rising in anger. "But we are *not* sorry! For anything! We love each other."

"I know that, Kyle."

"*How* could you know that? How can you know how we feel, for Christ's sake? What are you? Psychic?"

I made the decision in a split second to tell them the truth. "No, Kyle. I'm not psychic. I'm gay as well. Sam and I love each other too."

Both boys stared at me as if a crop of corn had sprouted from my ears.

"But you're a preacher," Kyle said.

"Yeah, well," I mumbled.

"And an uncle," Jesse added.

That made me smile. "Preacher uncles can be gay. *Anybody* can be gay. The two of you ought to know that if anybody does."

Kyle was the first to regain his footing. "If you and Sam can keep it a secret, so can we."

"Maybe," I said. "But you'll have to be a lot more careful than you've been recently."

"Fuck you," Kyle said. "Fuck everybody."

If he wanted to shock me, he failed. I've been known to drop the F-bomb occasionally, preacher or no. It was Jesse who came to my defense.

"Stop it, Kyle. He wants to help us." He turned to me. "Don't you?" He was pleading with his eyes.

"Yes," I said. "Sam and I, and Mrs. Shanahan too, we all want to help you." To Kyle, I added, "I saw the way you kissed. I saw the way you touched each other. I understand your feelings. Please believe me, I do. I'm not blaming you for anything. Neither of you. But I want you to understand what will happen if word of this gets out. You have two more years of high school ahead of you. Do you know what those two years will be like for you if people in this small town find out? You won't have a happy day between you. You'll be the butt of every homophobic joke the kids, and probably some of the adults, can think of."

Jesse was calming down. His tears had stopped. He still seemed to be regarding me as if he had never really seen me before.

"You and Sam make love?" he asked softly.

I smiled gently back at him. "Every chance we get, which isn't nearly enough. We have to be careful too."

"You should run away," he said. "Both of you. Move to the city where you can be yourselves. That's what Kyle wants us to do when we're old enough, when we get to college. Live together. Be ourselves. Be who we're supposed to be without being ashamed."

"Being yourself is the best way to live. I'm beginning to come to that conclusion myself."

"Are you leaving?" Jesse asked. "Are you and Sam leaving too?"

"I—I don't know." I wondered what Sam would say if he were present. As if I didn't know already.

Jesse looked from me to Kyle, then back to me. A wondrous smile spread across his innocent young face. "We're gay," he said. "We're all gay."

I nodded. "I know, son. That's the hand we've been dealt. We're stuck with it for life. But you have to learn how to live with the cards you're given. Calling yourself gay is putting a pleasant name to it, but being gay still isn't the norm. You are outside of the mainstream, and that puts you in a difficult position. Especially now, while you're still young. More especially here in this part of the world. Boys, this is the rural Midwest. They don't call our kind gay here. They call us by more hurtful names. They'll hate you for it."

"We can't be something we're not," Kyle said.

I smiled at him. "I know that. I wouldn't want you to be. I want you to be happy. But that's one thing you won't be if this gets out."

"Does Pop know about you and Sam?" Jesse asked.

"No, and I'd like to keep it that way."

"Gotcha."

An angry light still burned in Kyle's eyes. Not directed at me now. Directed—*everywhere*. His words were angry too. "We'll still have each other. Even if this gets out, we'll still have each other, Jesse and me."

"Yes, Kyle. But it won't be enough. You won't be there every minute of every day to protect each other. You have to deal with other people. Your friends. Your teachers. Your families."

Jesse jumped. "Do our dads know?"

I shook my head. "If they do, they didn't hear it from me. They never will. I promise you that. And I don't want them to hear it from anybody else. Do you?"

"God, no," Kyle said. "My dad would kill me."

Jesse gazed at the boy beside him, and I saw it there in his eyes as clear as day. Love. "My dad would be hurt, I think. He's been hurt enough, what with mom dying and all. I don't want to do anything to hurt him more."

"Good," I stated, sensing we were finally getting somewhere. "Don't *let* them hear it from someone else. Don't give anyone a reason to suspect it. You've got to be more careful. I'm not stupid enough to think you can stop seeing each other, although your dads might think differently. Just use more caution. You have to. For everyone's sake, especially your own. When you're both older, when you're away from this place, you can live your lives any way you choose. If you still want to be together, you can."

"We'll *always* be together, no matter what," Jesse said. To him it was a matter of fact. No questions asked.

"Maybe you will," I said. "Maybe your love for each other is strong enough to keep you together for a whole lifetime. That's a wonderful thing. But not here and not now. Do you understand what I'm telling you?"

"Yes," they both said. "Cool it."

"As far as discretion goes, yes. Cool it. If you don't want to do it for me, then do it for yourselves. Don't let the stupid people find a reason to destroy your lives. Believe me, that's exactly what they'll do if you give them a chance."

Jesse pushed his damp hair back out of his eyes and smiled a sweet smile, first at Kyle, then at me.

"I feel better already," he sighed. "Having someone know. Someone I can trust. Knowing we're not the only ones like this means a lot too. Thank you, Uncle Brian."

I reached out and caressed his cheek.

"So you're not going to send me away?" Kyle asked, watching us. "Send me back to town. Not let me stay at the lake anymore?"

I grinned. "No. Did you think I would?"

"I don't know what I thought."

"But your father might do exactly that. He might feel his only chance was to separate the two of you. Your dad too, Jesse. Don't give them a reason to do it. All right?"

Jesse nodded. "We won't. We promise."

"Are you using protection?"

"Protection?"

"Condoms. Are you using condoms?"

Kyle dismissed the question with a wave of his hand. "What's the point of using condoms if we've never been with anyone but each other?"

I didn't know how to respond to that, and I wasn't quite sure I wanted to follow that train of thought to its inevitable conclusion anyway. If they were having anal sex, I certainly didn't want to know about it, and I wasn't about to ask. On later consideration, I knew I probably should have, but it wasn't a subject I was ready to tackle at the time. I considered myself lucky matters had gone as well as they had, and I thought it best to quit while I was ahead.

Jesse sat up, hugging his legs and staring out across the lake. "It's hard being yourself."

"If you've learned that already," I said, "then I'm sorry. But you're right. The hardest thing in the world is to be yourself. To stand up for yourself. To never compromise yourself or your beliefs. Some people never learn how to do it."

He turned his gaze on me. My breath caught at the simple sweetness in his handsome face. "Life is scary, isn't it?" he asked.

"Yes," I said. "It is. We're all scared."

"Thank you for not hating me, Uncle Brian. And thank you for not hating Kyle."

I took his hand, then reached out and took Kyle's. We sat there like that for a second, holding hands in a circle.

"I could never hate either of you. Nothing you do could ever make me hate you."

Jesse took a long, shuddering breath and looked over at Kyle. "You all right?"

Kyle nodded. "Uh-huh. You?"

"Yeah," Jesse answered. Turning back to me, he added, "You didn't preach."

"Sam told me not to."

Jesse laughed.

"Well, let's go eat. Dinner should be ready by now," I said, trying to bring the cheer factor back down a notch. I wasn't so sure we had all that much to celebrate. The boys still had a lifetime of prejudice to confront. The prospect of it did not frighten them nearly as much as it did me. Not yet.

Mrs. Shanahan outdid herself that night. On Sam's return from town, she joined Sam and I and the boys at the table, shoveling food onto the boys' plates as if they hadn't eaten in a month. She called them baby names and patted their heads and embarrassed them by showing such affection toward them that by the time dinner was over they probably wanted to sink to the bottom of the lake and never surface again.

But they were relieved too. I could see it on their faces. They had shed a burden that must have been torturing them for a long time.

During dessert, Sam leaned in to my ear and whispered, "I owe you one."

"One what? What do you owe it to me for?" I asked.

"For not preaching."

"Well, what do I get? Is it like a door prize?"

"You'll see."

Later that night, with the warm summer breeze blowing across our bodies as we lay in bed, Sam made good on his promise. I did see. Twice. It was nothing like a door prize at all.

Hours later I awoke with a start, as if dragged from sleep by a sudden unconscious fear. Easing myself from beneath Sam's arm, I tiptoed naked onto the veranda and gazed down at the lakeshore, where the boys slept beneath the broad open sky.

Had I done right by them? Or had I committed a grievous sin by abetting the boys rather than helping them? Had I been a counselor or an enabler? Sam seemed to think I had done the right thing, but I wasn't so sure. In my mind I rehashed every word I had said to them as we lay on the pier that afternoon, and every word they said to me. Finally I returned to bed, and holding Sam close, for he was my rock, I tried to sleep. It was a long time coming.

During the days ahead, my thoughts would be taken up with other matters. Death for one. Fear, for another. And through it all, hovering constantly in the back of my mind, was a growing sense of guilt over how I had handled the situation with the boys. Not to mention the way I had been handling the situation with Sam.

My questions, my doubts, would go unanswered and unresolved.

The disappearance of Gordon Knowles, one week before the scheduled opening of camp, would see to that.

Chapter Fourteen

OUR LATEST trouble began with a phone call.

It was evening. Sam and I were helping Mrs. Shanahan organize her larder. A large shipment of canned and frozen goods had arrived that afternoon. It was enough food, hopefully, to feed fifty or sixty starving kids and counselors over a two-week period, beginning on the first of August, the date of the Methodist Youth Camp's grand opening. Fresh fruits and vegetables would arrive later.

Mrs. Shanahan seemed to find it necessary to either praise or gripe about each and every item. "Ooh, look at this. Lovely."

Two minutes later, it was "What the hell is *this* doing here? I wouldn't feed this to the cat."

Sam handled the inventory list. Lazarus had taken it upon himself to inspect every label for, presumably, valid expiration dates. I was actually doing the manual labor, stowing things on the shelves imperiously indicated by Mrs. Shanahan and breaking open fifty-pound boxes of chipped beef and hamburger to be stored in our industrial-size freezer.

"Careful with those flats of eggs, Reverend! My God," she said to Sam, "the man has hands like a gorilla."

"Don't I know it," Sam cooed, waggling his eyebrows like Groucho Marx and causing Mrs. Shanahan to snort in disgust. My ears burned red with embarrassment. I was not having a good time.

What to do with an entire side of pork, cut lengthwise from snout to tail, and frozen as solid as a boulder, left even Mrs. Shanahan stymied.

"Did you order that?" I asked.

Mrs. Shanahan eyed the carcass lying on the kitchen floor with a sad expression on her face, like maybe it was a distant relation of hers someone had recently dug from a glacier. "Well," she said, scratching her chins. "I ordered bacon."

Sam groaned. "It's still got teeth, one eye, and half a nose."

"And an ear," I pointlessly added.

The old lady prodded it with her foot. Being frozen solid, it didn't
have much give to it. "There must have been a mistake with the order."

"Oh, you think?" I asked.

Sam studied the invoice. "Here it is. Ninety pounds of bacon. It
doesn't say anything about feet or a tail. I wonder what happened to the
other half? The poor thing."

Mrs. Shanahan gave a sigh of exasperation. "Get hold of yourself,
Sam. You buy bacon all the time."

"Not in its original packaging."

"What do you suggest we do with it?" I asked. "Hang it up in the
smokehouse with the two dead moose I shot the other day with my
blunderbuss?"

"Very funny. Just drag it out on the back porch. We'll let it thaw
out for a couple of months. Then we can cut it into manageable
chunks."

"Poor thing," Sam said again.

"Oh, Sam, do be quiet. Come on, Reverend. Grab a hock."

She chuckled happily as she watched me drag it through the back
door. "Their loss, our gain. We got ourselves a free ham."

"Where's the ham?" Sam asked.

Mrs. Shanahan pointed to the carcass's haunch. "Right there.
That's a ham."

"It is?"

"Yes, dear."

I couldn't decide who was more annoying: Sam, Mrs. Shanahan,
or the poor unfortunate pig. I manhandled the rigid beast through the
door and dumped it unceremoniously on the back stoop. It didn't seem
to mind.

When the phone rang, I saw my chance for escape and ran for it,
snatching the receiver from the wall phone in the kitchen like a starving
hobo grabbing a stray chicken.

"Reverend, is that you?"

"Yes. Maggie?"

"Reverend, is Gordon there? I thought he might be working late."

I glanced at the clock over the stove. It was after 10:00 p.m.

"Why, no, Maggie. He left hours ago."

"Are you sure?"

I peeked through the kitchen window to the spot where Gordon always parked his truck, but I knew before I looked it wasn't there. I had seen him drive off at five o'clock just as he always did.

"I'm sorry, Maggie. He must have stopped off somewhere. Maybe he dropped into the Oodle for a beer and time got away from him."

The Oodle Inn and Waddle Out was Nine Mile's one and only drinking establishment. It was a seedy little beer bar perched at the junction of Highways 67 and 54, two blocks away from the church. It didn't look like the sort of place anyone would take visiting relatives, but on Saturday nights a live hillbilly band rocked the shingles and annoyed the neighbors for blocks around. The Oodle reportedly served the coldest beer in the county. I had seen Gordon's battered old pickup parked in the gravel lot beneath the tilted, half-lit neon sign on many occasions.

"I called there," Maggie said, worry evident in her voice. "They haven't seen him."

I didn't know what to say. It seemed Gordon was once again resuming his old practice of staying out late and giving his wife grief. The bastard.

Maggie tried to laugh it off. "Well, I suppose he'll come home sooner or later. Thanks, Reverend. Sorry I bothered you."

"If I see him I'll—"

But she had already hung up.

I braced myself for more abuse and headed back to the pantry.

Early the following morning, Maggie rang again. This time Mrs. Shanahan answered the phone. I listened to her side of the conversation while I ate my breakfast.

"Good morning, Maggie. Yes, it's me. No, he hasn't shown up yet. What do you mean, he didn't come home? Well I'm sure there's a reasonable explanation. How are you holding up? How's your father? What? Oh, I'm so sorry. Yes, of course. The minute he gets here."

Mrs. Shanahan replaced the phone in the cradle with the same motion one might employ to kill a rat with a cast-iron skillet.

"Men are pond scum," she mumbled to herself as she plunged a dirty pot into the sink, splashing herself with soapy water. "Shit fire and save the matches!" she fumed, impatiently flapping the soap off her apron and onto the previously spotless window above the sink. "God almighty hanging on a fence post!" She grabbed a dish towel and wiped the window clean, muttering curses under her breath.

After that, she turned to me and said, "Anything else, Reverend?" Sweet as pie. The woman was an enigma, as unfathomable as the farthest reaches of space and just as spooky to contemplate.

Gordon did not show up for work that day, nor did he go home or contact his wife. By that evening, Maggie was frantic, phoning every few hours and finally demanding Kyle return home to sit with her during her vigil as she waited to hear word of Gordon's whereabouts.

At my request, Billy Simmons gave Kyle a ride back to town. Kyle did not want to go—did not, I expect, want to leave Jesse—but he had no choice. I told him he had to go. His mother needed him. Jesse followed me around for the rest of the day like a lost puppy, worried sick about Kyle's father.

On the second morning, when Gordon again did not report for work, I knew we needed professional help. I phoned my brother.

"I thought you might be calling," he said.

"Why would you think that?"

"You have an employee missing, don't you? Maggie Knowles has been phoning this office every hour on the hour since Gordon went AWOL."

"What did you tell her?"

"That missing persons reports aren't acted upon until an unreasonable time of absence has passed."

"What do you consider an unreasonable time of absence?"

"Well, Bry, considering the fact that we've had three murders in the past six weeks, and considering the fact that Gordon Knowles's mother-in-law was one of the victims, I'd say ten minutes sounds about right."

"What the heck does that mean?"

"It means we've been looking for the man since the first time she called."

"You know, Boyd. He has a history of not being exactly punctual when it comes to returning home. According to Maggie, he's had a lot of late nights recently. Although she did tell me things were getting better."

"Hmmm."

Getting information out of Boyd was like pulling up trees with your teeth: a long, painful process.

"So what do you think?" I asked.

My brother surprised me by actually answering. "I think this time he seems to have done it up proper. Damn well disappeared without a trace. Him and his truck, as well, unless he simply drove off into the sunset and is now shacked up with some bimbo in a Motel 6 somewhere. Doesn't seem likely, though. I figure he's around someplace."

"Traffic accident, maybe?"

"That was my first thought, bro. We checked the hospitals of course. Nothing. I've got Morris following the routes he was known to take in case he drove off the road and is lying unconscious somewhere in that piece of shit truck he drives around in. Morris will be out your way later, unless he gets lost between here and there. I told him to check out that god-awful cow path that leads to your campground, maybe take soundings in some of those bottomless pits you call potholes. God knows what he might find. If not Gordon, then maybe Chinese treasure. I figure they're deep enough."

"You're taking this rather lightly."

"Not at all. Where's Jesse?"

"He's right here."

"In sight?"

"Yes. He's sitting next to me."

"Good. Keep him close."

"Why?"

"Why? He's my son. Do you need another reason?"

I eyed Jesse, who was intently listening to every word that came out of my mouth. "I suppose not," I said. "You think Gordon is dead, don't you?"

"Judging by past events, it would seem likely. But somehow I doubt it."

"Why? You don't still think he's the killer, do you?"

Jesse grabbed the phone from my hand before I knew he was on his feet. "Dad, you've got it all wrong. Kyle's dad didn't kill anybody."

I could hear Boyd's voice come faintly through the line even though Jesse was the one holding the receiver to his ear.

"Why do you say that, Jesse? Do you know something I don't?"

"No, Dad, of course not. I just don't think Gordon would kill anybody is all. Kyle says he's not like people say he is. He's a good person, Dad. He's not a murderer."

"Did Kyle say anything to you about where he thought his father might have gone?"

"He thinks maybe his parents had a fight and Gordon went off somewhere to blow off steam."

"For two days?"

"Well—he's not a killer! I know that!"

"All right, Jesse. Calm down. Put your uncle back on."

Jesse reluctantly handed the phone back to me. "I'm here," I said.

"Keep the boy close to you, Bry."

"I don't understand."

"I know you don't. I'm not sure I do. But something is not right, and I intend to get to the bottom of it. I can do my work a whole lot better if I know my son is safe."

"Don't worry," I said. "He's safe."

"Where's Kyle?"

"In Nine Mile. With his mother."

"Good."

I heard a click, and Boyd was gone.

Morris Carter arrived, sweating and puffing, an hour later. The trousers of his khaki uniform were stained with grass and dirt. His face was cherry-red from exertion and the heat. A leaf dangled from his hair like a sprig of mistletoe. I plucked it off.

"Did you fall?" Jesse asked.

"Yeah. Slid right down a goddamn hill." He gave me a guilty look. "Sorry, Reverend. Didn't mean to cuss." Pine needles clung to the cuff of his pants. I wondered if I should bend down and shake them out or leave them where they were. I left them.

Morris cast his eyes around the campground. "Is Kyle here?"

"No," I said. "He's in town."

"Thank God for that, Reverend. I found his daddy's truck about a half mile down the lane. He had driven it down into the trees, either on purpose or by accident."

"Was Gordon in it?"

Morris glanced at Jesse and shuffled his feet around, obviously uncomfortable. "Nope. Couldn't find him anywhere."

"That's odd."

He pulled a red bandana from his back pocket and mopped his brow. "I know."

"Then what are we waiting for?" Jesse blurted out. "Maybe he got sick and passed out or something while he was driving. He must be lying out there in the woods somewhere. We have to find him."

Jesse started to head off toward the lane, but Morris put his hand out and stopped him. "No, Jesse. You stay here."

"What is it?" I asked.

"Better send the boy into the house, Reverend. Orders from Boyd."

"Why?" Jesse demanded.

"Jesse," I said. "Go inside. Stay with Mrs. Shanahan until we get back. And send Sam out here."

"No!"

I laid a gentle hand on his shoulder. "Do it, son. Please."

Angrily, he stomped off toward the lodge. A moment later Sam came through the doorway and joined Morris and me.

"What's up?" he asked, eyeing Morris leerily. He didn't like the look of fear on Morris's face any better than I did.

I glanced back at the lodge and saw Mrs. Shanahan standing at the door with Jesse. "Keep him here, Elvie," I said. She nodded and took Jesse's hand. Together, they watched Morris and Sam and me climb into the patrol car and drive off down the lane.

I turned back to Morris. "Okay," I said. "What's happened?"

"You'll see."

Sam and I exchanged glances. A few minutes later, Morris stopped the squad car at the side of the lane. "Come on," he said. "It's right down here. Boyd's on the way."

Gordon's truck was parked about forty yards into the trees down a steep incline. I figured it would take a tow truck to get it back out again. There were deep tire tracks in the mulch. Beside them, I spotted skid marks where Morris had slid down the hill on his first approach. On this, his second approach, the deputy trod more carefully, daintily choosing his steps like a ballerina. By grabbing on to trees and brambles, the three of us made it safely to the bottom. The truck was undamaged.

Morris pointed to the cab. "There's a note on the seat."

Sam tensed beside me. "You mean there's been another murder?"

Morris leaned his bulk against a tree trunk. He was badly out of breath. The man really needed to lose some weight. "I don't think so,

Sam. It's a different kind of note. I left the truck door open when I was here before. If you bend in, you can read it. Just don't touch anything."

Shoulder to shoulder, Sam and I leaned into the truck together. The note lay on the tattered truck seat, written on the back of an old envelope in elegant, neat script. Gordon Knowles's handwriting was a heck of a lot better than my own. For some reason this surprised me. The precise penmanship didn't seem to fit the man I thought I knew. The words of the note, however, drove all thoughts of penmanship from my head.

I read it twice. Sam and I locked eyes.

"Oh no."

I gazed around the surrounding forest. "We have to find him. Maybe we're not too late."

Sam didn't look convinced. "He's been gone for two days, Brian. He's had plenty of time to do what he came here to do."

"Well, we can't just stand here waiting for Boyd to arrive. We have to search." I turned to Morris. "Don't we?"

"Feel free," he said. "I'll wait here and guard the truck."

"Right," Sam said, concerned. "Sit down, Morris. You look like you're going to pass out from the heat."

Morris nodded as if he knew it and agreed completely.

Still shoulder to shoulder, Sam and I moved off into the woods. The trees here were mostly pine, tall and dense, forming a heavy canopy overhead. The air felt humid and close. In the shadow of the trees, where the sun's rays could not penetrate, the ground was still moist from the recent rains. I studied the soil for footprints but saw none in the carpet of old pine needles. Our own feet left no mark. Only Morris's broad rear end had managed to leave a trail on the ground, a long furrow that started at the top of the hill and came all the way down to where I was standing.

I pointed to the west. "Go that way, Sam. The ground is level. It'll be easier to maneuver."

Sam reached and took my hand. "All right. Be careful."

I brought his hand up and pressed it to my lips. "I think whatever's happened here has already happened."

He nodded. "I think you're right." With a gentle chuck to my chin, he moved off into the foliage in the direction I had pointed.

I headed off the other way, continuing on down the hill, looking for signs of human passage. I saw none at first, but then farther down the hill I saw a spot of color on the ground at the base of a fallen tree. Drawing nearer, I saw it was a discarded pack of Marlboros, flung to the ground half-emptied. Unburned cigarettes were scattered around the box, now damp and discolored with dew and humidity.

Gordon smoked Marlboros.

I clambered over the trunk of the fallen tree and found myself approaching the lake. The trees opened up, and at a distance, across the water, I could see the lodge. Jesse and Mrs. Shanahan still stood on the porch, waiting for our return. As I watched, Mrs. Shanahan slipped her arm across Jesse's shoulder. Together they stood watching the lane, waiting for word. Wondering what had happened. Silent in their vigil.

I studied the mud at the side of the lake for footprints but saw only the imprints of birds. In one place I spotted the tracks of some small animal, perhaps a raccoon. I turned back to retrace my steps up the hill, but chose a different path, farther over, where I could cover new ground. I left the hot sunshine at the water's edge and returned to the shadows of the wood, weaving my way through the trees once more.

Then I turned back. I approached the lake on a different path, and from that vantage point I could once again see the lodge. I realized I was only a few dozen yards across the water from where the boys spent their nights camping out. From this angle I had a perfect view of where their sleeping bags still lay and where the cold pile of ashes, a reminder of their nightly campfire, was heaped up inside a circle of stones. From the lodge, because of the sloping hillside going down to the lake, their campsite could only be seen from my veranda. Even then, the distance was enough to make the flames of their campfire alone visible. Here, one could see the campsite close up. It was probably near enough to hear the conversation going on around the campfire.

Had Gordon stood here on those evenings when Maggie said he was not at home and watched the boys? Had he perhaps witnessed a scene such as I had seen that day by the trail?

I studied the ground around me. A few feet into the trees, I saw a place where the carpet of pine needles had been flattened and a small hole scooped out of the earth. The hole was filled with old cigarette butts. I sat down in the same spot where someone else had sat before me and looked around. The boys' campsite was clearly visible to me, but I would not have been visible to them. Especially at night.

I caught a whiff of something rancid, like putrefying meat. A small animal must have died somewhere in the underbrush. The sound of insects reached my ears. They swarmed somewhere nearby, likely feeding on the carcass. I rose and began searching, pushing bushes aside, peering into the undergrowth, seeking the source of the stench. The whine of hungry insects grew louder.

I looked up. My heart lurched inside my chest as I stumbled backward and tripped, landing hard on my back.

Above my head, Gordon Knowles's decomposing body twisted lazily in the breeze coming off the lake, suspended ten feet off the ground by a rope about his neck. The rope was tied to a thick branch jutting out from the side of an ancient oak tree; it creaked as the body continued its lazy, slow spin. Gordon's face was all but hidden by a swarming mask of insects. As I watched, fat maggots dropped to the ground at my feet, like some sort of ghastly snow. Still on my ass, I scrambled backward to get away from them.

Choking down bile and panic, I realized the ground around me was alive with maggots. Too bloated to hang on, they had fallen, one by one, until the forest floor was a writhing white mass of them. I sprang to my feet, brushing wildly at my clothes.

My heart began clanging away, the pulse of it throbbing behind my eyes. I swallowed back my growing fear and forced myself to look up at the body hanging above my head.

Gordon Knowles's face, what could be seen of it, was contorted in a grimace of pain. His blackened tongue protruded from his lips like the head of a snake peering out from its hole. Inside the open mouth, back among the shadows, more maggots feasted on rotting flesh.

Gordon still wore the dark gray Dickies he always wore to work. Matching slacks and shirt. His work shoes, neatly laced, hung even with my eyes, the toes pointing downward. His hands, limp at his sides, were bloated fat with the blood that had settled in them. His ankles, too, seemed to bulge over the tops of his shoes, where gravity had carried the blood to the lowest point.

His eyes were open, haunting and sightless, long empty of life.

I did not think he had died quickly. His neck did not appear to be broken. He had likely stood *there*, in the fork of the tree, and tied the rope to the jutting branch, then placed it around his throat and stepped out into nothing. No long fall, no sharp snap at the end of the rope bringing instant death. Dangling from the limb, he had simply choked to death. It could have taken several long minutes. I peered closely at his hands. The nails were broken; one was bent completely back. Had he tried to reach up and free himself? If he had, he must have realized escape was futile. There could be no going back. He could not have cried out for help. The pressure of the rope around his neck would have prevented it.

I jumped straight up into the air when a voice behind me said, "I see you've located our missing person."

It took every ounce of fortitude I possessed not to keel over in a dead swoon like some startled Victorian lady in crinoline and petticoats. I kept my feet and my honor. Barely.

Boyd stood there in the shadows, Sam at his side. They both ignored me, choosing to study the body instead. Sam appeared stunned. In Boyd's eyes I saw little pity at all.

"Did you read the note?" he asked.

"Yes. Morris showed it to me."

"Where *is* Morris?"

"The last time I saw him, he was guarding the truck."

"Is it true?" Sam asked quietly. "I mean, about the note Gordon wrote?"

Boyd hooked a thumb at the body before us. "When a person goes to this extreme to make a point, I believe we're fairly obligated to take them at their word, don't you think?"

"Then it's over," I said. "The killing's over."

"It would seem so," Boyd said. "By the way, little brother, your ass is covered with maggots."

"Oh, sweet Jesus!" For the second time in as many minutes I tried not to faint.

Sam grinned. "Stand still."

He pulled a handkerchief from his back pocket, wrapped it around his hand, and proceeded to brush me down. He looked fairly green doing it, and I probably didn't look much better.

"If either of you is going to puke," Boyd said, "do it somewhere else. This is a crime scene."

"I'm not going to puke," I said.

"Me either," Sam echoed.

Boyd didn't appear convinced. "You *look* like you're going to puke."

Sam said what I was thinking. "If you say 'puke' again, I just might."

"Well, don't. Where's Jesse?"

"At the lodge with Mrs. Shanahan."

"Is he all right?"

"Yes, of course he's all right. Why wouldn't he be?"

Boyd jutted his chin in the direction of the corpse. "That's his best friend's father hanging in that tree. This is going to be traumatic for Kyle. Jesse is very close to Kyle."

"Y-yes, I know."

Boyd pushed his cap back off his forehead and mopped his brow. "This will be hard on both of them. But it's Jesse I'm worried about. He's growing up too fast. He's had to, I reckon."

I wondered what my brother meant by that, but this wasn't the time to try to analyze it. "I would be more worried about Maggie if I were you. Not only is she suddenly a widow, but she's the widow of a murderer. After losing her mother a few weeks ago, this will kill her. She's not a strong woman."

"She'll cope. Women have more grit than we give them credit for."

"Let's hope so," I said.

Again I was drawn to the pitiable sight of Gordon's broken fingernails. They seemed to be the most heart-wrenching aspect of the horror before me.

"He tried to free himself, Boyd. Look at his nails."

"I know."

"Do you think it was guilt that drove him to do this?"

"That's the easy assumption, Bry. But tell me the truth. Did Gordon Knowles seem to be the sort of person who would let a little guilt get in his way? If it *was* guilt, it was a long time coming. Three old women are dead. Why should guilt suddenly kick in now?"

Sam blinked back surprise at the words. "But then why—"

"I'm more concerned with motive," Boyd said, stepping closer to the body, studying the shoes. "It's been the one thing this case has lacked from the beginning. Why kill those three old women? What the hell was the point of it?"

"With Gordon dead," I said, "I don't suppose we'll ever know."

Boyd pulled a pocketknife from his trouser pocket, flipped open the blade, clamped it in his teeth, and began to climb the tree. "That's not good enough," he said through clenched teeth. "There has to be a motive, and I intend to find out what it is."

With the murderer dead, I wondered how he intended to do that.

Later, as we climbed back up the hill toward the truck to reexamine the note and to direct the coroner to the body, I elicited a snicker from Boyd when I let a tree limb slap me in the face. I failed to see as much humor in the incident as he did, but it did serve to answer a question I had been asking myself for a long time. How did Gordon Knowles get those scratches on his face? Now I thought I knew.

SAM AND I, our heads together, reread the note, which was now encased in plastic.

> *Tell my wife and son how much I love them. Tell them I'm sorry. With my death, the murders will stop. I accept responsibility for each of them. Let sleeping dogs lie, Sheriff, and consider this my full and true confession. May God forgive us all.*

I handed the note back to Boyd, who slipped it into his shirt pocket. Gordon Knowles was en route to the morgue in Bloomfield, and Boyd, Sam, and I were waiting for the tow truck to arrive to winch Gordon's pickup back up the hillside.

Boyd pointed to a jumble of wheel ruts in the mulch.

"See this? He had parked here several times before. But not this far down. This time the truck got away from him and slid all the way down to where we found it. The flattened out place farther down, where you found the cigarette butts, tells us he was in the habit of coming here and looking out at the lake. Maybe it took him long hours of contemplation to build up the courage to do what he felt he had to do."

Or maybe he was watching the boys, I wanted to say, but didn't. That might open up a whole other kettle of fish, and Boyd had enough on his mind without suddenly being confronted with the fact that his son was gay, as Gordon, perhaps, had come to realize about both the boys. Or at the least suspected. Why else would he be watching them?

Boyd went on, talking first to Sam, then to me. "We have a full confession to the killings, as Gordon has made it a point of telling us, but we still don't have a goddamn motive. I don't fucking get it."

"Do you know about the will?" I asked. "Thelma Goldstone's will."

"Yes," Boyd said. "Maggie told me. That's a conceivable motive for Thelma's murder, but what about the other two? I find it hard to believe Gordon was making a couple of practice runs before getting down to the main event. If all he wanted to do was stop Thelma before she could finalize the will that would leave his family without a penny, why didn't he just kill her and be done with it? What was the point of the notes? What was the point of theatrically nailing poor Golda to her piano or making a pencil box out of Grace Nuggett's head?"

My brother had always had a flair for descriptive phrasing. Age had not lessened his talent. He also had a habit of thinking things through verbally, a most annoying habit when we were children. It seemed he never shut up. But now I was happy to hear his thoughts. At least it kept me in the loop.

Boyd shook his head. "I can't understand how the man could be so insensitive as to commit suicide here. By the lake. The first person to stumble along and discover his body could easily have been his own son. Can you imagine what that would do to a kid? My God, he'd be scarred for life."

"It will be a miracle if he isn't anyway," Sam said.

Boyd dipped his head in agreement. "True enough."

"Um… about the note…," I began.

A smile played at the corners of my brother's mouth. He knew what I was about to say before I said it. Another of his annoying habits. "Yes?"

"Well, the note. It seemed a bit different from the others."

"Did it?"

"Yes."

"You know, Bry, if you hadn't chosen the path to sainthood, you might have made a fair cop."

Here we go again, I thought. But Boyd let the matter of my chosen profession slide for the moment. "So tell me, your Holiness, what exactly was different about it?"

"Everything!" I stated with some heat, partially due to his attitude, but owing to the nature of the note as well, which bothered me deeply. "The handwriting is different. It's less verbose than the other notes. It's less melodramatic. Even the syntax is wrong."

"The syntax?"

"Yes. The way he expresses himself. The rhythm of the words."

"I *know* what syntax means."

"Well, then?"

"As for the handwriting, in the other notes it was obviously disguised to confuse the identity of the person who wrote it. They were printed out, rather than in longhand. But what's the point of disguising a suicide note? Defeats the whole purpose of the thing. As for the verbosity, he was no longer toying with us. No longer playing his little head games. That would explain the syntax as well, I should think. He no longer had an agenda. By the time he sat down to write his suicide note, the game was over."

"*Why* was the game suddenly over, Boyd? What turn of events brought it to a close? Did he figure he had accomplished everything he set out to do, and if he did, what the heck was it?"

"That, little brother, is what we need to find out."

DINNER THAT night was a somber affair. Sam, Mrs. Shanahan, Jesse, and I were the only ones in attendance. We sat around the kitchen table, pecking at our food, still shocked by Gordon's death on what was practically our doorstep.

Boyd had insisted Jesse stay at the lake, which seemed strange to me considering the fact the murderer was dead and the boy, or anyone else for that matter, could no longer be in any danger. With work still to be done before our opening, perhaps Boyd simply thought it best to keep the boy occupied. I selfishly wondered when Kyle would return, and if he didn't, where I would find another counselor to replace him on such short notice.

When Mrs. Shanahan figured we had played with our food long enough, she heaved herself to her feet and snatched our plates away, clucking all the while at the uneaten meal and grumbling to herself about the time she had wasted preparing it.

Later Jesse locked himself in my office and spent an hour on the phone with Kyle. Their conversation, overheard through the closed door, was at times tearful, at other times heated. I wondered what, at such a time, they could possibly find to argue about. It seemed doubly astounding considering the fact I had never heard a cross word pass between the two in all their years of growing up together. Boyd was right. They were growing up too quickly—on all fronts. This latest revelation concerning Kyle's father had to be difficult for them to accept. I wondered how Maggie was holding up.

When Jesse finally reemerged, he looked beaten down, as if the weight of the world rested squarely on his young shoulders. Mrs. Shanahan pressed a bowl filled to the brim with peach cobbler, Jesse's favorite, into his hands, along with a fork to eat it with. He halfheartedly accepted the offering and shuffled across the mess hall and out the front door. Later we saw a plume of smoke rise up from the edge of the lake, where Jesse had rekindled his campfire.

Sam pulled me aside. "Go talk to him," he said. "The boy shouldn't be alone."

I nodded. "Thank you, Sam."

It was not yet dark, but the sun had dipped behind the trees on the hillside, casting everything in shadow, when I wandered across the lawn to join the boy.

I found him sitting cross-legged on his sleeping bag, poking disconsolately at the flames with a stick. His appetite, perhaps, was not as dispirited as his mind. The dessert bowl was empty.

I pulled Kyle's sleeping bag to the opposite side of the fire and plopped myself down on it as if I had been invited. Jesse didn't object. We sat in silence for a long time. I watched the sun dip farther behind the hill and finally disappear. The shadows deepened into twilight, and twilight was becoming night when Jesse finally spoke. It was dark enough now for the campfire to light his face.

Thanks to the inroads of puberty, Jesse's voice, like Kyle's, still experienced periods of change. Tonight, due to either his galloping hormones or the emotional upheaval brought about by the catastrophic events of the day, his words came out nasal and ragged, with a crack in his voice of such monstrous proportions I feared it might silence him altogether.

"Kyle shouldn't be alone tonight," he said, still poking the fire with a stick.

"He's where he should be, Jesse. With his mother. Right now she needs him more than you do."

"That's not what I mean."

"Then what do you mean, son?"

He gazed out at the lake, shining blue in the growing darkness. A bullfrog croaked from its hiding place somewhere in the reeds, then dove into the water with a heavy splash.

"He's so torn up about his dad I'm afraid he might—do something to himself."

"Jesse, you know he wouldn't do that. Kyle is no fool."

Sparks shot up into the air as Jesse once again prodded the fire.

"But he's taking this really hard, Uncle Brian. He doesn't understand. He swears his father's not the killer."

"Son, Kyle loved his father. He doesn't believe the man committed these murders because he doesn't *want* to believe it. That doesn't mean he'll hurt himself over it. You don't really think he would do that to his mother, do you? Or to you?"

"Well...."

"Jesse, you'll have to trust Kyle. He's a sensible kid. I'm truly sorry you both can't be together right now. I know how much you want to be. But it just isn't possible."

His voice was sad when he said, "I know."

"Maggie doesn't know about the two of you, does she?"

He shook his head. "Only you and Sam and Mrs. Shanahan know."

Jesse tossed the stick into the fire and stared intently at me for a long moment before speaking. "What must it be like, Uncle Brian?"

I gave him a questioning look. "What must *what* be like?"

His gaze slid away from me then. He stared back into the flames. "Loving someone. Loving someone openly. What must it be like to walk down the street in town holding hands with the person you love and not caring what anybody thinks? Not feeling like you're doing something wrong. Something dirty."

"Jesse—"

"Kyle and I can't do that. Neither can you and Sam. We can't be honest about each other with anybody but ourselves. It shouldn't be like that when you love somebody, should it? You shouldn't have to feel ashamed in public about something that makes you so happy when you're alone. It's not fair."

"I know, Jesse. Maybe—maybe in some other place or at some other time, things will be fair. But unfortunately for you and me, it isn't here and it isn't now. I don't know what else to tell you."

"Do you think there *will* be a time when it's okay?"

"Absolutely. People accept it more and more every day. You just have to give the world time to catch up."

"And my dad," Jesse softly said.

"Yes. I think he'll need some time to catch up too."

I was pleased to see a grin soften the boy's face, but it didn't last long. "Do you think he'll hate me?"

"No, Jesse. No matter what you do, Boyd will never do anything but love you. He may need time to adjust, but his love for you will help him do that too. Jesse, your father loves you more than anything else in the world. Nothing you could ever do would make him risk losing you."

Tears sparkled in the boy's eyes, reflecting off the fire.

"Jesse, I want you to understand something. None of this is your fault. About the two of you, I mean. About me and Sam. The four of us aren't the only ones who ever felt this way. You and Kyle may have come to the realization of it a lot sooner than some do in their lives, me included, but that's because you had each other to sound off of. If it hadn't been for the fact that you had each other, and you both felt the same way, then this could have been much harder for you than it is now. It's kind of a miracle, if you think about it. Like Sam and I, you and Kyle grew up together, and you both were chosen to walk the same path."

"Chosen?"

"Yes, son. Chosen. It's not your fault you're gay any more than it's my fault I'm gay. Rack it up to a glitch in our DNA, or an errant enzyme. Or maybe it's not even that. Maybe it boils down to natural selection. Maybe this is nature's way of counterbalancing a global population that is quickly becoming too massive for our little planet to support. Who the heck knows *why* people are gay? It doesn't matter, does it? There's nothing anybody can do about it anyway. All you can do is try to live a good life in spite of it. You have to look at it as you would any other roadblock that pops up in front of you. Climb over it and carry on."

Jesse studied my face with troubled eyes as if trying to understand. I wondered if he really did.

"Jesse, this intensity of feeling you have for Kyle and Kyle has for you is a normal thing."

"Normal?"

"Well, normal in the sense that he's your first love. Jesse, you're still very young. There will be other people you'll fall in love with during the course of your life, but a person's first love is always special. It's an intense experience for anyone. Straight or gay."

"Was Sam your first love?"

I laughed. "No. That honor would go to Bobby Ketcham in the second grade."

Jesse was smiling now. "Did you ever tell him? What did he say?"

I groaned at the memory. "I tried to, but he didn't really say anything. He merely picked up a rock and beaned me in the head with a perfect sidearm pitch that almost knocked me out cold. See this?" I pointed to a tiny dent in my forehead.

Jesse leaned in and studied me in the firelight. His smile was broader now. He was beaming. "So he left you scarred for life."

I rubbed the dent and let the memory slip away. "That he did. Literally and figuratively."

"Did you stop loving him after he bonked you in the head?"

"Oh, yeah, he scared the hell out of me after that. I stayed as far away from him as I could get."

"So what happened to him?"

"He lives in Bloomfield. He has six kids and weighs about four hundred pounds. I still duck into a doorway when I see him coming."

"I guess I'd better not tell Sam about Bobby Ketcham."

"Please don't."

Jesse laughed and lifted his head to survey the emerging stars. "Moon's up," he said.

The moon indeed now hung, low and full in the western sky, above the treetops that crested the side of the hill. Both of us lost in our own thoughts, we watched it shine down on us. I couldn't recall ever seeing the moon so beautiful.

"Kyle thought he knew who the killer was. He was watching him."

I stared back at my nephew in the moonlight. "What do you mean, he was watching him?"

"Well, you know. When he got a chance. He had a theory."

I pondered this. "Who did he think the murderer was?"

"He wouldn't tell me."

"Why not?"

"He said he wanted to wait until he was sure. Then he would call everybody together and pull a Hercule Poirot. Lay out all his facts and then point his finger at the killer and say, 'And where were *you* on the night in question?' That sort of thing. Kyle reads a lot of mysteries."

I could see how that would appeal to a young man's sense of the dramatic, although I couldn't imagine how he could have been doing much snooping since he had spent most of the summer stranded at the lake.

"He never gave you so much as a hint as to who he thought the killer was?"

"No. But he wasn't happy about it. I think it was someone he knew. He wasn't just gathering clues, either. I think he was trying to prevent the third and last murder."

"Jesse, how could Kyle know the third murder would be the last?"

"He just did."

"He told you that?"

"Yeah."

Jesse was beginning to look like someone who wished he had never said anything to begin with.

"Did he say who he thought the last victim would be?"

"No. But I think he knew."

"Jesse, that's not possible, and you know it. Whatever Kyle's mysterious theory was, you have to realize now he had it all wrong."

"Why?"

"*Why?* Because his father was the real killer."

"Kyle and I don't believe that."

"Jesse, the man committed suicide because of it. He confessed to the killings in his note. How much more proof do you need?"

"We still don't believe it," he stated flatly.

"You're just being bullheaded because you can't stand the thought of Kyle being hurt. I understand that. I do. But you and Kyle are both going to have to face facts sooner or later because it's true. Gordon committed the murders. Period."

Jesse gave me a piercing stare. His face was growing redder by the second. He was suddenly furious. "What was his motive, then? Everybody thinks they're so smart, and everybody thinks they know everything, so tell me, Uncle Brian, why did he do it? He had to have a reason for it, didn't he? You don't just go around killing people because you want to. What was his *motive*?"

His sudden anger stunned me. I had never seen the boy like this before. I never knew there was any anger in him. But then, I had never seen him fighting for the person he loved, either. He was indeed growing up.

"Jesse, calm down. Your father hasn't figured out the motive yet."

"He hasn't figured out the motive because there *isn't* one. If Kyle's dad killed Kyle's grandmother, then why did Maggie say he was home all night? Do you really think she would lie to protect the person who killed her own mother?"

"Jesse—"

"Even if she was married to him?"

"Jesse, stop. Maggie doesn't want Gordon to be the killer any more than Kyle does. If she lied, and she must have, it was because she couldn't bring herself to believe the truth."

"That's pretty feeble."

I took a deep breath and tried to organize my thoughts. Try as I might, however, I had an uneasy feeling the boy was making more sense than I was. Why *would* Maggie lie? Was she so angry at her mother over the matter of the will she would actually let her husband get away with killing the woman? I couldn't believe that. Maggie led a Christian life. It would have gone against everything she believed in. According to Maggie, Gordon didn't know about the changing of the will. She had purposely kept it from him. Was that because she was afraid of what he might do? Could he have learned about it from some other source? Or did the will factor in as a reason for the killing of Thelma Goldstone at all? Was there another motive altogether? Even if there was, could it really be a reason to kill *all three* women?

Then I was struck by another thought. One far more disturbing. Did *Kyle* know about the will?

"Jesse, when did Kyle do all this detecting you say he did? When did he have time to follow this suspected killer of his if he was here at the lake most of the summer with us?"

Jesse was not comfortable with this line of questioning. I could see it in his face. "He made time, that's all."

"He might have made time, but how did he get into town?"

The boy's eyes turned cold in an instant. "Why did you come out here tonight? Have you been trying to worm information out of me?"

I was hurt by the resentment I saw on his face. I wanted to reach out and pull him close, to tell him I was only trying to help. But I wanted an answer to my question too, although I suspected I already knew what the answer would be.

Jesse glared at me, his face alight with the fire in front of him, his eyes locked onto mine. Suddenly he stood and began methodically removing every stitch of clothing he had on. When he was standing naked before me in the firelight, unashamed, insolent in the surety of his youth, he said, "I'm going for a swim. I'll see you in the morning."

With that, he padded out of the circle of light and dove into the lake.

I had been dismissed. Again.

Chapter Fifteen

THE FOLLOWING morning, under the pretext of performing my ministerial duties, I knocked on Maggie's back door. She had once told me only strangers and bill collectors ever used her front door, certainly not friends. I had used the back door that led into her kitchen ever since. Today I felt like an imposter doing so.

I was still hurt and reeling from Jesse's display of anger the night before, although the boy had been civil enough at breakfast. Civil, not warm. Sam hadn't seemed to notice, but Mrs. Shanahan, her radar up and sensing tension, had put cheese smiley faces on Jesse's muffins. They didn't seem to cheer him up much. He ate in silence, averting his eyes from everyone, and after licking the smiles off, mumbled a "thank you" and stalked out of the lodge.

Sam noticed that. He turned to me and said, "Brrr. What was that all about?"

"Nothing," I said, and he looked hurt that I had not tried to explain. A short time later, he too stepped away from the table without so much as a grunt of good-bye and headed out to do some work.

I knew I could salvage my relationship with Sam easily enough, but I was pretty sure I had destroyed any hope of recouping my losses and getting on the good side of Jesse again. I knew this was the case when he saw me climbing into the old Rambler and asked where I was going.

"I need to speak to Maggie," I said.

"Let me go with you. I want to see Kyle."

"I'm sorry," I said. "You'd better stay here."

His face once again red with anger, he spun and walked away.

Now, as I stood at Maggie's door waiting for an answer to my knock, I felt guilty and deceitful. I wondered if I would ever be able to regain the boy's trust. I was counting on the fact that he was a resilient kid and wasn't the type to hold a grudge. At least I hoped he wasn't.

After a second knock, the door was opened by a man in his sixties with a shock of white hair he obviously thought highly of. It was gelled and moussed and lacquered and coaxed and coerced into an elegant sphere of such perfect concrete symmetry I could have sanded plywood on it, and so white it flashed like a nuclear detonation when he stepped out of the door and into the sunlight.

The man was a stranger to me. "You're at the wrong door," I almost said.

Instead, I squinted against the blast of white light that ricocheted off the top of his head and stated blandly, "I'm Reverend Lucas. I'd like to see Maggie."

He gave me the once-over, like a man appraising a used car. Apparently I passed inspection. "My niece has been watching for you, Reverend. But don't expect to get much sense out of her. She's still in a state of shock. Hell, we all are. Gordon was a prick, but who would have dreamed he liked to murder little old ladies? My sister always said he would be the death of her. Jesus, she sure got that right."

"Your sister was…?"

"Thelma Goldstone, yeah. Anyway, the son of a bitch never had a decent job in his life—I'm in fertilizer myself—but Maggie loved the simpleminded bastard anyway. Go figure. So we all sort of accepted him for what he was worth, which wasn't much, let me tell you. I've always said love is blind, deaf, and dumb and usually pretty frigging stupid to boot. Am I right?"

"Uh—"

"Yeah, I thought you'd see it my way. Come on in."

"Nice to meet you too," I said—to the side of the house since he wasn't listening. Oblivious, he patted his hair as if reassuring himself it hadn't caught fire due to all the chemicals in it and ushered me through the door.

Inside the kitchen, every inch of counter space was covered with food in various containers. The dining room table, as well, was buried. In Greene County we eat our way through disasters. With sickness or death, neighbors come calling with armloads of provender and sympathy. Sound and sometimes not-so-sound advice was usually doled out at the same time. Reams of it. The advice might have been questionable, but the food was always good. The ladies of Nine Mile must have fired up their ovens the moment they heard of Gordon's death. Though their concern was heartfelt, they wouldn't have missed their chance to soak up some of the drama of the situation either. That meat loaf tucked under their arm was a ticket to the show. After all, our entertainment options were few. We had to make the best of what we were offered. In this instance, the good ladies of Nine Mile had both. This was Oscar-grade entertainment, and they hauled out the big guns. Maggie wouldn't have to cook for the rest of the year.

The house was packed with people. Aside from Maggie's uncle, whom I had never seen before and didn't much care if I ever saw again, every other face in the crowd was as familiar to me as my own. Most of them I saw every Sunday as I looked out over the pulpit. My flock, the female contingent of it at least, appeared to have descended on the house en masse.

The somber drone of voices abated a bit when I entered the living room. I received a chorus of muted greetings from the ladies of the church before all eyes turned to Maggie, who was sitting on the divan with a box of tissues in her lap. Upon seeing me she stood, and the tissue box tumbled to the floor. It was instantly snatched away from her feet by a well-meaning neighbor and placed on the end table out of harm's way.

Maggie reached out and took my hand. "I knew you'd come," she said. Her voice was hoarse from crying, her eyes bloodred. "Come sit with me, Reverend. Are you hungry?"

"No. Thank you, Maggie."

She led me to the divan and continued to hold my hand as we got comfortable. I caught the eye of Sharon Nolting, the church pianist, and with a discreet shooing motion of my head, indicated I would like to speak to Maggie alone. Sharon got the hint, although she didn't seem pleased about it, and began ushering everyone into the dining room. She closed the sliding door behind her, and the sudden clatter of plates and silverware told me the mob had laid siege to the food. Maggie and I were alone.

"Are you sure you're not hungry?" she asked again.

"I'm sure. Can I get you anything?"

She waved my question off as if it were inconsequential, which it was.

Maggie looked down at my hand, which she still held in her own. She wove her fingers between mine, and I watched, silent, as a tear slid down her cheek.

She wiped her eyes with a tissue and said, "It can't be true, can it? Did Gordon really kill those women? I knew he didn't like my mother, but…."

"Maggie, I'm sorry. You've experienced more loss in the past few weeks than anyone should have to suffer through. Your mother. Your husband. I'm proud of you for holding up as well as you are. My brother said you had grit. I guess he was right."

She impatiently flicked away another tear from her cheek. Her back stiffened. "Your brother. He suspected Gordon all along, didn't he?"

"No. That's not true. I'm not sure Boyd ever really suspected Gordon. Or not *just* Gordon. Boyd suspected everyone. I don't believe he ever pinned his suspicions down to one person. We're all shocked by the way things turned out, Maggie. No one wanted it to end like this."

She released my hand and began twisting the wad of tissue in her fingers. When it tore apart, she tossed it onto the end table and plucked another from the box.

"Gordon was a good man, Reverend. I know nobody believes that, but it's true. You can't know a man unless you live with him. Gordon had his faults, but I still don't believe murder was one of them. I *won't* believe it."

"I want to believe he was a good man too, Maggie. I want to believe it because you believe it. I know he loved you and Kyle."

Her face softened with an inner light. "Yes, he did."

"That's the thing you have to keep remembering. That's what will get you through this. Your faith in God and the knowledge that Gordon loved you. That's all you really need to remember."

"You make it sound so easy, Reverend."

"I don't mean to. I know it won't be."

She rested her head back on the sofa cushion and closed her eyes. "I miss him so much already. It's hard knowing Gordon will never come home again. Knowing what people think of him. That hurts even worse."

"Don't worry about what people think. Worry about yourself. And your son. Where *is* Kyle?"

She lifted her head and glanced toward the hallway. "He's in his room. He locked himself in there when people started arriving. Maybe you should go talk to him. See if you can get him to come out."

I was tempted to say, "He's already out. Him and my nephew both." The drama of it sort of appealed to me. But of course I didn't. That revelation would be left for another day, one of Kyle's choosing, and one I sincerely hoped I would not be present to witness. Although with Maggie, I imagined Kyle would get a much more understanding ear than he ever would have with his father. For the boy's sake, I hoped so.

"Maybe I will go speak to him," I said, patting her hand.

"The second door on the left. When you're finished, ask him to come in here. I want him with me."

"All right, Maggie. I will."

I excused myself, and halfway down the long hallway, I saw a guest room with twin beds. On one of the beds, Chester Goldstone lay sleeping. His shoes were off, but he was otherwise fully dressed. I knew he had not been well since his wife's death. This latest excitement must have been too much for him to deal with. His glasses had been carefully laid on the nightstand beside the bed.

I quietly moved on and rapped softly at the boy's door.

"Kyle, it's Reverend Lucas. May I come in?"

He must have been standing inside the door. Perhaps he had been listening as Maggie and I spoke. I could hear him clearly when he asked, "Is Jesse with you?"

"No, son. He wanted to come but I wouldn't let him."

The door swung open. Kyle was wearing sweatpants and a T-shirt. His feet were bare. His computer was on across the room, emitting low background music from a video game titled *Resident Evil*. I recognized it because Jesse had spent long hours playing it earlier in the summer before we moved out to the lake to complete the work there. He must have passed the game on to Kyle when he was finished with it.

"Why didn't you let him come?" Kyle asked suspiciously, as if maybe he thought I had decided to try to keep them apart.

"Kyle, I think you should be with your mother right now. When she's better, when she's got a grip on everything that's happened, you can come back to the campground with us. I'm not trying to separate the two of you, son. I wouldn't try to do that."

Kyle seemed appeased. He stepped aside and motioned me in. "We'll have to keep our voices down," he said. "Grandpa's asleep in the next room."

"I know. I saw him."

Kyle's room could have belonged to any teenager I ever met. There were posters on the wall of the *Star Wars* and *Lord of the Rings* movies, and exercise equipment on the floor in the corner: weights, barbells, and a rubber mat rolled up out of the way. His ever-present boom box sat silent on the bed. A metal sign that read Entrance in the Rear hung on one wall. I wondered if that meant what I thought it meant, or if I was seeing sexual innuendo where none was intended. Somehow I doubted it.

Kyle closed his door behind us and pointed to the bed. "Sit down," he said, pulling his desk chair around and straddling the seat, his arms resting on the back. He snuggled his chin down on his arms and studied me.

"Jesse's worried about you," I said.

"I wish I could see him."

"I know. Maybe in a few days, when things have calmed down a little, you can. Right now, though, I think you should be here."

"What did my mom say to you? Does she believe what everybody's saying?"

"I think she's beginning to. She doesn't have much choice, I'm afraid. Neither do you. The sooner you learn to accept what has happened, the sooner you'll be able to get past it and move on with your life."

Kyle tensed. "Why did he do it, Reverend? Why did he kill himself?"

"I don't suppose we'll ever really know. Maybe the guilt got to be too much for him."

"What did my dad have to feel guilty about?"

"Kyle—"

"He didn't kill anybody! I don't care what he wrote in that goddamn note! In the end, the only person he killed was his own stupid self! For what?"

"Jesse told me you had a theory about who the murderer was. Would you like to share that theory with me?"

His radar went up. "What else did Jesse tell you?"

I thought it best not to mention my suspicions about the car. Not yet. "Only that. That you had a theory."

"Yeah, well. It didn't pan out."

"What do you mean?"

"I thought I knew who the killer was. But, well, I guess I was wrong."

"What changed your mind?"

"Does it matter? Everybody and his dog think my dad's the killer, so what's the point of worrying about it now? I don't want to talk about it anymore. It's a waste of breath."

"Kyle, you're going to have to come to grips with this. You'll never have another happy day in your life if you don't."

"Oh, I've come to grips with it. I know exactly what's happened here. Nobody else does, but I do. A couple of decrepit old women are dead. Another old woman who should have been done away with years ago is dead. And for some reason my dad decided to take the blame for it all and hung himself from a tree, and now *he's* dead. How's that for a recap?"

I tried to ignore his sarcasm, but I was astounded and appalled by the contempt he showed for the victims. Especially his grandmother. Maggie too had almost seemed to hate her. Did Kyle know about the will? Had Maggie told him?

"Your mom tells me you plan on attending the university after you graduate from high school."

The anger on his face slowly melted away. "Yeah. I can afford it now. Jesse and I are going together."

"I know. Did your grandfather say he would help you with the tuition?"

The overly dramatic music of the video game continued to play on the computer behind him. It was beginning to annoy me. "Yeah. He said if I studied hard, he'd pay all the bills. That's the one good thing that came out of all this. Mom will never have to worry about money again. My dad wouldn't have either if he hadn't been so goddamn dumb."

"You shouldn't talk about your father that way, son. You know how much he loved you and your mom."

"If he loved us so much, why the hell did he leave us? He should have waited. Everything would have turned out all right." He slapped his fist on the back of the chair. "He should have fucking *waited*!"

I sighed. "Stop cursing. Waited for what?"

Kyle buried his chin in his arms again and mumbled, "Just waited. That's all. Everything would have turned out all right."

"Kyle, where did you go the night your grandmother died?"

His eyes narrowed as he lifted his head to look at me. "What do you mean?"

"You know what I mean. You took my car. Where did you go? Were you following the person you thought to be the killer?"

"Did Jesse tell you that?"

He might as well have.

"No. I saw you," I lied.

"If you saw me, why didn't you say something *then*?"

I was trying to think of a feasible response to that question when someone knocked at the bedroom door.

Without waiting for an answer to his knock, Chester Goldstone stepped into the room and quietly closed the door behind him. He had donned his glasses, but his shoes were still off. He did not look like someone who had just woken up.

"Reverend," he said, "this boy just lost his father. Do you think this is the best time to be giving him the third degree?"

"I wasn't," I lied again.

The old man ignored my protest. He turned to his grandson. "Kyle, go sit with your mother. She needs your strength right now. She needs to have you with her."

"But—"

"No buts. Go."

Kyle went.

I started to rise too, but Chester waved me back down onto the bed. "No, Reverend, you stay here. I'd like to have a word with you."

Chester reached over and clicked off the computer. "Hate that music."

"Chester, I wasn't grilling the boy."

"Sounded like it to me," he said, easing himself into the desk chair after he had turned it around the proper way. "The boy's been through enough. He doesn't need to be hounded by you or anybody else."

"I'm sorry if you thought I was."

Chester Goldstone appeared to have aged a dozen years since the last time I saw him. He looked tired and unwell. It took him a couple of tries with a palsied hand to tug his cuff down to cover his skinny wrist. His injured hand, the injury he had received on the night of his wife's death when he tried to pull the glass from her throat, was no longer bandaged. An angry welt still remained across the breadth of his palm.

"Kyle's an exceptional boy, Reverend. Maybe you didn't know that about him."

"I'm very fond of your grandson, Chester. I thought you knew that. But there are certain questions that need clearing up."

"Why?"

"I beg your pardon?"

"Why do they need clearing up? What's to clear up? The murderer has admitted his deeds and dealt himself the ultimate punishment for them. Kyle's just a boy. If he fancied himself to be Sherlock Holmes, or Nero Wolfe, or Charlie Chan, going around digging up clues and barking up the wrong tree all the time he was doing it, then where is the harm? That's what boys do. If he did any damage to your car the night he borrowed it, I'll be more than happy to reimburse you."

"You were listening," I said.

"I may be old, Reverend, but I'm not stupid, and I'm not deaf. Not yet. It's up to me to protect this family now, and if it means peeking through keyholes and listening at doors, then that's what I'll do. So tell me, was there any damage to your car?"

"No, of course not."

"Then what's the problem?"

He stared at me with benign patience as he waited for an answer. The confusion of mind he had demonstrated that morning weeks earlier, as Thelma lay dead in the other room, no longer appeared to afflict him. He seemed lucid and obstinate and more than ready to argue. A cantankerous old rooster, protecting his flock. But calm too. Calm and determined.

"Chester, the boy was in Bloomfield the night your wife was murdered. Morris Carter saw my car there."

"So?"

I was becoming a bit exasperated by his maddening obduracy.

"Chester, he might have seen something the police should know about."

"Like what?"

"Like the killer, for instance."

A tiny smile twisted the corners of his mouth. "But we know who that is, don't we?"

"Well, yes, but—"

"Then what does it matter what Kyle saw or didn't see? You don't think *he* committed those murders, do you?"

"My God, Chester, no. Of course I don't."

He laughed. "Then let sleeping dogs lie, Reverend."

"That's the same thing Gordon said in his suicide note."

"I know. I was quoting my former son-in-law when I said it. It's quite an apt phrase under the circumstances. Shows more sense than I would have given Gordon credit for. I don't mind telling you, Reverend, that upon his death my opinion of the man went up considerably."

"Why is that?"

"Let's just say he saw the problem and dealt with it in a truly self-sacrificing way. In the end, he was looking out for his family too. Most commendable."

"You consider his suicide to be commendable?"

"Absolutely. By doing so, he solved everyone's problems, including his own. I'm afraid he might have done it for all the wrong reasons, but the important thing is that he did it."

"I don't understand," I said.

"No, I'm sure you don't. But that doesn't really matter, does it? After all, it has nothing to do with you."

If his intent was to dismiss me, I didn't bite. Dismissal was something I was growing a bit tired of.

"The police are still concerned about a lack of motive for the killings."

"You can't be serious, Reverend. Even I understand the motive. Gordon wanted my wife's money. And mine. I would have been more than happy to pass it on to him and his family if my wife died first, but if the tables were turned and I went first, he would never have touched a penny of it. Thelma would have seen to it. Gordon wasn't willing to take that risk."

"Did she really hate him that much? Did she hate him enough to hurt her own daughter and grandson as well?"

"Oh, yes. She hated Gordon enough to do all those things. Gordon knew it, I suppose, or else why would he have done what he did?"

"But what about the other two women? What possible reason could he have for harming them?"

The old man chuckled. "Oh, well, now we come to the interesting part of the plan. The clever part. I don't really *know*, of course, but my guess would be the first two murders were simply a ruse. A means of drawing attention away from the real motive. Money. By making the murders seem random acts of madness, a motive would no longer be needed or looked for by the police. Madmen don't need motives. If they had one, their acts would no longer be considered mad. So in the shuffle of two motiveless murders, a third wouldn't be questioned at all. Even if there really was a motive for the third. You have to give the boy—the boy's *father*—credit for that one. It was really quite clever, don't you think?"

"It doesn't bother you that your wife was murdered, does it?"

"No, sir. It does not. She died quickly. She didn't suffer. And the world is all the better for having her gone. If I wasn't such a coward, I would have done it myself."

"You can't mean that."

He removed his glasses, held them up to the light to satisfy himself they were clean, then slipped them back on his head. "Oh, I suppose not," he said. "But it's nice to contemplate."

"I don't know what to say."

"Don't you? Look, Reverend, Thelma spent the long years of her life with seemingly only two purposes. To amass as much money as she could and to make everyone around her unhappy. She succeeded remarkably well at both. I suffered her barbs and arrows for forty years. I know what I'm talking about. In my opinion, it was a kindness on the murderer's part to end her life so quickly. She should have been made to suffer for the misery she caused her family and practically everyone else she ever came in contact with."

"That's a bit harsh, isn't it?"

He shrugged. "It's a harsh world."

"Chester, I don't believe you mean these things you're saying. You're tired. This has been hard on everyone."

"Let me finish," he said. "As for the first two women, were their murders really such acts of cruelty? They were old. They had lived full lives. They wouldn't have had much time left on this earth anyway. Who knows? Maybe they were spared long, horrible illnesses or years of neglect lying alone and forgotten in some miserable nursing home that for all the Lysol in the world still smelled of urine and feces and sadness. This way they died quickly in their own homes. True, if we had known Gordon would accept the blame and kill himself for the crimes, it would have been better if the first two women had not been harmed. But how could anyone know he would so readily lay the blame for it all on his own shoulders?"

"The blame?"

Chester blinked, as if surprised to see me there.

"The guilt, I meant to say. It was too much for him, I suppose. But he had accomplished what he had set out to do. Thelma was dead. His family was safe. By killing himself he made sure no more harm would come to them. In the end, Gordon protected his family the only way he knew how. It was a brave thing to do. Perhaps his plan could have been accomplished with less bloodshed, but at least it was done. He must have loved his family very much to do what he did."

I stared at this man I thought I knew as if he were a stranger. He stared back at me. His eyes were kind. Untroubled.

"Don't you understand?" he asked. "Crimes were committed, and justice has been doled out. An eye returned for an eye. Let's leave it at that."

He clapped his hands together and smiled. "Now, then. I understand we have quite a smorgasbord of delicacies out there. Let's go sample some of the offerings, shall we? All this talking has given me quite an appetite. I'm sure my daughter would like to spend more time with you as well, Reverend. She draws great comfort from you. She always has."

I watched him leave the room, shuffling out on his stockinged feet. I sat on the edge of Kyle's bed thinking about all Chester Goldstone had said. But more importantly, I began to think about what he had been extremely careful *not* to say.

Still considering his words, I gazed about me.

On the desk beside the computer, I spotted the corner of a notepad of blue-lined yellow paper peeking out from beneath a stack of mystery novels. Alongside the books lay a package, the top torn off, of yellow pencils. They were the sort of pencils every schoolkid needs. One pencil was missing from the cellophane pack. I stared at it for a long time while thoughts went skittering through my head. They were thoughts that up until now I might never have imagined. Thoughts that frightened me more than anything that had happened during the course of this long, remarkable summer.

Kyle's boom box sat beside me on the bed. Silent. I looked around for the boy's collection of CDs and found them neatly stacked on a bookshelf by the window. There were dozens. Cher. Madonna. Gilbert and Sullivan. U2. *Arias from the Met.* Pete Seeger. *Miss Saigon.* And one that read *Hymns for Piano.* My heart quickened. I doubted if Kyle's wide taste in music extended that far.

A white extension cord lying in a pool of blood beneath Golda Burrows's piano sprang to mind. I wondered if somewhere in this house I might not also find a toolbox with a hammer missing. Or had it been returned by now, freshly scrubbed and fingerprint free?

With the dawning of understanding, I felt myself rebelling against the direction my thoughts were leading me, rebelling too against the inevitability of my conclusions. I wanted to be wrong. *This can't be,* I tried to tell myself. But I knew it could. It made perfect sense.

I stared into the blank computer monitor, focusing my thoughts, or trying to. A cold drop of perspiration slid down my ribcage, making me shudder.

I thought of Kyle during the years I had known him. I had been away at college when he and Jesse became friends. They were young then. Children. Two years ago, when I returned to Nine Mile to take up the post of minister in the church I had worshipped in as a boy, Kyle and Jesse were already on the cusp of manhood. Still friends. Soon they would become lovers, although no one knew that at the time. Even now only a handful of people knew.

Perhaps if I had not been embroiled in my own love affair with Sam and spending every waking hour trying to keep it a secret, I might have noticed what was happening in the boys' lives.

I recalled the words Kyle said to me that day on the pier when I confronted them with what I knew. "We love each other, Reverend. And we're not sorry! For *anything!*"

I remembered the determined, stubborn look in his eyes when he said it, and the gentle way he had reached out to calm Jesse's fear. "Shhh," he had said to the boy beside him. "It'll be all right."

He had told me then, with that same cold certainty, that the two of them would always be together. Through college and everything. No matter what.

Had murder been the only way the boy could find to make that happen?

Was it Kyle's love for Jesse that pushed the boy over the brink? Was his obsession with my nephew so strong he was willing to risk everything to stay at his side? Attendance at a university is an expensive undertaking. Kyle could never have followed Jesse there unless his parents' finances were given a considerable boost. His grandmother's death would assure that. The deaths of Grace Nuggett and Golda Burrows, as Chester had so clearly pointed out, would serve to muddy the waters as far as motive went.

It stunned me to think that if not for his father's suicide, the boy might have gotten away with it. No one suspected him. The thought of it would have been inconceivable to anyone who knew the boy. With the implements of his crimes staring me in the face, I could barely believe it. How had he found the courage, the cold courage, to do what he had done? Was his love for Jesse so deep it buried his conscience? Did this boy with the face of an angel feel no pity whatsoever for the women he had killed? When did Gordon learn the truth? Was this why he had spent those long nights hunkered down among the trees, smoking cigarette after cigarette, watching the boys by their campfire? Did his suspicions about his son have more to do with murder than with sex? Was that when he formed his plan to accept the blame for the killings, and in accepting the blame, give his son the life the boy so desperately wanted? The life Kyle was willing to kill for? Tuition for college so he could continue to be with Jesse. Financial freedom for his parents. Was that when Gordon decided to make the greatest sacrifice a parent could make and forfeit his own life for his son's? He must have known the truth about the killings would come out sooner or later, and when that happened Kyle's life would be over. Gordon could not let that happen. He loved his son too much. Perhaps Gordon did blame himself for the murders, for the road his son had taken. If he had been more successful in his own life, none of this would have happened. Kyle would not have felt the need to commit murder to secure himself a place in the world. It was his own failings as a father that had driven the boy to do what he had done, but it was within Gordon's power to set things right. So he had done so. Unflinchingly. A brave act. An act of love. As Chester's was in sheltering the boy.

When had *he* learned the truth? Did he see the clues around him as I had done? Was Gordon's suicide the blessing he had been waiting for? A chance for Chester too to protect the boy? For his daughter, perhaps? For Maggie? A phone sat on the floor beside Kyle's bed. I reached out for it, then drew back my hand. If I phoned my brother now, there would be more lives ruined. The pain would go on and on, eventually filtering down to everyone involved, including my nephew. Jesse loved Kyle. Once again, I remembered their kiss by the lake. Their hunger for each other when they made love at the edge of the water. Both innocence and passion had brought the boys together. Who knew, I had told them, perhaps it would keep them together for a lifetime. Was I willing to steal that possibility of happiness from them? From Jesse?

But happiness could not be built on a foundation of deceit and murder. If Kyle could find it in himself to kill so easily now, would it ever stop? Would he one day kill again? Could Jesse, the person he purported to love the most in all the world, someday be at risk? The thought chilled me, but I knew there was truth in it. Dark, frightening truth.

For the second time, I reached for the phone, but once again I stayed my hand.

I closed my eyes to pray, but the words would not come. Billy Simmons had been right when he said prayer could not solve everything. But he had not been referring to murder when he said it. His imagination had not reached so far.

I heaved myself from the bed and stood looking down at the phone resting on the floor. I heard voices in other parts of the house. Words of condolence in the living room. Muted laughter from someone in the kitchen.

Life went on.

After a moment, after I did what I had to do, I strode from the room and firmly pulled Kyle's door closed behind me until I heard it latch.

With my heart aching inside me, I walked down the long hallway to join the others. Before stepping into the kitchen and facing the throng of Nine Milers who had come to give Maggie a shoulder to cry on, I thought of Kyle, and the moment I did, a question popped into my head. A question for myself.

How far would you go to hold on to Sam? What would you do to keep him at your side? The answer came instantly. *Anything. I'd do anything.*

Then a final question tore at my heart. *So why haven't you?*

HOURS LATER, back at the lodge, Sam followed me into my office. One look at my face had told him something was wrong.

"What is it?" he asked, one hand resting on my forearm, the other coming up to caress my face. "What's happened?"

I pulled him to me and breathed in his scent, drawing comfort from this man I loved so much.

"Two things," I said. "One good, one bad."

"Oh God," Sam groaned. "There's no humor in your eyes. Why do I get the impression they're both bad?"

"I love you, Sam."

"I love you too. You've always known that, I hope."

"Yes. I've always known."

He smiled gently. "Okay, Brian, give me the good news first."

"I have to leave this place. I have to leave Nine Mile. I can't live here anymore. I can't wake up every morning with a lie plastered on my face so people won't know the real me. I have to be who God made me to be."

Tears misted Sam's eyes as he faced me, his hand still on my cheek. "Who is that?" he asked softly, as if hoping he already knew the answer. "Who did God make you to be, Bry?"

"He made me to be the man who'll spend the rest of his life with you at his side. If you'll have me."

"You know I will. It's all I've ever wanted."

"Then you'll come with me? To the city? Any city? Preferably in a state that accepts gay unions. Gay… marriages."

Sam sucked in a shuddering breath. "Is this a proposal?"

"Yes."

"What about your church?"

"I don't mind how the church will think of me if they learn the truth, Sam. And someday they will. Someday we'll slip up and give ourselves away. But what I absolutely cannot bear to think about is how the church will think of *us*. These people here won't understand. We'll never be accepted. Never. Your aunt is the exception. I think you and I have both known that all along."

"Yes," he said simply.

"So you'll have me, then, Sam? You'll come with me? You'll leave your home here and begin a life somewhere else? Somewhere where we can walk down the street and hold hands if we want. Somewhere where we can commit to each other without shame, without fear?"

"Brian, I'll follow anywhere you want to go." His face gradually lit up. His eyes, still blurred with tears, flared brighter and brighter as the seconds passed.

He stepped closer into my arms and laid his forehead against mine. His breath was sweet on my face. He sniffed once, then laughed. "I need a hanky."

I laid my lips to the tip of his nose and smiled. "Me too."

A contented silence settled around us as we stood there in each other's arms, and just as my body was beginning to think of closer contact, something requiring the removal of clothing, Sam broke the mood with his next question.

"What's the bad news?" he asked, pulling far enough back to focus on my face. "What is it that's upset you so? What's going on?"

"I have to talk to Boyd."

"It's about the killings, isn't it?"

"Yes."

He studied my face for a long moment. "All right," he finally said. "Whatever it is, I know you'll do the right thing."

"Will I?"

"Yes, Brian. You will." He leaned in once again and laid his cheek to mine. Softly, in my ear, he whispered, "I'll leave you to it, then. Thank you."

I nodded. "Thank you, Sam. I'm sorry it took me so long to figure out what I had to do. About us, I mean."

He smiled. "I always knew you'd come around."

"Did you?"

He ran a thumb across my lips. "Yes." With that, he stepped away and left the room, quietly closing the office door behind him.

I closed my eyes for a moment to better hear the happy thudding of my heart. I drew comfort from the sound.

I picked up the Bible from my desk, hoping to draw comfort from that too, but somehow it lay like a dead thing in my hand. I looked through my window to the bright summer day outside. The roar of a lawn mower was the only sound to break the silence. Jesse was cutting the grass on that long slope of lawn leading down to the lake. His shirt was off, and his back glistened strong and brown in the sunlight as he struggled with the mower over the uneven ground. He was a man now. He would understand what I was about to do. He would have to.

I picked up the phone and dialed Boyd's number.

My brother's voice was crisp and businesslike. "County Sheriff," he barked, sounding a bit harried, as if his day was not going as well as he would have liked. It was, I knew, about to get much worse.

"It's me. I need to meet with you. We have to talk."

"About what, little brother?"

"About murder."

"Oh, shit, Bry, don't tell me you found another body."

"No."

"Well, thank Christ for that. Listen, I'm going to be tied up for a while. Working late. Meet me at the Oodle at eleven."

"The Oodle?"

"You got a problem with that?"

"Well, yes, actually. Boyd, I'm the town pastor. If anyone in my congregation should see me waltzing into the Oodle in the middle of the night, my career will be over." *Not that it won't be ruined quickly enough anyway when Sam and I pull up roots and elope.*

"Then don't waltz," Boyd said. "Trust me, oh righteous one. It'll be our little secret. I won't tell a soul."

"But—"

The line went dead.

BOYD DID indeed work late that day. Among the items on his rather colorless palette of criminal investigations since the matter of the murders had hit a quagmire was the theft of a prize breeding bull reported by Elmer Minks, a livestock breeder whose farm lay on the outskirts of Bloomfield.

Elmer Minks was one of our elite. His farm was not the usual motley collection of ramshackle sheds and drafty, listing old barns we were used to seeing around the township. No, the Minks farm was a modern beehive of concrete and steel that served the sole purpose of churning out some of the finest Hereford cattle to be found in the state. Elmer did not eke out an existence like the other farmers. He thrived. He had a PhD in animal husbandry from Purdue University, and he had put that knowledge to good use. Both of his sons had also attended Purdue in the same field of study and, after taking wives for themselves, had returned to their father's farm to join him in the family business. The Minks Ranch was the ideal all other farmers in Greene County aspired to but seldom attained.

The sweet, benign faces of Elmer's Herefords were scattered across the many acres of his spread, contentedly chewing their cuds and lifting their heavy heads every time a car passed along the gravel road that lined Elmer's property. Each and every one of Elmer's cattle was worth more money than I made in a month. While his cows might be prized, however, it was his bulls that were deified. They were worth more than a dozen cows combined. To Elmer, the loss of Nottingham, his favorite, was like the sudden and unscheduled removal of his spleen. Elmer wanted it back. He was a mere husk of a man without it.

Boyd received the frantic call at five, and by ten in the evening, he had solved the crime.

Nottingham, it seemed, while innocently pulling up weeds along Elmer's fence line and eyeing the members of his harem with a lascivious eye, as he was prone to do, had been enticed through a newly made hole in the fence by a handful of carrots.

The carrots dangled from the grimy paw of Elmer's neighbor, Jefferson Smits, who led Nottingham, a brawny beast but not of the highest intelligence, two miles down the road under the cover of twilight to be locked in a barn with Jefferson's one and only Hereford, Betsy.

Nottingham must have felt like the prince who awakens after being drugged at the ball and finds himself in the lowest hovel consorting with a woman of questionable beauty and morals. It was a step down for him, to be sure. But lust being what it is, and all men suffer from it, Betsy took the bull by the horns, so to speak, and enticed Nottingham into acts of nature that the poor noble beast had neither the will nor the strength to resist.

Following a trail of carrot tops and hoofprints by the light of his flashlight, Boyd found Nottingham there, nuzzling his new paramour as they shared a bale of hay, reveling in the afterglow of their insatiable lovemaking.

When confronted with his crime, Jefferson Smits was unapologetic. "Just needed a little sperm," he drawled, "and that damn bull has it dripping from his ears. Old Elmer ain't going to miss it now, is he?"

"No, but he missed the bull," Boyd said, chewing a fistful of aspirins.

They were standing at Jefferson's barn door, looking in.

"Bull's all right, Sheriff. Look at him. Happy as a clam. The way I see it, it's sorta like me borrowing a cup of sugar. Elmer ain't gonna begrudge me a cup of sugar, is he?"

When Boyd relayed this sentiment to Elmer Minks, Elmer said, "Expensive damn cup of sugar, Sheriff! Nottingham commands a six hundred dollar stud fee!"

Boyd rubbed the back of his neck. "Well, you and I both know Jefferson Smits doesn't have six hundred dollars to pay you with."

"Hell no, he doesn't! His whole damn spread ain't worth six hundred dollars on a good day!"

"You wanting to press charges, Elmer? I hope to hell not, because frankly I don't want to be writing down 'one load of jizm' on a stolen property report."

Elmer chuckled at that. "More like three, Sheriff. Ol' Nottingham never stops at one. He's a real horndog when it comes to the heifers. Damned if he ain't."

Boyd was losing patience. "So, what's it going to be? You going to press charges against Jefferson, or would you rather I just trot over there and shoot him?"

Elmer tapped his pipe clean on the side of a fence post and proceeded to refill it from a can of Prince Albert he extracted from his back pocket while he thought things over. When he had tamped the tobacco down to his satisfaction, he casually pulled a kitchen match from the chest pocket of his overall and lit the thing up.

With his head engulfed in smoke, he said, "Oh hell, Sheriff. Let it go. Nottingham's back safe and sound. That's the important thing. Tell that knothead Smits the next time he wants a cup of sugar to come and ask for it. He won't get it, but tell him to ask anyway. And while you're at it, tell him to plug that damn hole in my fence, and do it right, mind you, and I won't press charges."

"Hallelujah," Boyd said. "Now if you'll excuse me, I've got a date with a Budweiser. Have to meet my brother at the Oodle."

"Your brother the preacher?"

"That's the one."

"He frequents the Oodle, does he?"

"Only at night," Boyd said. "Can't seem to stay away from the place. It's a family problem. I'm sure you understand."

Elmer looked stricken with concern. "That's a damn shame, now, ain't it?"

Boyd cranked up the engine of his Bronco and drove off, leaving Elmer scratching his ass and shaking his head.

Boyd related this to me with a sparkle in his eye as he sipped his Bud from the bottle. We were parked in a booth in the darkest corner of the Oodle I could find.

"Our little secret," I snarled.

Boyd got a bang out of that. Judging by the insipid grin on his face, I suspect this was the happiest moment of his day.

"What's with the hat?" he asked.

I wore a baseball cap with Colts stenciled across the front and the brim pulled low over my forehead.

"Good Lord, little brother, if that's your idea of being incognito, it's not working. You still stand out like a dead squirrel in a punchbowl. Never saw anybody look so damned uncomfortable in my life. It's just a tavern, Bry. I don't see many Methodists sitting at the bar getting shit-faced, so relax and drink your beer and tell me why we're here."

I tossed the cellophane-wrapped package of pencils and the CD onto the table.

"What's all this?" he asked.

"Think about it."

He picked up the CD and held it out to the light to better see the label. "*Hymns for Piano,*" he read aloud. He flipped it over and squinted in the darkness to read the back. "'In the Garden.' 'Rock of Ages.' 'The Old Rugged Cross,' and many more." He gave me a quizzical look.

"Boyd. Remember what the neighbors said? Golda's neighbors? They said she played twice as long that night, well past dark. Remember? They also said her playing improved dramatically as the evening wore on. Became faultless, in fact. Boyd, Golda never played faultless piano in her life and you know it. It was the CD. The neighbors were listening to a CD."

Boyd said nothing, but continued to stare at me. I could see the realization dawning on his face. He glanced down at the opened package of pencils. Ticonderoga number two. Yellow. With one pencil missing from the pack. Grace Nuggett lying dead on her kitchen floor, that bloody pencil poking up from her ruined eyeball like a flagpole. The pencil that came from the package before him.

Was it my imagination, or did the Oodle suddenly grow a lot quieter?

"Bry, where did you get this stuff?"

"In Kyle's room."

Boyd gazed past me, seeing something only visible inside his mind. Fear woke in his eyes.

"Jesse," he breathed.

I reached out and touched his hand. "Jesse had nothing to do with it. Jesse didn't know. He still doesn't."

He focused on my face. I had never seen such pain in my brother's eyes. "How do you know that? How can you be sure? We have to be sure."

"I'm sure."

Boyd squeezed his eyes shut. I suspected he had finally found a reason for prayer. A prayer of thanks. When he opened them again, the pain had been replaced. By anger.

"So it was Kyle who took your car out the night Thelma Goldstone was murdered."

"Yes. Jesse told me. Well, sort of."

"Didn't he wonder where the boy was going? Didn't he ask Kyle why the hell he was stealing your car?"

"Kyle told Jesse he had a theory about who the murderer was. Said he had been following him ever since the killings started."

"And Jesse believed him?"

"Yes." I glanced at the items on the table. "I believed it too until I found those."

Boyd gazed again at the CD. "Kyle's boom box," he said, the words spoken so softly they barely stirred the air in front of his face. "He played this CD while he… while he killed Golda Burrows. He must have gone in after Chester dropped off the jewelry. With the CD of piano music playing, the neighbors thought she was still alone. Still… alive. It was dark. He could have gone in the back door. Nobody had to have seen him."

"Boyd," I interrupted. "This explains why Thelma went out alone that night. If Kyle called her and told her to meet him, she would have done it. She might not have done it for anyone else, but for her grandson she would have. He was her Golden Boy."

Boyd took a long pull from his beer. His face was ashen in the shadows of the bar, and his hands were shaking.

"My God," he said, his anger draining away to weariness. "This investigation has been a clusterfuck of suspicions from the very beginning. Too many suspicions. I must have suspected everybody at one time or another. Everybody but you, of course. And the boys."

I said it again. "It wasn't the boys. It was Kyle. Kyle alone. Jesse had nothing to do with it."

He nodded. "I know, Bry. I mean, I know Jesse could never have done any of the terrible things that have been done this summer. But up until two minutes ago, I would never have believed Kyle could be involved either. That sweet kid. Fifteen years old, for Christ's sake!"

He rubbed his eyes.

"The Golden Boy," I said, still only half believing the truths I had uncovered.

Boyd stared at me. "Golden Boy," he echoed. "You know, Bry, the only connection I could ever make between the three victims was their names."

"Their names?"

"Yes. Their names. Grace *Nuggett*. *Golda* Burrows. Thelma *Gold*stone."

Not thinking, I took a long pull of my own beer. I couldn't believe I had never seen it before. "Good Lord, are you saying the first two victims were picked because of their *names*?"

"Why else? Kyle's little inside joke, I guess. Kyle must have thought he could confuse the issue enough to cover up the real motive. That goddamn will."

"The cause of it all."

"Oh yeah," Boyd said. "That's why we were all so willing to believe Gordon was the killer. But Maggie swore he was home with her at the time her mother was killed, so I let it go. Couldn't believe she would lie to me about something like that. Turns out she didn't. She was telling the truth."

"Boyd, Gordon admitted to the killings to protect his son. It was a warning as well. He was warning the boy to stop."

"Looks like it. But how did he know?"

"He was watching him."

"Of course. The cigarette butts. That's why he was spying on the boys by the lake. I thought—"

"You thought what?"

Boyd slumped in his seat. "I thought it was… for other reasons."

"Then you knew about that as well."

Infinite sadness limned Boyd's reply. "Yes. I've known about it for a long time. I thought Jesse loved me enough to trust me to understand."

"He trusts you, Boyd. He just has to build up enough courage in himself to tell you. One day he will. Just give him time."

"It won't make any difference, you know. I'll still love him."

"The boy knows that, Boyd."

Boyd's eyes softened as he stared at me across the table. "When were *you* going to tell me, little brother? About you and Sam?"

My heart lurched inside my chest. "You know?"

He gave his head a disbelieving shake. "I've always known."

I sat speechless, plucking at the label of my beer bottle with a thumbnail. "Soon," I finally said. "I was going to tell you soon."

"You're leaving, then. You and Sam are finally leaving."

"Yes."

Boyd reached out and laid his great paw of a hand over mine. "It's about time, little brother. I'll miss you, but it's still about time."

"I know."

We let the silence reclaim us for a handful of heartbeats; then Boyd looked down at the evidence in front of him.

"Gordon was a good father, wasn't he." It wasn't a question. "Look what he did. Look what he did to shield his son."

"Yes. He surprised me."

Boyd's gaze returned to me. "Kyle must realize why his dad did what he did. I wonder how he feels about that."

I sipped my beer. It was warm. "I think it's tearing him apart. He never expected anything like that to happen. He was trying to give himself and his parents a better life, but it blew up in his face with his father's death."

"Are you sure about that?" Boyd asked. "There must have been something evil in the boy to begin with to do the things he's done. I've seen him time and again through the course of the summer, and not once did I see so much as a glimmer of guilt on his face. Not until his father died. He was able to keep what he had done from Jesse, and they were...."

His voice trailed away as another thought struck him.

"That night Susan and I brought him with us to the lake. After that weekend when Gordon made him go home to do his chores. Mow the yard and stuff. He was jabbering on and on about what a great summer he was having and how much him and Jesse were enjoying camping out and swimming and working for you. And all the while he had just come from Golda Burrows's house. Knew the things he had done there. He had washed her blood from his hands at Golda's kitchen sink, for Christ's sake. It was like... like he had washed all memory of his acts away as well. Like it never happened. There was no regret in him. No remorse. He was happy to be getting back to the lake. Back to... Jesse."

I remembered the boys on the vestibule steps the day of our basket dinner, scarfing down plates of food. What had Kyle done? Had he ridden his bike out to Grace's farm early that morning? It was only three miles. It wouldn't have taken him long. He could have been back before anyone missed him. Had he committed his first murder that day? Committed murder and then casually eaten a slab of persimmon pudding he found cooling on the countertop in Grace's kitchen.

There had been no remorse on his face that day either. No guilt.

"Boyd," I said. "What are we going to do? Do we really want Maggie to find out her son is a murderer? She's lost so much already. Her mother, her husband, and now her son too? She may be stronger than I give her credit for, but everyone has a limit. This will certainly kill her. She'll never get over it."

"Does anyone else know, Bry? Sam? Does he know?"

I shook my head. "I've told no one but you. But I think Chester suspects. In fact, I'm sure he does. He was trying to protect the boy earlier today when I started asking questions."

"In his shoes, I would have probably done the same thing," Boyd said.

I nodded. "I know."

"Bry, no one will ever believe Jesse knew nothing about this. You realize that, don't you? Kyle is lost to us already," he said. "We have to protect Jesse now. And Maggie."

"What do you mean, Kyle is lost to us?"

"There's only one way out of this, Brian. There's only one thing for us to do."

I couldn't imagine what he was getting at. "What's that? What do we have to do?"

But he wouldn't answer. Like a tired old man, he pulled himself up from the booth and went to the bar, where he ordered two more Buds, then carried them back to the table.

Later, when the bottles were almost empty, he finally spoke.

"Bry, there are secrets here that have to be kept. Letting the truth come out will help no one, but it will hurt a great many people if it does. You're right, it will kill Maggie, and Jesse will be ruined. We can't let that happen."

"Of course not, but—"

"There's nothing we can do to bring the victims back. There's nothing we can do to clear Gordon's name either, I'm afraid."

"All right. But what about the boy? What about Kyle?"

He stared at me for long moments before answering. When he did, his words were barely audible over the music of the jukebox. I had to lean forward to hear them.

"I'll handle it," was all he said.

Chapter Sixteen

THREE DAYS later Kyle returned to us, and to Jesse, at our campground at Sunset Lake. We worked hard that day, finalizing preparations for our long-awaited opening. In the evening, as the sun began to go down, I watched the boys head into the trees along the hiking trail. I let them go. During the course of the day, I had seen their need for each other. My heart went out to Jesse, his eager young face so alive with love and longing.

Kyle had been more subdued than usual, his mind perhaps weighted down with guilt over his father's death. The boys exchanged little laughter that day, but still their love for each other was a naked light that shone out of them every time their eyes came together. As darkness fully settled in, Boyd and Susan arrived. Once again, they joined Sam and me for dinner on the veranda. Susan and Sam carried the bulk of the conversation, when there was any, while Boyd and I ate in silence. Eventually even Susan and Sam grew quiet. Like the lull before a storm, an air of expectation seemed to settle over us. Boyd's eyes were continually drawn to the boys' campfire down by the lake.

Only once did my brother pull himself from his reverie and center his attention on Sam. To everyone's surprise, he stood formally and thrust out his hand for Sam to shake. Confused, Sam rose and took it.

"Welcome to the family," Boyd said as I watched from the sidelines, swallowing an appreciative lump in my throat. "You and my brother have been hiding your feelings for each other long enough. I'm glad the truth is finally out."

"Well, it isn't completely out. Or at least I hope it isn't. Not yet anyway," Sam said. "But thank you, Boyd. It's great for me to finally be able to tell you how much in love with your brother I am. He's my whole world. He has been for almost our entire lives."

Boyd stepped around the table and pulled Sam into his arms in a bear hug while Susan and I watched, both of us fighting tears and trying not to bawl.

When Boyd released him, Sam stepped toward me and took my hand. We could find nothing to say to each other, but there was a gleam of thank-you in Sam's eyes, knowing I had finally told my brother everything.

The four of us settled back around the table in our original positions and let the night sounds reclaim us. The buzz of insects. The hooting of an owl. A pigeon cooing somewhere in the eaves.

I still had no idea what Boyd intended to do about Kyle. If he knew, he did not offer to share the information with me. I knew the thought was preying on his mind. Susan, too, knew Boyd was troubled. She studied his face constantly when she thought he wouldn't notice. The tension in the air was not lost on Sam either. He left his hand in mine for the rest of the evening, even while we ate.

We were all relieved when the meal was finished.

After dinner, I was surprised when Boyd insisted he and I don our trunks and go down to the pier for a late-night swim.

"You stay here and entertain Susan," he pointedly told Sam, and Sam nodded his acquiescence.

Not sure what was going on, but knowing by the look of determination on Boyd's face that I couldn't alter the program if I wanted to, I ran up to my room and slipped into my trunks. Boyd peeled off his uniform on the veranda, showing he was wearing his swim trunks as underwear already, as we used to do when we were kids. He hailed the boys as we padded barefoot down the slope toward the water. They quickly slipped into their shorts and joined us on the pier.

For more than an hour, the sounds of our splashing and laughter echoed across the lake and into the trees on the hillsides surrounding us. The water felt warm on our skin until we reached the buoy line where the lake bottomed out. From that point on, the water was cold and unwelcoming. The knowledge of those endless fathoms of dark water beneath our feet quieted our voices and made us all a bit uneasy. We quickly dog-paddled closer to shore, where the water was warmer and less threatening.

Our playful swim had freed Jesse's mind of his recent troubles, and he seemed truly happy for the first time in days. Having Kyle at his side once again had a lot to do with it, I knew. Kyle, too, seemed more like his old self after spending the day with Jesse. They appeared to feed happiness into each other.

I could see their struggle not to reach out and touch each other every time their bodies brushed close beneath the water. Jesse and Kyle craved each other as badly as I craved Sam. It was an obsession I fully understood. The need of it was written plainly on their young faces, as I'm sure it was written on mine whenever Sam was near.

But as Kyle swam that night, as I listened to his laughter and watched the interaction between the boys in the flickering light from the campfire that illuminated us dimly in the water, a deep sadness welled up inside me. My brother must have felt it too. Our laughter was forced. Kyle's laughter was not. He was a fifteen-year-old kid having fun with the person he cared most about in all the world.

The terrible things he had done over the course of the summer meant nothing to him. Tonight even his father's death seemed forgotten. It was then I truly realized for the first time there was something deeply wrong with the boy. Grief did not register with him. Guilt did not exist inside his mind. He was completely childlike in his reactions to the storm of misery and murder he and he alone had unleashed.

He was immune to any emotion save one. Love. Love for Jesse. If he had once regretted his father's suicide, that had now slipped away from him. All he cared about was this one moment. I did not believe he felt a sense of relief in thinking he might have gotten away with it all because I doubted if the memory of what he had done, the murders he had committed, still dwelled inside him. His face was bright and happy and innocent. The black secrets buried behind that sweet face were lost to him in the cleansing darkness of his mind. They had been scoured away, as if they never existed.

Gordon, perhaps, had seen it first. I recalled the conversation we had on the veranda the morning after Golda's murder. He had spoken of black hearts as he stared out at the hail peppering the lake. He had spoken too of remorseless people. He had seen it even then, seen it in his own son. Was he already planning a way to protect the boy from the consequences of his actions? Had the act of suicide and a false confession to the murders, the decision to take the mantle of blame upon his own shoulders, already burrowed their way inside his mind? Could he see no other option for saving the boy? No other way out?

Did Kyle truly understand the sacrifice his father had made to protect him from his crimes? If he did, he didn't show it. Not tonight.

Tonight he was happy, blind to everything that had gone before. His father's death. The brutal murders. Everything. Tonight there was only—tonight.

Kyle's carefree laughter rang across the water, chilling me more than the coldest fathoms of the lake beneath my feet. There was madness in that laughter. Like the lake, one could drown in it. Like the lake, Kyle was beautiful to look at, but beneath the surface, somewhere deep in the cold shadows below the calm, beautiful exterior, horrors lurked. Death could be found there if one dove deep enough.

When we began to tire, we rested our arms on the edge of the pier and lazily hung in the water. A gentle breeze wafted down from the hills and dried our faces. It carried with it the sound of bullfrogs speaking to each other from one side of the lake to the other.

"Jesse," Boyd said, "go get us some Cokes."

"Okay," Jesse chirped, pulling himself onto the pier. "Cokes it is."

"Bry, you go with him," my brother said. "Four hands are better than two."

I gave him a questioning look.

"Go ahead," he said to me. "Kyle and I will wait here."

As I pulled myself out of the water, my brother's eyes met mine. "Take your time," he said. "Kyle and I will just take another lap around the buoy line."

He turned away from me and ruffled Kyle's damp hair. "Come on, son," he said. "I'll race you."

As Jesse and I started up the slope toward the lodge, dripping and sputtering, Boyd and Kyle shoved off from the pier and were quickly lost in the darkness.

Mrs. Shanahan bellowed in outrage when Jesse and I dripped through her kitchen, but I could tell her heart wasn't in it. She was too happy to see Jesse smiling again to put up much of a fuss. I suspected she only did that for show anyway. It was, after all, expected of her, and she was never one to disappoint.

She tossed towels over our heads and pushed us into chairs at the kitchen table. There, she doled out peach cobbler and ice cream. "The others can eat when they get here," she said. "You boys look hungry now." When she saw we had everything we needed, she rubbed her hands together and giggled like a schoolgirl. "Now back to the game. I'm teaching Susan and Sam how to gracefully lose their money."

So while Jesse and I attacked our cobbler and ice cream, Mrs. Shanahan rejoined Susan and Sam in the mess hall. There, with a pile of pennies in front of them, they laughed and slapped down cards like a trio of high rollers on a poker jaunt to Las Vegas.

Jesse and I were scooping the last dregs of ice cream from our bowls when Susan cried out in the other room. At the sound of chairs overturning, I rushed across the kitchen with Jesse on my heels. In the mess hall we saw Sam, Susan, and Mrs. Shanahan, speechless in shock, their cards forgotten in their hands, as they stared at the door leading to the outside.

Boyd stood there with the muscles straining in his neck and a pool of water forming at his feet. In his arms he held Kyle's lifeless body. The boy's head lolled back across my brother's arm, his eyes open but seeing nothing.

Jesse screamed, "No!" and ran toward his father. Together they lowered the boy to the floor.

My brother's eyes bored into mine. He held me locked in his gaze as the words tore out of him. "He must have cramped. He was out beyond the buoys. I couldn't find him in the darkness."

Mrs. Shanahan moaned and slumped into one of the chairs. Susan, crying now, rushed to her side. Sam rushed to mine. Together, in stunned silence, we all stared at the unmoving body.

Jesse dropped to the floor beside his lover and friend and swept the hair away from those unseeing eyes. He too began to sob, clutching Kyle's cold hand against his chest.

Boyd, blinded by tears, dropped to his knees at Jesse's side and wrapped his arms around his son's shoulders. "I'm so sorry, Jesse. I'm so sorry."

Jesse nodded, his young face ravaged with grief. He reached out with a trembling hand and brushed the tears from his father's face. Then he laid his head on Boyd's shoulder, but his gaze remained fixed on Kyle's face. "It wasn't your fault, Dad. Please. Stop crying now. It wasn't your fault."

Boyd looked across the room at me, his eyes wide with pain. He stared down again at Kyle's still body. He reached out and closed the boy's eyes with a gentle movement of his fingertips. His hand lingered there, caressing the damp forehead, stroking the ringlets of dark hair that still dripped with lakewater.

"Forgive me, Kyle," he said with a great shuddering sigh. "You sleep, son. Just sleep. It's all over now."

Once more, Boyd raised his eyes to me.

"It's all over now," he whispered again. Then he wept, his shoulders slumped and trembling.

I went to him, a prayer unbidden already forming in my mind. As I wrapped my arms around my brother's sobbing body, I remembered our father. A quiet, good man. A farmer. Buried these past five years in the same graveyard where Grace Nuggett now rested. He told me once to treasure kinship over all things. Kinship, after all, is sometimes all we really have, all we can truly call our own.

"Kinship," our father had told me as he lay dying, his body wasted away to sticks on the bed before me. "Remember that, boy. Faith might slip and love can falter, but kinship will always be there for you. Kinship and secrets. Keep them close to your heart."

After this night, I knew, Boyd and I would be bound together forever. By both.

Kinship and secrets.

Would God see it all through His eyes as we had seen it through ours? Would He understand? Would He forgive us for what my brother had done? For what, I now realized, I had known in my heart my brother was going to do?

In the days to come, we would do all we could to ease Maggie's grief at the loss of her son. Our only reward would be that she never learned the truth about the horrible crimes he had committed. But that would do little to ease our own grief. Or our guilt. We would watch helplessly as Maggie Knowles slowly withdrew. From us. From her father. From life. She would never really return.

As the years went by, as our own lives fell behind us, I wondered if Boyd and I would learn to live with the guilt we felt now. Would we ever accept the pain of it as the price we had to pay for what my brother and I had done on this warm summer night? Would we? I wasn't sure.

Tonight we mourned for the boy. For Kyle. Tomorrow we would mourn for ourselves, perhaps. The seemingly endless years of our lives might be spent and our deaths might be at last upon us before our judgments could ever *truly* be written, for they could only be written by God's hand on the day we faced Him. We would not be here by my beautiful lake when we did.

Epilogue

THE U-HAUL van had barely survived the trek down the potholed lane toward Sunset Lake. I wasn't so sure about the contents packed inside. Everything Sam and I owned was stuffed into the back of that truck. Sam's car was hooked to a hitch at the rear, and my car was in the hands of Billy Simmons, who, while he wouldn't be caught dead driving the old Rambler, thought it might be fun to try to restore it. So I had given it to him, every rattling bolt, rusting fender, and torn piece of upholstery.

Sam and I stood at the gateway to the church campground and stared up at the sign stretched across the lane. The sign with my name on it. Reverend Brian Lucas. At least I was a reverend for the moment. A reverend without a church, maybe. But a reverend nevertheless. I wasn't sure how much longer that would last. I remembered the cool, appraising expressions of the members of the Methodist board when I told them I was gay and forfeiting my post as minister in Nine Mile.

"The Methodist Conference will have my name off that sign before we're two miles out of Greene County," I said. "I saw it in their eyes."

"No, they won't," Sam said, bumping me with his hip as we leaned against the U-Haul's grill and held each other's hand. "I'll burn the place down before I let them take your name off that sign."

I chuckled. "I love you for that, Sam."

"I know," he softly said. "That and my dick."

I closed my eyes and inhaled the scent of pine. The air was cool on my face because the trees that framed the lane cast us in voluptuous shadow and filtered out the blazing noonday sun overhead.

In the distance, we could hear splashing and screams of laughter. It was the laughter of scores of young children, all enjoying this late summer day doing whatever it was they were doing. Swimming in the cool lake, canoeing, chasing each other down the broad sweeping lawn sloping down from the lodge to the water, their bellies full of Mrs. Shanahan's cooking. They would be going home soon. School would be starting. Their summer by my lake would be relocated to memory alone.

With the dying of summer, a lot would be relocated to memory, and much of it I wasn't sorry to see go. But now I was able to push it all behind me and let myself look forward instead. Forward to my future with Sam. An open, committed future. In the city and in the state where we were headed, we would be able to live the life God had decreed we should live when he made us the way we were.

"You'll miss this place," Sam said with a kind smile twisting his handsome face.

"There's a lot I won't miss," I answered truthfully.

"You're worried about Jesse," Sam said.

I nodded. "I hate to see him live a life like the one we had to live being here. I'd hate for him to become a victim of ignorance and hate. He doesn't really understand it yet, you know. He hasn't had to suffer it. Neither have we, really. We've all been lucky to escape the truth getting out. But as soon as they learn we've skedaddled off together hand in hand, I guess the truth will come out quick enough."

Sam's hand squeezed mine. "Brian, Jesse's a smart enough kid that when the time comes to do his own skedaddling, he won't think twice about leaving this place in the dust, with all the hate and narrow-mindedness and prejudice that goes with it. He won't grieve for Kyle forever. He'll find love again. Boyd will help see him through this. And Susan and my old aunt, who loves him like her own. The boy has the support he needs right now, and in three or four years, when he's ready to move on and be his own man, they'll let him go. Just as they should."

I turned toward Sam, and he let me pull him into my arms. "I'm sorry I've made you wait so long," I said.

Sam burrowed his face into my neck and murmured, "We're leaving now. That's all that matters. I'm sorry you have to give up so much to do it. Your ministry, your congregation, your Rambler."

I barked out a laugh. "Trust me, love. The Rambler I can live without. The rest of it too, Sam. I can still live a Christian life. I haven't abandoned God. If I have you with me, I know I'll be happy. That's all I've ever really wanted, Sam. A little happiness. And you."

He splayed his hands across my back and drew me closer. "Me too," Sam said, breathing the words against my neck.

"Hi," a voice said from behind us, and Sam and I both jumped.

We spun to find a young girl of perhaps eleven, with ropy red pigtails and dirty bare feet, staring up at us. She wore a pink bathing suit that was drying around her. Her mouth was so full of bubble gum she could barely talk.

"Hi back," Sam said while I tried to find my own voice. He did not pull away from my arms, but continued to hold me close against him.

She eyed us for a moment, then blew a fat bubble that exploded, covering her chin. She peeled it happily away and stuffed the gum back in her mouth. "Are you boyfriends?" she asked.

"Yes," Sam said, as fearless as always. "I'm Sam. This is Brian."

"So you love each other, then," the young girl said, all serious eyes and knobby knees.

"Yes," I said. "We love each other. Soon we'll be getting married."

She nodded her head, still studying us closely. "That's nice. My uncle married his boyfriend. They live in Maine."

She held out two squares of bubble gum. "Want some? They have cartoons on the wrappers."

"Thanks," I said, reaching out and accepting the gum.

When Sam and I were chewing away, she asked, "Wanna see the lake?"

"Sure," Sam said.

"Come on, then," the young girl said, and taking each of us by the hand, she led us down the rutted lane toward the campground and the sound of laughter in the distance.

Sam and I glanced at each other over the kid's head. I was stunned to see tears in his eyes as he stared back at me.

"Maybe there's hope for these people yet," he said.

"Maybe," I agreed. "This girl's on the right track at least. Not a homophobic bone in her body."

"My brother's here too," the girl said conversationally as we walked along the lane dappled with shadow. "In case you're wondering, he's not homophobic either. But he's still a pain in the butt."

"Don't worry," I said. "Someday he'll probably grow out of it. Being a pain in the butt, I mean. People change sometimes."

"More than you think they ever will. Or can," Sam said, still eyeing me as we walked along.

"About the wedding," the girl said, peeling another burst bubble off her chin and peering up into our faces, one after the other. "Will you have two boy statues stuck in the icing on top?"

"Probably," Sam said.

"That's good," the girl said. "It wouldn't make much sense if you had a girl on there."

"No," Sam said, grinning. "Not much sense at all."

A moment later she said, "Did I tell you my brother's a pain in the butt?"

"You might have mentioned it," I told her.

She nodded. "I thought I did."

JOHN INMAN has been writing fiction since he was old enough to hold a pencil. He and his partner live in beautiful San Diego, California. Together, they share a passion for theater, books, hiking and biking along the trails and canyons of San Diego or, if the mood strikes, simply kicking back with a beer and a movie. John's advice for anyone who wishes to be a writer? "Set time aside to write every day and do it. Don't be afraid to share what you've written. Feedback is important. When a rejection slip comes in, just tear it up and try again. Keep mailing stuff out. Keep writing and rewriting and then rewrite one more time. Every minute of the struggle is worth it in the end, so don't give up. Ever. Remember that publishers are a lot like lovers. Sometimes you have to look a long time to find the one that's right for you."

E-mail: john492@att.net
Facebook: http://www.facebook.com/john.inman.79
Website: http://www.johninmanauthor.com/

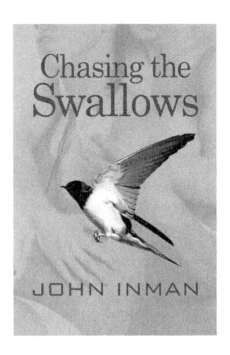

Sometimes an entire lifetime can be spent in the arms and heart of one person. It is not so with imaginations, for they go anywhere they wish.

David Ayres and Arthur Smith are about to find that out. When they meet as young men within the garden walls of the Mission of San Juan Capistrano, one man from one continent, one from another, an uncontrollable attraction brings them together. But it is something stronger than attraction that holds them there. It is love. Pure and simple.

After forty years, when the fabric of their existence together finally begins to fray because of David's imaginary infidelities, it is with humor and commitment that they strive to remain in each other's heart.

And turning fantasy into reality, they find, is the best way to do it.

http://www.dreamspinnerpress.com

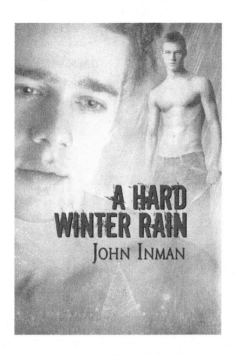

Sean Andros is tired—tired of hustling, tired of trying to make the rent, tired of running from his past.

But the past can chase you down in a heartbeat. Suddenly Sean's living a nightmare again and casualties are stacking up around him. The only person he can trust is Harry, a man twice his age and the closest thing to a friend Sean has ever known. Harry Connors has loved Sean since their first night together, and now, with danger hard at their heels, Harry will do anything to protect the tough, strangely vulnerable young man who begs him for help.

Harry had better be serious about offering protection, though, because the demons threatening Sean's life are no joke. Only a hard winter rain will wash away the evil that drove Sean Andros to the streets, and Sean and Harry are going to have to be strong if they plan on sticking around for the sun.

http://www.dreamspinnerpress.com

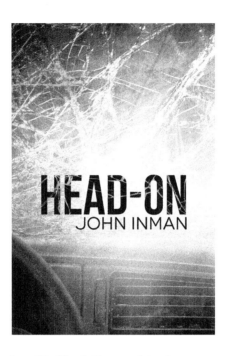

At twenty-six, Gordon Stafford figures his days are numbered. At least he hopes they are. Wearied by guilt and regret stemming from a horrific automobile accident two years earlier in which a man was killed, Gordon wakes up every morning with thoughts of suicide. While the law puts Gordon to work atoning for his sins, personal redemption is far harder to come by.

Then Squirt—a simple homeless man with his own crosses to bear—saves Gordon from a terrible fate. Overnight, Gordon finds not only a new light to follow, and maybe even a purpose to his life, but also the possibility of love waiting at the end of the tunnel.

Gordon never imagined he'd discover a way to forgive himself, and in doing so, open his heart enough to gain acceptance and love—from the very person he hurt the most.

http://www.dreamspinnerpress.com

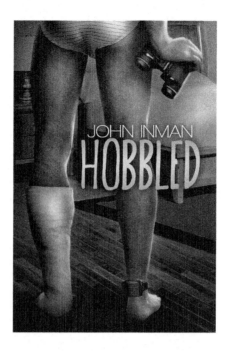

Thanks to fate and his own lack of good sense, eighteen-year-old Danny Shay is headed into what looks to be the worst summer of his life. It starts with a minor meltdown at work that leaves Danny under house arrest with a cast on one leg and an ankle monitor on the other, courtesy of the San Diego Police Department. On top of that, he's battling a chronic case of virginity, with no relief in sight.

Oh, and there's one more little glitch. A serial killer is stalking the city, murdering young men. And when strange sounds are heard in the house behind Danny's, the neighborhood kids think they've found the killer. But not until Danny learns he's next on the madman's list do things *really* begin to get desperate.

Damn! And Danny had plans to come out this summer—maybe even get laid! He doesn't have *time* for ankle monitors and serial killers!

Then ginger-haired Luke Jamison moves in next door. Not only does Luke solve a few of Danny's more *urgent* problems, he also manages to create a couple more that Danny never saw coming. Gee. If he can survive it, this summer might not be so bad after all.

http://www.dreamspinnerpress.com

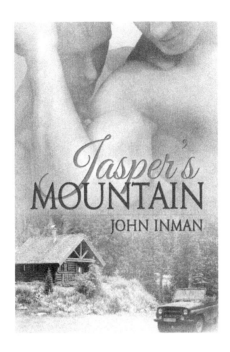

When small-time thief Timmy Harwell recklessly "borrows" a Cadillac for a joyride, he doesn't expect to find a cool $100,000 in the trunk. His elation turns to terror when he realizes the SUV and the dough belong to Miguel Garcia, aka El Poco, a Tijuana drug dealer with a nasty reputation. Timmy sees only one way out: leave the stolen car behind and run as fast as he can.

His getaway is cut short when a storm strands him outside Jasper Stone's secluded mountain cabin. Jasper finds Timmy in his shed, unconscious and burning up with fever, and takes care of the younger man, nursing him back to health. The two begin to grow close, but Jasper, a writer who seeks only solitude, is everything Timmy isn't. Straightforward, honest, and kind.

Timmy needs Jasper's help—and wants his respect—so he hides his dishonest habits. But when El Poco comes after him, Timmy realizes he's not the only one at risk. His actions have also put Jasper in harm's way. Honesty now could mean Timmy loses the man he's come to love, but not being honest could mean far worse.

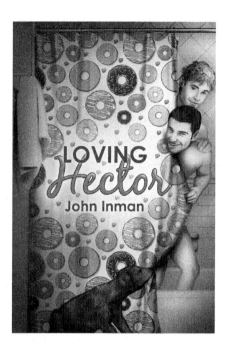

Dillard Brown has a mother who's determined he's straight, a writing career that's going nowhere, and at thirty, he's never been in love in his life. But thanks to a ten-pound ball of fluff and energy named Chester, one of Dill's circumstances is about to change. Maybe even all three.

Who would've thought one little stray dog could change Dill's world—and not by accident either. The damn dog has it planned. If not for Chester wandering into Dill's life and into his heart, Dill would never have met Hector Peña—and tumbled headlong into love at last!

But for all Chester's efforts, happiness for Dill and Hector is still not assured. Hector's evil ex, Valdemaro, is dead set on holding on—even if it means kidnapping Hector to keep him from Dill forever! Now Dill has to pull an army together to rescue Hector, and just where the hell is he supposed to find an army? Gads, if only Dill could write books this interesting!

http://www.dreamspinnerpress.com

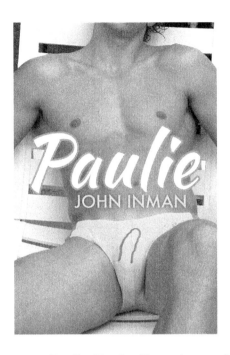

To the casual observer, Paulie Banks lives the perfect life. After all, he's young, handsome, and rich. But Paulie has a secret. He's madly in love with Ben, his old college roommate—and Ben is straight! Now Paulie has arranged a two-week reunion with his three closest friends to rehash their college years and get to know each other again. Jamie and Trevor are coming, along with their new lovers. And to Paulie's amazement, even Ben has accepted his invitation.

Beautiful Ben. The one non-gay apple in the old college barrel. Paulie will soon find out if Ben has forgiven him for overstepping the bounds of friendship on the last drunken night they spent together.

With his La Jolla mansion spotless, a stunning new houseboy hired for the duration, and his heart pounding in both fear and anticipation, Paulie welcomes his old friends back into his life. Thanks to a whole lot of liquor and a clothing-optional dress code, boy, do the festivities begin!

http://www.dreamspinnerpress.com

When Tyler Powell's life is torn apart by an unspeakable crime, the need for vengeance takes over. Every moment of every day, as he tries to pull his shattered existence together again, it's all he can think about—revenge.

Will he give in to his rage and become the very thing he hates most? A killer?

Only with the help of Homicide Detective Christian Martin, the cop in charge of his case, does Tyler see the possibility of another life beginning—the astounding revelation of another love reaching out to him. A love he thought he would never know again.

Will he let that love into his life, or is he lost already? Is payback more important to Tyler than his own happiness? And the happiness of the man who loves him? Tyler is determined to find a way to exact his revenge without sacrificing all hope for a future with Christian, but it will be difficult—if not impossible—and in the end he might be forced to make an unbearable choice.

http://www.dreamspinnerpress.com

With the world suddenly teeming with zombies, Charlie and Bobby are fighting to stay alive. Being about as gay as two people can be, they insist on doing it with panache.

Even with the planet throwing up its legs in submission, there is no reason a couple of style-conscious guys can't look good while saying good-bye to the age of man and ushering in the age of… God knows what. Amoebas, maybe. With their loyal zombie poodle, Mimi, at their side, they bravely face the apocalypse head-on.

Death, destruction, and the undead they can deal with. But without electricity, it's the depressing lack of blow-dryers and cappuccino machines that really pisses them off—until Bobby goes missing! Suddenly Charlie has more than fluffy hair and a good cup of coffee to worry about….

http://www.dreamspinnerpress.com

Dating is hard enough. Throw in an incontinent Chihuahua, an unrequited love affair, a severe case of social anxiety disorder, a dying father, and a man-eating hog and it becomes darned near impossible. Still, it takes two to tango—and when Tom Morgan, a mild-mannered assistant bank manager with a debilitating case of shyness, meets Frank Wells, who is straight off the farm and even shyer than he is, sparks start flying.

Just when Tom and Frank's burgeoning love affair is rolling along nicely, Frank must return to Indiana to oversee the farm while his father battles cancer. Tom tags along to help Frank out and finds himself slopping hogs and milking cows and wondering what the hell happened to his orderly citified existence. And what's with all the chickens? Tom *hates* chickens!

With Frank's help, Tom grits his teeth and muddles through. Funny what a couple of guys can accomplish when they're crazy about each other. Not even nine hundred chickens can stand in the way of true love.

http://www.dreamspinnerpress.com

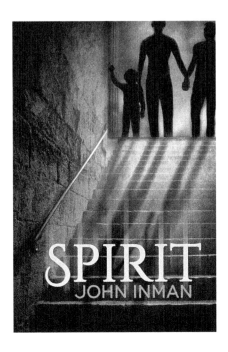

Jason Day, brilliant designer of video games, is not only a confirmed bachelor, but he's as gay as a maypole. One wouldn't think being saddled with his precocious four-year-old nephew for four weeks would be enough to throw him off-kilter.

Wrong. Timmy, Jason's nephew, is a true handful.

But just when Timmy and Uncle Jason begin to bond, and Jason feels he's getting a grip on this babysitting business once and for all, he's thrown for a loop by a couple of visitors—one from Tucson, the other from beyond the grave.

I'm sorry. Say what?

Toss a murder, a hot young stud, an unexpected love affair, and a spooky-ass ghost with a weird sense of humor into Jason's summer plans, and you've got the makings for one hell of a ride.

http://www.dreamspinnerpress.com

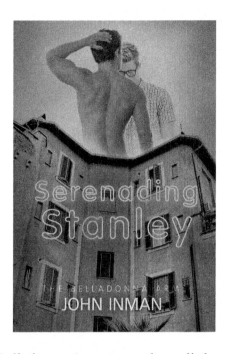

Welcome to the Belladonna Arms, a rundown little apartment building perched atop a hill in downtown San Diego, home to the city's lost and lovelorn. Shy archaeology student Stanley Sternbaum has just moved in and fills his time quietly observing his eccentric neighbors, avoiding his hellion mother, and trying his best to go unnoticed… which proves to be a problem when it comes to fellow tenant Roger Jane. Smitten, the hunky nurse with beautiful green eyes does everything in his power to woo Stanley, but Stanley has always lived a quiet life, too withdrawn from the world to take a chance on love. Especially with someone as beautiful as Roger Jane.

While Roger tries to batter down Stanley's defenses, Stanley turns to his new neighbors to learn about love: Ramon, who's not afraid to give his heart to the wrong man; Sylvia, the trans who just wants to be a woman, and the secret admirer who loves her just the way she is; Arthur, the aging drag queen who loves them all, expecting nothing in return—and Roger, who has been hurt once before but is still willing to risk his heart on Stanley, if Stanley will only look past his own insecurities and let him in.

http://www.dreamspinnerpress.com

Dumped by his lover, Harlie Rose ducks for cover in the Belladonna Arms, a seedy apartment building perched high on a hill in downtown San Diego. What he doesn't know is that the Belladonna Arms has a reputation for romance—and Harlie is about to become its next victim.

Finding a job at a deli up the street, Harlie meets Milan, a gorgeous but cranky baker. Unaware that Milan is suffering the effects of a broken heart just as Harlie is, the two men circle around each other, manning the barricades, both unwilling to open themselves up to love yet again.

But even the most stubborn heart can be conquered.

With his new friends to back him up—Sylvia, on the verge of her final surgery to become a woman, Arthur, the aging drag queen who is about to discover a romance of his own, and Stanley and Roger, the handsome young couple in 5C who lead by example, Harlie soon learns that at the Belladonna Arms, love is always just around the corner waiting to pounce. Whether you want it to or not.

But tragedy also drops in now and then.

http://www.dreamspinnerpress.com

COFFEE CAKE

MICHAELA GREY

http://www.dreamspinnerpress.com

FOR **MORE** OF THE **BEST** GAY ROMANCE

REAMSPINNER PRESS
dreamspinnerpress.com

CPSIA information can be obtained at www.ICGtesting.com
Printed in the USA
LVOW04s0530090715

445497LV00016B/146/P

9 781634 761376

SUNSET
LAKE

JOHN INMAN

Published by
DREAMSPINNER PRESS

5032 Capital Circle SW, Suite 2, PMB# 279, Tallahassee, FL 32305-7886 USA
http://www.dreamspinnerpress.com/

This is a work of fiction. Names, characters, places, and incidents either are the product of author imagination or are used fictitiously, and any resemblance to actual persons, living or dead, business establishments, events, or locales is entirely coincidental.

Sunset Lake
© 2015 John Inman.

Cover Art
© 2015 Aaron Anderson.
aaronbydesign55@gmail.com
Cover content is for illustrative purposes only and any person depicted on the cover is a model.

ISBN: 978-1-63476-137-6
Digital ISBN: 978-1-63476-138-3
Library of Congress Control Number: 2015905041
First Edition July 2015

Printed in the United States of America
∞
This paper meets the requirements of
ANSI/NISO Z39.48-1992 (Permanence of Paper).